YUMI
AND THE NIGHTMARE
PAINTER

TOR

TOR
PUBLISHING
GROUP

NEW YORK

BRANDON
SANDERSO

YUMI AND THE NIGHTMARE PAINTER

Copyright © 2023 by Dragonsteel Entertainment, LLC

Illustrations by Aliya Chen copyright © 2023 by Dragonsteel Entertainment, LLC.

Brandon Sanderson®, The Stormlight Archive®, Mistborn®, and Reckoners®
are registered trademarks of Dragonsteel Entertainment, LLC.

All rights reserved.

A Tor Book
Published by Tom Doherty Associates / Tor Publishing Group
120 Broadway
New York, NY 10271

www.tor-forge.com

Tor® is a registered trademark of Macmillan Publishing Group, LLC.

The Library of Congress Cataloging-in-Publication Data is available upon request.

ISBN 978-1-250-89969-9 (hardcover)

Our books may be purchased in bulk for promotional, educational, or business use.
Please contact your local bookseller or the Macmillan Corporate and Premium
Sales Department at 1-800-221-7945, extension 5442, or by email at
MacmillanSpecialMarkets@macmillan.com.

First Edition: 2023

Printed in the United States of America

0 9 8 7 6 5 4 3 2 1

ALSO FOR EMILY,

Who, for some amazing reason, gives me her love.

Contents

Acknowledgments

FIRST OFF, let's acknowledge Emily—the person this book is dedicated to—for being both my inspiration and my co-president at Dragonsteel. I think you would all be amazed by how much she does behind the scenes. She deserves praise, accolades, and no small thanks for sharing her book (which this is) with all of you.

Creative Development is our department focused on things like artwork for the books, concept art, and various cool things like that. In this department, I'd like to thank Isaac Stewart—VP, and my longtime partner in crime—for taking on the huge task of getting the artwork ready for all these Secret Projects.

And speaking of that, Aliya Chen was the artist for this book, and she did an amazing job. My goal for each of these books was to let the artists have extra freedom to create art for the story the way they want, and Aliya was really fantastic to work with. I hope those of you who listen to the audiobook will find time to go check out the beautiful pieces she did for this project.

Other members of this department include Rachael Lynn Buchanan (who brought Aliya's art to our attention), Jennifer Neal, Ben McSweeney, Hayley Lazo, Priscilla Spencer, and Anna Earley.

We also want to thank some of the people external to our organization here at Dragonsteel who helped on this project. This includes Oriana Leckert at Kickstarter, and Anna Gallagher and Palmer Johnson at BackerKit.

Also, a special thanks to Bill Wearne, our print rep, who worked miracles to get the premium edition printed on our schedule. At the JABberwocky literary agency: Joshua Bilmes, Susan Velazquez, and Christina Zobel. For the trade release at Tor in the US, I would like to thank Devi Pillai, Tessa Villanueva, Lucille Rettino, Eileen Lawrence, Alexis Saarela, Rafal Gibek, Peter Lutjen, Greg Collins, Hayley Jozwiak, and Sara Thwaite. In the UK I'd like to thank Gillian Redfearn, Emad Akhtar, and Brendan Durkin at Gollancz, as well as my UK agents, John Berlyne and Stevie Finegan, at the Zeno Agency. For the audiobook, many thanks to Kate Reading, Michael Kramer, and Erik Synnestvedt.

ΔOur Editorial department is headed by VP the Installed Peter Ahlstrom. His team also stepped up in a big way to get four extra books done on time, and they deserve huge props! They include Karen Ahlstrom, Kristy S. Gilbert (who did the layout), Betsey Ahlstrom, Jennie Stevens, and Emily Shaw-Higham. Deanna Hoak did our copyediting on this book.

Our Operations department VP is Matt "You're publishing how many books this year?" Hatch, who came on to our company just in time for us to do this huge project. Also on the operations team are Emma Tan-Stoker, Jane Horne, Kathleen Dorsey Sanderson, Makena Saluone, Hazel Cummings, and Becky Wilson. Thanks so much, folks, for keeping us all in line and focused!

The Publicity and Marketing department is headed by VP Adam Horne. These are the folks who helped me put together all the videos promoting the Secret Projects, and have been an invaluable resource in helping me get the news out about all of this! His team includes Jeremy Palmer, Taylor D. Hatch, and Octavia Escamilla. Nice work!

Last but not least is our Merchandising and Events department, headed by Kara Stewart as the VP. This team took on an extra-large burden for these four Secret Projects, as it was a *huge* endeavor to get it all put together, packaged, and shipped out to you all. They also spearheaded getting the digital products to everyone, and they handle customer service, so no matter which version of the book you ended up getting, these are the fine folks who got them to you! A huge thanks to them for all their work.

The team includes: Christi Jacobsen, Lex Willhite, and Kellyn Neumann.

Mem Grange, Michael Bateman, Joy Allen, Katy Ives, Richard Rubert, Brett Moore, Ally Reep, Daniel Phipps, and Dallin Holden.

Alex Lyon, Jacob Chrisman, Matt Hampton, Camilla Cutler, Quinton Martin, Kitty Allen, Esther Grange, Amanda Butterfield, Laura Loveridge, Gwen Hickman, Donald Mustard III, Zoe Hatch, Logan Reep, Rachel Jacobsen, and Sydney Wilson.

My writing group for this book included Emily Sanderson, Kathleen Dorsey Sanderson, Peter Ahlstrom, Karen Ahlstrom, Darci Stone, Eric James Stone, Alan Layton, Ethan Skarstedt, and Ben Olseeeen.

Alpha readers for this book included Jessie Farr, Oliver Sanderson, Rachael Lynn Buchanan, Jennifer Neal, Christi Jacobson, Kellyn Neumann, Lex Willhite, Joy Allen, and Emma Tan-Stoker.

Beta readers include Joshua Harkey, Tim Challener, Lingting "Botanica" Xu, Ross Newberry, Becca Reppert, Jessica Ashcraft, Alyx Hoge, Liliana Klein, Rahul Pantula, Gary Singer, Alexis Horizon, Lyndsey Luther, Nikki Ramsay, Suzanne Musin, Marnie Peterson, David Behrens, and Kendra Wilson.

Gamma readers include many of the beta readers plus: Brian T. Hill, Evgeni "Argent" Kirilov, Rosemary Williams, Shannon Nelson, Brandon Cole, Glen Vogelaar, Rob West, Ted Herman, Drew McCaffrey, Jessie Lake, Chris McGrath, Bob Kluttz, Sam Baskin, Kendra Alexander, Lauren McCaffrey, Billy Todd, Chana Oshira Block, and Jayden King.

And, obviously, I'd like to give a huge thanks to all of our Kickstarter backers, who made this project possible! Your enthusiasm has really propelled this project into the stratosphere. Thank you so very much.

Brandon Sanderson

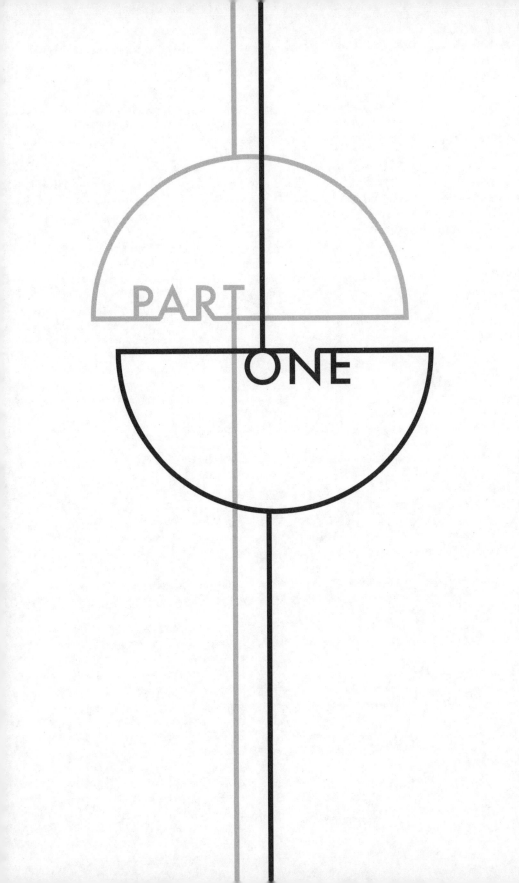

PART ONE

Chapter 1

THE STAR was particularly bright when the nightmare painter started his rounds.

The star. Singular. No, not a sun. Just one star. A bullet hole in the midnight sky, bleeding pale light.

The nightmare painter lingered outside his apartment building, locking his eyes on the star. He'd always found it strange, that sentry in the sky. Still, he was fond of it. Many nights it was his sole companion. Unless you counted the nightmares.

After losing his staring match, the nightmare painter strolled along the street, which was silent save for the hum of the hion lines. Ever present, those soared through the air—twin bands of pure energy, thick as a person's wrist, about twenty feet up. Imagine them like very large versions of the filaments in the center of a light bulb—motionless, glowing, unsupported.

One line was an indecisive blue-green. You might have called it aqua—or perhaps teal. But if so, it was an electric variety. Turquoise's pale cousin, who stayed in listening to music and never got enough sun.

The other was a vibrant fuchsia. If you could ascribe a personality to a cord of light, this one was perky, boisterous, blatant. It was a color you'd wear only if you wanted every eye in the room to follow you. A titch too purple for hot pink, it was at the very least a comfortably *lukewarm* pink.

The residents of the city of Kilahito might have found my explanation unnecessary. Why put such effort into describing something everyone knows? It would be like describing the sun to you. Yet you need this context, for—cold and warm—the hion lines were *the* colors of Kilahito. Needing no pole or wire to hold them aloft, they ran down every street, reflected in every window, lit every denizen. Wire-thin strings of both colors split off the main cords, running to each structure and powering modern life. They were the arteries and veins of the city.

Just as necessary to life in the city was the young man walking beneath them, although his role was quite different. He'd originally been named Nikaro by his parents—but by tradition, many nightmare painters went by their title to anyone but their fellows. Few internalized it as he had. So we shall call him as he called himself. Simply, Painter.

You'd probably say Painter looked Veden. Similar features, same black hair, but of paler skin than many you'd find on Roshar. He would have been confused to hear that comparison, as he had never heard of such lands as those. In fact, his people had only recently begun to think about whether their planet was alone in the cosmere. But we're getting ahead of ourselves.

Painter. He was a young man, still a year from his twenties, as you'd count the years. His people used different numbers, but for ease let's call him nineteen. Lanky, dressed in an untucked buttoned grey-blue shirt and a knee-length coat, he was the type who wore his hair long enough to brush his shoulders because he thought it took less effort. In reality it takes far more, but only if you do it right. He also thought it looked more impressive. But again, only if you do it right. Which he didn't.

You might have thought him young to bear the burden of protecting an entire city. But you see, he did it along with hundreds of other nightmare painters. In this, he was important in the brilliantly modern way that teachers, firefighters, and nurses are important: essential workers who earn fancy days of appreciation on the calendar, words of praise in every politician's mouth, and murmurs of thanks from people at restaurants. Indeed, discussions of the intense value of these professions crowd out other more mundane conversations. Like ones regarding salary increases.

As a result, Painter didn't make much—merely enough to eat and have some pocket cash. He lived in a single-room apartment provided by his employer. Each night he went out for his job. And he did so, even at this hour, without fear of mugging or attack. Kilahito was a safe city, night-mares excluded. Nothing like rampaging semisapient voids of darkness to drive down crime.

Understandably, most people stayed indoors at night.

Night. Well, we'll call it that. The time when people slept. They didn't have the same view of these things that you do, as his people lived in per-sistent darkness. Yet during his shift, you'd say it *felt* like night. Painter passed hollow streets alongside overstuffed apartments. The only activ-ity he spotted was from Rabble Way: a street you might charitably call a low-end merchant district. Naturally, the long narrow street lay near the perimeter of town. Here, the hion had been bent and curved into signs. These stuck out from shop after shop, like hands waving for attention.

Each sign—letters, pictures, and designs—was created using just two colors, aqua and magenta, the art drawn in continuous lines. Yes, Kilahito had things like light bulbs, as are common on many planets. But the hion worked with no need for machinery or replacement, so many relied on it, particularly outdoors.

Soon Painter reached the western edge. The end of hion. Kilahito was circular, and its perimeter held a final line of buildings, not *quite* a city wall. Warehouses mostly, without windows or residents. Outside of that was one last street, in a loop running around the city. No one used it. It lay there nonetheless, forming a kind of buffer between civili-zation and what lurked beyond.

What lurked beyond was the shroud: an endless, inky darkness that besieged the city, and everyone on the planet.

It smothered the city like a dome, driven back by the hion—which could also be used to make passages and corridors between cities. Only the light of the star shone through the shroud. To this day, I'm not a hun-dred percent certain why. But this was close to where Virtuosity Splin-tered herself, and I suspect that had an effect.

Looking out at the shroud, Painter folded his arms, confident. This was his realm. Here, he was the lone hunter. The solitary wanderer. The man who prowled the endless dark, unafraid of—

Laughter tinkled in the air to his right.

He sighed, glancing to where two other nightmare painters strolled the perimeter. Akane wore a bright green skirt and buttoned white blouse, and carried the long brush of a nightmare painter like a baton. Tojin loped beside her, a young man with bulging arms and flat features. Painter had always thought Tojin was like a painting done without proper use of perspective or foreshortening. Surely a man's arms couldn't be *that* big, his chin *that* square.

The two laughed once more at something Akane said. Then they saw him standing there.

"Nikaro?" Akane called. "You on the same schedule as us again?"

"Yeah," Painter said. "It's, um, on the chart . . . I think?" Had he actually filled it out this time?

"Great!" she replied. "See you later. Maybe?"

"Uh, yeah," Painter said.

Akane walked off, heels striking stone, paintbrush in hand, canvas under her arm. Tojin gave Painter a little shrug, then followed, his own supplies in his large painter's bag. Painter lingered as he watched them go, and fought down the urge to chase after them.

He was a lone hunter. A solitary wanderer. An . . . unescorted meanderer? Regardless, he didn't want to work in a pair or a group, as a lot of the others did.

It would be nice if someone would ask him. So he could show Akane and Tojin that he had friends. He would reject any such offer with stoic firmness, of course. Because he worked by himself. He was a single saunterer. A . . .

Painter sighed. It was difficult to maintain a properly brooding air after an encounter with Akane. Particularly as her laughter echoed two streets over. To many of his colleagues, nightmare painting was not as . . . solemn a job as he made it out to be.

It helped him to think otherwise. Helped him feel like less of a mistake. Especially during those times when he contemplated a life where he would spend his next six decades on this street every night, backlit by the hion. Alone.

Chapter 2

YUMI HAD always considered the appearance of the daystar to be encouraging. An omen of fortune. A sign that the primal hijo would be open and welcoming to her.

The daystar seemed extra bright today—glowing a soft blue on the western horizon as the sun rose in the east. A powerful sign, if you believed in such things. (An old joke notes that lost items tend to be in the last place one looks. Conversely, omens tend to appear in the first place people look for them.)

Yumi did believe in signs. She had to; an omen had been the single most important event in her life. At her birth, a falling star had marked the sky—indicating that she had been chosen by the spirits. She'd been taken from her parents and raised to accomplish a holy and important duty.

She settled down on the warm floor of her wagon as her attendants, Chaeyung and Hwanji, entered. They bowed in ritual postures, then fed her with maipon sticks and spoons—a meal of rice and a stew that had been left on the ground to cook. Yumi sat and swallowed, never so crass as to try to feed herself. This was a ritual, and she was an expert in those.

Though today she couldn't help feeling distracted. It was nineteen days past her nineteenth birthday.

A day for decisions. A day for action.

A day to—maybe—ask for what she wanted?

It was a hundred days until the big festival in Torio City, the grand capital, seat of the queen. The yearly reveal of the country's greatest art, plays, and projects. She had never gone. Perhaps . . . this time . . .

Once her attendants finished feeding her, she rose. They opened the door for her, then hopped down out of the private wagon. Yumi took a deep breath, then followed, stepping out into sunlight and down into her clogs.

Immediately her two attendants leaped to hold up enormous fans, obscuring her from view. Naturally people in the village had gathered to see her. The Chosen. The yoki-hijo. The girl of commanding primal spirits. (Not the most pithy of titles, but it works better in their language.)

This land—the kingdom of Torio—couldn't have been more different from where Painter lived. Not one glowing line—cold or warm—streaked the sky. No apartment buildings. No pavement. Oh, but they had *sunlight*. A dominant red-orange sun, the color of baked clay. Bigger and closer than your sun, it had distinct spots of varied color on it—like a boiling breakfast stew, churning and undulating in the sky.

This scarlet sun painted the landscape . . . well, perfectly ordinary colors. That's how the brain works. Once you'd been there a few hours, you wouldn't notice the light was a shade redder. But when you first arrived, it would look striking. Like the scene of a bloody massacre everyone is too numb to acknowledge.

Hidden behind her fans, Yumi walked on her clogs through the village to the local cold spring. Once at the spring, her attendants slipped her out of her nightgown—a yoki-hijo did not dress or undress herself—and let her walk down into the slightly cool water, shivering at its shocking kiss. A short time later, Chaeyung and Hwanji followed with a floating plate holding crystalline soaps. They rubbed her once with the first, then she rinsed. Once with the second, then she rinsed. Twice with the third. Three times with the fourth. Five times with the fifth. Eight times with the sixth. Thirteen times with the seventh.

You might think that extreme. If so, have you perhaps never heard of religion?

Yumi's particular flavor of devotion, fortunately, did have some practical accommodations. The later soaps were only such by the broadest definition—you would consider them perfumed creams, with a deliberately moisturizing component. (I find them especially nice on the feet, though I'll probably need them for my whole body once I arrive in the Torish version of hell for abusing their ritual components for bunion relief.)

Yumi's final rinse involved ducking beneath the water for a count of a hundred and forty-four. Underneath, her dark hair flowed around her, writhing in the current of her motion as if alive. The compulsory washing made her hair extremely clean—which was important, as her religious calling forbade her from ever cutting it, so it reached all the way to her waist.

Though it wasn't required of the ritual, Yumi liked to gaze upward through the shimmering water and see if she could find the sun. Fire and water. Liquid and light.

She burst out of the water at the exact count of one forty-four and gasped. That was *supposed* to get easier. She was *supposed* to rise serenely, renewed and reborn. Instead she was forced to break decorum today by coughing a little.

(Yes, she saw coughing as "breaking decorum." Don't even ask how she regarded something truly onerous, like being late for a ritual.)

Ritual bathing done, it was time for the ritual dressing, also carried out by her attendants. The traditional sash under the bust, then the larger white wrap across the chest. Loose undergarment leggings. Then the tobok, in two layers of thick colorful cloth, with a wide bell skirt. Bright magenta, her ritual wear for that day of the week.

She slipped her clogs on again and somehow walked in them, natural and fluid. (I consider myself a reasonably adroit person, but Torish clogs—they call them getuk—feel like bricks tied to my feet. They aren't necessarily hard to balance in—they're only six inches tall—but they grant most outsiders the graceful poise of a drunk chull.)

With all of that, she was at last ready . . . for her next ritual. In this case, she needed to pray at the village shrine to seek the blessings of the spirits. So she again let her attendants block all view of her with their fans, then walked out and around to the village flower garden.

Here, vibrant blue blossoms—cuplike, to catch the rain—floated on thermals. They hovered around two feet in the air. In Torio, plants rarely dared touch the ground, lest the heat of the stone wither them away.

Each flower was maybe two inches across, with wide leaves catching the thermals—like lilies with fine dangling roots that absorbed water from the air. Yumi's passing caused them to swirl and bump against one another.

The shrine was a small structure, wood, mostly open at the sides but with a latticed dome. Remarkably, it *also* floated gracefully a few feet off the ground—this time by way of a single lifting spirit underneath that took the physical shape of two statues, each with grotesque features, facing one another. One vaguely male crouched on the ground; one vaguely female clung to the bottom of the building. Though divided once made physical, they were still part of the same spirit.

Yumi approached among the flowers, the soft thermals causing her skirt to ripple. Thick cloth didn't rise enough to be embarrassing—merely enough to give shape and flare to the bell of her outfit. She removed her clogs once more as she reached the shrine, stepping up onto the cool wood. It barely wobbled, held firm by the strength of the spirit.

She knelt, then began the first of the thirteen ritual prayers. Now, if you think my description of her preparations took a while, that's intentional. It might help you understand—in the slightest way—Yumi's life. Because this wasn't a special day, in terms of her duties. This was *typical*. Ritual eating. Ritual bathing. Ritual dressing. Ritual prayers. And more. Yumi was one of the Chosen, picked at birth, granted the ability to influence the hijo, the spirits. It was an enormous honor among her people. And they never let her forget it.

The prayers and following meditations took around an hour. When she finished, she looked up toward the sun, slots in the shrine's wooden canopy decorating her in alternating lines of light and shadow. She felt . . . lucky. Yes, she was certain that was the proper emotion. She was blessed to hold this station, one of the very fortunate few.

The world the spirits provided was wonderful. The sun of vivid red-orange shining through brilliant clouds of yellow, scarlet, violet. A field of hovering flowers, trembling as tiny lizards leaped from one to another. The stone underneath, warm and vibrant, the source of all life, heat, and growth.

She was a part of this. A vital one.

Surely this was wonderful.

Surely this was all that she should ever need.

Surely she couldn't want *more*. Even if . . . even if today was lucky. Even if . . . perhaps, for once, she could ask?

The festival, she thought. *I could visit, wearing the clothing of an ordinary person. One day to be normal.*

Rustling cloth and the sound of wooden shoes on stone caused Yumi to turn. Only one person would dare approach her during meditation: Liyun, a tall woman in a severe black tobok with a white bow. Liyun, her kihomaban—a word that meant something between a guardian and a sponsor. We'll use the term "warden" for simplicity.

Liyun halted a few steps from the shrine, hands behind her back. Ostensibly she waited upon Yumi's pleasure, a servant to the girl of commanding primal spirits. (Trust me, the term grows on you.) Yet there was a certain demanding air even to the way Liyun *stood*.

Perhaps it was the fashionable shoes: clogs with thick wood beneath her toes, but sleek heels behind. Perhaps it was the way she wore her hair: cut short in the rear, longer in the front—evoking the shape of a blade at each side of her head. This wasn't a woman whose time you could waste, somehow including when she *wasn't* waiting for you.

Yumi quickly rose. "Is it time, Warden-nimi?" she said, with enormous respect.

Yumi's and Painter's languages shared a common root, and in both there was a certain affectation I find hard to express in your tongue. They could conjugate sentences, or add modifiers to words, to indicate praise or derision. Interestingly, no curses or swears existed among them. They would simply change a word to its lowest form instead. I'll do my best to indicate this nuance by adding the words "highly" or "lowly" in certain key locations.

"The time has not quite arrived, Chosen," Liyun said. "We should wait for the steamwell's eruption."

Of course. The air was renewed then; better to wait if it was near. But that meant they had time. A few precious moments with no scheduled work or ceremony.

"Warden-nimi," Yumi said (highly), gathering her courage. "The Festival of Reveals. It is near."

"A hundred days, yes."

"And it is a thirteenth year," Yumi said. "The hijo will be unusually active. We will not . . . petition them that day, I assume?"

"I suppose we won't, Chosen," Liyun said, checking the little calendar—in the form of a small book—that she kept in her pouch. She flipped a few pages.

"We'll be . . . near Torio City? We've been traveling in the region."

"And?"

"And . . . I . . ." Yumi bit her lip.

"Ah . . ." Liyun said. "You would like to spend the festival day in prayer of thanks to the spirits for granting you such an elevated station."

Just say it, a part of her whispered. *Just say no. That's not what you want. Tell her.*

Liyun snapped her book closed, watching Yumi. "Surely," she said, "that *is* what you want. You wouldn't actively desire to do something that would *embarrass* your station. To imply you regret your place. Would you, Chosen?"

"Never," Yumi whispered.

"You were honored, of all the children born that year," Liyun said, "to be given this calling, these powers. One of only *fourteen* currently living."

"I know."

"You are *special.*"

She would have preferred to be less special—but she felt guilty the moment she thought it.

"I understand," Yumi said, steeling herself. "Let us not wait for the steamwell. Please, lead me to the place of ritual. I am eager to begin my duties and call the spirits."

Chapter 3

IT'S TERRIFYING how nightmares transform.

I'm talking about ordinary nightmares now, not the kind that get painted. Terror dreams—they change. They evolve. It's bad enough to encounter something frightening in the waking world, but at least those mortal horrors have shape, substance. That which has shape can be understood. That which has mass can be destroyed.

Nightmares are a fluid terror. Once you get the briefest handle on one, it will change. Filling nooks in the soul like spilled water filling cracks in the floor. Nightmares are a seeping chill, created by the mind to punish itself. In this, a nightmare is the very definition of masochism. Most of us are modest enough to keep that sort of thing tucked away, hidden.

On Painter's world, those dark bits were strikingly prone to coming alive.

He stood at the edge of the city—bathed from behind in radioactive teal and electric magenta—and stared out at the churning darkness. It had substance; it shifted and flowed similar to molten tar.

The shroud. The blackness beyond.

Nightmares unformed.

Trains traveled the hion lines to places like the small town where his family still lived, a couple of hours away. He *knew* other places existed. Yet it was difficult not to feel isolated while looking into that endless blackness.

It stayed away from the hion lines. Mostly.

He turned and walked the street outside the city for a short time. To his right, those outer buildings rose as a shield wall, with narrow alleyways between. As I said before, it wasn't a true fortification. Walls didn't stop nightmares; a wall would merely prevent people from stepping out onto the perimeter.

In Painter's experience, no one came out here but his kind. The ordinary people stayed indoors; even one street farther inward felt infinitely safer. The people lived as he once had, trying hard not to think about what was out there. Seething. Churning. Watching.

These days, it was his job to confront it.

He didn't spot anything at first—no signs of particularly brave nightmares encroaching upon the city. Those could be subtle, however. So Painter continued. His assigned beat was a small wedge that began several blocks inward of the perimeter, but the outside portion was the widest—and the most likely place for signs of nightmares to appear.

As he did his rounds, he continued to imagine that he was some lone warrior. Instead of, essentially, an exterminator who had gone to art school.

To his right he passed the capstone paintings. He wasn't certain where the local painters had come up with the idea, but these days—during dull moments on patrol—they tended to do practice work on the outer buildings of the city. The walls facing the shroud didn't have windows. So they made for large inviting canvases.

Not strictly part of the job, each was a certain personal statement. He passed Akane's painting, depicting an expansive flower. Black paint on the whitewashed wall. His own spot was two buildings over. Just a blank white wall, though if you looked closely you could see the failed project beneath peeking through. He decided to whitewash it again. But not tonight, because he caught signs of a nightmare at last.

He stepped closer to the shroud, but didn't touch it of course. Yes . . . the black surface here was disturbed. Like paint that had been touched when near to drying, it was . . . upset, rippling. It was difficult to make out, as the shroud didn't reflect light, unlike the ink or tar it otherwise appeared to be. But Painter had trained well.

Something had emerged from the shroud here and started into the city.

He retrieved his brush, a tool as long as a sword, from his large painter's bag. He felt better with it in hand. He shifted his bag to his back, feeling the weight of the canvases and ink jar inside. Then he struck inward—passing the whitewashed wall that obscured his latest failure.

He'd tried four times. This last one had gotten further than most of his attempts. A painting of the star, which he'd started after hearing the news of an upcoming voyage intended to travel the darkness of the sky. A trip to the star itself, for which scientists planned to use a special vessel and a pair of hion lines launched an incredible distance.

In this, Painter had learned something interesting. Contrary to what everyone had once assumed, the star wasn't merely a spot of light in the sky. Telescopes revealed it was a *planet*. Occupied, according to their best guess, by other people. A place whose light somehow cut through the shroud.

The news of the impending trip had briefly inspired him. But he'd lost that spark, and the painting had languished. How long had it been since he'd covered it over? At least a month.

On the corner of the wall near the painting, he picked out steaming blackness. The nightmare had passed this way and brushed the stone, leaving residue that evaporated slowly, shedding black tendrils into the night. He'd expected it to take this path; they almost always took the most direct way into the city. It was good to confirm it nonetheless.

Painter crept inward, reentering the realm of the twin hion lights. Laughter echoed from somewhere to his right, but the nightmare probably hadn't gone that direction. The pleasure district was where people went to do anything *other* than sleep.

There, he thought, picking out black wisps on a planter up ahead. The shrub grew toward the hion lines and their nourishing light. So as Painter moved down the empty roadway, he walked between plants that looked as if they were reaching arms up in silent salute.

The next sign came near an alley. An actual footprint, black, steaming dark vapors. The nightmare had begun evolving, picking up on human thoughts, changing from formless blackness to something with a shape. Only a vague one at first, but instead of being a slinking, flowing black thing, it probably had feet now. Even in that form they rarely left footprints, so he was fortunate to have found one.

He moved onto a darker street, where the hion lines were fine and thin overhead. In this shadowy place, he remembered his first nights working alone. Despite extensive training, despite mentorship with three different painters, he'd felt exposed and raw—like a fresh scrape exposed to the air, his emotions and fear close to the surface.

These days, fear was layered well beneath calluses of experience. Still, he gripped his shoulder bag tightly in one hand and held his brush out as he crept along. There, on the wall, was a handprint with too-long fingers and what looked like claws. Yes, it *was* taking a form. Its prey must be close.

Farther along the narrow alley, by a bare wall, he found the nightmare: a thing of ink and shadow some seven feet tall. It had fashioned two long arms that bent too many times, the elongated palms pressed against the wall, fingers spread. Its head had sunk *through* the stone to peek into the room beyond.

The tall ones always unnerved him, particularly when they had long fingers. He felt he'd seen figures like that in his own fragmented dreams— figments of terrors buried within. His feet scraped the stones, and the thing heard and withdrew its head, wisps of formless blackness rising from it like ash from a smoldering fire.

No face though. They never had faces—not unless something was going very wrong. Instead they usually displayed a deeper blackness on the front of the head. One that *dripped* dark liquid. Like tears, or wax near a flame.

Painter immediately raised his mental protections, thinking calm thoughts. This was the first and most important training. The nightmares, like many predators that fed on minds, could sense thoughts and emotions. They searched for the most powerful, raw ones to feed upon. A placid mind was of little interest.

The thing turned and put its head through the wall again. This building had no windows, which was foolish. Nightmares could ignore walls. In removing windows, the occupants trapped themselves more fully in the boxes of their homes, feeding their claustrophobia—and making the jobs of the painters more difficult.

Painter moved carefully, slowly, taking a canvas—a good three-foot by three-foot piece of thick cloth on a frame—from his shoulder bag. He set it on the ground in front of him. His jar of ink followed—black and runny. Nightmare painters always worked in black on white, no colors, as you wanted something that mimicked the look of a nightmare. The ink blend was designed to give excellent gradations in the grey and black. Not that Painter bothered with that much nuance these days.

He dipped the brush in the ink and knelt above his canvas, then paused, gazing at the nightmare. The blackness continued to steam off it, and its shape was still fairly indistinct. This was probably only its first or second trip into the city. It took a good dozen trips before a nightmare had enough substance to be dangerous—and they had to return to the shroud each time to renew, lest they evaporate away.

Judging by its appearance, this one was fairly new. It probably couldn't hurt him.

Probably.

And here was the crux of why painters were so important, yet so disposable. Their job was essential, but not *urgent*. As long as a nightmare was discovered within its first ten or so trips into the city, it could be neutralized. That almost always happened.

Painter was good at controlling his fear with thoughts like these. That was part of his training—very pragmatic. Once his breathing calmed, he tried to consider what the nightmare looked like, what its shape *could* have been. Supposedly if you picked something that the entity already resembled, then painted that, you would have more power over it. He had trouble with this. Or rather, during the last few months it had felt like more trouble than it was worth.

So today he settled on the shape of a small bamboo thicket and began painting. The thing had spindly arms, after all. Those were kind of like bamboo.

He'd practiced a great number of bamboo stalks. In fact, you could say that Painter had a certain scientific precision in the way he drew each segment—a little sideways flourish at the start, followed by a long line. You let the brush linger a moment so that when you raised it, the blot the brush left formed the end knob of the bamboo segment. You could create each in a single stroke.

It was efficient, and these days that seemed most important to him. As he painted, he fixed the shape in his mind—a central powerful image. As usual such deliberate thought drew the thing's attention. It hesitated, then pulled its head out from the wall and turned in his direction, its face dripping its own ink.

It moved toward him, walking on its arms, but those had grown more round. With knobbed segments.

Painter continued. Stroke. Flourish. Leaves made with quick flips of the brush, blacker than the main body of the bamboo. Similar protrusions appeared on the arms of the thing as it drew closer. It also shrank in upon itself as he painted a pot at the bottom.

The painting captured the thing. Diverted it. So that by the time it reached him, the transformation was fully in effect.

He never lost himself in the painting these days. After all, he told himself, he had a job to do. And he did that job well. As he finished, the thing even adopted some of the sounds of bamboo—the soft rattle of stalks beating against one another to accompany the omnipresent buzz of the hion lines above.

He lifted his brush, leaving a perfect bamboo painting on his canvas, mimicked by the thing in the alley, leaves brushing the walls. Then, with a sound very much like a sigh, the nightmare dispersed. He'd deliberately transformed it into a harmless shape—and now, trapped as it was, it couldn't flee to the shroud to regain strength. Instead, like water trapped on a hot plate, it just . . . evaporated.

Soon Painter was alone in the alley. He packed up his things, sliding the canvas back into the large bag, alongside three unused ones. Then he returned to his patrol.

Chapter 4

THE LOCAL steamwell erupted right as Yumi was passing—at a safe distance—on the way to the place of ritual.

A glorious jet of water ascended from the hole in the center of the village. A furious, superheated cascade that reached forty feet at its highest—a gift from the spirits deep below. This water was vital; rain was scarce in Torio, and rivers . . . well, one can imagine what the superheated ground did to prospective rivers. Water wasn't *rare* in Yumi's land, but it was concentrated, centralized, elevated.

The air nearest the steamwells was humid, nourishing migratory plants and other lively entities. You often found clouds above the steamwells, offering shade and occasional rainfall. The water that didn't escape as steam rained down on large bronze trays set up in six concentric rings around the geyser. Elevated from the ground to keep them cool, the metal funneled the water down the slope toward the nearby homes. There were some sixty of those in the town—with room to grow, judging by how much water the steamwell released.

The homes were built a good distance back, of course. Steamwells were vital to life in this land, yes, but it was best not to fraternize.

Farther out from the city were the searing barrens. Wastelands where the ground was too hot even for plants; the stone there could set clogs afire and kill travelers who lingered. In Torio you traveled only at night, and only upon hovering wagons pulled by flying devices created by the spirits. Needless to say, most people stayed home.

The loud pelting of drops against metal basins drowned out the murmurs of the watching crowds. Bathing finished, prayers proffered, Yumi could now be gawked at officially, so her attendants followed with fans withdrawn.

She kept her eyes lowered, and she walked with a practiced step—a yoki-hijo must glide, as if a spirit. She was glad for the sound of the steamwell, for though she didn't dare *mind* the whispers and murmurs of awe, they did sometimes . . . overwhelm. She quickly reminded herself that the people's awe wasn't for *her*, but for her calling. She needed to remember that, needed to banish pride and remain reserved. She most certainly needed to avoid anything embarrassing—like smiling. Out of reverence for her station.

The station, in return, did not notice. As is the case with many things that people revere.

She passed homes, most of which were in two tiers: One section built upon the ground to benefit from the warmth and heat. Another built on stilts, with air underneath to keep it cooler. Imagine two large planter boxes built against one another, one elevated four feet, the other resting on the ground. Most of them had a stocky tree or two—about eight feet from the tips of their branches to the bottom of their wide, webbed roots—chained to them, riding the thermals a few feet in the air.

Lighter plants hovered high in the sky, casting variegated shadows. During the daytime, you found low plants solely in spots like gardens, where the ground was cooler. That and places where humans worked to keep them nearby, so they didn't float away, or get float*ed* away. Torio is the only land I've ever heard of with tree rustlers.

(Yes, there's more to the flying than the thermals alone. Even in Torio the trees are made of heavy wood. So they need specific local adaptations to float. But we're not going to get into it right now.)

At the far side of the town was the kimomakkin, or—as we'll phrase it in this story—the place of ritual. A village usually had only one, lest the spirits get jealous of one another. A few flowers floated nearby, and when Yumi entered, her passing caused them to eddy and spin in her wake. They immediately shot up high into the sky. The place of ritual was a section of extra-hot stone, though not nearly on the level of the outlands.

(If you've ever been to the Reshi Isles, where sand lines the beaches on bright and sweltering summer days, you might have a frame of reference. The stones in the place of ritual felt the same as walking across that beach sand on a particularly sunny day. Hot enough to hurt, but not so hot as to be deadly.)

In Torio, heat was sacred. The village people gathered outside the fence, their clogs scraping stone, parents lifting children. Three local spirit scribes settled on tall stools to sing songs that, best I can tell, the spirits never noticed. (I approve of the job nonetheless. Anything to gainfully employ more musicians. It's not that we're unable to do anything else; it's more that if you don't find something productive for us to do, we'll generally start asking questions like, "Hey, why aren't they worshipping *me*?")

Everyone waited outside the small fenced portion of ground, including Liyun. The songs started: a rhythmic chanting accompanying a percussion of sticks on paddle drums, a flute in the background, all of it growing more audible as the steamwell finished relieving itself and stumbled off to sleep.

Inside the place of ritual was only Yumi.

The spirits deep underground.

And a whole lot of rocks.

The villagers spent months gathering them, setting them throughout the city, then deliberating over which ones had the best shapes. You may think your local pastimes are boring, and the things your parents always forced you to do mind-numbing, but at least you didn't spend your days excited by the prospect of ranking rock shapes.

Yumi put on a pair of kneepads, then knelt in the center of the rocks, spreading her skirts—which rippled and rose in the thermals. Normally you did not want your skin that close to the ground. Here, there was something almost intimate about kneeling. Spirits gathered in warm places. Or rather, warmth was a sign they were near.

They were unseen as of yet. You had to draw them forth—but they wouldn't come to the beck of just anyone. You needed someone like

Yumi. You needed a girl who could call to the spirits. There were many viable methods, but they shared a common theme: creativity. Most self-aware Invested beings—be they called fay, seon, or spirit—respond to this fundamental aspect of human nature in one way or another.

Something from nothing. Creation.

Beauty from raw materials. Art.

Order from chaos. Organization.

Or in this case, all three at once. Each yoki-hijo trained in an ancient and powerful art. A deliberate, wondrous artistry requiring the full synergy of body and mind. Geological reorganization on the microscale, requiring acute understanding of gravitational equilibrium.

In other words, they stacked rocks.

Yumi selected one with an interesting shape and carefully balanced it on end, then removed her hands and left it standing—oblong, looking like it *should* fall. The crowd gasped, though nothing arcane or mystical was on display. The art was a product of instinct and practice. She placed a second stone on the first, then two on top at once—balancing them against one another in a way that looked impossible. The contrasting stones—one leaning out to the right, the other precariously resting on its left tip—remained steady as she pulled her hands away.

There was a deliberate reverence to the way Yumi positioned rocks—seeming to cradle them for a moment, stilling them like a mother with a sleeping child. Then she'd withdraw her hands and leave the rocks as if one breath from collapse. It wasn't magic. But it was certainly magical.

The crowd ate it up. If you find their fascination to be odd, well . . . I'm not going to disagree. It *is* a little strange. Not merely the balancing, but the way her people treated the performances—and creations—of the yoki-hijo as the greatest possible triumphs of artistry.

But then again, there's nothing intrinsically valuable about *any* kind of art. That's not me complaining or making light. It's one of the most wonderful aspects to art—the fact that *people* decide what is beautiful. We don't get to decide what is food and what is not. (Yes, exceptions exist. Don't be pedantic. When you pass those marbles, we're all going to laugh.) But we *absolutely* get to decide what counts as art.

If Yumi's people wanted to declare that rock arrangements surpassed painting or sculpture as an artistic creation . . . well, I personally found it fascinating.

The spirits agreed.

Today Yumi created a spiral, using the artist's sequence of progress as a kind of loose structure. You might know it by a different name. One, one, two, three, five, eight, thirteen, twenty-one, thirty-four. Then back down. The piles of twenty or thirty rocks should have been the most impressive—and indeed, the fact that she could stack them so well is incredible. But she found ways to make the stacks of five or three delight just as much. Incongruous mixes of tiny rocks, with enormous ones balanced on top. Shingled patterns of stones, oblong ones hanging out precariously to the sides. Stones as long as her forearm balanced on their tiniest tips.

From the mathematical descriptions, and the use of the artist's sequence, you might have assumed the process to be methodical. Calculating. Yet it felt more a feat of organic improvisation than it did one of engineering prowess. Yumi swayed as she stacked, moving to the beats of the drums. She'd close her eyes, swimming her head from side to side as she *felt* the stones grind beneath her fingers. Judged their weights, the way they tipped.

Yumi didn't want to simply accomplish the task. She didn't want merely to perform for the whispering, excitable audience. She wanted to be worthy. She wanted to sense the spirits and know what they desired of her.

She felt they deserved so much better than her. Someone who did more than she could, even at her best. Someone who didn't secretly yearn for freedom. Someone who didn't—deep down—reject the incredible gift she'd been given.

Over the course of several hours, the sculpture grew into a brilliant spiral of dozens of stacks. Yumi outlasted the drumming women, who fell off after about two hours. She continued as people took children home for naps, or slipped away to eat. She went on so long that Liyun had to duck out to use the facilities, then hastily return.

Those watching could appreciate the sculpture, of course. But the best place to view it was from above. Or below. Imagine a great swirl made up of stacked stones, evoking the feeling of blowing wind, spiraling, yet made entirely from rock. Order from chaos. Beauty from raw materials. Something from nothing. The spirits noticed.

In record numbers, they noticed.

As Yumi persevered through scraped fingers and aching muscles, spirits began to float up from the stones beneath. Teardrop shaped, radiant like the sun—a swirling red and blue—and the size of a person's head. They'd rise up and settle next to Yumi, watching her progress, transfixed. They didn't have eyes—they were little more than blobs—but they could watch. Sense, at least.

Spirits of this sort find human creations to be fascinating. And here, because of what she'd done—because of who she was—they knew this sculpture was a gift. As the day grew dark and the plants began to drift down from the upper layers of the sky, Yumi finally started to weaken. By now her fingers were bloodied—the calluses scraped away by repetitive movement. Her arms had gone from sore to numb, to somehow both sore *and* numb.

It was time for the next step. She couldn't afford a childish mistake like she'd suffered in her early years: that of working so hard that she collapsed unconscious before binding the spirits. This wasn't simply about creating the sculpture or providing a pious display. Like a fine-print rider in a contract, there was a measure of practicality attached to this day's art.

Too tired to stand, Yumi turned from her creation—which contained hundreds of stones. Then she blinked, counting the spirits who surrounded her in their glory—in this case they looked a bit like a series of overly large ice cream scoops that had tumbled from the cone.

Thirty-seven.

She'd summoned *thirty-seven*.

Most yoki-hijo were lucky to get six. Her previous record had been twenty.

Yumi wiped the sweat from her brow, then counted again through blurry eyes. She was tired. So (lowly) tired.

"Send forth," she said, her voice croaking, "the first supplicant."

The crowd agitated with excitement, and people went running to fetch friends or family members who had fallen off during the hours of sculpting. A strict order of needs was kept in the town, adjudicated by methods

Yumi didn't know. Supplicants were arranged, with the lucky five or six at the top all but guaranteed a slot.

Those lower down would usually have to wait for another visit to see to their needs. As spirits typically remained bound for five to ten years—with their effectiveness waning in the latter part of that—there was always a grand need for the efforts of the yoki-hijo. Today, for example, had begun with twenty-three names on the list, though they'd expected only a half dozen spirits.

As one might imagine, there was a fervor among the members of the town council to fill out the rest of the names. Yumi was unaware of this. She merely positioned herself at the front of the place of ritual, kneeling, head bowed—and trying her best not to collapse sideways to the stone.

Liyun allowed the first supplicant in, a man with a head that sat a little too far forward on his neck, like a picture that had been cut in half and then sloppily taped together. "Blessed bringer of spirits," he said, wringing his cap in his hands, "we need light for my home. It has been six years that we have been without."

Six years? Without a light at night? Suddenly, Yumi felt *more* selfish for her attempt to escape her duties earlier. "I am sorry," she whispered back, "for failing you and your family these many years."

"You didn't—" The man cut himself off. It wasn't proper to contradict a yoki-hijo. Even to compliment them.

Yumi turned to the first of the spirits, who inched up beside her, curious. "Light," she said. "Please. In exchange for this gift of mine, will you give us light?" At the same time, she projected the proper idea. Of a flaming sun becoming a small glowing orb, capable of being carried in the palm of her hand.

"Light," the spirit said to her. "Yes."

The man waited anxiously as the spirit shivered, then divided in half—one side glowing brightly with a friendly orange color, the other becoming a dull blue sphere so dark it could be mistaken for black, particularly at dusk.

Yumi handed the man the two balls, each fitting in the palm of one hand. He bowed and retreated. The next requested a repelling pair, as was used in the garden veranda, to lift her small dairy into the air so that it would stay cooler and she could make butter. Yumi complied, speaking to the next spirit in line, coaxing it to split into the shape of two squat statues with grimacing features.

Each supplicant in turn got their request fulfilled. It had been years since Yumi had accidentally confused or frightened off a spirit—though these people didn't know that, and so each waited in worried anticipation, fearing that their request would be one where the spirit turned away.

It didn't happen, though each request took longer to fulfill, each spirit longer to persuade, as they grew more detached from her performance. Plus, each request took a little . . . something from Yumi. Something that recovered over time, but in the moment left her feeling empty. Like a jar of citron tea being devoured spoonful by spoonful.

Some wanted light. A few wanted repelling devices. The majority requested flyers—hovering devices about two feet across. These could be used to help care for crops during the daytime, when the plants soared out of reach of the farmers and needed to be watched by the village's great crows instead. There were some threats the crows could not manage, so flyers were a necessity for most settlements. As always, the spirit split into two to make the devices—in this case a machine with great insectile wings, and a handheld device to control it from the ground.

One could make basically anything out of a spirit, provided it was willing and you could formulate the request properly. To Torish people, using a spirit for light was as natural—and as common—as spheres are for you, and candles or lanterns are on other worlds. You might consider the Torish wasteful of the great cosmic power afforded them, but theirs was a harsh land where the ground could literally boil water. You'll have to forgive them for making use of the resources they had.

Getting through all thirty-seven spirits was nearly as grueling as the art itself—and by the end, Yumi continued in a daze. Barely seeing, barely hearing. Mumbling ceremonial phrases by rote and projecting to the spirits more with primal need than crisp images. But eventually, the last supplicant bowed and hurried away with his new spirit saw. Yumi found herself alone before her creation, surrounded by cooling air and floating lilies that were drifting down to her level as the thermals cooled.

Done. She was . . . done?

Her sculpture would be allowed to fade with time as all art does, and eventually would be taken down before the next visit of a yoki-hijo to this town. The power of the devices created in the ritual would eventually weaken, each spirit's bond remaining in effect for a different length of time. But in general, the more spirits you bound in a session, the longer all of them would last. What she had done today was unprecedented.

Liyun approached to offer congratulations. She found, however, not a magnificent master of spirits—but an exhausted nineteen-year-old girl, collapsed unconscious, her hair fanning around her on the stone and her ceremonial silks trembling in the breeze.

Chapter 5

THE NIGHTMARES had originally come from the sky.

Painter had heard the accounts. Everyone had. They weren't *quite* histories, mind you. They were fragments of stories that were likely exaggerations. They were taught in school regardless. Like a man with diarrhea in a sandpaper factory, sometimes all available options are less than ideal. One account read:

I watched it rain the blood of a dying god. I crawled through tar that took the faces of the people I had loved. It took them. Their blood became black ink.

Those are the words of a poet who, after the event, didn't speak or even write for thirty years. Years later, another woman wrote:

Grandfather spoke of the nightmares. He doesn't know why he was spared. He stares at nothing when he tells of those days spent crawling in the darkness, that terror from the sky, until he found another voice. They met and huddled, weeping together, clinging to one another— although they had never met before that day, they were suddenly brothers. Because they were real.

And then this one, which I find most unnerving of them all:

It will take me. It creeps under the barrier. It knows I am here.

That was found roughly a hundred years later, painted on the wall of a cave. No bones were ever located.

The accounts are sparse, fragmentary, and feverish. You'll need to forgive the people who left them; they were busy surviving an all-out societal collapse. By Painter's time, it had been seventeen centuries—and as far as they were concerned, the blackness of the shroud was normal.

They'd only survived because of the hion: the lights that drove back the shroud. The energy by which a new society had been forged—or, in the parlance of the locals, painted anew. But this new world required dealingwith the nightmares, one way or another.

"Another bamboo?" Foreman Sukishi said, sliding the top canvas from Painter's bag.

"Bamboo works," Painter said. "Why change if it works?"

"It's lazy," Sukishi replied.

Painter shrugged. The small room where he turned in his paintings after his shift was lit by a hanging chandelier. If you touch opposite lines of hion to either side of a piece of metal, you can make it heat up. From there, you're barely a little sideways skip away from the incandescent bulb. As I said, not everything in the city was teal or magenta—though the hion overhead outside obviated a need for streetlights of any other color.

Sukishi marked a tally by Painter's name in the ledger. There wasn't a strict quota—everyone knew that encountering nightmares was random, and there were more than enough painters. On average, you'd find one nightmare a night—but sometimes you went days without seeing a single one.

They still kept track. Too long without a painting to turn in, and questions would be asked. Now, the more lazy among you might notice a hole in this system. In theory, the rigorous training required to become a painter was supposed to weed out the sort of person who would paint random things without actually encountering any nightmares. But there *was* a reason Sukishi hesitated and narrowed his eyes at Painter after retrieving the second canvas and revealing a *second* bamboo painting.

"Bamboo works," Painter repeated.

"You need to look at the *shape* of the nightmare," Sukishi said. "You need to match your drawing to *that*, changing the natural form of the nightmare into something innocent, nonthreatening. You should only be drawing bamboo if the nightmares you encounter *look* like bamboo."

"They did."

Sukishi glared at him, and the old man had an impressive glare. Some facial expressions, like miso, require aging to hit their potency.

Painter feigned indifference, taking his wages for the day and stepping out onto the street. He slung his bag over his shoulder—with his tools and remaining canvases—and went searching for some dinner.

The Noodle Pupil was the sort of corner restaurant where you could make noise. A place where you weren't afraid to slurp as you sucked down your dinner, where your table's laughter wasn't embarrassing because it mixed like paint with that coming from the next one over. Though less busy on the "night" shift than during the "day," it was somehow loud even when it was quiet.

Painter hovered outside the place like a mote of dust in the light, seeking somewhere to land. The younger painters from his class congregated here with the sort of frequency that earned them their own unspoken booths and tables. A double line of hion outlined the broad picture window in the front, glowing, making it appear like a futuristic screen. Those same lines rose like vines above the window, spelling out the name in teal and magenta, with a giant bowl of noodles on top.

(Technically, I was a part owner of that noodle shop. What? Renowned interdimensional storytellers can't invest in a little real estate now and then?)

Painter stood on the street, absorbing the laughter like a tree soaking up the light of hion. Eventually he lowered his head and ducked inside, looping his large shoulder bag on one of the prongs of the coatrack without looking. Fifteen other painters occupied the place, congregated around three tables. Akane's place was in the back, where she was adjusting her hair. Tojin knelt low beside a nearby table, solemnly adjudicating a noodle-eating contest between two other young men.

Painter sat at the bar. He was, after all, a solitary defense against the miasma outside the city. A lone warrior. He preferred eating by himself, obviously. He wouldn't have stopped in, save for his tragic mortality. Even solemn, edgy warriors against darkness needed noodles now and then.

The restaurant's manager flitted over behind the bar, then folded her arms and kind of hunched as she stood, mimicking his pose. Finally he looked up.

"Hey, Design," he said. "Um . . . can I have the usual?"

"Your usual is so usual!" she said. "Do you want to know a secret? If you order something new, I'll write it down and wrap it up, then put it in your noodles. But I'll also tell you what it is, because the paper will get soggy in the noodles, and you won't be able to read it."

"Uh . . ." Painter said. "The usual. Please?"

"Politeness," she said, pointing at him, "*accepted.*"

Design . . . did not do a good job acting human. I take no blame, as she repeatedly refused my counsel on the matter. At least her disguise was holding up. People did wonder why the strange noodle-shop woman had long white hair, despite appearing to be in her early twenties. She wore tight dresses, and many of the painters had crushes on her. She insisted, you see, that I make her disguise particularly striking.

Or, well, I should say it in her words: "Make me pretty so they'll be extra disturbed if my face ever unravels. And give me voluptuous curves, because they remind me of a graphed cosine. And also because boobs look fun."

It wasn't an *actual* body—we all kind of learned our lesson on that—but rather a complicated wireframe Lightweaving with force projections attached directly to her cognitive element as it manifested in the physical realm. But as I was getting pretty good at the technical side of all this, you can pretend it functioned the same as flesh and blood.

I'll admit to some pride regarding the way Painter's eyes followed Design as she walked over to begin preparing his meal. Granted, he did overdo it—his eyes lingered on her the entire time she worked. Don't judge him too harshly. He was nineteen, and I'm a uniquely talented artist.

Design soon returned with his bowl of noodles, which she set into a circular nook carved into the wood. The hion lines—one connected to either end of the bar—ran heat through the element at the bottom of the bowl to keep the broth warm on chill Kilahito nights.

From behind, laughter and chanting picked up as the noodle competition progressed. Painter, in turn, broke his maipon sticks apart and ate slowly, in a dignified way, as befitted one of his imaginary station.

"Design," he said, trying not to slurp too loud. "Is . . . what I'm doing important?"

"Of course it is," she said, lounging down across the bar from him. "If you all didn't *eat* the noodles, I think I'd run out of places to store them."

"No," he said, waving to his bag where it hung from one arm of the restaurant's curiously shaped coatrack. "I mean being a nightmare painter. It's an important job, right?"

"Uh, yeah," Design said. "Obviously. Let me tell you a story. Once upon a time there was a place with no nightmare painters. Then the people got eaten. It's a short story."

"I mean, I know it's important in *general*," Painter said. "But . . . is what *I'm* doing important?"

Design leaned forward across the bar, and he met her eyes. Which was difficult for him, considering her current posture. That said, you may have heard of her kind. I suggest, if you have the option, that you avoid trying to meet a Cryptic's gaze. Their features—when undisguised—bend space and time, and have been known to lead to acute bouts of madness in those who try to make sense of them. Then again, who hasn't wanted to flip off linear continuity now and then, eh?

"I see what you're saying," she told him.

"You do?" he asked.

"Yes. Noodles seven percent off tonight. In respect for your brave painting services."

It . . . wasn't what he'd been talking about. But he nodded in thanks anyway. Because he was a young person working a vitally important, relatively low-paying job. Seven percent was seven percent.

(Design, it should be noted, only gave discounts in prime number increments. Because, and I quote, "I have standards." Still not sure what she meant.)

She turned to see to another customer, so Painter continued slurping down the long noodles in the warm, savory broth. The dish was quite good. Best in the city, according to some people, which isn't that surprising. If there's one thing you can count on a Cryptic to do, it's follow a list of instructions with strict precision. Design had little vials of seasoning she added to the broth, each one counted to the exact number of grains of salt.

Halfway through the meal, Akane stepped up to the bar, and Painter glanced away. She was gone a moment later, carrying festive drinks to the others.

He ate the rest of the noodles in silence. "Rice?" Design asked when she noticed he was almost done.

"Yes, please."

She added a scoop to soak up the rest of the broth, and he scarfed it down.

"You could go talk to them," Design said softly, wiping the counter with a rag.

"I tried befriending them in school. It didn't go well."

"People grow up. It's one of the things that makes them different from rocks. You should—"

"I'm fine," he said. "I'm a loner, Design. You think I care what others think of me?"

She cocked her head, squinting with one eye. "Is that a trick question? Because you obviously—"

"How much?" he said. "With the discount?"

She sighed. "Six."

"Six? A bowl normally costs two hundred kon."

"Ninety-seven percent off," she said. "Because you need it, Painter. You sure about this? I could go talk to them, tell them that you're lonely. Why don't I go do it right now?"

He laid a ten-kon coin on the counter, with a quick bow of thanks. Before she could push him further to do something that was probably good for him, he grabbed his bag from among the others hanging on the rack. He'd always found the statue coatrack a strange addition to the restaurant. But it was a quirky place. So why not have a coatrack in the shape of a man with hawkish features and a sly smile?

(Unfortunately, I had been quite aware of my surroundings when my ailment first struck. I had screamed inside when Design—thinking me too creepy otherwise—spray-painted me copper. Then, ever practical, she'd added a crown with spikes on it for holding hats, and several large bandoliers with poles on them for holding bags or coats.

As I said, I owned the restaurant. Part owner at least. Design ransacked my pockets for the money to build the place. I didn't run it though. You can't do that when you've been frozen in time. For your information, I have it on good authority that I made an excellent coatrack. I prefer not to think of it as an undignified disposal of my person, but rather as pulling off an incredible disguise.)

Painter stepped outside, heart thumping. A passing shower of rain had left puddles and given the street a reflective sheen—lines of light hanging above, their reflections ghosts beneath the ground.

Painter breathed in, and out, and in again. Having fled from Design's offers, he found it difficult to maintain the pretense. He knew he wasn't a loner. He wasn't some proud knight fighting the darkness for honor's sake. He wasn't important, interesting, or even personable. He was just one of likely *thousands* of unremarkable boys without the courage to do anything notable—and worse, without the skill to go underappreciated.

It was an unfair assessment of himself. But he thought it anyway, and found it difficult to stomach. Difficult enough that he wanted to retreat toward his easy lies of self-imposed solitude and noble sacrifice. But a part of him was beginning to find those attitudes silly. Cringeworthy. That left him afraid. Without the illusion, how would he keep going?

With a sigh, he started off toward his apartment, his large painter's bag across his shoulder and resting against his back. At the first intersection though, he spotted a telltale sign: wisps of darkness curling off a brick at the corner. A nightmare had passed this way recently.

That wasn't *too* surprising. This was the poorer section of town near the perimeter. Nightmares came through here with some regularity. Another painter would find this one eventually; he was off shift. Hands in pockets, absorbed by his personal discontent, Painter walked on past the corner. If he hurried home, he could catch the opening of his favorite drama on the hion viewer.

Another light rain blew through the city, playing soft percussion on the street, making the reflected lines dance to the beat. Those dark wisps began to fade from the corner brick, the trail going cold.

Two minutes later, Painter reappeared, stepping through a puddle and following after the nightmare instead of returning home—all the while muttering to himself that the first part of the drama was always a recap anyway.

Chapter 6

ALL RIGHT, let's talk about me.

Uncharacteristically, I don't *want* to discuss the topic. This isn't a bright point in my career, and I would rather the attention be on other less statuesque people for the duration of the narrative. That said, I know it's going to distract some of you unless I explain at least a tad.

What had happened to me?

I didn't know. It's complicated. I arrived on the planet, and immediately froze in place. Unable to move.

Was I aware?

Yes, at first. As the months passed, my senses began to dull. I fell into a kind of trance. Unaware, almost asleep. By the time the events of this story took place, Design and I had been in Kilahito for a bit over three years, Roshar time.

So, how do I know this story?

It started as voices. Dialogue. Lines spoken by Painter, who was near me. Others from Yumi—whose comments were softer, warped, more distant. From there my perception sparked, and I became aware of images, visuals, like they were . . . well, painted for me. In magenta and teal. Directly into my brain. Sometimes I saw what happened as faint representations, just two lines vaguely in the shapes of people. Other times I saw paintings or full-motion images. I seemed to have some control over which it became, depending on my level of attention.

To this day, I can't completely explain why this happened. Something to do with the Connection between us, though the intricacies of how these things interact sometimes baffle even the most astute arcanists. Regardless, I could tell that whatever was happening with Painter and Yumi was tied to what had happened to me—that their story was my story, only without the whole "frozen in place, painted copper, unable to interact with one's surroundings" part.

So kindly keep your attention on them. Because I most certainly wasn't going anywhere or doing anything interesting, not anytime soon.

Yumi awoke on the floor of her wagon, a blanket over her. She had been bathed, dressed in her formal sleeping gown, and placed here. Surrounded by flower petals in a circle, along with a ring of seeds for luck. Starlight cut around her in a square, reaching in through the window to gawk.

Sore, still exhausted despite her hours of sleep, Yumi curled up beneath her blanket. They had to be at a halt in their travels. The chill air of night had driven back the worst of the ground's heat, and her wagon had been lowered so that its stone floor could soak up the remaining warmth. She usually loved this. There was a unique comfort to being able to drape a blanket over her and bake in the floor's radiance. It was almost like the planet itself was feeding her strength.

Yumi huddled there for some time, trying to recover. She knew she should feel pride at her accomplishment, and virtually any other person would have.

But she just felt . . . tired. And guilty over her lack of proper emotions.

And more tired, because guilt of that sort is an immense burden. Heavier than the rocks she'd moved earlier.

Then she felt ashamed. Because guilt has a great number of friends and keeps their addresses handy for quick summons.

Heat seeped up around Yumi, but seemed not to *enter* her. It cooked her, but she remained raw in the middle. She stayed there until the door opened. You might have heard clogged footsteps approaching first, but Yumi didn't notice.

The figure in the doorway—in the deep of night, that figure was little more than a blot of ink on black paper—waited. Until Yumi looked up at last, realizing she'd been crying. The tears hit the floor and didn't immediately evaporate.

"How did I do today, Liyun?" Yumi finally asked, rising to her knees.

"You did your duty," Liyun replied, her voice soft yet rasping. Like ripping paper.

"I . . . have never heard of a yoki-hijo summoning thirty-seven spirits in one day," Yumi said, hopeful. It wasn't her warden's job to compliment her. But . . . it would feel good . . . to hear the words nonetheless.

"Yes," Liyun said. "It will make people question. Were you always capable of this? Were you holding back in other cities, refusing to bless them as you did this one?"

"I . . ."

"I'm certain it is wisdom in you, Chosen," Liyun said, "to do as you did. I am certain it is not you working too hard, so that the next town in line gets a much smaller blessing and therefore thinks *themselves* less worthy also."

Yumi felt sick at the very thought. Her arms dangled at her sides, because moving them was painful. "I will work hard tomorrow."

"I am sure you will." Liyun paused. "I would hate to think that I trained a yoki-hijo who did not know how to properly pace herself. I would also hate to think that I was such a *poor* teacher that my student thought it wise to pretend to be of lower potential, in order to have an easier time."

Yumi shrank down farther, wincing at the throbs of pain from muscles in her arms and back. Even in great success, it appeared she did not do enough.

"Neither is true, fortunately," she whispered.

"I will tell Gongsha Town," Liyun said, "that they can look forward to a visit from a strong yoki-hijo tomorrow."

"Thank you."

"May I offer a reminder, Chosen?"

Yumi glanced up, and from where she knelt, the perspective made Liyun seem ten feet tall. A silhouette against the night; a cutout with blank space in the middle.

"Yes," Yumi said. "Please."

"You must remember," Liyun said, "that you are a resource to the land.

Like the water of the steamwell. Like the plants, the sunlight, and the spirits. If you do not take care of yourself, you will squander the great position and opportunity you have been given."

"Thank you," Yumi whispered.

"Sleep now, if it pleases you. *Chosen.*"

It takes real talent to use an honorific as an insult. I'll give Liyun that much; it's professional courtesy, from one hideous bastard to another.

Liyun turned to leave, then hesitated, glancing over her shoulder at Yumi. "I feel like . . ." she said, with an odd haunted cast to her voice, "this will happen again. Unless I do something. I am failing as your warden. Perhaps . . . I will seek advice. There must be something I can do."

She shut the door with a click, and Yumi lowered her eyes. She didn't go back to sleep. She felt too much. Not just pain, not just shame. Other, rebellious things. Numbness. Frustration. Even . . . anger.

She hauled herself to her feet and walked across the warm stone floor of the wagon to the window. Since her wagon hadn't left yet, the next town must be close; otherwise they'd be on their way.

From here she could see a starlit collection of hundreds of individual plants that had lowered from the sky as the thermals cooled. They spun and drifted lazily near the stone, their gas pockets—one under each of four broad leaves per plant—slowly reinflating, the stalks supporting clusters of seeds growing on top. Scadrians would have called it rice, a type of grain that is smaller and thinner than the ones you eat on Roshar. It wasn't exactly rice. The local word was "mingo." But it boiled up nearly the same except for the deep blue-purple color, so I'll use the more familiar word.

As Yumi watched, some dozen rice plants caught a rogue night thermal and jetted into the air, then drifted lazily back down. Small creatures scurried underneath looking for something to nibble on while avoiding serpents. Both prey and hunter slept in trees during the heat. If they were fortunate—or unfortunate, depending on the perspective—they picked different trees.

A gust across the field made the plants shiver and sway to one side, but night farmers moved along, waving large fans to keep the crops contained. Somewhere distant in the town, a giant crow cawed. (They aren't as big as everyone says; I've never seen one the size of a full-grown man.

More like the size of a seven- or eight-year-old.) A village corvider soon hushed the animal with soothing words.

Yumi wished she had someone to comfort her. Instead she rested aching arms on the windowsill and stared out at the placid crops as they turned lazily, occasionally jetting into the air. A tree leashed to the side of the wagon quivered in the breeze, its branches casting lines of shadow across Yumi's face.

She could maybe just . . . crawl out of the window and start walking. No night farmer would stop a yoki-hijo. She should have felt ashamed at the thought, but she was full up with shame at the moment. A cup filled to the top can't hold anything more. It spills out over the rim, then boils onto the floor.

She wouldn't leave, but that night she wished she could. Wished she could escape the prison of her ceremonial nightgown. She wasn't allowed to *sleep* as a normal person. She had to be reminded even by her undergarments of what she was. Chosen at birth. Blessed at birth. Imprisoned at birth.

I . . . a voice said in her mind. *I understand* . . .

Yumi started, spinning around. Then she felt it. A . . . a spirit. Her soul vibrated with its presence, a powerful one.

Bound . . . it said. *You are bound* . . .

Spirits understood her thoughts. That was part of her blessing. But they very, *very* rarely responded to anything a yoki-hijo thought. She'd heard of it happening only in stories.

I am blessed, she thought toward it, bowing her head, suddenly feeling *extremely* foolish. How had she let her fatigue drive her to such insane contemplations? She would anger the spirits. Suddenly she had a terrible premonition: The spirits refusing to be drawn to her performances. Villages going without light, without food, because of her. How could she reject—?

No . . . the spirit thought. *You are trapped. And we* . . . *we are trapped* . . . *like you* . . .

Yumi frowned, turning back to the window. Something was different about this voice. This spirit. It seemed . . . so very tired. And it was distant? Barely able to reach her? She looked up to the sparkling sky—and the bright daystar, stronger than them all. Was . . . the spirit . . . talking to her from there?

You worked so hard today, the spirit said. *Can we give you something? A gift?*

Yumi's breath caught.

She'd read that story.

Most cultures have something similar. Some are terrible, but this wasn't one of those places. Here the boons of spirits were always associated with wondrous adventure.

She shouldn't want adventure though. She hesitated. Teetered, like a stone unbalanced. Then, in what was the most difficult moment of her life, she lowered her eyes.

You have already blessed me, she said. *With the greatest gift a mortal can have. I accept my burden. It is for the best of my people. Forgive my idle thoughts earlier.*

As you wish . . . the distant spirit said. *Then . . . could you give . . . us a boon?*

Yumi looked up. That . . . never happened in the stories.

How? she asked.

We are bound. Trapped.

She glanced toward the corner of the room, where a spirit light—the spheres touching to turn the light off for sleep—lay on a counter. It was identical to those she'd made earlier today. One light sphere, one dark. Trapped?

No, the spirit thought. *That is not our prison . . . We . . . have a more terrible . . . existence. Can you free us? Will you . . . try? There is one who can help you.*

Spirits in trouble? She didn't know what she could do, but it was her duty to see them cared for. Her life was to serve. She was the yoki-hijo. The girl of commanding primal spirits.

Yes, she said, bowing her head again. *Tell me what you need, and I will do whatever I can.*

Please, it said. *Free. Us.*

All went black.

Chapter

PAINTER WOUND through the next set of streets, tracking the nightmare as the rain tapped him on the head. The trail was difficult to follow; the dark wisps seemed to vanish in the haze. He backtracked twice as the streets grew narrower, winding through the huddled tenements of the city's outer rings.

The hion lines overhead here were as thin as twine, barely giving him enough light to see by. It got so bad that he eventually decided he'd lost the trail and turned to go home, passing a slit of a window he'd neglected to glance through earlier.

He checked it this time and found the nightmare inside, crouched at the head of a bed.

The room was lit by a faint line of teal hion tracing the ceiling, making shadows of the room's meager furniture and frameless mattress, which held three figures: parents the nightmare had ignored, and a child who made for more . . . tender prey.

The little boy was perhaps four. He huddled on his side, eyes squeezed shut, holding to a worn pillow that had eyes sewn on it—a poorer family's approximation of a stuffed toy. Treasured regardless.

The nightmare was tall enough that it had to bend over, or its head would have hit the ceiling. A sinuous, boneless neck. A body with lupine features, legs that bent the wrong way, a face with a snout. With a sense of dread, Painter realized why this one had been so difficult to track. Virtually no smoke rose from its body. Most telling, it had *eyes*. Bone white as if drawn in chalk, but as deep as sockets in a skull.

This nightmare barely dripped darkness from its face. It was almost fully *stable*. No longer formless. No longer aimless.

No longer harmless.

This thing must have been incredibly crafty to have escaped notice during so many trips to the city. It took around ten feedings for a nightmare to coalesce to this level. Only a few more, and it would be fully solid. Painter stepped backward, trembling. It already had substance. Things like this could . . . could *slaughter* hundreds. The entire city of Futinoro had been destroyed by stable nightmares only thirty years earlier.

This was above his pay grade. Quite literally. There was an entire specialized division of painters tasked with stopping stable nightmares. They traveled the land, going to towns where one was spotted.

The sound of a small sniffle broke through Painter's panic. He ripped his eyes from the nightmare to look at the bed, where the child—trembling—had squeezed his eyes closed even tighter.

The child was awake.

At this stage, the nightmare could feed on conscious terror as easily as it did the formless fear of a dream. It ran clawed fingers across the child's cheek, trailing streaks of blood from split skin. The gesture was almost tender. And why shouldn't it be? The child had given the thing shape and substance, ripped directly out of his deepest fears.

Now, the story thus far might have given you an unflattering picture of Painter. And yes, much of that picture is justified. Many of his problems in life were his own fault—and rather than trying to fix them, he alternated between comfortable self-delusion and pointless self-pity.

But you should also know that right then—before the nightmare saw him—he could have easily slipped away into the night. He could have reported this to the foreman, who would have sent for the Dreamwatch. Most painters would have done just that.

Instead, our painter reached for his supplies.

Too much noise. Too much noise! he thought as he slapped his bag onto the pavement and scrambled for a canvas. He couldn't wake the parents. If anyone started screaming, the stable nightmare *would* attack and people *would* die.

Calm. Calm. Don't feed it.

His training barely held as, trembling, he spilled out canvas, brush, and paints. He glanced up.

And found the thing at the window, long neck stretching out toward him, knife-fingers scraping the wall inside the room. Two white eye-holes seemed to suck him into them, pull him through to some other eternity. Before this day, he'd never seen a nightmare with anything resembling a face, but this one smiled with bone-white lupine teeth.

Painter's fingers slipped on the ink jar, and it struck the ground before him with a clink, spilling. He struggled to keep his calm as he fumbled for the jar, then frantically decided to simply dip his brush into the ink puddle.

The nightmare stretched forward . . . but then caught. It wasn't used to having so much substance, and had trouble pulling itself through the wall. Its claws proved particularly difficult. The delay, though brief, probably saved Painter's life, as he managed to get his umbrella out and open to shelter his canvas so he could begin.

He started with bamboo, naturally. A . . . a blob at the bottom, then . . . then the straight line upward with a swipe. Just the briefest pause then to make the next knob . . . Like clockwork. He'd done this a hundred times.

He looked toward the nightmare, which slowly slid one hand out through the wall—leaving gouges in the stone. Its smile broadened. Painter's mind, in his current state, was most certainly not beneath its notice. And bamboo was *not* going to be enough this time.

Painter tossed aside his canvas and pulled the last one from his bag. Nails ground stone as the thing pulled its other hand through the wall. Rainwater connected with its head, running down the sides of its grinning face: crystalline tears to accompany the midnight ones.

Painter began painting.

There's a certain insanity that defines artists. The willful ability to ignore what *exists*. Millennia of evolution have produced in us not merely the ability to recognize and register light, but to define colors, shapes, objects. We don't often acknowledge how amazing it is that we can tell what something is simply by letting some photons bounce off us.

An artist can't see this way. An artist has to be able to look at a rock and say, "That's not stone. That's a head. At least it will be, once I pound on it with this hammer for a while."

Painter couldn't see just a nightmare. He had to see what it could be, what it *might* have been, if it hadn't been produced by terror. In that moment he saw the child's mother. Though he'd barely glimpsed her face in the bedroom next to her son, he recreated her.

Turn something terrible into something normal. Something loved. He'd been warned that painting the nightmares as people was dangerous, because a person could still hurt you. But tonight it felt right. Even with a few brief strokes, he evoked the shape of her face. Stark eyebrows. Thin lips, faint brushstrokes of ink. The curve of cheeks. For the briefest moment, something returned to him. Something he'd lost in the monotony of a hundred paintings of bamboo. Something beautiful. Or if you were a nearly stabilized nightmare, something terrible.

It fled. An event so incongruous that Painter slipped on his next brush stroke. He looked up and barely caught sight of the thing running away through the alley. It could have attacked, but it wasn't *quite* stable yet. So it chose to flee rather than risk letting him bind it into a passive, harmless shape. In seconds, it was gone.

He breathed out and let the paintbrush drop from his fingers. He was relieved, on one hand. Worried on the other. If it knew to escape . . . it was dangerous. Extremely dangerous. He had basically no idea how to deal with something like that—and doubted his skill would have been enough to defeat it. Only the most talented painters could bring down a stable nightmare, and he'd learned—painfully—that wasn't him.

Fortunately, he'd done enough to frighten it away. Now he could go and tell his superiors about the encounter, and they'd send for the Dreamwatch. They could hunt it before it finished its last few feedings, and the city would be safe.

He left the canvas on the ground beside the umbrella and stepped up to the wall, wrapping his arms around himself to try to force some warmth into his core. Inside the room, the child had opened his eyes and was staring out the window at him. Painter smiled and nodded.

The kid immediately started screaming. That was a more violent reaction than Painter had been expecting, but it had the desired result: a pair of terrified parents comforting the boy, followed by a hesitant father in shorts opening the tiny window.

He regarded the supplies on the ground—paintings slowly losing their ink to the rain—and the wet young man standing in the alleyway.

". . . Painter?" he asked. "Was it . . ."

"A nightmare," Painter said, feeling numb. "Feeding off your son's dreams."

The man backed away from the window, eyes wide. He searched the room, as if to find something hiding in the corners.

"I frightened it away," Painter said. "But . . . this was a strong one. Do you have family in another city?"

"My parents," the man said. "In Fuhima."

"Go there," Painter said, speaking words he'd been taught to say in such a situation. "Nightmares can't track a person that far—your son will be safe until we can deal with the horror. There is a fund available to help you during this time. Once I register what happened, you'll be able to access it."

The man looked at the child huddled in his mother's arms, weeping. Then at Painter—who knew what would come next. Demands, asking why he'd let the thing escape. Why he hadn't been strong enough, good enough, practiced enough to capture the thing.

Instead the man dropped to his knees, bowing his head. "Thank you," he whispered. He looked back up at Painter, tears in his eyes. "*Thank you.*"

Huh. Painter blinked, stammered a second. Then found his words. "Think nothing of it, citizen," he said. "Just a man doing his job." Then, with as much decorum as he could manage in the rain—and with hands still trembling from the stress—he gathered up his things.

By the time he finished, the family was already packing their meager possessions. You'd forgive Painter for walking a little swiftly, often checking over his shoulder, as he wound through the narrows. He had the feeling of one who had nearly been crushed by a falling piece of stone. A part of him couldn't believe he had escaped with his life.

He breathed a sigh of relief as he stepped out onto a larger road and saw other people—the regular foot traffic of the morning shift. The star was low in the sky, barely visible over the horizon at the end of the street.

He looked toward the foreman's offices, but suddenly found himself unnaturally tired. His feet like clay, mushy, his head a boulder. He teetered. He needed . . . sleep.

The nightmare would not return to the city tonight. It would run to the shroud, regenerate, then slink in the following . . . night. He could tell the foreman . . . when he woke . . .

Sluggish, his mind a haze, he turned toward home, which was fortunately nearby. He barely registered arriving, climbing the stairs, and walking to his apartment. It took him four tries to get the key in, but once he stumbled into his room and threw on his pajamas, he paused.

Dared he sleep? The family . . . needed his report . . . for the funds . . .

What was happening to him? Why did he suddenly feel like he'd been drained of strength? Abruptly gasping for breath, he flung open his window for fresh air, leaning out. Then he heard something odd. A rushing sound? Like . . . water?

He looked up toward the star.

Something came from the sky and struck him. Hard.

All went black.

PAINTER blinked. He was hot. Uncomfortably hot, and something was shining in his face. A garish light, like from the front of a hion-line bus.

He blinked his eyes open and was immediately blinded by that terrible overpowering light.

What was (lowly) going on? He'd hit his head perhaps? He forced his eyes open against the light and pushed himself with effort to a sitting position. He was wearing . . . bright cloth? Yes, some sort of bulky formal nightdress made of bright red-and-blue cloth.

Beside him lay a young woman. You'd recognize her as Yumi.

She opened her eyes.

Then screamed.

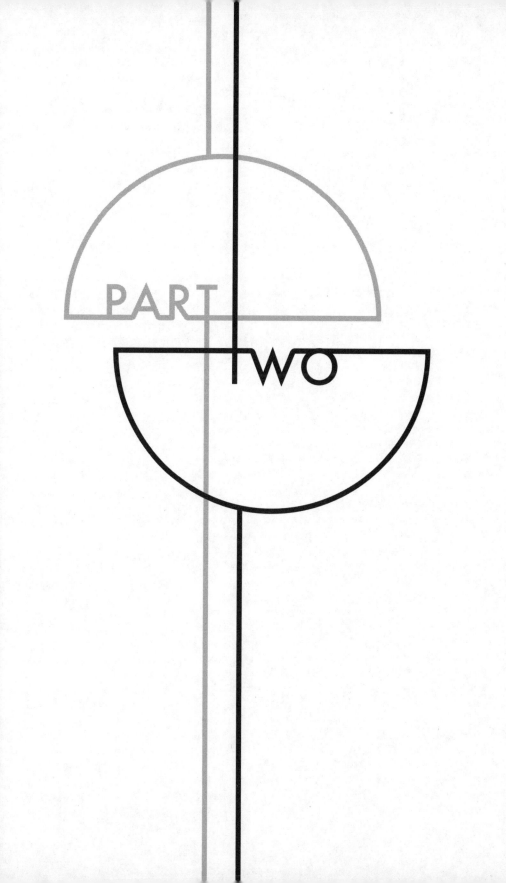

PART TWO

Chapter 8

PAINTER BOLTED to his feet. He was in a small room with a stone floor, wooden walls, and no furniture.

That *impossibly* bright light—flooding in through the room's single window—washed everything out, making it difficult to see. He raised his hand against the bizarre red-orange glare. That was a color that light should never be. To him, seeing it was like seeing someone spill the wrong color of blood.

Plus, that girl. How had he ended up lying next to her? She scrambled to her knees and grabbed at her blanket.

Her hands went straight through it as if she weren't there.

Right. Okay. This was . . . a dream, maybe? Painter knew dreams. His classes—which he'd mostly paid attention to while secretly drawing in his notebook—had covered their nature in detail. This didn't feel at *all* like a dream, but he knew you couldn't trust yourself while in one.

He needed to find some writing. According to his classes, that was one possible way to prove he was dreaming—you usually couldn't read in a dream.

"Attendants!" the girl shouted. "Attendants!" She continued scrabbling at the blanket, but it kept passing through her fingers. As if . . .

Oh no. Was she a nightmare?

Paper. He needed paper. Still shading his eyes against the garish light from the window, he did another scan of the room—but this place was completely empty. Who lived in a room with no dressers, no futon, not even a table?

Wait. Book over there, on a shelf. He snatched it and flipped through the pages. Looked like a bunch of prayers? He could read them without trouble.

The girl fell silent as her cries for help fortunately brought no response. If she *was* a nightmare, she . . . well, she defied his knowledge. One that was fully stable like she was should have been physical. She also shouldn't have had color, or the shape of a girl, but should have taken the form of something twisted and imaginary.

Unless she was *beyond* stable. There were stories of the last days of some of the cities that had been attacked, of solid nightmares that had begun to change color, more like flesh tones . . . But no, this girl wasn't crazed, lashing out in a maddened frenzy, trying to kill. She couldn't be a nightmare.

He glanced back at the book. He could read it. That wasn't sure proof, and yet . . . well, he knew dreams. He knew nightmares. He wasn't dreaming. Time was linear. Causality was in effect. He could read, feel, and—most importantly—consider whether this was a dream without feeling a disconnect.

Somehow, this was real.

The girl, who was wearing a nightdress identical to what he had on, frantically clawed for her blankets. Painter didn't know how to respond. He'd never woken next to an incorporeal girl before. While that's far more pleasant than some of the things *I've* woken up in bed with, it can still be rather disorienting.

"You wear my clothing . . ." the girl whispered. "You . . . you're not an intruder, are you? You're the spirit I talked to. You've taken shape?"

Painter wasn't certain what she was talking about, but—on account of it being better than being screamed at—he decided to play things cool. "Cool" in this case meant pretending that he knew what was going on. He closed the book and put it back on the shelf. Then he folded his arms and gave her his best confident "I am a dark and mysterious warrior" look.

She bowed her head. "You *are* the powerful spirit. Please forgive me for my attitude earlier. I was surprised, confused. I did not mean offense."

Wait.

That had *worked*?

Wow. What next?

Well, if someone thought he was cool, then he shouldn't undermine or contradict that. It felt like a good rule to live by. Even if this was his first real chance to experiment with it.

"Where am I?" he said.

"You are in my wagon," the girl said. "The wagon of a yoki-hijo. I am Yumi, and this is my chamber."

"And . . . where is your furniture?"

"I need no furniture," she said, "as my sole purpose is to serve and to contemplate your greatness."

That . . . felt like it went too far. He shuffled uncomfortably, then considered that maybe he could see where he was by checking out that window. He'd been deliberately avoiding that too-powerful red-orange light. This entire experience was impossible, but that light . . . it was *incomprehensible*. How could anything so bright exist?

With trepidation, Painter approached the window, though part of him was certain the light would burn him. It seemed so much more . . . well, just *more* than the twin hion lines. It was like the very essence of flame. He put his toe into it, cringing—but nothing happened.

He stepped fully into it and felt like he'd slipped into a warm bath. How strange. Blinking against the brightness, he raised his hand to shade his eyes and looked out. I wouldn't call that a *mistake*, not really. But like a ten-year-old asking for the explanation of where babies came from, he did *not* know what he was getting himself into.

Painter gazed up into a sky that was not dark. Instead it was a washed-out blue extending into infinity, dominated by an enormous ball of light. Like a huge light bulb in the sky except not soft and white, but angry and red-orange.

As if that weren't enough, *plants* dotted the sky. Big bunches of them, tended by great black crows that fanned them toward each other if they strayed. Fly objects buzzed around, organizing the crows and chasing away undomesticated birds.

The land went on forever, brown stone occasionally sprinkled with hovering flowers. It was a lot to take in. More than he could manage. He didn't even notice, for example, that Yumi's wagon was floating in the air.

What he *did* notice overwhelmed his remaining skepticism like a group of thirsty customers shoving open the door to the bar right before opening. This was real. But it wasn't any place he knew about, or any place he'd read about. It wasn't like his home at all. It was like . . . another planet?

"The star," he said, pointing at a gleam on the horizon.

"The daystar, spirit?" Yumi asked from behind.

"The news report said that *people* live on the star! That it's another world, like ours. I remember . . . a nightmare coming down from the sky, engulfing me . . ."

It had taken him to this place, perhaps? Then was that his home, up in the sky, visible from this position?

"Powerful spirit," Yumi said from where she knelt. "I don't understand what you're saying, but please. Could I know what you've done to me? And . . . how long you intend it to continue? That I might know your will, and properly worship it."

Yeah . . . acting cool was one thing. Making a young woman think he was some powerful divinity was another. "Look," he said. "I'm, uh, not—"

He was interrupted as a knock came at the door. Yumi raised her head in a panic, then glanced at Painter. "Please, spirit," she said, "restore me. *Please.*"

The door opened and two women entered. One was short and squat, in her twenties, the other in her thirties and more willowy. They were dressed in similarly strange, too-wide dresses, their hair up in buns. Painter felt a bit of Yumi's same panic. She might assume he was some kind of important spirit, but surely these older people would respond differently. What was the punishment in this land for being caught invading a young woman's bedchamber?

The only thing he could think to do was fold his arms again in a confident posture. He thought it was impressive. It might have been—if you were a four-year-old wanting tips on how to pout.

The two women, however, walked straight through Yumi as if they couldn't see her. They carried a small table, for sitting on the floor while eating, and a bowl of rice. They approached Painter and knelt, bowing.

He eyed Yumi, who stood up, her long hair snarled from sleep. She cocked her head, then walked forward and waved her hand in front of the women. "Chaeyung?" Yumi asked. "Hwanji? Can you hear me?"

The two gave no response. They remained kneeling, though one looked up at Painter. "Chosen?" she asked. "Are . . . are you well?"

Yumi gasped, her eyes widening. "Spirit . . . you've taken my *shape*?"

Had he?

Wait, no. He wasn't a spirit.

He had *no* (lowly) *idea* what was happening.

(As a reminder, Yumi's and Painter's languages have this curious feature that makes narratives rather hard on a storyteller speaking to a crowd of people without high or low variations in their boring languages. Conveying this can be awkward, but I'm doing my best. You're welcome.)

Anyway, while Painter was confused, he *was* also hungry. And these women appeared to be waiting for him to eat. He decided that the confident thing to do—the way of the solitary warrior—was to get some sustenance so that he could continue being mysterious without his stomach growling. So he settled down and took the bowl of rice from the hands of one of the women.

"Thanks," he said, taking the maipon sticks from another. He started eating. "You have anything to go with this?"

The two women gasped.

"Why, spirit?" Yumi begged. "Why have you taken my form? You . . . cast me out? I am only a soul, and you have my body? But why can *I* see you in the shape of a young man?" She knelt before him, in line with the others. "Please. I don't understand. *Please.* Tell me your will."

He hesitantly stopped, the mouthful of rice half-chewed. One of the women reached for the bowl and he shied back, then took another bite, judging their reaction. Horror?

"Is it . . . poisoned or something?" he said. "Not that I mind. I am strong enough to stomach any poison, of course."

The two women fled, abandoning the table and other dining implements. They left the door swinging—spilling in more garish light—and ran off, their feet clopping on the stone ground. Were they . . . wearing wooden shoes?

Yumi watched him with tears in her eyes. Then remarkably, subtly, her expression shifted. Drooping lips went taut. Teeth clenched. Her muscles tensed.

"That's *it*," she said (lowly). "I'm *done!*"

Chapter 9

I'S A common mistake to assume that someone is weak because they are accommodating. If you think this, you might be the type who has no idea how much effort—how much *strength*—it takes to put up with your nonsense.

Yumi wasn't weak. She wasn't a pushover. Don't assume fragility where you should see patience. Beyond that, she did have her limits. They had just been reached.

"I've served you all my life!" Yumi said, standing tall. "I've given *everything* to you!"

The spirit blinked. And, well, Yumi hadn't *intended* to make an outburst. I think that is rather part of the definition. The words simply gushed out.

"I made a mistake!" she said. "I somehow worked *too hard* yesterday. Is that why you decided to rise? Why you demanded my help, then took my shape? Is *that* what this is? Punishment? You're here to embarrass me! You *know* how someone like me is to act. You decreed it! So the sole reason you'd grab that bowl and start eating is to humiliate me!"

Yumi finished, sucking in deep gasps, filled with a remarkable species of anger. She'd never let herself act like this before. One might have assumed it to be refreshing, but for her, it was more . . . inevitable. You dropped a brick and it fell. You dropped a flower and it floated. You pushed a person too far and . . . well, they exploded. Like a steamwell. The pressure had to go somewhere.

She squeezed her eyes shut, hands making fists, and braced herself. She wasn't certain what happened when you defied the spirits in such a terrible, insolent way. There were all kinds of *implications* of course, but few explicit answers. An ordinary person could have escaped with only some bad luck, but she was a yoki-hijo.

She expected to be ripped to pieces. Perhaps to be compressed to the size of a marble. Maybe she'd be fortunate and the spirit would merely curse her to spit lizards when she tried to talk. But she couldn't have stopped the outburst. She was exhausted, sore, overwhelmed.

She waited. An uncomfortably long time.

Then finally, the spirit spoke.

"Let's pretend," it said, "that I'm *not* a spirit like you think I am. How bad would that be?"

Yumi cracked one eye. He sat there, a piece of rice sticking to his cheek. As soon as he noticed she'd opened her eye, he puffed up a little, sitting straighter, and made a strange face. As if . . . nauseated? She couldn't read it.

"I don't understand," she said.

"I wish that I did," he said. "But I'm not a spirit. I'm a person. Granted, a *mysterious* one."

"Mysterious?"

"Incredibly," he said. "Look, I don't know what this place is or why I'm here. But I think . . . I might be from another planet." He winced when he said it. "Does that sound crazy?"

She cocked her head.

"That star in the sky?" he said, standing up and pointing at the window. "The one you called the daystar? I'm from there. Maybe. It's my best theory."

"You're . . . human?"

"A hundred percent."

"Born from a mother?"

He nodded.

"You eat? You sleep? You . . . deposit the spirits' gifts back into the ecosystem to be reused?"

"Excuse me?" he said.

Yumi was barely listening. Was it possible she'd gotten this wrong? Well, of course. She was, as has been established, exhausted, sore, overwhelmed. Not the best state of mind for logical thought.

She reflected on what had happened the night before: The spirit talking to her, saying it was trapped. Asking her to free it. It hadn't sounded angry at her weakness. It had said, *There is one who can help you.*

"They *sent* you," Yumi whispered. "They sent you to help me! The spirits are in danger. There are stories like this—great heroes tasked with quests by the spirits." Her eyes widened. "They needed a boon from me. They needed my body? I couldn't do what they needed, so they've put you in my place . . . Tell me, are you a great warrior among your kind? The people of the daystar?"

He considered a moment. Longer than she'd have predicted. He was humble, evidently. Finally he nodded. "Yes. I'm among the greatest."

Her state made some sense then. The spirits had no substance until she called them. It stood to reason that in taking her form for this hero, they had given her a form as insubstantial as a spirit herself. She could feel her nightdress, but nothing else. Even the floor beneath her feet seemed to have no substance. She wasn't certain how she walked or moved on it.

"My attendants will return soon, hopefully," Yumi said. "Tell them what has happened." She reached out absently to take his hand in supplication. "They will know how to help. Please, we must . . ." She trailed off as her hand touched his.

She felt an immediate shiver, like when she stepped into cool water—but heat followed. Warmth *flooded* her, moving up her fingers in a rush, accompanied by an almost electric tingling. It surged through her, overwhelming her, driving away all other thoughts, feelings, and sensations.

When she'd touched the blanket, she'd felt nothing. Not even a tingling as her fingers passed through. The same when her attendants had walked through her.

But this other effect was completely unexpected. She let go and jumped back, sucking in a breath, sweat prickling on her brow. He gaped at his hand, and his posture made it obvious he'd felt it too. A connection between her spirit and her body, perhaps? She found it difficult to speak for a moment, gasping for air—though without a body, that metaphor didn't quite work. But when she looked at him, she felt like she was blushing all the way from her toes to the roots of her hair.

All right, she thought. *Maybe don't touch him. It is . . . distracting.*

"That was *crazy*," he said. "Touching you was like touching a raw hion line . . ."

She backed away, embarrassed. "Maybe," she said, "I could go see what's happening in the town? It's possible that in my current state, I might be able to communicate with the spirits."

"Sure. Um, I mean . . . a valiant suggestion."

She nodded and hesitantly stepped out of the wagon. She had slept barefoot and was worried about not having clogs, but her feet didn't feel the ground's heat. Only a yard past the door, however, she felt a sudden pulling sensation. She was unable to move any farther, as if she was tethered to him. She backed up, then tried running to escape the pull—but when she hit the edge of it she was yanked backward, as if on an elastic rope.

She spun and stumbled into the wagon. He stepped forward as if to catch her, and her chest brushed against his.

That warmth flooded her again, radiating deep into her core. With a yelp, she managed to leap away, then fell to the floor. Having no body, it didn't hurt, but her blush was hotter this time. Celibacy was a fact of a yoki-hijo's life, naturally. And she was very much in control of that aspect of her emotions. Absolutely in control. Yes indeed.

She was rescued from her embarrassment as a severe figure stepped up to the door of her wagon, which was still swinging open. Liyun wore yellow on black today, as was the ritual for the fourth day of the month. As usual, she didn't *appear* angry. One did not speak in *anger* to a yoki-hijo.

Besides, Liyun was expert at expressing emotions without speaking them.

"I hear, Chosen," she said, leaving her clogs and swooping up onto the floor of the wagon, "that you have, in your wisdom, decided to violate ritual today." She walked past Yumi, in a heap on the floor.

"Oh," the hero said. "Right. So, I'm supposed to tell you that I'm not who you think I am. I'm a hero, er, that the spirits brought? Look, my home is on that star out there, a place where the light is normal? Teal and magenta? Not . . . whatever is out there."

Yumi crawled on her knees to Liyun, then stumbled to her feet and nodded eagerly. Surely the warden would know how to approach this. Surely she could help the two of them understand what the spirits wanted.

"You realize," Liyun said softly, "that a Chosen must continue to serve, even through personal difficulties."

"Sure?" the hero said. "I guess?"

"If a Chosen," Liyun continued, "were to try to *escape* her duties through fabricated nonsense . . . why, it would only make life harder for her. And for everyone. The guilt of such lies would eventually tear her apart within." Liyun bowed her head, as if in subservience. "Chosen. I apologize for my boldness in explaining to you that which you already know quite well."

Yumi sank back to her knees, a sick lump in her throat. That was . . . that was exactly what she should have expected from Liyun. If she'd been less out of sorts, she would have realized that sooner.

"I see," the hero said. He thought a moment, then he . . . posed? With arms folded? Did he think that looked dramatic when he was wearing a nightgown? "I don't think you are taking me seriously enough. I—"

"Please," Yumi said, interrupting. "Please, hero. My previous plan was flawed. Just . . . just go along with what she is saying."

He frowned, glancing at Yumi.

"Liyun," Yumi said, "will never believe that I, of all yoki-hijo, was blessed in this way by the spirits. Just . . . for now, could you do as I say?"

"Who is she?" he asked.

"My head servant."

He seemed skeptical about that. Liyun, who had only heard his part of that conversation, opened her mouth to offer another passive-aggressive piece of "advice." Yumi spoke first.

"Tell her this: 'I am sorry, Warden-nimi. I felt remnants of a dream, and was speaking according to them. By overtaxing myself yesterday, I've left myself weakened, as your wise counsel indicated. Forgive my indiscretions.'"

He reluctantly repeated the words, cutting Liyun off.

The warden fell silent, studying him.

"Kneel," Yumi whispered. "Please? And bow your head? I know it's not very heroic, but . . ."

He obeyed, doing as she asked.

"Then shall I order the rituals to continue?" Liyun said. "Without interruption? It is, of course, your prerogative, Chosen."

The hero glanced at Yumi, as if to ask whether she actually had a choice. Which she didn't.

"I will continue the rituals," she said, and the hero repeated it. "Please send the attendants back. And apologize to Hwanji that I addressed her directly."

Liyun accepted this, and turned and slipped out, her clogged feet clomping on the stone as she went to search for Hwanji and Chaeyung. Yumi pulled her hands to her breast and bowed her head, trying to still her racing heart. She always felt so *tense* when Liyun was serving her. More so now. The woman was already convinced that Yumi was trying to dodge her responsibilities . . . and with good reason. Yumi was, she knew, a poor representative of the Chosen.

But the spirits had come to her for help. They had sent a hero. That meant something, didn't it?

"I don't get it," the hero said. "She's your servant?"

"Everyone serves me," Yumi said softly, "so that I may serve the world. It is my honor and duty to call the spirits, and bind them to the service of the people of Torio. As such, the people are . . . deeply invested in freeing me from worldly concerns, so I may focus solely on my important obligations."

"It's not just the sky that's weird here, then?" he said. "It's the (lowly) people too?"

"I must say," Yumi told him, bowing further, "that you are taking this well, hero. Many would insist this is nothing but a dream. Your adventures in your land must have been great and interesting for this experience to be mundane to you."

"I wouldn't call it mundane," he replied. "I just . . . have experience with dreams. My name is Painter, by the way."

"Painter," she said, mouthing the word. "It means 'one who paints' in our language. That is interesting."

"I . . . I think I said it that way, in your language. Which I appear to be able to speak and read. Anyway, it's more a title than a name." He thought a moment. "So . . . I'm going to have to pretend to be you? At least until we get this all sorted out?"

"Yes," she said. "If we can make it through the early part of the day, we should be able to approach the spirits and find out from them what we are to do. Perhaps . . . perhaps then we will know how to explain this to Liyun?"

That didn't seem likely to Yumi, but the hero—Painter—didn't know enough to object. Instead he scratched his head. She found it odd, naturally, that the spirits had sent a youth of her own age as the hero. Perhaps their ages had to match for the transfer to occur. And likely a hero this young was *more* incredible, to have accomplished so much in only two decades of life.

"Those other women were offended," he said, "when I took the food. Was it for them to eat, then?"

"They must feed you," Yumi said.

"What? Like a baby?"

"You must be free," she explained, "of all worldly concerns. Others will do everything for you that you need."

"That . . . sounds extremely patronizing," he said. "Maybe even humiliating."

She blushed. Well, as she considered it, perhaps to an outsider it would give that impression. Never to her, of course.

Despite his reservations, Painter didn't object when the attendants returned and set out their things. They'd prepared a new bowl of rice, and—with Yumi's coaching—he did the appropriate ritual moves, letting them feed him bite by bite. Liyun haunted the doorway, though she normally wouldn't come to Yumi until after morning prayers.

As the meal progressed, Yumi managed to calm herself. Painter took direction well. She would have expected a hero to be more arrogant, but he did as she asked. By the end of the meal, Yumi was feeling far more composed and confident. They could manage this. They could approach the spirits, and receive direction. All they needed to do now was . . .

Was . . .

Oh.

Oh no.

The attendants rose and fetched their fans. Liyun gestured for Painter to stand and leave.

"Okay," he whispered to Yumi as she stood up with him. "I think I'm getting the hang of this. What's next?"

"Next," she said, "we need to take our ritual bath."

Chapter 10

RITUAL BATH?" Painter said, thoughtful. That sounded nice. This place was much hotter than back home. A little refreshment would be welcome. "I suppose I could use a bath. It won't be too hot, will it?"

"The ritual bath is in the town's cool spring," Yumi explained. "Each day I work in a new town, so I do not know the layout—but the spring should be upon high ground. While you are here, it will be reserved exclusively for you, hero."

That *did* sound nice, particularly following what he'd been through. How could a simple meal be so taxing?

Unfortunately, his conscience was working on him. Painter had gotten himself into some trouble with issues like this—expectations from others, warranted or not—in the past. While thinking of those days brought pain, he'd sworn he would never get into that kind of trouble again.

Nonetheless, here he was. As the two attendants were out of the room, he found himself standing and staring at the strange ghostly girl with long hair. And words came out.

"You asked if I'm a great warrior," he said. "Are you needing me to fight something, then?"

"I don't *think* it will require that," she said. "I don't know, honestly. The spirits will need to be formed, and then asked. They said they're trapped somehow; perhaps you can rescue them?"

"By forming them?" he said, relaxing a little. "Does this require painting?"

"Painting?" she said, cocking her head. "We call them. Through art."

Through art.

Right. Okay. That he could do. Maybe even something other than bamboo. Was it true—had he been summoned to an entirely different world simply to . . . to paint? He should probably make sure, he thought. He looked to the girl to explain more, but . . .

She was just so *hopeful*. Emotions flowed inside him like blood from wounds, warm and sharp. How long had it been since he'd felt *needed*, *wanted*? He didn't mean to lie. He wasn't *really* lying, was he? Her spirits had chosen him, brought him here, perhaps to paint them.

In that moment, he wanted *so badly* to be the hero someone needed. To have a chance to make up for the mistakes of his past. To become something. It wasn't arrogance, as some of you might assume. It was more desperation.

Deep down, Painter saw himself as a ruined canvas—the painting spoiled by spilled ink, then tossed into the trash. This was his chance to spread himself out and start a new drawing on the back. He seized that opportunity like a ravenous man at his first bowl of rice in days.

"Lead on," he said, dropping his mysterious loner affectations and speaking with a heartfelt passion. "I'll do it. Whatever it is you need, I promise, I'll *do* it."

Yumi gestured to the doors. The attendants and that awful woman— Liyun, Yumi had called her—had gone that way. He leaned out of the doorway and looked around, hoping he'd be able to walk this part rather than being carried or something. Curiously the building—indeed a wagon as Yumi had said—appeared to be floating. That was . . . odd. But not much more than—

He stepped on the ground.

Barefoot.

Painter yelped and leaped back onto the wooden steps, shaking the wagon-room. The ground was *hot*. Extremely hot; like as hot as a *stove*.

For the first time, he looked specifically at the clogs everyone was wearing. Liyun and the attendants, in turn, stared at him with horrified expressions. It was the same sort of expression you might have given a person who sat down to dinner, then started eating the plate.

"What is wrong, hero?" Yumi asked. "I recognize you are mighty and strong, but there is no reason you need to walk without shoes." She frowned, glancing down at his bare feet.

"This place is . . ." He trailed off, not wanting to spoil the illusion for Liyun and the attendants. Finally, he took a deep breath and slipped on the pair of clogs by the door. It seemed he hadn't burned himself too badly, as the pain was fading, but he was still timid as he stepped onto the ground.

The procession started off. Painter felt proud of how well he walked in the thick clogs; they looked more awkward than they actually were. He merely had to be deliberate with each step. He looked to Yumi, but she lowered her gaze and seemed reticent. Even more than earlier. What had he done this time?

There were plenty of other oddities to occupy his attention. For example, the attendants held out big fans to hide him from the eyes of the gathering townspeople. That left gaps through which he could be seen though, and apparently the entire town had lined up to catch a glimpse of him.

Why the pageantry? Couldn't they have pulled him in the wagon to this new location? This halfway measure with the fans felt deliberate—like pretending not to care if anyone noticed your new haircut, but running your hands through it every time anyone glanced your way.

There were also those floating plants—but at least he'd seen those from the wagon. So he didn't gawk. Much. But then there was a very odd contraption at the center of the town—a big shiny metal thing made of wide sets of plates, as big across as a building. What was *that* all about?

At least the people looked human. He would have expected aliens from another planet to have . . . he didn't know. Some extra appendages? Seven eyes? Instead they were just people. Mostly eager-eyed, in bright clothing of a completely different fashion and design than he was used to. It reminded him of formal dresses and wraps worn at weddings among his people—at least the colors were similar. But these outfits were far bulkier, particularly on the women, whose dresses were bell-shaped instead of sleek and tight as was common in Kilahito. The men wore clothing that was loose and baggy—often pastel, with a watercolor softness—tied closed at the ankles. They accented these with the occasional black hat, and many wore neat short beards, which you rarely saw among Painter's people.

The townspeople stayed behind as Painter was led to some nearby hills. Close to the top, his attendants and he entered a secluded alcove where a pool of water filled a natural basin perhaps fifteen feet across. It looked to be only about waist-deep, and no steam rose from it. That was a good sign. Painter was already sweating. How did these people live here with that giant ball of fire in the sky constantly glaring at them?

His attendants drew to a halt outside as he stepped up to the edge of the pool. Yes, this part should be nice. He looked to Yumi, who had followed him past rocks that provided privacy. She was blushing furiously. Why . . .

Ah. Suddenly it made sense. She couldn't get more than ten feet or so from him, but he had to take a bath.

"It's all right," he whispered to her. "Just go behind those rocks over there and sit down."

"Hero?" she said. "That wouldn't be appropriate."

Then she began to disrobe, undoing the bow on her dress. She was some type of ghost, but it seemed her clothing was part of whatever she was, because she was able to remove the overdress and set it down, leaving her in an underdress akin to a thin nightgown.

"Wait," he said. "*That* wouldn't be appropriate? But *this* is?"

"I may be in spirit form," Yumi explained, "but I am still the yoki-hijo, and must follow the directions of the spirits. I must do my ritual cleansing. If we're going to figure out what it is they have sent you to do, then I must be pure before their eyes."

Painter tried to forcibly stifle his blush. He figured that heroes didn't blush. Unless they . . . what, had just slain their fourth dragon and had too much to drink?

"Well then," he said, "we could simply bathe in clothing."

"You can't be ritually cleansed that way," she said. "Besides, Chaeyung and Hwanji would think that very strange."

She nodded to the side, where his two attendants were walking up to join him. He'd assumed they were staying behind to give him privacy, but in fact they'd stopped to gather some soaps. And evidently to disrobe.

Because neither was wearing a scrap of clothing.

For a moment, Painter was rooted in place. Naturally it wasn't out of embarrassment, as he was a mighty hero or some such rubbish. It was probably something far more heroic. Like indigestion.

"At least they see you as me," Yumi said, "so you will not embarrass them."

Embarrass *them*.

Right.

That was what he was worried about.

The two set aside their soaps and began to undress him, because of course they did. Now, if you should ever find yourself in a similar position, *this* would be the place to call a stop to it. It doesn't matter if you're in a story, or if the fate of the world is at risk, or if it's merely the result of a few stupid decisions. You never need to let someone undress you if you're against the idea.

Painter, however, was *determined* to help. To not mess up this chance like he'd messed up his real life. So he tried to play it off as nothing. He did so poorly, mind you, but one might admire his gumption. You *could* have assumed his blush to be due to the heat, and he *almost* managed to look stoic. Until he glanced at Yumi, who had pulled off her underdress but clutched it awkwardly to her chest. Her long, shimmering black hair falling over her shoulders and around her arms.

"You . . . must have done this hundreds of times," Yumi said to him, her eyes lowered. "Been . . . in situations like this. With women. A hero like you would be revered and lauded."

"Uh . . ." Painter said. The attendants glanced at him. "I'm talking to a spirit," he said to them. "Please, um, ignore me."

They frowned at this, but pulled off his own undergarment.

"It's . . . something *very* new to me," Yumi said. "Do you suppose maybe you could . . . avert your gaze?"

Oh. Right. That was an option, wasn't it?

Now, you might be a little upset at Painter for not realizing this earlier, as it was the obvious gentlemanly thing to do. Please do remember, this had all come upon him rather unexpectedly. It's hard to be gentlemanly when the world isn't being particularly gentle with you.

But if you can't be a gentleman, you can at least not be a creep. Painter closed his eyes.

The attendants led him into the water, which he found warm. This was the *cold* spring? They began bathing him with the ritual soaps, and didn't exclaim or run screaming at the discovery of certain unexpected bits, so Painter assumed that the illusion—or whatever it was—worked absolutely, even to those touching him.

He did his best to relax. They didn't see him as him, so there was nothing to be embarrassed about. He figured that Tojin, back home, probably would have been *thrilled* to be in a situation like this. It would give him all kinds of opportunities to flex his muscles for everyone. Or who knew; maybe Tojin bathed with women all the time. He did always have Akane hanging off him.

Yes, Tojin would probably relish the experience. Painter wondered if he shouldn't try to do so as well. Wasn't that what a great hero would do? He could put his back to Yumi and enjoy looking at the other two.

But that idea disgusted him. The attendants didn't know who he was. It wasn't right.

You're a coward, a part of him thought. *This might even be a dream. Enjoy it.*

But . . . well, he just couldn't. Yumi was one thing. She'd chosen to come bathe here, knowing what he was. The attendants were another thing entirely. So he kept his eyes closed as he was washed. Unfortunately, he lost his footing while standing up, and started to slip. Through no fault of his own, his eyes popped open.

He found Yumi standing in the water nearby, looking at his waist— well, below it—her head cocked. As soon as she saw his eyes open, she squeaked and squeezed hers closed.

"Sorry. Sorry, sorry, sorry!" she said. "I didn't mean to do that. I—"

"It's fine." He closed his eyes again. "It's a . . . difficult situation." He meant that. After all, he'd basically done the same thing.

As the attendants finished his current rinse and he leaned back into the water, his hand drifted to the side and accidentally touched Yumi's. Again the powerful sense of warmth thrummed through him. Overwhelming, even *exhausting*.

But with it, this time, came emotions. Her emotions. He could feel her fear, her embarrassment, her shame. Her deeper terror that something was very, *very* wrong—and that she didn't know how to fix it.

(She, in turn, felt much of the same from him—though when she sensed the shield he put up to protect his natural shyness, she interpreted it as confidence. She felt his own embarrassment, and the shame buried so far beneath his surface emotions it might as well have been magma churning beneath the crust of the planet.)

Then, as they broke the touch, both felt better. The situation was horribly awkward, but in that moment they realized it was a *shared* experience of horrible awkwardness that they had to get through together. Trauma doesn't decrease with company, but it does grow easier to work through when you know someone else understands.

The attendants dunked him, and he—at Yumi's instruction—did his best to stay underwater for the ritual amount of time. After that, the attendants withdrew from the pool to dry off, then stepped outside to dress and prepare the yoki-hijo's tobok, which would take a few minutes. Alone with Yumi, Painter tipped his head back and relaxed into the warm water, his eyes closed. He let his hand drift out, kind of hoping it would touch Yumi's again.

"I truly *am* sorry," she whispered, somewhere nearby. She hadn't gotten out, then. "I . . . don't have much experience . . . with men, you see. It's not part of my training."

"Is it part of anyone's?" he asked.

"I don't know," she said. "Did you . . . lead a normal life when you were young? Before you became a hero?"

"Depends on what you call normal. I'd say it was . . . unremarkable in most ways. But not you? You've lived with *this* all your life?"

"This has been my duty since I was chosen by the spirits as a baby." She paused. "You may think it confining, but it's an *enormous* honor. I provide such an important service to the people. Our society could not exist without the yoki-hijo. Thousands would starve."

He wanted to be encouraging, but words eluded him. He'd pretended to be a hero for so long that now that he had to live up to that ideal, even deciding what to say was difficult. Still, as he drifted there, somewhere near her, he found himself increasingly thrilled to be stolen from his other life and brought to this strange place.

This, you might note, is somewhat different from many stories. Painter wasn't reluctant. He wasn't eager to get back to his life. What was there for him at home? Instead he was excited to find a way to actually help Yumi. To change the world.

But wait, he thought. *There was a stable nightmare. I never reported it.* He could only vaguely remember trailing back to his apartment, struck by what now seemed a supernatural exhaustion, his mind a fuzz.

He had to find a way home, or that nightmare could do serious damage. Kill and rampage. It was a sudden, cruel irony that the one time in his life where his otherwise monotonous job was urgent . . . was the same time he'd found himself in a mystical adventure.

He had to help Yumi quickly, so he could get to Kilahito and report that nightmare. Unless he could find a way to send a message. For now, he focused on Yumi. How could he fix her problem? She needed a painting?

Then his mind drifted a bit. Back to when he'd opened his eyes briefly and seen her standing there in the pool . . . her hair and skin glistening in the light . . .

Wait.

"Wait!" he said, splashing and righting himself, opening his eyes by instinct to double-check. "Yumi, your hair is wet!"

She opened her own eyes, then stood and touched her long black hair. Which *was* wet.

"Why?" he asked. "You can't touch anything else, but you can touch the water?"

She frowned. "I . . . didn't *feel* like I was getting wet when I stepped into the pool. I felt nothing, like when I tried to touch the blanket or the wall. Now though, I *do* feel it. I'm floating. I feel the water's coolness like every other time I've entered a pool like this." She cocked her head. "It means something. You're right."

They met one another's eyes. Then, at basically the same moment, they realized where they were and what they weren't wearing. Both blushed and squeezed their eyes closed.

Yes, I know.

But you were once young and nervous too. We all were. There's nothing wrong with being a tad awkward. It is a sign of a new experience—and new experiences are among the cosmere's best forms of emotional leavening. We shouldn't be so afraid of showing inexperience. Cynicism isn't interesting; it is often no more than a mask we place over tedium.

"Your attendants have dressed and are returning to dry you, hero," Yumi said softly. "They will wait until you're ready—it is traditional to allow you time here. I will get dressed, then turn and let you know you may approach."

The water sloshed a bit as she left the pool. True to her word, she called out a short time later. He opened his eyes and found her dressed in her nightgown again, with her back toward him.

Reminding himself that he wasn't *actually* exposing himself to the attendants, Painter climbed out of the pool and let the women dry him. One had prepared new clothing, even more ornate than what he'd been wearing before. An undergarment followed by one of the bell-shaped skirts, with a separate top that came down over it in a matching—but darker—color. Bow across the front, though that was less to hold it together and more to ornament the ensemble.

The clothing was made of a stiff, starchy silk that practically crinkled when handled. It was all so loose that it fit him, though he was several inches taller than Yumi and far from her measurements.

He did notice that her own phantom clothing, now replaced, was darkened with the water seeping through from her skin. She hadn't had a towel to dry herself. How had the water gotten her wet, then gotten her ghostly *clothing* wet?

He tried to think of an explanation, but once more began to feel strangely tired. As the women tied Painter's bow, the odd sensation increased, accompanied by nausea. That heat from the sky . . . the heat from below . . . the layers of clothing . . .

It all came together in an otherworldly moment his body was *not* prepared to handle. Heroic or not, Painter swayed, felt his vision go dark, then fainted.

HE blinked awake to the sound of pounding on a door.

Painter groaned and found himself on his futon. He shook his head, looking around his apartment. Strewn with clothing, a half-eaten box of cereal on the table, hion lights—teal and magenta—shining from the line outside his window, painting the place familiar modern colors.

It had been a dream after all?

The door continued to thump angrily. "Coming!" he shouted as the beating persisted. "I said I'm coming!" He shifted, sitting up, and put his hand to his head.

Yumi sat up from the floor beside his futon, dressed in a pair of *his* pajamas—the oversized shirt exposing her shoulder, the sleeves long enough that her hands barely stuck out the ends. Her hair was a frizzy mess, and she looked baffled.

He gaped, then reached for her. His arm passed through the edge of his short dining table.

Painter froze, then waved his hand through the table. He couldn't touch it. Or the sock that was sitting on it for some reason. Or the pillow, or . . .

Yumi stumbled to her feet, knocking against the table, causing an old noodle bowl to rattle and one of the maipon sticks to fall off it and clatter to the wood. She glanced at it, then at her hands, then met his eyes with her own panicked ones.

Oh *no*.

Chapter 11

YUMI WAS in the darkest place of dead spirits.

That was the only explanation for the strange hostile lights coming in through the window—not warm like the sun, instead cold and terrible. That was the only explanation for the chill air, particularly under her bare feet.

The door thumped and rattled. Some beast was out there. No, some terrible force from beyond life.

She must be dead. But if that was so, why was she so very hungry? She felt like she'd been *weeks* without food. Was that another part of the torture? Had . . . had she been taken to the cold skies, where the souls of the unworthy drifted? Was she forbidden the embrace of the warm earth below? Was . . . was she *that* bad a yoki-hijo? Had she failed the spirits that terribly?

Nearby, the hero groaned.

The hero. He was here. Hope surged. Was this part of their quest? She'd learned in the histories that many heroes traveled to the place of cold, frozen spirits. She tried to contain her terror and make herself feel strong. Perhaps this was what the spirits wanted. Maybe . . . maybe she wasn't dead, but on their path?

The door pounded again, louder.

"Nikaro!" a voice shouted outside. "You answer this door!"

"Great," the hero said (lowly). "It's the foreman. Yumi . . . you're going to have to answer that."

"What?" she said, her voice going shrill.

"I can't touch things," he said, proving it by waving his hand through a table beside the strange altar he'd been lying on when they awoke. He then seemed to notice her confusion. "This is my room in my world, Yumi. Like I was in yours?"

"Your . . . world?" she said. "You live in the land of frozen souls? The land of the sky?"

"Yeah, kind of."

"Are we dead?" she whispered.

"I . . . don't think so. But if the foreman is forced to break in here, he might strangle one of us . . ."

The door pounded once more. "I can hear you talking in there!" the terrible voice shouted. Some kind of demon, perhaps half person, half animal. Yumi stepped back, and only then realized what she was wearing. Some kind of loose trousers and a buttoned shirt, made of a thick but soft material.

She gasped. You could see the exact *shape* of her— That and the curve of her—

"Yumi," the hero said. "Look at me. Are you all right?"

"No!" she said. She glanced around again, and as her eyes adjusted to the darkness—it must be night here, but what was that strange light?— she picked out things she hadn't seen earlier. Wadded-up clothing on the floor. Unwashed bowls in piles on a counter. Refuse.

The hero . . . was a slob?

Well, of course he wasn't. Heroes didn't clean up after themselves. Servants did that. So his servants had grown lax in his absence. This *was* a small room. Surely this wasn't his sole quarters. She leaned toward the window and glanced outside. There she saw a dauntingly dark sky. No stars at all. A grim *nothing* up above that felt eager to swallow her. But she was in some kind of large building.

A palace? It was certainly bigger than any building she'd ever been in before. Yet the street was *lined* with them. A dozen or more palaces in a row! Taller than steamwell eruptions. How did these buildings get so big—ten stories—without collapsing? How did they live without heat from the ground?

It's the land of the heroes, she thought. *Rules are different here.* It was colder and darker than she'd imagined, but at least she *probably* wasn't dead.

The door thundered again.

"Go," the hero said. "Answer it and get rid of him."

"I can't answer the door like this." She gestured to her outfit. "The clothing outlines my form! It's so immodest!"

"Yumi, we were *just* taking a bath."

"In the service of the spirits," she said, increasingly frantic. "Ritual cleansing. That's *completely different*!"

"He'll see you as me," the hero said. "Don't you understand? Everyone looked at me and saw you. Now I'm the one that's incorporeal. They won't see *you* being immodest."

It was . . . a valid point. So, trying to control her anxiety, shoving aside her famishing hunger, she stepped to the door and eased it open. Doing that for herself would have been a novelty if the situation were different. Now she barely gave it a thought as she found a giant of a white-haired older man on the other side. He wore thick trousers and a buttoned shirt made of some material she didn't recognize.

He froze immediately, fixating on her. "What the . . . ?" He looked past her into the little room. "Well, slap me silly," he muttered. "Would never have expected to find a girl answering Nikaro's door . . ."

Yumi stiffened.

He saw her.

He saw *her*?

Painter groaned behind her. But this foreman seemed unable to see him, for he focused again only on Yumi. "Where is he?"

"Tell him I'm sick!" Painter said, sounding panicked.

"He's sick!" she said quickly, then felt a stab of anguish at the untruth. Liyun would be disappointed in her.

"Huh," the foreman said, narrowing his eyes. "You . . . all right? Everything good here?"

"I . . ." Then she drew in a breath and gave a deep ritual bow of conciliation. "O great being of the cold skies, forgive any slight or offense I have given. It is not my intent. Please ask of me what you will. I will do all in my power to see it delivered to you."

"Oh. Uh . . ." The foreman shuffled from one foot to the other. "Just, have him report in, okay? He didn't do his rounds yesterday, and we're already short-staffed. He's supposed to send word if he's sick."

"I will see this message delivered with all due soberness and courage," Yumi whispered, lowering her bow. "Please go with the blessing of the spirits and find peace in your life."

"Thanks," he muttered, sounding . . . embarrassed?

"Wait," Painter said, stepping up beside her. "You need to tell him something important. Um, repeat this. 'Painter says he saw a stable nightmare, and—despite being sick—is so diligent at his job that he is out hunting to get more information. He wanted me to inform you that this is an emergency, and that you must send for the Dreamwatch.'"

She repeated the words exactly as spoken and glanced up from her bow. The foreman frowned deeply.

"He said that?" the man asked her.

"Yes," she said. "I vow it." She knelt and touched her forehead to the floor in solemn consummation of the words.

"Huh. Right, okay then," the foreman said, then tromped away down the hallway.

"Thank you," Painter said, relief evident in his voice. "That's one thing taken care of, at least. I can stop worrying."

Yumi stood upright, glancing down the hallway as the foreman vanished. She felt herself blushing with the heat of a thousand stones.

A man had seen her. Like *this*. Not merely wearing . . . whatever this was she was wearing, but also with her hair disheveled. She was supposed to represent the spirits in every way, but today she would have had trouble properly representing a pile of *dust*.

"That was strange," the hero said, wandering around the room. "Why did he see you, Yumi? None of this makes any kind of sense."

Yumi moved to close the door, but as she did, a door directly across the hallway opened. And a goddess stepped out. Wearing almost no clothing at all.

Her skirt ended *mid-thigh*, and was made of some kind of glossy black material. Her shirt was filmy and drooped low, exposing the depth of her bosom. Yumi would have thought her a demon but for her beauty.

The woman was perhaps Yumi's age, but her black hair shone with a luster that no amount of combing would *ever* provide Yumi. She wore makeup that—instead of lightening her face to pale white, as was used for formal situations in Torio—outlined her eyes in dark colors, making them wide and inviting. Her lips were cherry red, her cheeks dusted with a hint of blush.

Yumi gaped at the gorgeous person, barely noticing when Painter cried out behind her, then waved his incorporeal hands through the door as if to try to shut it.

The woman turned to Yumi and paused, then cocked her head. "Oh," she said, taking in Yumi's state of dress. "Um . . . hello. Are you . . . a friend of Nikaro's?"

"She's going to think we're sleeping together," Painter said. "This is bad. She'll *never* talk to me again. Quick, uh, tell her you're my sister!"

"I'm his sister," Yumi whispered. "Yumi."

Then immediately panicked.

Her earlier lie about Painter being sick had been a . . . stretch of the truth. He was sick in a way—he was incorporeal. So while it wasn't strictly the sort of behavior proper for a yoki-hijo, she could rationalize it.

This was different. This was a deliberate untruth. The sort that she'd never spoken since having impressed upon her—as a toddler—the gravity of her duties and the requirements of the spirits. She cringed, expecting the spirits to rise up and destroy her. She had to be better than such behaviors.

However, no divine recrimination seized her.

The woman across the hall relaxed. "Of course you are," she said, evidently amused that she'd considered otherwise. "That makes sense. I'm Akane. Are you visiting Nikaro for the first time?"

"Yes," Painter said quickly. "Tell her that you came to see the big city."

Yumi repeated the words, numb. Maybe . . . well, if the hero was telling her to say these things, maybe they didn't *count* as lies. After all, the spirits had sent him to her. He must know what he was doing. So instead of worrying, she tried to figure out this woman with the strange dress and kindly smile.

"Close the door," Painter said.

Instead Yumi asked the woman, "Do you know Painter well?"

"What, Nikaro?" the woman asked. "Well, I knew him in school, and we live across from each other. So . . . I suppose, maybe?"

Yumi frowned, cocking her head. But then it clicked. Akane lived in his palace. She dressed like this. Painter was concerned she'd think that Yumi was sleeping with him.

"Oh!" Yumi said. "You must be one of his concubines!"

"His *what*?" Akane asked.

Painter groaned, flopping back onto the altar he'd been lying on before.

"He told me that he'd been with *many* women," Yumi said. "Er, intimately, I mean. A hero like him has many such conquests in stories. I apologize for my blush. I am . . . not experienced. He explained it to me when we were bathing together earlier. He told me all about the hundreds of women he'd been with! I should have realized when I saw you that you were one of his concubines!"

Yumi bowed. It was only proper to show the concubine of an important hero such deference. When she came up from her bow, however, she noticed the look of disgust on Akane's face. Which quickly became a look of violent anger, Akane's nose wrinkling in a sneer.

"He said all of that," Akane said, her voice as cold as the air in this strange place.

"I . . ." Oh no. She'd misjudged, hadn't she? Perhaps this was a woman he'd known intimately, but hadn't made his concubine. That would explain her anger. Except something about the way she was fuming . . . "You're . . . not one of his conquests?" Yumi asked.

"Girl," Akane said, "your brother has trouble conquering a bowl of noodles if it has too much spice."

"He's . . . a mighty hero though. Right?" Yumi asked.

In the other room, Painter groaned louder.

"Hero?" Akane laughed. Then she turned and stalked away down the corridor, wearing shoes that did *not* look like they would survive the ground's heat. But then, Yumi was beginning to think maybe this place wasn't *ever* hot.

She shut the door, then put her back to it. "I . . . did poorly, didn't I?" she asked.

Painter just continued staring at the ceiling.

"Painter," Yumi said, "are you a hero? Like you've been telling me?"

"I . . ."

"*Painter*," she said, her voice growing firm as she stepped toward him. "Have you been telling me *untruths*?"

He turned his head and met her eyes. "Look," he said, "I'm a very good painter. Well . . . okay, I'm a weak painter. But I'm capable enough, right? So you said you needed someone like me, and I figured . . ."

He held her eyes a moment, then turned away with obvious shame, flopping back down on his altar again.

"It's not my fault," he muttered, "what you assumed."

Yumi felt a crushing sensation inside her, something squeezing the air from her lungs, her chest constricting.

He wasn't . . . She . . .

She gasped in and out for several breaths, then sat on the floor. It wasn't warm. How did they live without warmth underneath to bolster them?

"What was I supposed to do?" Painter said. "I got home from work, and next thing I knew, I was in your world. In your *body*. And there you were, asking for help. And I do consider myself kind of heroic, you know? So . . ."

"You lied," she said. "You *lied*. And now . . . now I have no idea what's going on. I thought the spirits sent you to me, and . . . and that you'd know what to do . . . and . . ." She focused on him. "And you peeked at me when I was bathing!"

"*You* peeked at *me*."

"You're not a holy vessel chosen by the spirits!" she said. "*I am*. I . . . I need to stack something."

She stormed through the small chamber, gathering up bowls of various sizes, some plates, other kitchen . . . things. She didn't really know what went into cooking. She'd never done it before.

She plopped down on the cold, lifeless floor near his table, which was low like the ones she knew. Why make low tables if the floor was *cold*?

Her stomach growled.

She ignored it, instead stacking the dishes. And mind you, this wasn't normal stacking. No simple largest-to-smallest tower. No, this was expert-level ceremonial, *artistic* stacking. With a vengeful air.

Painter watched her, transfixed as the stack grew higher. Then he sat up, staring as she positioned several bowls on their edges, with maipon sticks used to balance them and make the stack seem to teeter on stilts—though if you were to touch it, you'd have found it surprisingly sturdy.

"Wow," Painter eventually said.

Yumi ignored him. She waited, praying, hoping the spirits would see this creation and visit. Offer wisdom, explain what they wanted of her. Why was she here in this terrible place? Why had they sent her a liar instead of a hero?

No spirits visited. She felt nothing other than a ravenous hunger. "I need something to eat," she said.

"Rice cakes in the cupboard maybe?" he said, waving. "Some dry instant noodles. You can eat them raw. I do."

She followed his vague gesture. The food she found—wrapped in a strange clear material she was too famished to wonder about—proved to be a nasty, crunchy substance, like something proper that had been left on the ground to steam for far, far too long.

She ate the entire thing anyway, then carried five more cakes—all he had left—back to the table and continued eating. Why hadn't the spirits answered her? Did they not exist in this place? Were they ignoring her offering?

Or . . . or was there a more terrible answer? Maybe they'd rescinded her gift, taken from her the blessing of being the yoki-hijo. The possibility terrified her.

"That's amazing," Painter said, still staring at her tower. "How did you manage to (highly) stack them *rim on rim* like that?"

"I managed nothing," she whispered around bites of strange rations, "save the exercise of the talents the spirits gave me. I am nothing. Merely a vessel for their will."

"Look," he said. "I'm sorry that—"

"I do not want to hear your lies, nor your excuses for lies," she said. "Please keep both to yourself."

"Fine."

A moment later the building trembled (as it often did when a bus passed by outside). That was enough to shift the balance of the stack, and it came tumbling straight down in a clatter of wood and ceramic. Yumi, even in her state, was shocked it didn't all break and shatter.

"Sorry," Painter whispered.

"The creations are unstable," she replied, "unless blessed by the spirits. Which mine . . . might never be again . . ."

She wiped crumbs from her mouth, then pulled her arms close, feeling like she was shrinking down into her strange clothing. Wishing she could vanish.

But she had not been chosen because she was weak. She had to believe—at least had to pretend—that she could fix her situation.

"So . . . what now?" Painter asked. "Not to sound rude, but you *basically* ruined my chances with Akane back there. I've been working on repairing my relationship with her for *months*. I'd rather not let you put a wrecking ball through the rest of my life."

"The spirits came to me," she replied, "and said they needed help. I have to believe they picked me for something special, regardless of how this looks or feels. But why did they pick *you* to help me?"

"Beats me," he said (lowly). He sat up, then heaved a sigh. "I need to know how much time I lost. I felt like I was on your world only a few hours, but the foreman says I didn't check in for an entire day."

"How do you know what day it is here?" she asked. "Do you check the stars?"

"The *star*, you mean?" he asked. "Your planet is the only thing we can see in the sky here. It wouldn't tell us anything even if I could see it right now." He stood up and moved to a piece of glass affixed to one wall. He tried to touch it, then muttered softly as his hand passed through it. "I keep forgetting. Here, come turn this knob."

She did so, making two lines of light—soft purple and blue—appear behind the glass. They vibrated and shook, taking on the shapes of . . . people? Yes, small people barely two feet high, but incredibly detailed. Sound came from the glass as the two people talked—a woman made of the blue, and a man made of the violet.

"—But your brother," the woman said, moving to touch the man's arm. The image grew more detailed, zooming in on her face, though it remarkably appeared to all be made of a single continuous line. "What will he say?"

"Lee? Why should I (lowly) care what *he* says? I live my own life. I have to."

"Ah," Painter said. "*Times of the Night.* That means it's Samday evening. I haven't seen this episode, so it's the first showing. So I missed one day, didn't report to work last night, and the foreman came to check on me in the evening."

Yumi settled on the floor and stared at the moving lines with wide eyes. "How . . . What happened to those people? Why did they turn into lines of light?"

Painter chuckled. "They're fine. Those two are actors. You know, like a play? You've seen a play, right?"

She shook her head. "Too frivolous for a yoki-hijo," she whispered. "But I've heard of them."

"Don't you get *any* time to relax?"

"I have plenty of time to meditate and pray."

"No, I mean . . . have fun?"

"If I waste time having fun, people starve," she said, still watching the two figures made of light. "How are actors doing this?"

"They're standing in another place," Painter explained, "and projecting onto the hion lines. Uh . . . I don't know how it works. Kind of like a photograph, maybe?"

She looked at him blankly.

"Right," he said. "I guess you don't have those. Just . . . imagine a pair of people standing in a room somewhere acting out this play. And these lines mimic the actions they're making. Anyone in the city with a hion viewer can watch."

"Is . . . that what the glass is? A hion viewer?"

"Nah, the viewer is these boxes on the side, which manipulates the shape of the lines. The glass is to keep you from touching the hion."

She nodded absently, mesmerized. The play, she pieced together, was about a man who had woken up one day without memories. This was important because he'd been the only one who knew the location of a fantastic treasure. But the story didn't seem to be about the treasure. It was about all the different people trying to persuade the man that they'd been his good friend, and about the man piecing together the fragments of who he'd once been and discovering—bit by bit—who was actually an ally and who was lying.

She knew that she should have been doing something else. Meditating, at the very least. But for some reason the story *connected* to her. The man with a blank life. Everything he tried was new . . .

She was so tired. Overwhelmed. There was something incredibly *therapeutic* about sitting, pulling a blanket around herself, and watching someone else's problems for a while.

When the story finished she gasped softly. "It can't end there!" she said. "What is in the safe?"

"It always does this," Painter said. "Every time. It ends right before it's going to reveal something important or interesting. I think they want to make it so you have to watch the next episode."

"We *have* to!" she said. "When is it?"

"This one is weekly," he said. "Some are daily, others every other day. For this, the actors have other obligations, so they can only do it once in a while."

"A whole *week*?"

The spirits were surely punishing her.

Yumi pulled the blanket close, trying to keep warm. Maybe this was for the best. She wouldn't be distracted by the story . . . except the lines remarkably started vibrating again and forming new shapes.

"It's returning!" she said.

"That's the next program," he said. "*Seasons of Regret*. It's one of the best."

"Another program . . . How many are there?"

"A different one every hour," he said. "All day. Though in the late night and early morning, they're mostly reruns. Which is nice, in case you miss an episode."

Every hour? All day?

This device was dangerous. She reached up and flipped it off before it could draw her in. She *had* to focus on her predicament. The spirits needed her.

"Did anything happen to you?" she said. "Anything unusual before you woke up, having stolen my body?"

"I didn't *steal* anything," he said, lying back on his plush altar, rubbing his eyes with the heels of his palms. To be honest, Yumi was feeling a little worn out herself.

"There *was* something," he eventually continued. "Like I had you tell the foreman. A nightmare—one that was almost fully corporeal. That's rare. I've never seen one like that."

"Nightmare?" Yumi said, frowning. "You were asleep?"

"Nightmares walk in my world, Yumi," he said. As if that weren't the most terrifying thing someone had ever said. But he seemed unafraid. So maybe he wasn't a complete waste. "But normally they're formless, without the strength or ability to hurt people. I told you, I'm a nightmare painter. My kind keep them in control."

"That . . . actually does sound a little heroic," she admitted.

"See?" he said, sitting up. Then he wilted. "But I'm not a warrior. We use ink, and . . . it's normally not dangerous. Boring and mundane, really. But I did encounter one. The foreman will take care of it though. Send for experts that . . ."

He stood up suddenly, causing her to yelp and pull back.

"The Dreamwatch!" he said. "They're warriors, Yumi. They fight stable nightmares. Maybe if they come to the city, we can talk to them about your problem. Maybe the spirits want us to meet with them?" He hesitated. "That doesn't make sense though. How would they help with your world? And why wouldn't the spirits send one of *them* to you instead of me? So . . . I don't know."

Yumi nodded, though she was barely listening. She found her mind oddly cloudy. She . . . she had to . . .

Suddenly she was tired. Incredibly tired. Though she intended to respond to Painter, she instead stretched and curled up on the floor, nestled in the blanket. And fell asleep.

YUMI awoke to delightful warmth underneath her back. As her eyes fluttered open and she moved to sit, her hand—unfortunately—passed through the floor.

She could feel the warmth, but her body was again incorporeal. Next to her Painter sat up, disturbing blankets, wearing one of her thick, enveloping sleeping gowns. He looked toward the window, where sunlight streamed in, and groaned.

"I guess," he said, "we're going to have to do something about that bathing issue . . ."

Chapter 12

'VE OFTEN wondered at the purpose of nightmares. Again, the normal kind, not the stalking kind. Why do we have them? Is there a point?

Maybe it's a brutal way of making us more resilient.

Humans are incredibly malleable. Despite my breadth of experience, I've never stopped being surprised at how durable human beings can be. They can survive in almost any environment. They can recover from debilitating loss. They can be crushed physically, mentally, emotionally—and still ask you how your day is going.

Perhaps nightmares are Cultivation's method of giving us a way of surviving trauma in a strangely safe environment. (At least safe physically.) A way to put it behind us, forget the details, but retain the growth. Nightmares are vicarious living done in our own minds.

In that way, nightmares serve much the same function as storytellers. Evolution doing a favor for those who, unlucky and unfortunate, never encountered me.

Painter finished his meal and barely managed to keep himself from wiping his mouth—his attendants had to do that for him.

Yumi paced behind him, invisible to everyone else. She'd barely spoken to him since they'd awoken. He kept trying to catch her eye, but she ignored him like one would a bad scent made by someone too important to stink.

Eventually the two attendants retreated—and were replaced by Liyun, in her strict formal outfit, her hairstyle impeccably symmetrical. There was a certain art to the way she loomed over him. He wondered if she practiced. How else would one explain her perfect posture, looking down at him without tipping her head, which made even the act of studying him seem like a huge inconvenience. The way she folded her arms to make her shadow expand across him, isolating him in darkness. The way she lingered *just* a tad longer than was comfortable . . .

It was impressive. Like a beautiful gourmet dish. Made from mud.

She settled down on her knees. "The people of the town," she said, "are concerned about you, following your . . . episode yesterday."

"I'm . . . sorry?" Painter said.

"I doubt I need to explain," Liyun continued, "the indignity it would bring upon them to be refused the blessings of the spirits. They would see it as a terrible omen. They would be the town that caused the yoki-hijo to collapse. The shame would run deep, Chosen."

"Look," Painter said, "it's not like I fainted on *purpose* just to—"

"*No,*" Yumi said stepping up to him.

He turned, frowning. She was finally acknowledging him? He opened his mouth to reply, but she cut him off.

"You will repeat *only* the words I say," she told him. "You are not to interact with Liyun without my *explicit* guidance."

"But—"

"*You,*" she said, "will *repeat* only the *words I say.*"

He had admired Liyun's ability to loom. But in one moment, Yumi eclipsed her master. She stepped up to him, eyes wide, daring, hands in tense fists. *Threatening.*

Painter felt a sudden jolt of disconnect. He was . . . elevated, you might say, to a higher realm of understanding. Like a child painter who at long last gained enough skill to see the true artistry of a master, Painter was confronted by looming that was somehow more grandiose. While Liyun had loomed with exactness, it had felt performative.

Yumi was passionate. The timid girl who had bowed before the foreman had now been completely consumed by . . . this creature. He'd faced nightmares, but in that moment he would have chosen to defy any of them before he did Yumi.

He nodded.

"Honored attendant," Yumi said, nodding for him to repeat the words—which he did. "The failing is entirely mine. My flesh has been made weak by my foolishness two days ago, when I overextended myself. My soul, however, trusts in the spirits. It is my deepest wish to continue my duties today. I will give all effort to avoid a repeat of yesterday's failing."

Painter finished the recitation. Which he admitted was likely a better way of handling Liyun. He'd never been particularly good at apologizing for things that weren't his fault. To be honest, he'd never been that good at apologizing for things that *were* his fault . . .

He gave a bow as Yumi indicated he should. When he looked up, he was surprised to see Liyun *considering*. She actually seemed to need to *deliberate* whether or not Yumi deserved forgiveness. For fainting. After pushing herself to serve while *obviously* unwell.

What kind of twisted society produced people who thought this was reasonable?

Liyun finally nodded. "You are wise, as always, elevated one. We will pretend that yesterday is unworthy of attention. Come, let us proceed with a *proper* day's summoning."

She led the way out, and Yumi glared at Painter until he wordlessly followed. As they trekked through the town, obscured by the fans, he was again left wondering how these people lived in this sweltering *heat*. Even with the clogs lifting his feet from the ground, he felt it radiating, making his bell-shaped skirt ripple with thermals. Perhaps that was why they used such thick cloth—to prevent accidents.

He kept his composure despite the heat, until they reached the base of the rise leading to the cold spring. Then a sudden noise like an explosion from near the center of the town made Painter spin, gaping as a jet of superheated water erupted and sprayed some thirty or forty feet into the air. The entire procession stopped to let him watch.

It was like the ground was so inhospitable that the very laws of nature were corrupted. Instead of falling from the sky, water came *up* from *below*. It dispersed, part becoming steam, releasing a rumble and even a faint whine—as if tortured.

"What (lowly) is *wrong* with this place?" he whispered.

Yumi stepped between him and the sight. "Continue," she said firmly. "But—"

"A yoki-hijo does *not* break composure," she said. "A yoki-hijo remains controlled, calm, and deliberate. If something startles you, look down or away. Do not stare. Do not gawk. You are not here to indulge. You are here to serve."

"I," he hissed, "am *not* a yoki-hijo."

"No," she said in the lowest form of speech, reserved for speaking of things like the slime between your toes. "You are a *liar*."

She held his gaze until he turned away and continued the procession. Painter found himself simmering, a little like the superheated water. Yes, he'd . . . overstated some things. But he didn't deserve this kind of treatment. He'd offered to help. Were those the actions of a *liar*? Of someone who deserved the lowest form of speech?

They reached the cold spring. He stood and thrust his hands to the sides until his attendants removed his clothing. Then he shut his eyes—without even glancing at Yumi—and strode into the bath. There he suffered the ministrations of the attendants while stewing in the broth of the not-so-cool spring.

Was it too much to want acknowledgment of how tough this was for him? Some thankfulness for his willingness to help? Though he might not have recognized it at the time, these were familiar thoughts. Characteristic, even. They weren't *wrong*—though a thought can be correct but still unhealthy.

The several scrub-downs with various soaps and scents, anointing and preparing him, took longer than he remembered. Followed by that long dunk according to Yumi's order. Finally the attendants withdrew. He lingered—half floating, half standing. Enjoying the water, trying to let it wash away his bad attitude.

And eventually . . . well, he ended up peeking.

He found Yumi standing right in front of him, eye to eye, so close that if she'd been corporeal he would have felt her breath. He jumped despite himself, splashing away.

Had . . . had she been doing that the entire time? Staring at him? Glaring? Just waiting to see if he peeked?

(The answer is yes. Yumi was, as you might have noticed, a special kind of stubborn.)

Painter's first inclination was to take in the sights. She stood there completely unashamed, in direct—or shall we say *stark*—contrast to how she'd been acting while wearing his pajamas. Despite not striking the most intimidating of postures—standing waist-deep in a pool of water, her wet hair plastered to her skin—there was *confidence* in her eyes.

So, deliberately not ogling, Painter met her gaze. He stepped toward her, leaning forward until he feared touching noses and experiencing that surreal warmth again.

She could glare, yes. Even loom with aplomb, despite being shorter than him. But Painter was an artist, and one thing artists learned to do was *look*. There's something unnerving about the stare of someone trained in shadows, shapes, and anatomy. An artist has a gaze like a knife, separating the layers of skin, fat, and muscle. His were the eyes of a person who could rip out your soul and recreate it on the page in ink or graphite.

After a minute of this, Yumi's eyes narrowed and her lips cocked slightly to the side. While there are many ways to interpret that kind of expression, Painter picked the right one. This time it was a mark of surprise that he'd held the stare—accompanied by the very faintest measure of respect.

"So," he said, "is this what we're going to do all day?"

"The spirits picked you," she said. "And then they sent you to me. I *have* to believe that they were correct to do so. To accept otherwise is to accept that *I* was chosen for no purpose—and that is lunacy."

"All right," he said. "But that doesn't tell us what we're supposed to *do*."

"We have to commune with them," she said. "Which means *you* have to summon them. I can't—not without being able to touch the things around me. We bring them to us, and maybe that will be enough to prove ourselves. Perhaps that alone will end this . . . association the two of us have been forced into."

"And if it isn't enough?"

"Then the first step is *still* to summon them," she said. "So we can get some answers. Spirits who have been formed and dedicated to a service can no longer speak—or perhaps they choose not to. But newly summoned ones can; they respond when I make requests of them. Our best hope is to learn from them what they want of us."

"Fine," he said, leaning a little closer.

"*Fine,*" she said, leaning even closer.

A contest of pride, then. He leaned in a titch. She responded. Then he got just a hair's distance from her, smiling, as there was no space remaining.

So she inched forward and stubbornly touched her nose to his.

Enveloping warmth.

Understanding.

A sharing of frustration, anger, confusion.

Connection.

Passion.

They both splashed backward, and Painter gasped. It was completely unfair how—

"Aargh!" Yumi shouted at the sky. "It is *ridiculously* unfair how . . . distracting that feels!" Then she looked at him, glaring still, and sullenly sank into the water down to her chin, covering herself as best as one could under the circumstances. She didn't blink once as she did it.

"Don't stare," she muttered.

"Stare?" he said, turning away, feigning indifference. "At what? There'd need to be something worth looking at before I'd be tempted to stare, Yumi."

Then, because he wasn't actually a heel despite what saying those words implied, he felt guilty. He walked out of the pool, telling himself—and his blush—that he didn't care if she watched him. Chaeyung and Hwanji approached, bringing him towels and clothing.

"Just don't faint this time!" Yumi called from behind. "We have work to do today, liar."

Chapter 13

YUMI WAS daunted by the number of towns she'd visited but couldn't name. She was a servant of the people of Torio; shouldn't she be able to *name* the places she'd helped?

Yet she saw so little of them. Only their cold springs—or bathhouses, for those that didn't have a spring—and their shrines and places of ritual. The different towns blurred together, interchangeable in her memory. At times she almost thought they could be the same town over and over—that she went to sleep and her wagon was pulled around in circles to give the illusion of motion before stopping right back where she'd begun.

She was ashamed of that thought, because the places were important and unique to the people who lived in them. Take this shrine, where Painter knelt today per her instructions. Most shrines were in gardens, with cold stone so the flowers could spin low to the ground.

This one was instead in the middle of an orchard. Nearby, trees drifted and bumped against one another, chained in place to keep them from floating off but given enough slack to always be in motion. The air was cooler than she liked, and the dim light of the sun behind so many branches reminded her of Painter's world. However, this was a different *kind* of dimness: broken up instead of absolute, like sunlight made festive. The trees in turn were spangled with fruit. The celebration here was a quiet one.

Though the workers had been cleared out to give the yoki-hijo silence for her meditations, this was plainly a cultivated spot. Any fallen fruit had been collected before it could bake into sticky tar. People worked in here frequently.

Which meant the people of this town didn't strictly obey tradition by setting the shrine off from commonly trafficked areas. She'd seen it before, and . . . well, a rebellious part of her approved. These people wanted their shrine near as they worked. There were spirit statues on the roof, created by a yoki-hijo to have no purpose beyond watching over the workers to give them comfort.

Why shouldn't people adapt tradition to their needs? It was a dangerous line of thinking—so when Liyun noted the cultivated trees and the statues on the roof of the shrine, she frowned. Then, fortunately, she bowed and withdrew—leaving the yoki-hijo to her ritual prayers.

As Liyun retreated, Painter let out a long sigh. "Something's wrong with that woman."

"Liyun-*nimi*," Yumi said, "is an *immaculate* warden. You will expunge such terrible ideas from your mind."

"Why?" he said. "It's not like I'm saying it to her face."

"Thinking it is as bad," Yumi said. "You are a yoki-hijo. *You* are better than such thoughts. You must be pure, not just in action, but in *mind* and *soul.*"

"But—"

"Complaining is for those lesser. Back straight. Head bowed."

"I'm not a yoki-hijo."

"Today you are," she said, walking around him as he knelt in the open-sided shrine. "If you want to end this, you must do what I cannot. Beyond that, there are consequences—rarely implemented—for a yoki-hijo who cannot serve. We are in danger of provoking Liyun to extreme measures, which will make it impossible for us to accomplish our goals. So unless you want to be stuck like this forever, you need to follow the protocol and *do* what I *tell* you."

He let out a long, annoyed breath. "Fine," he said (lowly).

Yumi nodded. During her bathing she had come to a realization. A reason why the spirits might have sent this seemingly useless person to take her place. Shortly they would test her theory. But first, meditation.

"Now," she said, "you will say the proper prayers. Because you are new to this, we will say only the six that are strictly necessary."

"Six?" he said. "How long will this take?"

"Half an hour," she said. "Roughly."

"A half hour of *praying*? But—"

"Do you want out or not?"

He grumbled, but as she began to recite the prayers, he repeated them. She wondered if perhaps she should be kneeling too. So she knelt beside him, hands laced in the pattern of reverence before her, head bowed. It would give him a good model at the least.

Was it the words or the heart that mattered in a prayer? Perhaps the spirits would accept his words and her heart.

The half hour was over in no time—saying only six of the prayers was novel, and barely felt like it was enough. But at the end Painter groaned as if she'd made him do something terrible, like carry his own luggage. He flopped to the side, and she decided to let him rest before making him—

"Hey!" she snapped. "Don't close your eyes."

"Just for a moment," he said, his eyelids flickering.

"If you fall asleep, we might swap again!"

"You don't *know* that's true . . ." he mumbled.

So she did the only thing she could think of to wake him. She stuck her finger through the middle of his forehead.

The immediate effect was that overwhelming warmth, spreading through her body with a ripple—a tingling *shiver* riding before it, like a flower on a thermal. Then the blurring of self, that connection to him. She felt his fatigue, his concern, his frustration. His emotions washed against hers, mixing like overlapping prayers—blurring together, but still distinct.

It wasn't *terrible*. But it was unnerving, as it mashed them both together in a way that was utterly unnatural.

He sat bolt upright, pulling away from her. "Hey! What are you (lowly) *doing*?"

"Keeping you awake," she said. "We must meet the spirits. You can't afford to nap."

He huffed, but stood and shook his arms, the moment of drowsiness apparently past. "Fine. Let's get on with it."

"We have to meditate," she said, "until the ritual time."

"Ritual time," he said. "Ritual bathing, ritual clothing, ritual place. When do I get my ritual tote bag? My ritual underpants? Ritual fingernail clipper?"

"Levity," she said, "is *not* becoming of a yoki-hijo. Your duty is to our people. To make light of your position is to make light of their lives."

"It's a shame then," he said gravely, "that their lives are all so (lowly) ridiculous that mockery is inevitable."

"Enough!" she shouted, pointing at him. "You *will* take this seriously."

"What happened to you?" he muttered, backing away before she could poke him again. "I liked the demure version of you better."

"Nothing *happened* to me," she said. "This is who I am. The person I *have* to be. If I grow lax, then people die, Painter. Do you understand that? Farming among my people *ends* without the yoki-hijo. If I am not my best self, then people will *starve*. Forgive me if it's a little *stressful*, therefore, that I can't do my duty without the cooperation of a liar who finds all this funny!"

He glanced away, looking ashamed. As he should have been. This was the way she'd been trained—with relentless conditioning toward solemnity. With unyielding strictness. Until the desire for levity and individuality had been drained from her like pus from a boil.

It had worked for her. She'd turned out fine. Rather, she'd turned out to be what she had to be.

It would work for him. She merely had to remain stern. For his good and the good of the spirits as well.

"We wait, then," he finally said.

"We meditate," she said, kneeling.

He knelt beside her. "Meditate, eh? So . . . we just kneel here and think?"

"No thinking," she said, spreading her hands to the sides and tipping her head toward the sky. "Meditation is the opposite of thinking."

"Uh . . . I can force myself to be calm. Will that work?"

She glanced at him, and he seemed genuinely confused. Did . . . she really have to explain something so simple?

"It is more than calmness," she clarified. "It is an utter rejection of all emotion, sensation, and individuality. You often start by fixating on something rhythmic, like your breathing or the deliberate stretching and relaxing of a muscle. Some find it helpful to vocalize a tone or a mantra. The goal is to empty your mind of all thought—abandoning even the initial focus that started the meditation."

"What's the point of that?"

She cocked her head, baffled. "To center yourself in the cosmere," she said. "To wash your mind as you wash your body. To expel emotional refuse, as your body does with physical excrement. To be clean, down to your soul, and to renew. You've never done it before?"

He shook his head.

No *wonder* he was so . . . well, him. How backward must his society be to know nothing about a need so fundamental?

She started him out—as you might with a child—with a focus on breathing. She centered herself, let herself simply exist. The familiar sense of drifting enveloped her, followed by the sensation of . . . nothing.

Complete emptiness. Being. Nothing else. She was as the rocks, the trees in the air. The . . .

He was there next to her.

She could *feel* him. Now that she was centered, she sensed him *pulling* on her. She cracked an eye; his own eyes were closed, but he was smiling, his mouth twitching.

"You're thinking about something," she said to him.

"I can't help *thinking*," he complained. "I don't want to stop, regardless. I like thinking about things."

"You will control even those enjoyable thoughts better," she said, "when you are experienced at meditation."

"There's more to life than control."

"Try it," she said, centering herself again. "Practice. You'll see. The best artists can focus far better on their art after training to meditate. Control leads to focus and focus to accomplishment."

"Depends on what you want to accomplish."

The two continued to kneel, and now *Yumi* found it difficult to stop thinking. About him. Not that there was anything specifically appealing about Painter. It was just that she'd never imagined kneeling in a shrine beside someone. It was . . . a thing that married couples did.

Not an experience for her. To marry would be to defy the spirits and the gift they'd granted. To have a love, to have a family, would be to turn her back on her duty. She was a precious resource, and *absolute* dedication was required.

Yet strangely, many of her world's favorite stories involved a yoki-hijo falling in love. Liyun had rightly tried to keep them from her, but Yumi had heard the tales from Samjae—a yoki-hijo she'd been friends with when they were young—who had relayed them with a gleeful air of transgression.

Samjae said transgressive stories were the best. Because forbidden love somehow tasted the sweetest.

"Nice," Painter said, shaking the shrine as he stood up. Yumi started, thinking he'd somehow sensed her thoughts. But he was referencing Liyun approaching up the path. "This means we're done, right?"

"Right," Yumi said, standing. "Let's go summon the spirits."

He nodded and took a step forward. Then he paused. "Wait. I can't believe I've never asked this, but *how* do we summon them? You said something about art the other day?"

"Yes, it's easy," she said. "All you have to do is stack some rocks."

IT was time to test Yumi's theory.

She considered it as Painter entered the place of ritual, the fenced-off section of ground where stones had been placed for him. Townspeople gathered along the fence, musicians at the ready, and Yumi remained behind with them—until Painter was distant enough that she was pulled, against her will, a few steps inside.

He looked back at her, noticing the pull. She nodded to him encouragingly. Earlier she'd said that his task would be easy. That was *sort of* an untruth. Learning to properly stack rocks was difficult, and had been a large part of her training.

But she had a suspicion that it would be easy for *him*. That was the realization she'd come to while bathing, and it would explain so much. The spirits had come to her begging for help—yet Yumi had not been enough. She wasn't skilled enough; wasn't good enough. She was inadequate.

So they had sent someone who could do what she couldn't. Painter might not be a hero . . . but he might be a *prodigy*. That would explain why they'd picked him. She was now confident that he'd prove to be a natural at stacking, blessed with talent beyond her own even though he'd never known it on his world. The answer was so obvious it made her smile.

She was able to maintain this happy delusion right up to the moment he "stacked" his first rock. It fell.

The very *first* rock he placed fell. Somehow he managed to fail at balancing a large flat piece of stone on the *ground*. It toppled to the side and rolled away.

The townspeople behind Yumi gasped. Painter didn't notice—just gave a goofy smile and piled up some other rocks like he was . . . pushing blocks into a heap. He didn't even manage this without squishing his finger, which made him yelp and shake it.

Yumi glanced to Liyun, who watched with a slack jaw, horrified.

Painter put a rock on top of his pile, which collapsed. Then he looked to Yumi and gestured. "Like this?" he asked. "How's it look?"

Oh no, Yumi thought. *Oh, spirits. No.*

They were in serious, *serious* trouble.

Chapter 14

PAINTER WOKE in his rooms back in his world, the indignity of the rock fiasco fresh in his mind.

He still didn't understand what he'd done wrong.

No, wait.

He didn't understand what would have been *right*. Rocks? What had been the point of those rocks?

Yumi sat up from the blanket on the floor, her hair a twisted mess. "Ow," she said softly. "I think I . . . somehow slept on my nose . . ." She focused on him, and despite the frizzy hair and rumpled pajamas, she became more commanding. "You have failed."

"I stacked the rocks!" he said, sitting up. "I did it six different ways before you had me leave."

As the people watching had grown increasingly distraught, Yumi had told him to plead fatigue to Liyun. The dignified woman, plainly troubled by whatever it was he'd done wrong, had led him back to the wagon, where he'd succumbed to sleep. He probably hadn't even been awake six hours. Something about this transfer seemed to require a lot of energy, and they tired far faster than normal.

"The stacking," Yumi said, standing up and putting her hands on her hips, "must be done with *skill* and *artistry*."

"Stacking," he said, "does not require artistry."

"To do it ritually does."

"Ritually. Of course. I should have known!"

She stalked over and pointed at his face as if threatening to touch him. But he lay down on his futon and shrugged. "Go ahead. I'm feeling a bit of a chill anyway. Might warm me up."

She set her jaw, then stalked away, arms folded. She appeared to be shivering. The apartment looked as they'd left it, but he had a suspicion that they'd lost another day. Which meant the foreman would be furious.

Hopefully the foreman had dealt with the stable nightmare. Painter hadn't warned him about the family who might need money to relocate. The foreman would put it together, right?

Maybe he should check in anyway. Make certain the Dreamwatch had arrived and everything was under control. It wasn't his problem, now that he'd reported it, but he kept remembering that little boy with blood on his cheek from the nightmare's claws. He at least wanted an update.

How, though? He didn't have a phone—those required expensive dedicated hion lines and were beyond a mere nightmare painter's wages. So to get information from the foreman, they'd have to find a public phone and wait in line, or—since the office was so close—simply walk over. Both would require them to leave the apartment, however.

Yumi was talking again. "To properly stack, one needs years of training."

"And you just expected me to do it with none?"

"I . . . hoped you would have natural talent," she admitted. "I was wrong, obviously. The only solution remaining is a difficult one. We *must* contact the spirits, which means you're going to have to learn. We'll come up with some excuse to Liyun, then train you, like I was as a child. Until you're good enough to draw spirits."

Delightful. Training under her sounded about as much fun as a hornet-eating competition. And these spirits? Were they even real? Everyone on her world seemed to think so, and she *had* shown him some kind of goblinlike statues underneath her wagon that made it float. Those came from somewhere.

Regardless, he had his own troubles. "I want to go talk to the foreman," he said. "And check in. Make sure I still have a job . . ."

"No," she said. "We're going to stay in here and I'm going to start training you. Your education begins now."

"My education? My training? To do what? Stack?" He sat up and waved his hand through the table. "Wow. That's going to be *so* effective, Yumi."

"I can demonstrate," she said. "Instruct."

"No," he said, standing. "This is my world. I should get to make the rules. There's a dangerous nightmare out there, and I want to be certain it's been dealt with. Foreman doesn't always . . . think the most highly of me—"

"I wonder why."

"Yumi," he said. "That nightmare is dangerous. It could be fully stable by now, and violently murderous! It could kill dozens or more if not stopped, and no regular painter is equipped to deal with one so strong. It requires talent beyond what someone like me has.

"We are going to go make sure the foreman understood my warning, then get him to check on a family I helped. Who knows—maybe those spirits sent *you* to *me*, not the other way around! Maybe they need *you* to do something here! You ever consider that?"

She huffed, arms still folded, but then glanced away. "Fine," she said softly. "But . . . I can't go out like this. I look, and feel, grimy. I don't think bathing when I'm a spirit cleans this body."

"Well, we can fix that," he said, walking across his living room to the small bathroom. He waved to it, and she sullenly stepped over and pulled open the door. He showed her the knobs on the shower, which she turned. Then she yelped, her eyes wide as the water sprayed down.

"You have a geyser," she said. "But . . . the water seems cold?"

"It will warm," he said. "Unless Mrs. Shinja used it all up again—avoid showering at nine in the morning, unless you like to freeze. Also, warning, she gets very possessive over the water. Be careful not to use too much yourself."

"Shower," she said softly, letting the water run over her hand.

"Soap here," he said, pointing. "Shampoo and conditioner here. Clean towel there." He nodded to her, then stepped toward the door.

"Wait," Yumi said, then turned, looking at him.

"What?"

"I'm . . . supposed to do it myself?" she asked. "You don't have any . . . attendants I can call?"

"Uh, no. Not a thing in my world."

"Right," she said, and appeared strangely daunted. How could you be intimidated by something like *showering*? He smiled, finding it cathartic to see her, the tyrant, suddenly terrified of something so trivial. It was like finding out that a fearsome tiger was scared of getting its nails done.

He shut the door, but then—because he couldn't get too far from her—leaned against it. He did so absently, but then was shocked to discover he didn't fall straight through. Just like he didn't fall through the floor. So . . . why did he sometimes pass through things, but not always?

(I could have explained. Unfortunately, at that moment I was being used to hold a large overstuffed coat, three bags, a puppy in a carrying case, and *three* boiled eggs. Don't ask.)

The sound of the water grew louder in the bathroom, then the telltale noise of splashing followed as Yumi stepped in. A few moments later, Painter was pretty sure he heard her sigh in satisfaction.

"Nice, eh?" he said.

"It's warm," Yumi's voice said, echoing in the small bathroom. "I'd begun to think you people had no idea what it was to feel properly warm." She paused. "Um . . . what is shampoo?"

"For your hair," he said. "Lather it up in your hair to clean it. Then use the conditioner to . . . uh . . . It's good for the hair somehow. Trust me. It, um, moisturizes?"

"Right. I'll . . . shampoo, then? Do I do it now? Or after I've used the soap? And to what count do I lather before rinsing?"

"There aren't rules, Yumi," he said. "You've *really* never done this before on your own? What about when you were a kid?"

"I told you I was chosen by the spirits as a baby," she replied. "Taken from my parents, raised by the wardens to my singular purpose."

"That's terrible," he said (lowly). "You didn't get a childhood at all?"

"A yoki-hijo is not a child," she said, her voice bearing the air of an oft-recited line. "Nor is she an adult. The yoki-hijo is a manifestation of the will of the spirits. Her entire existence is service."

No wonder she was so strange. Didn't excuse her being the human manifestation of what it felt like to miss the last bus home, but—considering all of this—at least she made more sense to him now.

"How is it," she asked, her voice echoing, "that your people have captured this geyser and channeled it to your will?"

"It's not a geyser. It's water pumped from the lake, filtered and heated."

"Pumped? Are there people working those pumps right now to deliver this?"

"No, it's machines powered by the hion lines," he said. "The heating too. Touch opposite hion lines to metal and it will heat up. It's basic science to turn that into a bus engine or a simple heater."

"How do you know all this?"

"School," he said.

"You are a painter."

"School teaches more than just painting."

"I was not taught anything but my duties," she said, her voice softer. "It is better that way. I must keep focus. Other things might . . . cloud my mind with frivolities."

The conversation died off, and he let her linger in the shower—longer than he'd have let himself. Eventually Yumi stopped on her own. A few minutes later she said, "Do I put these clothes back on?"

"Please don't," he said. "They haven't been washed in days. Put on a towel for now."

She stepped out a moment later, wrapped in *three* towels. Well, fair enough. Painter led her to his pile of clean clothing. "I didn't get around to folding these."

She cocked an eyebrow.

"I intended to," he said. "I usually fold everything right after it's washed."

"I'm sure," she said, nudging the pile with her toe. "This is all going to be too big on me, isn't it?"

"Yumi, in your world, you wear a dress that's roughly the size of a bedspread. I think you'll be fine."

She put a hand to her towels, then paused. But he was already walking to the bathroom, which was close enough that he didn't hit the end of his leash. He stepped inside, giving her privacy.

"Thank you," she said from outside. "For being so . . . thoughtful."

"This isn't being thoughtful," he said. "It's basic decency."

"Still, I didn't expect it."

"It's almost like it's unfair to judge a person based on how they react after being forced into someone else's body, towed off to a strange location, then forcibly stripped. Eh?"

"I guess," she said, "we've both been under . . . unusual amounts of stress." A few minutes later she continued. "All right. I don't like it, but this will have to do."

Painter stepped out to find her wearing . . .

Well, it certainly met the definition of an outfit. It was *clothing*, at least. Worn on a body. She'd found one of his longer shirts—a thick turtleneck—and had put that on. He wasn't too surprised by that, but she'd put a sweatshirt on *over* that, and the combination of long turtleneck and shorter sweatshirt was comical. In fact, the sweatshirt puffed out a little, as if she had another smaller one on underneath *it*. How many layers was she wearing?

Regardless, it was the sweater she was using as a *skirt*—the sleeves tucked into the waist—that really threw him for a loop. She had put on some trousers underneath that as well, which was good he supposed. But . . .

Wow. The total effect was truly something.

"Do women *actually* go out like this?" she asked him. "Among your people? Wearing trousers?"

"Not exactly like this . . ." he said. "Um, you realize that's . . . a shirt, not a skirt."

"I needed to improvise," she said. "To keep up *some* semblance of modesty." She lifted up one foot. "At least your sandals fit, so long as I put on three pairs of socks. But I didn't see any clogs."

"You won't need clogs here . . ." he said, then trailed off, trying to find something else to say. How could her clothing look so baggy, yet so overstuffed at the same time? It was swallowing her completely, like her head was peeking out the mouth of some bizarre fish made of cloth.

She stepped over to the mirror on the door of the bathroom and seemed to deflate a little at the sight. Well, after how much he'd been through in her world, it was hard to feel sorry for her. Maybe this would help her build a little empathy.

"You aren't too hot in that?" he asked.

"Your world is unnaturally cold," she said. "I think it's best to be prepared. I'm ready to go petition your foreman. Please lead the way."

He had to show her how to lock the door after herself—apparently that was another thing she didn't understand. "People would come in?" she said, turning the key. "To your home? When you're not there? Why? To wait for you?"

He shook his head and led her down the steps to the ground floor. Here, she froze at the exit to the building, looking up at the dark sky.

I don't blame her. There was something inherently moody about Painter's world.

In Kilahito it always felt like you'd stepped out right after it finished raining. In Kilahito the streets perpetually felt too empty—but in a way that made you think you were encountering a brief lull, with activity echoing from the next street over. In Kilahito, it always felt like the lights were turned down low to let the land sleep.

In Kilahito you noticed absences. It was a city made from negative space.

"Come on," Painter said, waving to her from the street.

She stayed in the doorway. "It's so . . . empty."

"Comfortingly so," he said. "You *really* find this more unnerving than your world, with that big ball of fire in the sky? With all those things flying around up there? *That's* unnerving. It makes me feel like I'm going to get crushed!"

"At least we can see what's above," she said. "Here . . . there's just nothing."

"That's the shroud," he said. "Scientists have flown beyond it; they found more stars and things up there." He softened his tone. "Look there. See that? The one that shines through the shroud?"

She hesitantly stepped out onto the street with him and gazed up at the star. "Do you think that's *actually* my world?"

"It must be," he said. "Whatever grabbed me came from the sky, and scientists say there are people there. It's a planet like ours—they've taken pictures of what look like small cities, but they're vague, too far away to make out much. Whoever lives there doesn't seem to have radios or anything. They're . . . not as advanced as we are."

She didn't take this as an insult, instead staring up at the star, then turning her eyes to follow the hion lines above the street, their light painting it the contrasting blue and violet of progress.

"This stable nightmare," she said. "You said it will . . . hurt people? Unless we do something to stop it?"

"Yes," he said. "But *we* don't have to do anything to stop it. My job is to report it. We did that, but I forgot to warn the foreman about a family that the nightmare threatened. I need to see they've gotten the assistance I promised them."

"You mentioned that others would come to stop the nightmare," she said. "Didn't you say we could recruit them? *Actual* heroes?"

The words felt like a punch to Painter's gut, but she apparently didn't realize that, so he controlled it. "The foreman will send for a member of the Dreamwatch. Maybe two, with their companions. They're spectacular artists, but I don't think they can help with your problems. Come on."

She took a deep breath and nodded, then caught up to him. It was early evening, according to the clock in the bank window, and a decent number of people were out. Main thoroughfares like this were wide enough for an emergency vehicle to drive through, but the idea of personal vehicles would have been baffling to the residents of Kilahito. Most people traveled by bus or trolley, which connected to the hion lines and used them for power and guidance.

"The foreman's office is nearby," he said as they walked, "so fortunately we won't need to take the hion trams. The idea of talking you through the daytime tram schedule does *not* appeal to me."

She nodded again, although he doubted she knew what he was talking about. She seemed to be trying very hard not to look at the sky and was instead watching everyone they passed. She drew more than a few stares.

It's often said that nothing fazes people in a big city, and that *does* tend to be true—to an extent. Big-city people tend to be unfazed by *ordinary* sorts of strangeness. You don't give a second glance to the drunk wearing no pants since, well, that's the third one this week. But an oddity like Yumi? No pants was somehow less strange than what she'd opted to wear.

"They know what I am," she whispered to Painter. "They can sense the girl of commanding primal spirits."

"Uh . . . no," he said. "We don't have those here. They just think you look strange."

"They know," she said, firm. "They stare at me like the townspeople do. Even if you don't have yoki-hijo, these people can *feel* something is different about me. It is my burden. And my blessing."

Being weird was apparently her primary burden, though he wasn't certain what was blessed about it. As they passed a shop selling many varieties of hion viewers, with actors moving across the windows in unison, she paused.

"I thought yoki-hijo didn't gawk," he noted.

"Oh, sorry," she said softly, glancing down. "You are correct. I have shamed myself."

Painter grimaced. He'd been hoping for a more satisfying reaction. Giving someone a jibe, then having them *internalize* it, felt awful: the conversational equivalent of going for a comedic burp and accidentally inducing yourself to vomit.

Regardless, he navigated her without incident to the foreman's office— a small room with its own entrance at the corner of the general Painter Department headquarters. At his prompting, she entered. Foreman Sukishi didn't care about knocking.

Fortunately, he was in. The older man sat at his usual place behind the small room's single desk, feet up, reading his paper. Behind him, the many slots where he stored the paintings turned in for the day—tagged and sorted—were mostly empty. Ready for the night's offerings.

As Yumi entered he lowered his feet and folded his paper, frowning at her. "You look familiar."

"You met me the other day," she said softly, "at Painter's house. Um . . . Nikaro, the painter? I'm his sister."

The foreman blinked, then recognition hit him and he sat back. "Sister? Of course. That makes *so* much more sense."

Painter winced. Why did people keep saying that?

"He didn't work last night either," the foreman said. "Is that why you're here?"

"He's sick," Yumi said.

"Yeah. So sick that when I saw you the other day, he wasn't sleeping on his futon—but was out somewhere. And had to leave his sister to cover for him."

Yumi blushed, lowering her eyes. "I apologize for him, honored Foreman-nimi."

"Oh, it's not your fault," the foreman said, softening his tone. Which was horribly unfair. This man had always treated Painter with some shade of contempt—but Yumi, the tyrant? *She* got his sympathies?

Then again, she *did* seem to be an expert at milking these kinds of situations. Today she knelt down on the ground and gave the foreman a full ritual bow.

"Honored Foreman-nimi," she said, her eyes toward the floor, "I am here to ask for information. You said my brother was out doing something the other day, but I remind you: He encountered something he called a *stable nightmare*. He was watching out for that. He sent me to ask if perhaps you have an update?"

The foreman leaned forward, eyeing her. He tapped his fingers on the tabletop. "Right," he said. "Stable nightmare."

"He did send for the Dreamwatch, didn't he?" Painter asked, feeling a spike of alarm.

"Did you send for the Dreamwatch, Foreman-nimi?" Yumi asked, looking up. "Have they found the thing? Painter says that it could grow dangerous in a matter of days if not dealt with."

The foreman leaned backward in his seat, which gave a plaintive creak. "Tell me more about this thing he supposedly saw. Nikaro. Was he wounded, facing a stable nightmare?"

"No," Painter snapped. "I fought it off, thank you very much."

"He used his powers," she said, "to drive it away."

The foreman squinted his eyes. "Nikaro. Used those half-rate paintings of his to drive away a *stable nightmare*?"

"That's what he said." Yumi looked to Painter, who nodded firmly.

The foreman studied her, then sighed. "I should have expected this . . ."

Painter frowned. Expected? A stable nightmare?

"Nikaro always likes to be so dramatic," the foreman said softly—as if more to himself than to Yumi. "Always needs to be at the center of everything. And we know how much he likes a good lie . . . Doing his job never has been good enough for that one. Needs people paying attention to him, telling him how great he is."

Painter stepped back, his stomach turning over. He'd long known what the foreman thought of him, but hearing it still hurt.

"Foreman-nimi?" Yumi asked. "There was a family. They saw it, and Painter wants to check on them. He promised them financial help? He gave me an address . . ." She stood and wrote it quickly, able to write in his language as he was able to write in hers.

The foreman grunted and read the address. This finally seemed to give him pause. But then he tucked it away in his pocket and shook his head. "I'll take care of it."

"Thank you," she said, bowing again. "Thank you *so* much."

She left, holding the door long enough for Painter to slink out behind her.

"There," she said, halting at the curb. "We handled *that.*"

"Except we didn't," Painter said. "He didn't believe you."

"What? He said—"

"He said what he needed to," Painter explained, "to get you out the door. But he thinks I made up the story about the stable nightmare in order to get attention. That (lowly) man!"

Yumi appeared to shrink farther into her oversized clothing. "So he's not going to stop the creature?"

"Doubt it," Painter said. "If we're lucky, he'll check on the address. But it's been three days—and I told the family to get out of town. They'll likely have found a way, even without the money I promised them."

"He might look into it," Yumi said. "Maybe he'll find them and see evidence of the nightmare?"

"Maybe," Painter said, sighing. "Hopefully. Unless he decides to 'take care' of things by writing me up."

"Your world makes no sense," Yumi said. "People simply . . . mislead one another?"

"I'll bet they do the same on your world," Painter said. "Just not around you. People are people, Yumi. Your world is different, yes, but I doubt it's *that* different."

She started toward his flat again, and he gave minimal guidance as he walked beside her, fuming. And, deeper inside, feeling utterly humiliated. Based on the foreman's expression and attitude, the man wasn't going to investigate at all.

That nightmare had been crafty, powerful. Painter had given it a fright, so it might stay away a few days. But it *would* be back.

"What if you're right?" Yumi said as they walked. "What if the spirits sent me here to help you with this nightmare? What do we do?"

"I'm thinking about it, okay?" Painter snapped.

By the time they neared the apartment building though, he still didn't have any good answers. Maybe . . . the nightmare would get noticed by someone else? But if it had gone this long without being captured, then it must be distinctly cunning. It would probably only draw attention once it started killing . . .

"Hey!" a voice said. "It's you!"

Painter and Yumi stopped on the street by the apartment building as Akane came out the front door. Gorgeous as always, she was wearing street clothing again—skirt, blouse, makeup—rather than her work gear. She went out most evenings before their shift began, clubbing, or . . . other normal-person things?

He didn't really know, to be honest. Perhaps this was what she wore to go to the grocery store.

"Yumi, was it?" Akane said, looking her up and down, lingering on the sweater-turned-skirt.

"Yes," Yumi said. "Um . . . I lost my trunk of clothing on the way here. I had to borrow my brother's things."

"Good save," Painter said. "Get rid of her. We need to get back to the flat and discuss what to do."

"I haven't seen Nikaro around," Akane said. "What's up with him? He hasn't been reporting to his shift."

"Oh!" Yumi said. "He has . . . um . . . some big project he's been doing. Somewhere else."

"Your brother," Akane said flatly, "invited you to the city, then *left* you *alone. After* you'd lost your luggage?"

"Yes?" Yumi said, shrinking down in her—his—clothing.

Painter groaned as he saw his chances with Akane fading even further.

(Which proved him to be an optimist, since he assumed he'd ever had chances in the first place.)

"Quick!" he said. "Let's go."

"Thank you and excuse me," Yumi said, with a quick bow, then slipped past Akane into the building.

Akane lingered, holding the door. Before Yumi and Painter could reach the stairs, she rushed in after them and caught up to Yumi.

"Hey," Akane said, "this is probably none of my business, so tell me to go stick my head in the shroud if you want. But . . . are you all right, Yumi? Could you maybe use some help? Someone to take you shopping for some new clothes?"

Painter sighed. Akane was always—

Yumi, shockingly, *burst into tears.* "Yes," she said between sobs. "Oh, yes, *please.*"

Chapter 15

YUMI, OF course, instantly felt mortified at her breakdown. She tried to control her tears as she took Akane by the hand and bowed to her in thanks.

Surprisingly, it wasn't against the rules for a yoki-hijo to cry. Many of these rules had been instituted by older yoki-hijo themselves, after all—and so they'd made crying *in front of others* the thing that was against protocol.

I find it telling. They all understood. For one living the life of a yoki-hijo, breakdowns were basically inevitable. You just had to hide them as best you could.

Regardless, Yumi knew she shouldn't act this way. It was just such a *relief* to have someone pay attention to her needs. Akane's attempt to help, albeit in a small way, was physically overwhelming.

This place was just so *strange*. That sky felt like it would swallow her, but that was somehow the least of it. She'd seen enormous vehicles—carrying tons of people—moving through the nearby streets. These buildings towered around her, stacks of stones piled so straight, glued together. They could have been mountains. And then there were those twin lines of light glowing and hovering in the air above every street, connected to every building, forming garish glowing signs.

She'd been dumped into all of this without any direction. She felt lost, even when she knew where she was. She felt terrified even though she wasn't in danger. Worst, she'd had to go out wearing . . . wearing this *mess*.

Akane patted her hand as if troubled. Nearby, Painter stared at her, frowning. He seemed baffled. Well, Yumi understood both of their emotions.

"Right, then," Akane said, towing Yumi out the door. "I know a place." Her shoes made a sharp clopping sound on the strange black-stone street. It didn't sound like a pair of clogs, but it was comforting nonetheless.

Yumi seized her emotions in a death grip and wrangled them under control. As soon as her tears stopped, however, she found she was still humiliated—not merely because of her outburst, but because of what had happened the last time she'd met this woman.

"Akane," she said. "Last time we spoke . . . I embarrassed myself by exposing, flagrantly, my ignorance. Please accept not just my apologies, but my sincere remunerations—anything I can do in your favor, I will extend."

"It's not your fault your brother is a creep, Yumi."

"He's not a creep!" Yumi said quickly. Then paused. Was that a lie? She wasn't completely certain. "In truth, I misunderstood what he was saying. He was speaking of . . . of the dramas he likes to watch. Not of anyone he knows. In addition, I was overwhelmed. People in the city are . . . different from the way people are back home."

"I've heard about the smaller towns," Akane said with a laugh. "I know things are more traditional there. We must look a sight to you!"

"It's more the city itself," Yumi said, staring to the right as they crossed a road. "The streets seem to go on *forever*. So many people all in one place, building monoliths toward a dark sky. Living atop one another, piled like stones in a wall . . ."

Akane smiled.

"Did I say something wrong?" Yumi asked, lowering her eyes. "I gravely apologize for my foolishness."

"You're not foolish," Akane said. "Actually, I was thinking that I like the way you talk. It has a kind of . . . poetic feel to it."

Poetic? She was merely speaking with proper formality. Still, it would not be polite to correct Akane, so she held her tongue. Akane led her to a large structure with bigger windows and brighter lights than many.

Yumi glanced over her shoulder toward Painter, who was following along behind, hands in his pockets. He didn't seem to want to talk, but she made sure to linger at the door so he could follow her.

Then all her attention was captured by the place inside those doors: a vast open room full of displays and statues wearing clothing. Hundreds of skirts hanging in artfully arranged racks. Shirts piled high in cubbies on the walls. Shoes in a thousand different varieties, raised up on tables to show them off.

"So," Akane said, "you'll need at least a couple of outfits. Three, maybe? That could keep you going until you can send for something from home."

Yumi simply stared. Bright lights presented it all, of a whiter light than the lines outside. Dozens of people moved among the racks, chatting, pointing at different options. Was this . . . this all just here for people to take?

"What do you like to wear?" Akane said gently, nudging her. "Yumi?"

"I . . ." she whispered. "There's so much . . ."

"Their selection," Akane said, "is *acceptable*." She leaned in. "Shinzua Shopping Center has more cutting-edge trends, but the prices there are *insane*. This place is a good balance."

Prices.

Right, *money*. Normal people needed *money* to buy things.

Yumi panicked. "I have misled you, honored Akane! I don't possess any money for—"

"It's fine," she said. "I'll cover it and charge your brother. Trust me. He'll pay me back. I'll make *sure* of it."

Oh. Well, she supposed that he owed her that much. She pointedly didn't look toward him as she nodded.

"So, three outfits?" Akane said. "One skirt, two pairs of pants, some shirts?"

"No!" Yumi said, too forcefully. "Um, dresses? Full dresses? Is that acceptable?" Maybe she could find something similar to what she'd worn at home. Even though . . . she had yet to see a single woman wearing anything of the sort.

"Sure," Akane said. "This way."

They wove between racks of clothing, and the garments all appeared so ... slight. Shirts that fit tightly on the torso, skirts so light and flowing they seemed made of air and clouds. She and Akane emerged into a section selling dresses, and Yumi's feeling of intimidation built. How did anyone choose? She had always worn what she'd been dressed in—never voicing an opinion. Because why would she need one of those?

She was about to tell Akane to find her the thickest, bulkiest dress—when she froze. Just ahead, a statue of a woman with no face stood on a pedestal, wearing something *gorgeous*. Flowing, but not insubstantial, the light blue dress deepened to a darker color near the floor—like it was the blossom of a flower. It did outline the form, as all of the dresses in this place did, but didn't *hug* it like the skirts that Akane favored. Instead it had a fluid, rippling sense to it.

To wear something like that ... It would flare when she turned. It would leave her shoulders mostly bare, save for two straps, though the neckline wasn't nearly as daring as the other dresses'. It would show more of her than she had ever exposed.

But it was like the gown a *queen* would wear. A queen from a story. A woman, not a girl of commanding primal spirits.

"Ah," Akane said, stepping back to join her. "*Someone* has *remarkably* good taste. What's your size? I'll go get one off the racks."

"No!" Yumi said, taking her by the arm. "I can't, honored Akane. It's too ... daring."

Akane glanced toward the dress, then back at Yumi, who blushed. (Perhaps Akane was thinking that wearing a sweater as a skirt was the actual daring maneuver.)

"Look," Akane said, patting her hand. "I won't force you to do anything you're uncomfortable with. But you're in the city now, Yumi. There's no better time to try out something new—be a little *daring*, so to speak. It might not seem so to you, but that dress is actually pretty conservative here."

Yumi refrained from eyeing Akane's own skirt, which appeared about one yawn-and-stretch away from flipping up and turning into a belt instead. Perhaps ... the other one *was* conservative. And the spirits hadn't punished her for the lies she'd been forced to tell ... so maybe they *knew* she'd have to do things differently here. To accomplish their designs?

That was her excuse, at least. In truth, looking up at that dress—and realizing she could simply *choose* to wear it—awakened something in her. This inclination hadn't been sleeping deeply, hadn't been hidden far underneath the surface. It had been lurking, even back in her world. Liyun would have called it dangerous.

Liyun wasn't here.

"Let's try it," Yumi whispered, clinging to Akane.

"Great! What's your size?"

Yumi felt herself blushing. "I . . . don't know. I've never been shopping before."

"*What?*"

"I just always wore what was given to me."

"Siblings?" she said (lowly). "You're the youngest then? That's rough, always wearing hand-me-downs. I know how it feels. So this is your first time?"

Yumi nodded.

"No wonder you look like a moth in a light bulb factory," Akane said. "How about this: you point out a few other mannequins with a style you like, and I'll gather together a selection of similar things, then bring them to your changing room to try on. That way you don't have to pick from hundreds of options, only a dozen or so."

"That sounds wonderful," Yumi said (highly). "Thank you, Akane. You are an honor to your family, your lineage, and the spirits themselves."

"And you," Akane said, "are an *absolute* charm bracelet of a person."

Akane led her to a servant who worked at the place, and there they took some very personal measurements of Yumi. Akane seemed to think this would embarrass her, but standing there and being prodded was the first thing Yumi found *familiar* about this entire experience. Despite not being particularly fond of doing it in front of Painter.

"Don't suppose you know your bra size?" Akane asked after that part was done.

"Uh . . ." Would saying she didn't know what that was make her seem too odd? She didn't want to act *too* strange, lest people realize she was literally an alien. "No?"

The next measurements were even more personal. But Yumi suffered it, and soon found herself deposited in a small hallway with a set of rooms apparently for trying on clothing. Painter sat outside as she stepped into one, though she didn't have any clothing to try on yet—Akane was still gathering it.

"What," Yumi hissed at Painter through the open door, "is a 'bra'?"

"Undergarment," he said. "For women." He hesitated, then gestured toward his chest.

"Oh," she said. "Why not a bosom band?"

"That . . . might be a better question for Akane than me."

"I suppose," she said, "that you find all of this a frivolous distraction."

He shrugged, looking out toward where Akane passed by, now leading *two* different shop servants. "You need clothes, Yumi. And I don't know anyone better to help you get them than Akane."

"She's very pretty," Yumi said.

"Prettiest in our class at school," he agreed.

"Tell me what you like about her, *other* than the fact that she's pretty."

He paused, and took an embarrassing—for him—amount of time to reply. "She has great fashion sense."

"That's basically another way of saying she's pretty."

"Why do you care?" he snapped.

"Well, *I've* already noticed that she's a tender and helpful person," Yumi said. "I was simply curious if that is why you're so infatuated with her."

"I'm not infatuated," Painter said, and sounded serious, not defensive. "I just have a lot of time to think. Maybe too much time to think. And dream." He shook his head as Akane passed back the other way, the two servants laden with clothing, and . . . was that a *third* hurrying along after them?

Hadn't she said she was only going to get a *few* outfits for Yumi to try on?

"She was nice to me," Painter finally said. "Even though I was from a small town. When we first met in class three years ago, a few of the others made fun of me. Akane instead asked what made me want to be a painter . . ."

When he didn't continue, Yumi asked, "You had a choice?" It sounded stupid when she said it. It seemed obvious in retrospect that he'd chosen to become a painter. Yet few people in Torio actually got to decide what they did. You generally just inherited your family's trade. Unless you were a yoki-hijo.

"It's how we do things here," he said.

"And you became a painter of nightmares?" she said. "Why?"

Before he could answer, Akane came striding back—four servants in tow, all laden with clothing. Yumi was accepting the first armload, listening to Akane's instructions, before she realized that Painter could have simply answered her. No one could hear him but her, so why fall silent when others were near?

Soon Yumi was closed in her little room, surrounded by too many options. She began by peeling off the layers she'd chosen to wear, finding her skin sweaty underneath. She hadn't really been paying attention, but it felt nice to be out of that clothing—it had actually been *too* warm. Perhaps she was adjusting to this semifrozen land.

The first undergarment made sense, but the bra . . . well, that was formidable. She could see how it was to be worn, but there were straps and a clip and . . . well, it took some work. She did pause while putting it on, marveling at the stretchiness of some of the cloth. How did they make it do *that*?

She got the thing on finally, though she had to put it on backward to get the clip fastened, then twist it around and fit herself into it. It felt kind of constrictive, and it outlined her form instead of flattening it as was normal. She supposed that was how Akane and the others made their figures look so . . . prominent. Why would they want to be *more* conspicuous?

The bra seemed a purely vain thing, and she almost took it off to go without. But then she turned, and cocked her head. Then she tried jumping. And . . .

That felt *nice*. Not that it was *comfortable* really, but it certainly prevented *discomfort*.

"Yumi?" Akane asked from outside. "You okay?"

"This bra," she said, jumping again, "is *incredible*."

"Never had one that fits right, eh?" Akane asked. "You'd be surprised the difference it makes."

It was her intention to try on the pretty dress last, but . . . well, her curiosity got the better of her. She pulled it on, then looked at herself in the changing mirror. It was beautiful, like clouds above a deep blue sky—like the wind itself given shape and sent to embrace her.

But there was a magnetism to it beyond its overt beauty. It transformed her into someone else. Someone who could make a choice. It was the first time in her *entire life* that she'd made a decision just for *herself.*

Akane had brought her a small bag of toiletries, and inside was a brush. Yumi stroked her hair with this a few times, getting rid of the frazzles, then stood and stared at the mythical being in the mirror, feeling a disconnect, trying to accept that it was her.

"Well?" Akane called. "Come on! Let me see!"

Yumi blushed immediately, putting her hands to her bare shoulders. The previous layers had been too hot, but this was undoubtedly too cold. "I don't know if I can," she called out. "My shoulders are naked!"

"Ah!" Akane said. "Well, you're lucky. Because *I* thought of that. Look at the first hook on your right for the matching top."

Yumi looked and saw a short buttoning top. You might call it a dress cardigan, but it was a bit fancier than that—a little more stiff (of a denim blend) and shorter, not even reaching to her navel. It reminded Yumi a little of the top part of the tobok she wore among her people, only with shorter sleeves.

She removed it from its hanger and hesitantly pulled it on. It matched the dress nicely. The fit was close, and she sported a *distinctly* feminine silhouette. She tried not to be embarrassed about that as she opened the door.

Akane beamed at her. That gave Yumi a surge of confidence, like a flower rising high into the sky. One of the attendants had stayed, and this woman nodded thoughtfully and seemed approving as well.

Behind the two of them, Painter stood up straight, gawking at her. He probably thought she looked silly, as he knew the type of clothing she *should* be wearing.

"That is *wonderful*," Akane said. "We're getting that one for *sure*. But here, try on the others! You *have* to see this pink one . . ."

Akane stepped in and dug through the dresses to find a specific choice. Yumi raised her chin and met Painter's eyes. He was still staring at her.

Well, for once she didn't care if she looked improper. The spirits had demanded a lot of her these last few days.

It was blasphemous, but she had decided it was time for her to demand something in return. She wanted *possessions* for the first time in her life. So it was that an hour later, she trotted out of the store wearing the blue dress and clutching a package containing two other outfits of slightly different styles. Hers. Actually *hers*. Granted, she wouldn't be able to bring them back to her land, where her life—once this was over—would go back to the way it always was.

For now, she got to live a dream. That almost made all of this chaos worth it. And as she walked home with Akane, she noticed something else. No one was staring at her anymore.

Painter had been *right*, she realized with amazement. No one here knew what she was. No one here cared. Now that she wasn't dressed in such ridiculous clothing, now that she fit in, she was just . . . normal.

It was the most exciting thing that had ever happened to her.

"All right," Akane said, stopping outside the apartment building. "I need to get ready for work. The foreman throws a fit if I go painting in a miniskirt. You have food? Upstairs?"

"Um . . ." Yumi said. "Technically it *counts* as food."

"Uh-huh. Come back to the lobby in ten minutes. I'm meeting friends for lunch before shift at a noodle shop nearby. You'll join us."

"I'm being too much of a burden," Yumi said, lowering her head.

"You? A burden?" Akane laughed. "Please, Yumi. You're not going to deny me the chance to show off my fashion pupil to my friends, are you?"

Nearby, Painter was shaking his head urgently. That, mixed with her growling stomach, was the decider.

"Of course I'll go with you," Yumi said. "Let me go drop these things off at my brother's room."

Chapter 16

WHAT'S A noodle shop?" Yumi asked, arranging her new outfits on the floor.

"Place where you can pay," Painter explained, "and people bring you food." He lingered in the doorway, watching her. It was surreal how a simple outfit change made her seem like she belonged. All of a sudden he could picture her here, in his life.

"People bring you food," she said. "You don't have to make it yourself?"

"No."

"Do they . . . feed you?"

Why did she sound *hopeful*? "No," he said. "You need to do that part on your own."

"Well, as long as I don't have to make it," she said, hands on her hips as she surveyed the clothing she'd laid out.

"You're just going to leave it there?" he asked.

She hesitated, then glanced at him. "Is there . . . another place where it should go?" She looked at the heaps of clothing.

"Closet," he said, gesturing, "has hangers and a rod."

"Oh!" She walked over. "How clever! Your people think of so many interesting things."

"I . . . suspect your people have closets, Yumi," he said.

She cocked her head. "I guess maybe they do. I've never been inside another person's home." She began hanging the clothes. "Is there money here somewhere I can use at the noodle shop?"

"In the can on the counter," he said. "But Yumi, I don't think you should go. So far we've been lucky. Akane hasn't asked too many questions, and hasn't noticed the oddities about you. But the longer you spend around people, the more dangerous it gets."

"Dangerous?" she said. "Getting clothing? Eating dinner?"

"Someone's bound to ask questions you can't answer," he said. "They might start poking around, getting suspicious. Eventually someone will find out I don't *have* a sister. Then things start getting awkward."

"This is why lies are bad," she said, shutting the closet doors. "We should have told them the truth at the start."

"Oh? And how did it go telling Liyun the truth? And telling the foreman about the nightmare? How well did that work?"

"These mistakes are due to our inadequacy," she said. "We should try again, presenting Liyun with the truth in a more convincing way."

"No," he said. "She'll just think we've decided to make her life terrible for some reason."

Yumi averted her eyes.

"It could be even worse here, if you tell the truth," he said. "They'll demand proof you can't provide. What if they think you're insane? Or that you've killed me?"

She looked at her feet. "I thought . . . maybe the other painters could help me. Figure out what I'm supposed to do. It sounded . . . nice to talk to them."

"That group?" Painter snorted. "They're too exclusive for people like us, Yumi. You might be a novelty to them now, but they'll drop you as soon as something more interesting comes along. Trust me."

"Akane is nice. You said she was nice to you."

"She was. At first." He turned away, not wanting to think about those times.

Yumi was quiet for a moment, then retrieved the money and brushed past him, heading toward the stairs. "I want to do it anyway."

A second later, he was yanked after her. *That* aspect of this was extremely unfair. How was it that he got bullied by her when he was physical, but then he ended up being pulled along like a dog on a leash when *she* was the one with the body?

They met Akane below, now in a simpler outfit of slacks and a blouse. Not exactly what he'd call painting gear, but it was as dressed down as she got. Akane led Yumi around the corner to the Noodle Pupil, and Painter followed sullenly. He couldn't have said what made him want to avoid this place. Perhaps it was the way that Akane had adopted Yumi so easily. Reminded him of how easily he'd been dropped.

Not that he could, in all honesty, blame them.

He felt better though when they stepped into the restaurant. The place was familiar, and even without a body he could smell the warm scents of broth and green onions. In here, the clatter of bowls and utensils felt somehow *softer* than it did in other restaurants.

Akane hung her oversized painter's bag on the arm of the statue in the front of the shop, the one that (in case you've forgotten) contained the body of an exceedingly bored storyteller. At least the eggs were gone by that point.

Painter's former friends sat at the rear, in their usual place. As he followed the two women over, he felt . . . annoyed. He'd wanted for so long to be invited to this table. To rejoin in this familiar laughter, as he had during school.

It turned out there was an easy way to get the others to let him back in: he just had to be invisible.

Akane presented Yumi with a flourish. "Behold," she said, "Nikaro's *little sister.*"

There were three others in the group: two girls, one guy. That meant Tojin was outnumbered three to one in the clique—unless you went by sheer muscle mass. Painter was reasonably certain Tojin outweighed the other three combined.

"No (lowly) way," Tojin said, sitting backward on his chair as he usually did, sleeves rolled up as if they were too intimidated by his massive forearms and had shriveled out of respect. He was squeezing some kind of hand exercise device, ten reps in each hand before swapping, because of course he was.

"That's Tojin," Akane said, gesturing to him.

"Hey," he replied, swapping hands.

"Tojin," Painter said, leaning in toward Yumi, "is exactly what he appears to be. The type of guy who would roll up his sleeves and do exercises at the dinner table to get a better chance at showing off to the women. He *never* misses a chance to display his body to the girls."

"This is Masaka," Akane said, gesturing toward a girl all in black, huddled in her chair with her knees up, sketchpad in front of her. Masaka hated showing skin, and wore a scarf to hide even her neck. She peeked over the top of the sketchpad with narrowed eyes, dark beneath her bangs.

Yumi stepped back in shock. Masaka had that effect on people.

"Rumors in school were," Painter whispered, "she had to become a painter as part of a plea deal with the judge after stabbing someone during her lower school years. She doesn't talk much. Too busy plotting."

Masaka punctuated something on the page at that moment, then looked up again at Yumi—who took another unconscious step backward.

"Don't let her stern demeanor get to you," Akane said with her usual cheerfulness. "She's a softy inside. Besides, staring only makes her angry. And finally, here is Izumakamo!"

A girl in trousers and a sweatshirt stood up, proffering her hand. Yumi stared at it.

"You take it," Painter explained, "and bow. It's a kind of greeting."

Yumi hesitantly did as he said, taking Izzy's hand and bowing as the other girl did likewise. Then Yumi glanced toward Painter, as if expecting an explanation of who this was, like he'd given for the other two.

"Just watch," Painter said instead.

"Yumi . . ." Izzy said, thoughtful. Then she dug into a thick encyclopedia-style book, flipping pages quickly. "Starts with a *Y* . . . two syllables . . . Birth year and month?"

"Say you're year of the dragon," Painter told her. "It would look strange if we're the same age. And, let's say, the month of rain. For fun."

"Um . . ." Yumi said. "Year of the dragon. Month of rain?"

"Ah yes . . ." Izzy continued, flipping a few more pages. "Oh, here it is. Guri and Shishi's wedding episode! The first wedding, I mean. You will have very good luck today, Yumi. Very good indeed. Great day for making promises."

Yumi regarded the young woman, baffled. Nearby, Tojin snickered, swapping hands again with his exercise device.

"Don't you laugh, Tojin," Izzy said. "This is a *totally* legitimate science."

"Don't worry about her, Yumi," Akane said, leaning in and whispering. "She's special."

"My talent *is* special!" Izzy declared. "You wait and see. Soon people are going to catch on, and *everyone* will be getting their dramascope. I'll be famous for inventing it, and you all won't be able to make fun of me any longer. You'll have to wait in line."

"Wait in line," Tojin said. "To make fun of you."

"No. Um . . ."

"Presumably," he said, flexing his hand, "because so many other people will want a chance to do so?"

"That is *not* what I meant," Izzy said. She then leaned toward Masaka and whispered conspiratorially, "When I'm rich and famous, want to be my bodyguard?"

Masaka shrugged.

"Great," Izzy said. "Your first job will be to beat up Tojin when he tries to tell everyone he knew me before I was famous."

"I'm . . . confused," Yumi said.

"Not surprising," Akane said. "It's just a game Izzy plays."

"It's *not* a game," Izzy replied.

"She thinks," Akane said, "that she can predict people's fortunes using episode guides for hion-line programs."

"It's an ancient art," Izzy said.

"You made it up!" Tojin said, pointing.

"I made it up a long time ago," Izzy said. "During a previous life. So it's ancient. Do you want to see the dramascope that explains it? Here, let me show you."

She grinned as Tojin rolled his eyes. Painter never had been able to figure out how serious she was about her crazy ideas. In moments like this— smiling as if she'd gone too far on purpose—he was left uncertain.

Standing there though . . . listening to Tojin joke while Masaka drew and Izzy rambled on about something incredibly random . . . he felt a painful nostalgia. For something he'd lost, like a misplaced note you keep remembering you wrote something important on, but you can never quite recall what pocket you left it in.

These *weren't* his friends anymore. This feeling he felt? It was false. He turned to go as the food arrived, brought by one of Design's assistants. Two bowls for Tojin—no noodles, just extra eggs and pork—and a small one for Masaka.

There was nothing for Painter here. Why had he yearned so long to come back to this?

He walked off. Yumi gave him a panicked look as he did, but she was the one who had wanted to come down here and talk to this crew. She could do it without him. He wanted to be as far away as he could get— well, as far away as he could get without being yanked every time Yumi shifted. He made it to the bar, where he settled on an empty stool, facing away from the group.

Yumi joined him a few minutes later. "They said," she told him softly, "I should come up here to order? Which means . . . tell them what food I want, right?"

He nodded.

"Is there a specific dish I'm supposed to have?" she asked.

"You pick any you want," he said.

She drew in a breath, appearing nervous about that idea.

"Get a small mild pork with salt," he said. "No add-ons. My guess, from what I've been fed in your world, is that you'd like something with a more . . . non-complex taste."

"Thank you," she said, then held up a sheet of paper. "Um . . . Masaka gave me this . . ."

It was a picture of a rabbit drawn with deep, cavernous holes for eyes and a stare that seemed like it wanted to swallow the world. Text underneath said, "Yumi reminds me of a cute bunny."

"Oh dear," Painter said (lowly).

"What?" Yumi asked, her voice rising.

"She likes you."

"Is that bad?"

"Never can tell with Masaka," he replied.

Yumi settled down on the stool next to his. "You were right," she said softly. "I shouldn't have come here. I don't . . . know how to be a person, Painter."

"Well, maybe *I* was wrong. Because you need practice."

"No," she said. "I don't need practice to become something I shouldn't. I'm *not* a person, Painter."

He frowned, looking toward her. "Of course you're a person, Yumi."

"No, I'm a concept," she said. "A thing, owned by society. I would be better as a machine, like that box that shows stories in your room. If I didn't think, if I didn't feel, I'd do my job far better." She gazed downward, concentrating on the counter. "The nibbles at freedom I had today are dangerous, Painter. They taste of things I *shouldn't* want. If I let them control me, then what? I still have to go back. Take up my duties again. Do you think maybe the spirits sent me here to warn me? Or maybe . . . to test me?"

"No," Painter said. "I think they sent you here as a reward, Yumi. So that you *could* taste these things. Enjoy them, for once in your life."

She glanced at him, then smiled. And suddenly he felt ashamed for his earlier joy at her discomfort. Perhaps he should have seen it before, but this was a person who somehow felt more isolated than he did.

He'd thought himself alone. He'd barely understood the word.

Her smile faltered, and she averted her eyes. "I wish I could believe you were right. But the spirit that came to me, Painter . . . it was *hurting*. It *needed* something. This isn't a reward. It might not be a punishment or a test, but it's no reward."

"You could still enjoy it," he said. "While you can."

She glanced back at him. And instinctively, he reached his hand toward hers. She looked like she could use something to hold. But . . . then he stopped, because he couldn't touch her even if he wanted to. He blushed, feeling foolish.

A bowl clattered to the floor.

They both jumped, turning toward Design—who had just left the kitchen. She didn't seem to notice the bowl of soup she'd dropped; instead she stood there slack-jawed.

"Storms!" Design said, staring *directly* at Painter. "Nikaro? Are you *dead*?"

Chapter 17

IT TOOK Yumi a moment to register what had happened.

This strange woman with the white hair and the outrageously full figure was looking at Painter. She'd called him by name.

She could see him.

Someone could *see Painter*.

"Design!" he said, leaping to his feet. "You can *see* me?"

"Um . . ." Design said, glancing to the sides at the nearby patrons, who were staring at her because of the dropped bowl. "Nope. Nope, can't see any ghosts here. Mortals *hate* talk of ghosts." She raised her eyes and spoke louder. "Just an accident with my clumsy, inefficient meat-fingers! I did *not* see a ghost. Everyone, enjoy the noodles!"

"Design!" Painter said, pained.

Design nodded toward the ground in an exaggerated way. Then she crouched to begin cleaning up the noodles. Painter rushed around the bar, and Yumi—feeling awkward—grabbed some bar cloths and did the same, kneeling down.

This left the three of them all out of sight but perfectly audible—except maybe Painter. This method seemed *more* suspicious to Yumi. But she didn't know how normal people acted, so maybe she wasn't the best judge.

"Painter!" Design said. "How did you die? Did you choke on an overly large noodle?"

"I don't think I'm dead," he said, whispering for some reason. "A couple days ago, I started waking up on *her* world! I think it's the star—like, I think I'm visiting it. Then when I fall asleep, I wake up back here—but I'm like a ghost, and somehow she's here now."

Design looked at Yumi, then stuck out her hand. "Hello! Would you like to shake meat-appendages?"

"Uh . . ." Yumi took the hand, then bowed. Strangely, Design didn't bow back, but only waggled her hand a little.

"Nice to meet you," Design said. "You're not a ghost."

"We haven't been able to figure out what's going on," Painter said. "Or why I wear her body when I'm in her world, but she doesn't wear mine when she's here."

"Uh, Painter?" Design said, nodding her head toward Yumi. "Yeah, that's totally your body."

"But . . ." he said. "It looks like her. Even to you, right?"

"Yup," Design said. "But I can see the line of Connection from you to it. I've got this, um, strong Cognitive aspect? Hard to explain without numbers, and mortals get cross-eyed when I use those instead. I'm not *really* here, like I've told you, so I can see Cognitive Shadows even when they don't want to be seen. Also, your body is a girl's body now."

"*What?*" Painter said.

"Who are you?" Design said, ignoring Painter and looking at Yumi. "You've got a *storming* strong Spiritual aspect, highly Invested in some strange way. Otherwise you wouldn't have been able to rewrite his body with your soul and warp it to match your sense of self. Shrinking and reshaping the bones, stretching and shifting the muscles . . . Fun stuff."

Painter's face paled.

Yumi tried to take it in stride. "I . . . didn't mean to do any of these things, honored hostess. It was done by the spirits because of some kind of desperate need."

"Yeah," Design said. "Um, that's some seriously hard work you did. Bet you're hungry."

"Ravenous," Yumi admitted. "Though not so bad today as the last time I came to your world."

"Should get easier each time," Design said. "The body will fight you less and waste less energy trying to snap back to looking like him. Still, I should feed you. It's, like, my job. I'm *employed*!" She popped up from behind the bar and shooed Yumi back to a stool, though they'd barely cleaned up half the mess. Design did the rest quickly and efficiently, while Painter stood morosely nearby.

"I don't *want* to be a girl," he said.

"Oh hush," Design said, quickly mopping the floor. "I've been pretending to be one for years now, so I'm an authority—and it's really quite nice. Except for the sexism. But it's hard to blame that on being a woman instead of on, you know, *morons*." She paused, then smiled at Painter. "Don't look so glum. Your body will probably snap back to your shape once she's no longer attached to it."

"Probably?" he asked.

"Definitely probably." She handed him the mop, which slipped through his incorporeal fingers as soon as she let go of it. Which caused her to snicker. "What?" she asked at his offended expression. "Just doing some tests."

She gathered the bucket and mop and stalked into the kitchen again. Painter rounded the bar, then slumped down next to Yumi. She, in turn, glanced around the room—but no one seemed to be paying much attention to them. Akane was gazing toward Yumi as if to check on her, so Yumi gave her what was hopefully an "I'm good" gesture.

"Why is no one bothered," Yumi whispered, "by the things Design is saying and doing? Ghosts? Dropping a mop? Talking to the air?"

"This place is mostly full of longtimers," Painter explained, his voice sullen. "They're . . . accustomed to Design. She acts like this even on normal days."

"I ignore social boundaries," Design said, bustling out of the kitchen with a bowl of soup for Yumi. "It's endearing."

She set the bowl down and leaned forward. People on this planet . . . really liked their low-cut tops, didn't they?

"Eat," Design said, pointing.

Yumi started eating. It was a stronger flavor than she was used to—in fact, it was also a *stranger* flavor than she was used to. Spices she'd never tasted mixed in her mouth, making it wake up from a long slumber.

The first spoonful was a lot. The second was satisfying. The third . . . divine.

"Usually," Painter said, "you use the maipon sticks to eat the noodles."

Yumi glanced at the sticks, which she'd seen her attendants use to feed her. She'd never held any herself. So she stuck with the spoon.

"I still don't understand," Painter said to Design, "why you can see me."

"It's technical," Design said. "It's mostly because I'm not actually human, but an immortal essence of pure Investiture with an imitation human fleshy-type shell stapled on."

Yumi paused, her spoon trailing noodles halfway to her mouth. She tried to parse that sentence—which was difficult—but came to the obvious conclusion.

"Are you . . . a spirit?" she asked.

"Depends," Design said, "on what definition of the word you're using. What is a spirit to you, Yumi?"

"They're the soul of my world," Yumi explained between bites. "They rise up from the ground at my summons if I—as the intercessor between the divine and the mortal—please them with my stacks of stone, arranged to their liking. In return, they will do as I ask and take shapes of power and utility, serving for a time to bless the lives of my people."

"Stacks of stone, eh?" Design said.

"Arranged in patterns," Yumi replied. "For reasons beyond the knowledge of mortals, the spirits love to see order made from chaos. There are other ways, but stacks of stones have proven among the most attractive to the spirits."

"It's the mixing of math and art," Design said. "Plus the human aspect—the concentration, the satisfaction, the emotion. This entire region is littered with Splinters that Virtuosity left behind. Regardless, it seems that, yay, I can answer you. Yes! I'm absolutely a spirit. Basically the same thing."

Yumi had suspected, but still she found the idea daunting. She reverently put down her spoon, and after a moment of trying to decide what to do, she started one of the prayers.

"Stop that," Design said, smacking her on the head with a spoon. "I'm not an honorspren. What's wrong with you?"

"I . . ." Yumi said (highly), "should show you devotion."

"I'm not one of *your* spirits," Design said. "Besides, I'm on vacation. No worshipping the bits of God when they're on vacation. It's a rule I just made up."

Well, that was going to be difficult, but it *was* Yumi's duty to do as the spirits asked, so . . . she hesitantly picked up her spoon and continued eating. As she did though, she shot a glare at Painter.

"You had a spirit here," she said, "and you didn't *mention* it to me?"

"I didn't know she was a spirit," Painter said.

"I've told you," Design said, lounging with her elbows on the bar. "I've told basically everyone. They ignore me. If I were a more vengeful bit of God, I'd be offended. Fortunately, I'm eccentric instead. It's endearing."

"She always says strange things like that," Painter said, still addressing Yumi. "How was I to know she was being truthful rather than crazy?"

Design leaned in toward Yumi and spoke in a conspiratorial tone. "I don't think Nikaro paid much attention to what I was saying. In his defense, he was staring at my butt the whole time."

Painter blushed something fierce. "That's in my *defense*?"

"Sure," Design said, turning, "it's an honest explanation. I mean, it is a remarkably nice butt, isn't it?"

"I didn't think you'd noticed I'd been . . . looking," Painter said, wilting.

"Kid, women *always* notice. I've only been one for a few years, and even *I* know that."

"I . . ." Yumi said, "don't think *I'd* notice." She continued eating the food, which was more incredible with every bite. But now that her hunger had finally begun to be satiated, she was feeling drowsy. She'd lasted far longer this excursion into Painter's world than last time, but she wasn't certain how much longer she could remain awake.

"Can you help us, Design?" Painter was asking. "Can you find a way to fix what has happened to us?"

"I don't know," Design said. "I'm . . . not terribly good at this sort of thing. The guy you want is Hoid. He's a pain in the butt—remarkable ones and common ones alike—but he understands Realmatic Theory better than anyone I know."

(It's nice to be appreciated.)

"Great," Painter said. "So where is he?"

Design pointed. Yumi turned to see the statue by the door, posed to hold people's coats and bags when they entered. That . . . was an actual person? Or perhaps another spirit? That made sense to Yumi, as the spirits she called often became stone or metal when transformed.

"Oh," Painter said. "Him. You . . . told me about him the other day. I didn't believe you."

"Can we wake him up?" Yumi asked.

"You're welcome to try," she said. "I've been trying *forever*. Granted, as I told you, I'm not the best at this sort of thing. I *have*, however, established a reputable restaurant with a loyal clientele and learned to make *seventeen* kinds of noodles. That was on my list of human experiences to try, so I have to say, the visit here has been rather successful."

(Sigh. Of all the spren I could have bonded . . .)

"So," Painter said (lowly), "you're saying you're useless?"

"Painter!" Yumi hissed. "You can't speak to a spirit that way."

"Yes he can," Design said. "I've insulted him like twice today already. He's owed a shot back."

"My apologies, honored spirit," Yumi said (highly).

"Stop that." Design rapped her on the head again. Which was *demonstrably* unfair.

"Painter," Design continued, "I'll try to think of something I can do, but this world of yours? It's *strange*. The strangest I've visited—and I've been to *Threnody*. You have nightmares that come alive? Creeping out of a miasma of raw Investiture? That's the kind of stuff you get on a planet when a *god* has been *killed*.

"It's what we came here to learn about. Well, what *Hoid* came here to learn about. But he turned into a statue the moment we arrived, and *I* was left to experiment at being a small business owner running one of the most notoriously difficult varieties of startup. Here, have a coupon."

She actually delivered one to Yumi, who naturally had no idea what to make of it.

"Anyway," Design continued, "I'll need time to think. Maybe the shroud and the nightmares are connected to what has happened to you two? I didn't realize the other planet was involved. That might explain some of this. Regardless, for now I have other customers. And your body, Nikaro, is about to fall asleep in its soup."

Indeed, Yumi was beginning to droop. She finished a few more bites, then went to excuse herself to Akane and the others—feeling mortified that she'd spent the entire meal apart from them after being invited. She told them that she'd been grabbed by Design and hadn't wanted to be rude by leaving. They appeared to accept that, but Yumi could tell—as she and Painter walked out—that the group thought she was odd.

"I've offended them," she said softly.

"They're the popular kids," Painter said—as if she was supposed to know what that meant. "Everything offends them." He looked over his shoulder into the restaurant. Then he shook his head and the two of them trudged back to his flat.

Yumi went into the bathroom and changed into the pajamas—which he'd been wearing this entire time in spirit form—then sat down on the ground and began arranging blankets. Painter, seeming pained, said, "We haven't even been awake six hours yet, Yumi. Can't you fight it off a little longer?"

She yawned. "I'm at my limit. Besides, we need to return to my world and get to work."

"Do we?" he said. "I don't fancy being yelled at by Liyun again. Here, what about this?"

He went to the hion screen and tried to get it to turn on. Oddly, though he couldn't touch other items, a little *zap* of light appeared at his fingertip—and the thing activated. "Ha!" he said. "That's something. See! I'm learning."

A pair of actors appeared in the blue and magenta. A man and a woman. *Holding hands.* Yumi's eyes widened.

"*Seasons of Regret*," Painter explained. "It's quite good. It's a historical, Yumi, taking place like a hundred years ago. They're old-fashioned, like you are! You're going to enjoy this one. Just watch."

She did so, ignoring her fatigue. It still seemed hedonistic how there were stories on this screen, all hours of the day, played out for anyone to watch. This world was so intoxicating, with its strange conveniences, wonderful flavors, and something even better than either: The dangerous allure of anonymity. Of living a normal life.

"No," she said, rising and switching the screen off. "No, I *cannot* have this, Painter. I am a *yoki-hijo*. I have a *duty*. And so long as you're in my body, you do as well!"

He sighed, sitting on the cushioned altar thing.

"We are going to fix this, whatever it is," Yumi said, doing her best to summon Liyun's force of will and sternness. "You will travel to my world, and you will *learn* the art of stacking. When we're in your world, instead of indulging in frivolity, I will learn your art."

"Painting?" he said, frowning. "Why?"

"In case you are right," she said, "and the spirits sent me here to deal with this stable nightmare you discovered."

"You'll be no match for a nightmare. It would be foolish to even try."

"Then I'll learn your art, so that I can go out in relative safety. There, I will then find a way to persuade others the nightmare is real—so they can deal with it. Either way, this is not a chance for us to relax. No more watching dramas. No more shopping. I am sorry for not listening to you before about going to meet those others."

"Yumi . . ."

"Do we have an agreement?" she demanded. "We do this as quickly as possible? You will subject yourself to my training in my world, and I will do the same in yours?"

His expression hardened. "Yeah, sure, fine. Not my fault if you don't want to take even a *single* moment to relax."

"It's not about what I want," she said. "It can *never* be about what I want. This is what must be. You agree."

He nodded curtly. "I just want my life back."

I don't, she thought. Then quashed that thought immediately, instead lying down in the cold bed she'd made on a floor with no heat.

She'd resisted temptation. She felt sick at having to do so. Yet she knew, in this one thing, Liyun would have been proud of her.

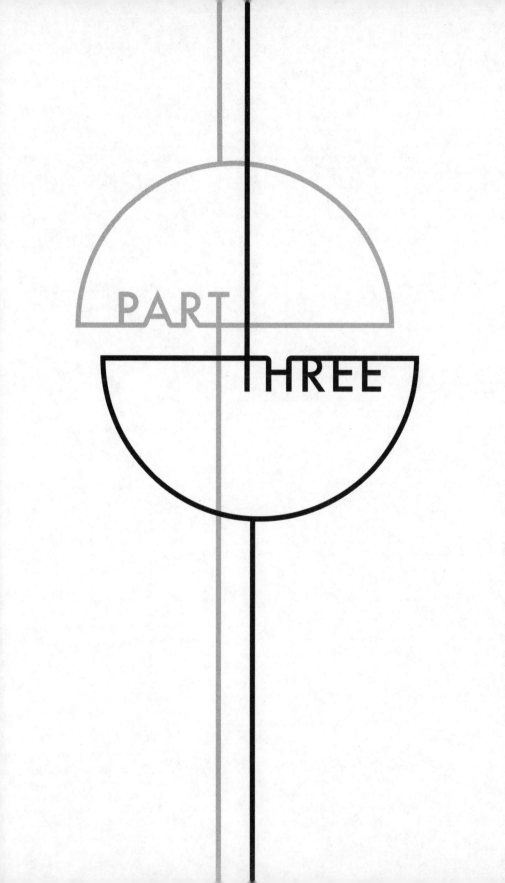

PART THREE

Chapter *18*

PAINTER STEPPED up to the cold spring, then turned his back toward Yumi. She, in turn, did the same to him. The attendants removed his clothing, and he entered the water, turning his back once more when he settled.

They bathed in silence. He still wasn't certain why she insisted on doing this at the same time as him. She was so shy in some situations, but then ridiculously brash in others. Why?

What point is there in trying to understand her? He'd *almost* felt like they were connecting. She'd almost started to act like a *person*, instead of some kind of machine. Yet here they were, on her world again—which meant a return to orders and stern curtness.

He finished the formal portion of his bathing, with its ceremonial dunk, and the attendants left him to soak while they dressed. He floated on his back, staring at the strange blue sky, with plants hovering some hundred feet or more in the air. It almost felt like *that* was the surface, and he'd somehow sunk far beneath it . . .

"Liyun didn't come speak to us in the morning," Yumi said from where she floated somewhere nearby. He didn't look toward her. "So she's probably having trouble deciding what to say. We utterly failed at our duties yesterday. She will be humiliated. The thought of it twists my insides."

"You worry about *her*?" Painter said. "What about me?"

"You are nothing," Yumi said, her voice stern. "The yoki-hijo is nothing.

When she arrives to speak with us—which she will inevitably do very soon—you will get down on your knees and bow to her in ritual apology."

"And if I don't want to?" he asked.

"My world," she said, "my rules. You *will* do it."

He sighed as a flock of distant specks fluttered around the plants. Insects of some sort, like moths, only more colorful.

"This way you act," he said softly, "won't get you what you want, Yumi. Not in the long run. You'll just end up pushing people away."

"As is appropriate," she said. "I am set apart."

He grunted, then righted himself and stalked out of the bath up onto the stones. The attendants rushed in from outside as he called to them—though they weren't quite ready—and began gathering his clothing for the day. Then, aggravatingly, Yumi proved correct—for Liyun strode up the path a short time later. Painter felt he should have been embarrassed for his state of undress. Even if they couldn't see him as him, it was awkward.

He was growing tired of that emotion. He couldn't summon the motivation to feel ashamed. Unfortunately, Yumi hurried over in a distracting state of half-dress herself—and that was far more difficult to ignore.

"Bow!" she said.

He reluctantly sank to his knees and bowed forward, putting his hands on the ground and touching his forehead to his knuckles. "I'm sorry," he said.

Oddly, Liyun knelt and bowed as well. He could see the motions even with his head lowered. She seemed just as ashamed.

"What is happening, Honored One?" Liyun said.

"Repeat this," Yumi said. "I cannot explain what has happened to me. It is as if another soul has taken residence inside of me, and it has lost all ability to stack."

"Your collapse," Liyun said softly after he repeated the words, "a few days ago. It has . . . left you affected."

"That may be true," Yumi said, with Painter repeating. "I fear I must take time, Warden-nimi, to practice. Perhaps even relearn the things I have lost."

Liyun knelt in silence. Painter felt his back ache from the unnatural posture, but when he tried to straighten, Yumi hissed at him.

At last, after a painful pause, Liyun spoke. "I will go to the leaders of the town we are now inhabiting. I will beg that they let us use their place of ritual for practice until you recover. They will be . . . shamed further by this, as they already believe their unworthiness before the spirits is the cause of your strange malady."

"I understand," Yumi said through Painter. "I am deeply sorry."

"That is well," Liyun said. "Perhaps your shame will lead to the spirits forgiving you." She stood up. "I will prepare the place of ritual, as you will want to start immediately."

Painter finally stood, and wasn't chastised this time. The attendants continued dressing him, their heads down, seeming humiliated by proxy. He didn't know much about them, having barely spoken to them despite all they'd done for him. The younger of the two was probably several years his senior, with an extremely pale complexion and a round face. The other was older, maybe in her thirties, with a longer face.

"You should not have gotten out of the bath until the attendants were ready for you," Yumi said, continuing to dress. "Next time, do not be so thoughtless."

He turned toward her to object, then blushed and turned away again.

"Do not speak," she continued. "The attendants will think it odd."

He forced down his words, and found they tasted unpleasant. When the attendants finished with him, they stepped beyond the stones to continue their preparations.

"Liyun does whatever you say," he hissed at Yumi, "doesn't she? So why don't you tell her to let you eat for yourself and dress yourself? Everything would be so much easier."

"Why do you think what is *easier* has any relevance for us?" Yumi asked, having finally put on her top. "Come, it's time for your first lesson."

THE first problem was that Painter couldn't kneel on the stone like she said he should be able to. Even with the kneepads, it was just so *hot*. The air got underneath his skirt and made him swelter from within.

"Instead of kneeling, then," Yumi said, walking around him in a circle, "you will squat, allowing you to move more frequently and perhaps ventilate a little more."

"The rocks are uncomfortably warm to the touch," he said, gesturing. "I need gloves or something."

"You will adapt," she said.

"You want to wait for that and get nothing done today?" he said. "Other than me picking up rocks and dropping them?"

She regarded him with something akin to contempt, then told him to request gloves of Liyun, who fetched some from the town—it was nearby, mere steps away really. This place of ritual was an exposed section of too-hot stone with a little fence built around it and rocks strewn about inside that looked like the remnants from a quarry.

Liyun, fortunately, had managed to clear away most of the gawking townspeople. For his audience today he had only his attendants and a few of the town's higher-ups, who watched and whispered with confused expressions. The men wore beards like they did in old paintings on his world, but with clothing that was unfamiliar and too colorful for the bland or black-and-white image of the past he'd formed from old photographs.

The town itself was a huddle of barely under a hundred homes, with that strange water-collecting thing in the center. An orchard of hundreds of trees drifted and bumped against one another off to Painter's left.

"Why can't we go in there to practice?" he whispered, wiping his brow at the heat. "I'd like to be in the shade. It wouldn't be quite as sweltering that way."

"Most of the heat comes from the ground," Yumi said, frowning. "It's not that much cooler in the trees. Besides, *this* is the place of ritual. You'd have the people of the town move all the rocks just for your convenience? That would be a shameful act."

Of course it would be.

His gloves arrived, and he pulled them on—feeling annoyed at being forced to put on *more* clothing. He swore it was hotter this day than it had been on the others, and the light of that sun overhead did *not* help.

"All right," Yumi said. "Step one is to learn to evaluate rocks. To stack properly, you must balance—and to do that, you need to be able to judge each rock. Pick up one and heft it."

He did so. It felt like a rock.

"Note how," she said, walking around him again, "it is bulbous on one end, narrower on the other. Its center of gravity, then, will be toward the bulbous side. Using that, you can create spectacular illusions of stacking where it *looks* like one side is hanging out impossibly in the air, while the other side is heavy enough to balance it out. Precision work using other stones can enhance this."

"Center of gravity," he said, "and precise work. I thought you called this stacking of yours an *art*."

"Art is all about precision."

"No it's not," he said, passing the rock from hand to hand. "Art is about feelings and emotion. It's about letting them escape, so they can be shared. It's about capturing a truth about yourself. Like you're ripping a hole in your chest and exposing your soul."

"Pretty words," she said, "but meaningless. Poetry is a luxury. And we—"

"—have no claim upon luxuries."

"Exactly," she said.

"This is stupid," he said, dropping the rock. "This entire world is stupid, Yumi. You don't need a hero. You need an *accountant*."

She glared at him. Silent. Intense. Until finally he picked the rock back up. "Fine," he said. "How do I stack it?"

"You don't, not yet," she said. "Drop it and pick up another one. Today we will focus only on weighing rocks."

"Seriously?" he said. "I'm going to spend all day just *picking them up*."

"Yes," she said. "We'll likely do that tomorrow as well. Might spend as much as a week getting a feel for the stones. In my training, we spent multiple months."

"You're . . ." He stopped himself. He'd been about to say, "You're kidding." But of course she wasn't. Because kidding—indeed, smiling or joking in any way—was a luxury. She wouldn't understand such things.

Too bad. Because the greatest joke *he'd* ever experienced was the one the cosmere was playing on him right now.

Chapter 19

YUMI WAS terrified.

She wasn't trained for this. Teaching another yoki-hijo? This wasn't appropriate. It wasn't what the spirits had chosen her to do.

She was going to screw it up. She felt herself screwing it up as Painter proved to be a stubborn student. She'd been stubborn too, hadn't she? Liyun talked about how willful she'd been as a young girl, always demanding explanations before doing as she was told.

And yet . . . that tone in the spirit's voice when it had spoken to her before beginning their swap—something was terribly wrong, or was going to go terribly wrong, and *she* had to stop it. Possibly through Painter.

The spirits depended on her. She was terrified she was going to fail them.

"Pay attention," she said to Painter, trying to give her voice the same weight that Liyun gave hers. "Don't daydream."

He sighed, dropping his current rock. She'd caught him staring off into space, likely pondering clever ways to aggravate her.

"How," he said to her, "am I supposed to 'feel' the stones and 'know' them if I don't take some time to contemplate?"

"You don't need time to contemplate now," she said. "That's what meditation time is for."

"It doesn't have to be that strict," he said. "You can't just force every part of your life into some neat little box, with no overlap." He'd found a larger boulder to perch on, ignoring her reasonable instruction that he practice squatting or kneeling.

"Life," she said, "would be *chaos* without proper boundaries and guidelines."

He rolled his eyes. "You claim this is art, but there's not the slightest allowance for an artistic inclination?" He picked up a rock. "If I really wanted to *understand* this stone, I'd think about where it came from, how these nicks got in the side. I'd look at the shadows created when the light falls on it, and the individual veins running through it."

"None of that is relevant," she said. "You need to know the weight of the item and how it balances. *That* is your art now, Painter."

"Stupid," he said (lowly). "*So* stupid . . ."

Each minute of training felt like an hour, with Painter needing repeated correction. As the day wore on, Yumi felt nothing but frustration. They had made *no* progress. Even after all her work, Painter couldn't tell her how a given stone balanced.

Eventually he dusted off his gloves and removed them. She wanted to tell him to keep going, but his eyes were drooping. Considering how quickly they'd lost strength the first few days, it was remarkable how long he'd lasted: a solid eight hours.

Liyun entered the place of ritual. She'd spent almost the entire day outside it, watching, her normally unflappable expression growing more and more disturbed. Now she led the way back toward their wagon.

Should I, Yumi wondered, *let Liyun take over instruction?* The woman was certainly better at it than Yumi was.

Except . . . well, the spirits hadn't chosen Liyun for this duty. They'd chosen Yumi. As terrified as she was of getting it wrong, it *was* her responsibility.

But what if Liyun did something drastic? That concern on her face had Yumi unnerved.

In storytelling, we pretend you can read all kinds of things from a furrowed brow or a fleeting expression. This is shorthand for a real phenomenon, but it's more complex than we pretend. The longer you spend with a person, the more you know them. But beyond the obvious details like learning their favorite foods, we internalize the way that *they* react. The way that *they* express worry.

For some, it's the archetypal furrowed brow. For others it's the way they linger, the way they won't meet your eyes. It's more than eyes, more than posture, more than brow. Human beings are bundles of emotion puppeting muscles like a marionette. We emote not only with our bodies, but with our very souls.

Yumi could read what Liyun was thinking as they walked together. The woman was contemplating something dangerous. There *was* a fate worse than going back to basics with Painter. In an emergency, a yoki-hijo could be removed entirely from duty.

Yumi could see herself frantically trying yet again to explain the truth of her situation to Liyun—and the woman taking it as fancy brought on by overwork. Liyun did not like fancy. No, Painter was right in this. She would never accept some tale of a man from another planet invading Yumi's body. Push too far, and Liyun would be forced to call her superiors and have Yumi . . . removed. Locked away, forced to do spirit summonings in a prison environment.

Yumi wished she could be as calm and positive as Painter. He yawned as they reached the wagon. But the disappointment, even anger, on Liyun's face as she watched him step in, exhausted after a mere eight hours awake . . .

"Please," Yumi said to Liyun. "Please, let me *try*. Don't remove us from duty. Don't send for the executors."

"Hmmm?" Painter said, turning in the wagon. He'd forgotten to remove his clogs.

"Nothing," Yumi said as he flopped down. The attendants hurried in to begin feeding him. They were too slow because a second later—

—Yumi opened her eyes and found herself in the jumble of blankets on Painter's floor. It was a uniquely surreal experience, as moments ago she'd been standing outside the wagon. Yet she felt groggy, as if she'd been asleep. Likely this body slumbered while they were on her world. Plus, they did lose time with every transfer, hours that were unaccounted for—probably spent with both of them unconscious.

Painter ran a hand through his hair, looking scruffy and out of sorts, dressed in the fuzzy cloth material that passed for night clothing here. Each time she'd been here, he'd spent all day in the same thing. The clothing Yumi was currently dressed in.

"You should try seeing if you can put on some other clothes," she said. "The souls of them, at least."

"The souls," he said groggily, "of the clothing?"

"When I'm a spirit, I'm able to touch the soul of the clothes I'm wearing to take them off, then put them back on. You might be able to do something similar with your other outfits." She turned and eyed the bathroom. So convenient to have a room like that, where the water flowed directly into the home. "I am going to experience another of those showers."

She strode in that direction, intent on starting off this day right. No more wasting time as she had the last time she'd been in his world. Painter yelped as she got far enough away that he was towed off the plush altar and to his feet. She glanced at him, but he just crossed the room and groggily waved for her to continue. She nodded, then shut the door and turned on the lights. Time for focus.

Unfortunately, as soon as she stepped into the steaming water—responsive to her touch upon the knobs, turning the perfect temperature at her command—she caught herself sighing and melting into the luxury. This place was so dangerous. Reluctantly, she turned the knobs until the water was uncomfortably cold. That chill seeped into her, deep down in her soul, dousing the rebellious heat within. That would encourage her not to linger.

She washed—an awkward act without an attendant—then stood shivering in the cold water and said her prayers.

Finally she stepped out and wrapped herself in a towel, then stood in front of the mirror to brush her hair. Here she missed her attendants even more. Chaeyung was expert at getting out snarls without it hurting, and Hwanji would hum while they worked, which was so comforting. They weren't her friends, as she wasn't allowed friends. Indeed, if she grew too familiar with them, they would be changed. Regardless, she missed spending time with them.

Strange, she thought, *how they barely touch Painter's hair when they get him ready. They see him as me, but instead of doing a hundred strokes, they run the brush through his hair a few times and are done.*

Curious. Design hadn't been surprised that Yumi could make this body look like hers. Yumi had rewritten Painter's shape somehow—and the method apparently had to do with her calling as a yoki-hijo. Perhaps if Painter were more skilled, he'd be able to make *her* body look like *his*? That would be a disaster of incredible magnitude, but perhaps it was what the spirits wanted?

She didn't know. But she *would* find out.

She finished her brushing, so frigid she felt like she'd never be warm again. This was her duty. She stepped toward the door, then paused. She was wearing only a single towel. But . . . well, it *was* just Painter. She pushed out into the main room, which was even colder than the bathroom. Her skin immediately puckered with goosebumps. She still half believed this place was the land of the dead and frozen spirits.

Painter stood near his heaps of clothing, and had changed. He wore stiff trousers, a simple shirt, and then a second shirt over that with long sleeves, untucked and unbuttoned. It looked . . . sloppy, but in a managed way? A little like him, actually.

"You were right," he said, holding his hands to the sides. "I couldn't touch them at first, but then I . . . I don't know, I cleared my mind, then thought only about a specific article of clothing. When I reached for it that way, I could grab it. A copy of it, at least."

"Its soul," she said. "You *meditated!*"

"No!" he said defensively. "I was thinking about something. What I wanted to wear."

"You cleared your mind first," she said, pointing. "You *learned* something!"

He shrugged indifferently, then noticed her picking through the clothing Akane had bought her, so he turned his back toward her to allow her to dress with some privacy.

"Today," she said as she strapped on the bra, "you will teach me how to paint."

"I'm not certain I want to," he said, arms folded, facing away. "What I do is dangerous, Yumi. *Especially* if a stable nightmare is involved."

"We already decided this," she said, trying to dress as quickly as she could, to get covered in something that would hopefully keep her warm. "The spirits might have sent me to stop the stable nightmare."

"We *didn't* decide that," he replied. "We discussed the *possibility*. You can't face a stable nightmare, Yumi. They require the expertise of extremely talented painters—far beyond my skill level, let alone that of a neophyte."

"But we can't let it roam. You're the one who said that it will be out there hurting people."

"It *might* be," Painter said. "Or it might not. It appeared close to becoming fully stable, but what do I know? I've never seen one like that before. It could take weeks to complete the process, particularly if it's clever and careful. If that's true, someone else is bound to discover it eventually. Then the experts will get called."

"And if it kills someone first?" she asked.

He didn't respond.

"I'm r-ready," she said.

"Fine," he said, turning around. "I'll teach you, but *only* so you can defend yourself against . . ." He frowned, looking at her standing there in one of her dresses and tops, arms wrapped around herself. "Are your teeth chattering?"

"Is th-that what you c-call it?" she asked, her jaw trembling from the cold. "I've never been this c-cold before."

"*Never?*" he asked, seeming surprised.

"No," she said, shivering. "If you get c-cold, you just l-lie down. D-depending on how h-hot the floor is."

Perhaps showering in that cold water hadn't been the smartest idea. Her body was *not* dealing with it well.

"Here," he said, walking to the wall. "See this dial? Turn it up to increase the heat in the room."

"From the floor?" she asked, hopeful.

"Uh, no," he said, pointing at the top of the wall. "Vents from a small hion heater."

Pity. But she shook her head, and would have done so even if it had heated the floor. "No."

"No?" he said. "I can *see* you shivering, Yumi."

"I g-got used to this place after a l-little while before," she said. "Besides, it is d-dangerous for me to get t-too comfortable in your w-world. I will instead accept w-what the spirits have g-given me."

Painter gaped at her as if she'd sprouted leaves and started flying like a tree. "You," he said, "are *so* (lowly) strange." He inspected the dial on the wall, then stuck his finger at it, fiddling. Soon after, a hum came from the vent.

"Ha!" he said. "I made the viewer turn on last time, so I *thought* I might be able to do this too. I can *feel* the hion lines. I couldn't move the dial, but I can tweak them somehow, make them activate . . ."

A knock on the door interrupted further conversation. Timid, Yumi answered—worried she'd have to lie again. Fortunately, this time all she found was a large envelope taped to the door.

She returned to the room and opened the envelope at Painter's insistence. Inside was a single sheet full of words. She'd rarely read anything other than prayers, but oddly this felt as if it had some of the same tone or formality to it.

"This is bad, isn't it?" she asked after reading it to herself. "I don't understand all the words, but . . ."

"It's a letter of suspension," Painter said softly, staring at the page with an uncharacteristic solemnity. "From the foreman. Relieving me of duty for a month without pay, as punishment for lying about my work."

"It says he went to the address provided but found nothing? Just an unoccupied home?"

Painter turned away, waving a hand flippantly in the air. "I'll bet he barely gave it a cursory inspection; might have even sent someone else. He's been *waiting* for a chance to reprimand me. Thinks I've been turning in fake paintings for some time now. Idiot."

"So he really *doesn't* believe you about the stable nightmare," Yumi said. "You were right about that."

"He's never liked me. Feels I shouldn't have been able to enter the job lottery out of school in the first place; hates that I drew his sector." He put a hand to his forehead, eyes closed. "At least I won't have to come up with some excuse for missing my rounds this next month."

"What . . . happens next?"

"It's my first offense," Painter said. "To the other painters, this will be described as medical leave. At least I won't have to suffer the embarrassment of *them* knowing I've been suspended." He paused. "Unless this lasts longer than a month. Unless I'm unable to consistently do my job. Then I'll get fired. Lose the apartment."

"We'll just fix our problems before then," Yumi said, confident. "Even if it requires me to find a way to deal with that stable nightmare." She stared at him, defiant. She wasn't certain if it was what he'd done with the heat, or if she was again growing accustomed to this place. But her shivering had subsided. That let her maintain some confidence as she met his eyes when he turned back toward her.

"I'll teach you," Painter finally said, and walked over to a large trunk beside his fuzzy altar. "But you're *not* going to face the stable nightmare, Yumi. I will train you to deal with an ordinary nightmare in an emergency. Then we'll go out at night and try to find proof of the stable nightmare's existence. Maybe we can spot it moving through the city, then lead someone else to it. If we have another witness, the foreman will *have* to accept that it's real. That will prove I wasn't lying to him, and he'll be forced to revoke my suspension and send for help."

"An excellent plan," Yumi said, nodding as she walked up beside the trunk as well.

"There's something odd about that nightmare, Yumi," Painter said softly. "When I found it, it *was* almost fully formed. I know I said otherwise, but . . . my gut says this one should have started rampaging by now. When the nightmares destroyed Futinoro, they didn't do it quietly. Yet this monster is subtle, sneaky. It's been days since I spotted it, and not a single attack has been reported . . ." He shook his head, then gestured to the trunk. "Open it."

She did so, revealing a collection of large paintbrushes. Some were nearly as tall as a person, like a broom with a brush on the end. Most were somewhat shorter, perhaps two feet long.

There were also jars of ink, all of the same dark shade, and some canvases. Painter directed her to get out one of the shorter brushes, along with a large pad of paper rather than the canvases—which he said were for painting when "on duty." The paper was for practice.

Judging by the fact that the pad was pristine, never opened, it didn't seem that Painter did much practicing himself. After setting the things out, Yumi noticed something else at the bottom of the trunk, easy to miss in the shadows. A large black portfolio tied with a cord. She reached for it.

"No!" Painter said, reaching to take her hand.

The transcendent warmth chased away the chills, erasing them from her body like the wrinkles in a blanket suddenly stretched tight. She gasped, then let out a soft sigh at the way the heat warmed her to the core.

Painter didn't snatch his hand away as quickly this time as he had before. He looked down at their hands, where he'd tried in vain to take hold of hers. Instead they had merged, the heat pulsing like a heartbeat and washing away all other thoughts and sensations.

Finally he withdrew his hand. "Sorry," he said. "But you can't touch that portfolio. *Ever.*"

"Why not?"

"Because I say so," he snapped. "My world. My rules. You don't touch that. Understood?"

She nodded.

"Right, then," he said, stepping back. "I'll teach you how to paint bamboo."

"Wait," she said, frowning. "You have bamboo on your planet?"

"Sure we do," he said. "Wait, you have bamboo? It doesn't fly . . . does it?"

She shook her head. "It grows where the stone gives way to soil. Out beyond the searing stone, in the cold wastes. Few people live there because there's no heat, but I've seen bamboo around cold springs also." She frowned. "How do plants live here? There's no sunlight."

"What does sunlight have to do with anything?" he asked.

"It . . . makes plants grow."

"It does?" he said. "I guess that's how you survive without hion lines. Our outer cities have enormous farms where little lines of hion crisscross the fields and sustain the plants."

She tried to imagine that. There were places here other than Kilahito? How did one reach them? It seemed like everything out there was pure darkness.

Yumi put aside her questions as Painter began coaching her through painting bamboo. She still didn't understand why *painting* had anything to do with *nightmares*. They were ... scared of art?

Well, she would get those explanations when Painter decided to disclose them. For now she tried to be a good student, to give him an example of how he should be. She did as he asked, kneeling beside the pad of paper to draw straight lines with the brush, and did not interrupt or ask questions.

(It's infuriating how many cultures think this is the best way to teach. They make it as convenient to the instructor as possible. As if learning were somehow a performance for their benefit alone.)

"You start," he explained, "by getting a feel for how the ink flows. Notice how it's dark at the top, then grows lighter the longer you draw the line, finally running out at the bottom. When you paint, you're not just creating something from your mind. You're seeing what the ink *wants* to become. You ..."

He trailed off, and she glanced toward him.

"Never mind that," he said. "Here's how you make bamboo." He snatched his fingers a few times at one of the brushes and managed at last to pull out a copy of it. With some work, he procured the souls of some paper and ink as well, then knelt beside her and showed her a specific method for painting bamboo. It was actually quite clever how he used the natural way the ink filled the brush to create a darker top for the bamboo, the lighter middle, then another blotch at the bottom where he paused briefly. There was something organic about the painting style, as if he were *growing* the bamboo.

He did it again, exactly the same way.

Then again.

And again.

"Bamboo," he said, "is easy. It's great because you can simply memorize the pattern—then create something that looks good with minimal effort."

"All right," she said, nodding. "I like how structured that feels. But ..."

"What?" he asked.

"Nothing." Yumi lowered her eyes. "I should not question."

"How do I know you're learning if you don't ask questions?"

It wasn't the proper way ... but it *was* his world. His rules. "You said in the place of ritual," she explained, "that art is about emotion. I disagreed, and I like this way of making bamboo you showed me. I merely find it odd to hear you speak of memorizing a pattern, then creating without effort. I guess . . . I expected something different."

Painter stared at the soul of the paper in front of him. And then it vanished into smoke, drawn back to the body of the paper nearby. It appeared he couldn't keep something that way very long. Fortunately, his clothing remained in place . . . She covered a blush.

"Never mind that," he said to her, standing up. "Just practice what I've shown you. Draw a thousand of them until you can do it by rote."

She nodded and began, though her fledgling efforts were pathetically out of proportion. How had he made it seem so easy?

Well, she could absolutely do this a thousand times. That sounded like the perfect way to learn. She took the role of a dutiful student, proud of her example. She kept going, not saying a word, until her wrist ached and her knees hurt from kneeling. She didn't speak, didn't ask for a break. She would wait for him to offer one.

He didn't. He sat on his altar, expression distant, the entire time. He . . . did know he was supposed to be supervising her, right?

Finally she was interrupted by another knock on the door. Painter shook out of his trance, then looked toward her, finding that she was surrounded by dozens of papers.

"Yumi," he said (lowly), "are you still going?"

"You said to do a thousand," she said. "I am at three hundred and sixty-three."

He put a hand to his head as if befuddled. The knock came again, and he gestured toward her. She took that as permission to pause her work, so she rose to go to the door. She only cracked it open so whoever was there wouldn't see what she'd been doing, just in case.

"Hey!" Akane said. "Dinner?"

"Oh," Yumi said. Her stomach growled. But she would survive on rice cakes and dry noodles today. Painter had shown her where he kept more. "No thank you."

"Yumi," Akane said, folding her arms and leaning forward. "Have you spent all day in here?"

"Uh . . ." Yumi said.

"You can't come to Kilahito and hide yourself away!" Akane said. "I won't allow it."

Painter groaned. "She does this," he said softly from behind. "Adopts people. Um . . . quick, tell her that you've got to study."

"Study?" Yumi asked.

"Oh," Akane said. "You haven't placed in upper school yet? How much younger than Nikaro are you?"

"Say three years. But you just missed the cutoff."

"Three years," she said, though surely she didn't look *that* young, did she? "But I just missed the cutoff."

"So you have entrance tests in a few months," Akane said. "Well, those are *not* as important as everyone makes them out to be." She fidgeted. "I'll bring you some noodles. But don't work yourself too hard, all right?"

Yumi nodded, then bowed deeply, glad as Akane finally retreated.

"What lie," Yumi said, closing the door, "did I just tell?"

"When you finish lower school at age sixteen or seventeen," Painter explained, "you take tests to place in upper school for professional training. It's kind of a big deal around here. The last few months before the tests, people spend most hours of the day studying. It will give us a good excuse for why you aren't letting her adopt you."

Yumi nodded, grateful at least that Akane might bring her something to eat other than rice cakes. She knelt to return to her training.

"Yumi," he said, "don't you want a break or something?"

"Only if you offer it, Master Teacher," she said, touching her forehead to the ground.

He snorted. "Master? Do I look like a master of *anything*?"

"You fill the role nonetheless," she said, still bowed.

"So, wait," he said. "You'd have simply kept going? Until what? Until you collapsed?"

"If it is required for my instruction."

"And . . . you'd do whatever I asked?"

"If it aids in my learning."

"I just remembered," he said, "that it's *essential* to the painting process that you learn to do it while standing on your head." She glanced up and saw him settle back on his altar. "With one finger up your left nostril. We should practice that now. Go ahead."

She almost did it. Almost tried standing on her head, while wearing a skirt, to test whether he *actually* wanted her to waste her time flailing around and likely hurting herself. It would have served him right.

But she wasn't about to establish a precedent by playing games. She instead rose to a kneeling position and met his gaze, feeling a frustration that she *should* have been able to control. "You," she said, "are not treating your position with its due respect."

"My world," he said lightly. "My rules."

"Your world," she said, "is (lowly) stupid. I'm taking a break."

She walked to the window, which she fiddled with and managed to open. Cold or not, she wanted some fresh air. Why did he get under her skin? She had legendary patience—Liyun had trained her to that end. Now she was snapping at a boy after he tossed a few half-witted jibes in her direction?

She breathed in the outside air, cool in contrast with the room, which had now heated up considerably. There was a strange *scent* to the air, crisp and inviting. Like the smell of freshly washed clothing. And the street below . . . was wet. She looked to the sky as wind blew water into her face. Rain. Rain that lingered on the ground rather than hissing away the moment it hit. How utterly bizarre. Why didn't the city drown in a flood of water?

That scent . . . was that what rain smelled like when it pooled? As much as she disliked the cold, there was something intriguing to scents and sights like these. Exotic and mesmerizing. Water that covered the ground . . . rain you could smell . . . and a street lit violet and blue.

She looked up and down the street, watching the people pass, carrying bright umbrellas and wearing clothing so varied it made her wonder how they ever decided upon anything. Perhaps that was why some women wore those indecent skirts that cut off mid-thigh, despite the cold air. Too many options overwhelmed the brain. It wasn't immorality; it was decision paralysis.

As she watched, her eyes were drawn to an alley across from the apartment building. She couldn't say why. Something about the pooling darkness, though there wasn't anything to see. Indeed, there was literally nothing to see. Just shadows.

The cold of the night air assaulted her right then. The cut of the wind, which seemed to have found a sharpening stone. The bite of the rain, suddenly hungry. She closed the window and returned to her practice—six hundred and thirty-seven more bamboo paintings to go.

If she had looked closer, or if she'd called to Painter, perhaps they would have noticed a living darkness in the alley—one that brushed the bricks with its too-real substance and left clinging wisps of smoke trailing upward in the rain, as if from a candle recently snuffed.

Chapter 20

YUMI MADE Painter wait a week—eleven whole days—before she let him move to the next step of his training.

Eleven. Days.

He spent each and every one just sitting there. Picking up rocks and trying to judge their weight, their balance. Studying them, trying to "understand" them. Ad nauseam.

This was a new kind of boredom for Painter. It wasn't the indecisive boredom of someone with a hundred things to do, none of them particularly appetizing. It was old-school, despotic boredom—the kind forced upon you by a society lacking choices. A place where "free time" was a sin and "leisure" was a word used only in conjunction with the rich.

That sun made it so much worse. The heat from both above and below, Painter pressed between the two, the pancake between hot plates. There was a certain enervating effulgence to the sunlight, sapping away strength, leaving him lethargic. Perhaps, Painter thought, that was what the sun subsisted on—burning as fuel the willpower of those who lived beneath it.

"You must understand the stone," Yumi said, walking around him in a circle. Each time she passed in front of the sun, her form briefly diffused its light like a pane of stained glass.

Understand. One week later, and he still didn't grasp what she meant by this term. In fact, today—despite having promised that he could finally move to the next step—she made him do some weighing to "warm up."

Who would need any further warming up in this place?

"Close your eyes," she said, striding around him, wearing a bright green-and-blue dress, bell-shaped, with an enormous bow across the front that trailed its ends almost to her knees. It was shorter on him of course, but didn't look *bad* really. He'd worn skirts as part of formal wear during celebration days, and while these colors were a little bright to be masculine among his kind, the people of Torio didn't care. Here men commonly wore pinks and yellows.

So he didn't find the clothing humiliating. At least it was reasonably comfortable. And today for once, the heat didn't seem . . . overwhelming. Was he changing, or was the weather just better today? Odd. And yes, the ground was hot, but at least those thermals constantly blowing upward were pleasant. They fanned out the bell and gave some semblance of a breeze.

(I haven't figured out how the thermals worked. My current theory is microfractures in the stones, with air being forced up through them and out. The plants also had something odd about them, to float as they did.)

While Painter didn't mind the clothing, Yumi's instruction *was* humiliating. One week, and still she didn't trust him to do anything without direct, condescending instruction.

"Close your eyes," she said, leaning forward to glare at him. "Now."

He sighed and complied.

"Now, pick up a stone."

He selected one. Most were new today, having been replaced overnight by the townspeople. His thick gloves protected his hands from the stone's heat.

"Feel it," she said. "Weigh it. Find the center of balance."

"You don't need to explain each step. I—"

"Hush," she said. "You are the student. You listen, I speak. That is the way."

Well, at least he knew why the spirits had made them unable to touch one another. Because he absolutely would have strangled her at some point during this.

"Do you understand the stone?" Yumi asked. "You may speak to answer me."

"Center of balance," he said, weighing the stone on his gloved hand. "Right here, when holding it on this side. Here when holding it the other direction. Three nooks—here, here, and here—where I can catch it on another stone for stability."

"Good," Yumi said.

"Shadows cling to this dimple here," he said, his voice softer, "and the grain goes this direction here—rougher near the top, creating tiny jagged shadows. It's not quite oblong, but shadows pull in at the sides, like a waist—and that's also where the single vein of quartz runs."

Yumi was silent for a moment. "How did you know that?" she asked. "I told you to close your eyes."

"I looked it over earlier, knowing you'd make me pick up a stone near me," he said. "You want me to understand the rock? That's how I do it."

"All of that is immaterial to stacking."

"It works for me." He cracked an eye to look at her.

"I should make you do another week of this," she said, folding her arms. "*I* had to do it for months."

"Go ahead," he said with a yawn. "Torment me out of spite. Waste our time when the spirits are waiting, perhaps in pain, for you to finish training me."

"Couldn't the spirits," she said (lowly), "*possibly* have sent me a man who wasn't so smug? There was *no one* else available?"

"Maybe," he replied (highly), "you're just such a *wonderful* teacher that they wanted to give you a challenge."

She glanced away, as if that barb had for some reason actually stung. He hesitated, frowning. "Yumi?"

She held herself a little tighter, still looking away. "The next phase of your training," she said, "is low stacks, focused on stability. The base of your stack needs to be the sturdiest part. Take fewer chances with the base; use it to give yourself as solid a foundation as possible, allowing for more daring choices later. Here, let's begin."

She knelt and grabbed the soul of one of the stones, then demonstrated stacking it on another, with their flat portions touching. Painter smiled, thrilled at being able to start at last.

Excitement for *stacking rocks*. Who would have thought? He squatted down carefully—even with kneepads on, he'd burned himself multiple times—and picked up a stone. He tried making a stack. The stones were unstable, so he tried again, this time aligning the centers of gravity.

He eventually got it. At her prompting, he added another stone. And it stayed on.

"Oh no," he said under his breath.

"What?" she asked.

"This is definitely easier now," he said, grabbing another rock and balancing it too. Then another. "A week ago, I could barely get three rocks on top of one another." He removed his hand, letting the fifth stone balance. It was precarious, but didn't topple. He looked toward Yumi and heaved out a long, annoyed sigh. "I can't believe that your training actually worked."

"It did," she said, her eyes widening. "It *did*." She smiled, eager. It was an intoxicating smile, for how genuine it was. Smiles, like radiation, are made more potent by proximity.

He added a sixth rock, and the whole thing collapsed. But she eagerly pointed for him to try another stack, so he did, and managed to get five again.

"It worked," she said, her voice soft. "I . . . actually . . . I actually trained you."

"I could have used a less tyrannical approach. But I guess I have to admit that you *kind of* know what you're talking about."

Staring at his stack, she looked like she might burst into tears. He managed to get a sixth, very small rock balanced on top before the whole thing fell down again.

"Six," he said, folding his arms. "Not bad, eh? So when do the spirits show up?"

"You'll need thirty stones or more per stack to draw them consistently," she said. "And one stack by itself is never enough. To be certain, you'll need twenty or so different stacks, in a pattern, arranged artistically."

"Twenty or more stacks," he said flatly, "of *thirty or more* stones."

"You can go less high with challenging stacks that look interesting," she said. "It's a relatively easy task to get forty stones straight up—but that should be done sparingly, as it's the interesting balances and odd-shaped stones that truly please the spirits."

He gazed at his little stack of fallen stones. He . . . didn't feel so excited anymore.

"Don't get discouraged," Yumi said softly. "That's what you need to *consistently* draw them. My first spirit came to me after only two weeks of training—but the next took another four months. It was years before I could do it every time, but we don't need you to hit that level of skill. I keep feeling that even a single spirit could give us guidance."

He heaved out a sigh, then nodded and gave her a smile. Unfortunately, she fell back into strict proctor mode, launching him into his next phase of training: forming solid bases for stacks. It wasn't *quite* as mind-numbing as the previous week's work. Neither was it exhilarating. It reminded him of his anatomy classes, where he'd drawn the same muscles over and over again.

Yet a little success brews eagerness, and the hours passed quickly. Particularly because Yumi seemed to catch the taste of success herself, and was somewhat less demanding. Instead of looming over him and snapping out instructions, she spent more time showing him examples. Sadly, she couldn't manage to build anything higher than a handful of stones before what she'd stacked started disintegrating to smoke. Her incorporeal creations had a lifespan of a couple minutes.

They stopped periodically for drinks of water, and remarkably Painter found as the day wore on that he was almost *enjoying* himself. He still didn't understand what was artistic about piling up rocks, and the spirits were an erratic bunch if they responded to it. But . . . it was moderately fun.

Besides, Yumi's enthusiasm was infectious. Halfway through the day he paused to watch her make a little stack of ten stones, her lips pursed, her eyes focused, but her posture relaxed—as opposed to rigid with worry in anticipation of a collapse like he was as he stacked. She moved with a flowing suppleness—scooping the stones up instead of seizing them. Encountering them instead of seeking them.

She placed many of her stones on their short edges and let pieces hang out to the sides to stack other stones on, forming little towers. Instead of making the obvious choice with each stone, she somehow accounted for its individual irregularities and fit them all together into an unexpected puzzle. Each new stone was like a key change in a symphony: Abrupt, yet immediately *right*. So delightful you were left surprised you had enjoyed the song before that.

She was right, he thought (highly). *It is an art. In her hands, at least.*

She was part of the art—her motions a performance to be relished, then remembered. It was . . . beautiful. If he'd been a spirit, he would absolutely have been drawn to this.

Unfortunately, her bottom rock vanished at that moment, and the entire stack collapsed into swirling black smoke. She sat back on her heels and released a long, trailing sigh—exhaled like a eulogy. You know the sort. They're fashioned from the corpses of dreams.

Painter stared at Yumi, pained for her. That emotion, the one he saw in her face—he *knew* that emotion. He'd never thought he would meet another who understood it the same way he did.

Her passion, he realized, *is the same passion* I *used to feel.* Realizing that recontextualized everything, and he started to wonder if there were other things she knew that he once had. That worry she displayed . . . was that the same worry he had always felt about getting things wrong—about not being the person everyone thought he was?

Loneliness, even in a group. Shame and its stalwart companion: those whispers that say you aren't worthy of attention or love.

He understood. Without needing to touch her, he understood.

She glanced at him and he fumbled, collapsing the stones he'd been stacking.

"Put the heaviest on the bottom," she suggested. "That's not *always* the biggest, depending."

He nodded, hoping she hadn't seen him staring. As he tried again, he wondered how the last week had been for her. Forced to give him instructions rather than doing what she loved—she could have been constructing stone towers all the while. It felt more tragic if *both* of them had been having such a bad time.

He tried to see the stones as she did for his next few constructions, but that was less effective and he felt himself backsliding. He didn't have her effortless ability to evaluate, to see the placement for a rock, to visualize a larger whole. So he returned to piling flat ones.

She shook her head. "You'll need to learn to judge a center of balance for the entire tower, not just individual stones. You keep perpetuating imbalances instead of correcting for them with new stones."

"I . . ." He hesitated as he saw townspeople gathering outside. He looked to Yumi, who frowned. Liyun was supposed to keep the people away so he could practice in peace. What was . . .

They weren't gathering for him. Something was happening. He could sense noise. A disturbance.

"It probably doesn't involve us," Yumi said. She said it in a half-hearted way though.

Painter heaved himself to his feet, stiff from having worked so long in basically the same posture. He crossed the place of ritual to the fence, outside of which Chaeyung and Hwanji were also distracted by the crowding people. It seemed that a wagon had arrived? Yes, another floating wagon, larger than Yumi's, pulled by the flying devices made from spirits.

Painter absently pushed out of the place of ritual, noticing that Liyun had vanished somewhere. His two attendants yelped and hurried to catch up, trying to obscure him with their fans as he walked toward the crowd. Although he was clothed, he wasn't technically on display now, and their duty was to hide him.

"We should stay at the place of ritual," Yumi said, yanked after him. "Painter. We aren't to leave!"

But he'd seen crowds like this before. At the scene of a disturbance. A nightmare appearance. He pushed the fans away, and when they returned he pushed them more forcefully—and the attendants fell back. The crowd made way for him, speaking in hushed tones as he approached the source of their consternation.

It wasn't a scene of violence or fear, thankfully. The wagon had deposited a group of men with long mustaches, beards on their chins, and white clothing. Their most striking feature was their strange hats. Black, with tall backs and shorter fronts, like . . . well, kind of like little chairs. Only there were wings at the sides too.

"Scholars," Yumi said, stepping up beside him. She put a hand to her lips. "From Torio City. The *university*. I've . . . always wanted to see them."

". . . heard of the unfortunate nature of your plight," the lead scholar was saying, "even all the way in Torio City. So we have come to bless you."

He addressed the town's pudgy mayor, though the words were obviously for the entire crowd. The mayor, in turn, bowed to the scholars, then bowed again as if worried the first one might not stick. "Honored scholars," he said in the highest and most flowery of forms, "you are welcome to our humble town."

Painter frowned. Those were the kind of linguistic forms they used in the historical dramas to address a *king*. It left little ambiguity about how scholars were regarded.

Behind the four scholars, a group of younger men in smaller hats—simple black caps—opened the doors on the rear of the wagon, then heaved something out. Roughly the size of a clothing dresser, it was a metal construction with a great number of long rods. Spiderlike, if said spider had grown a few dozen extra legs.

"This town," the tallest of the scholars said, "has suffered an embarrassing flaw in our system. The most (highly) appreciated yoki-hijo"—he bowed to Painter—"is of course a revered member of our tradition. However, human beings are limited in their capacity, and it is *highly* inefficient that we must depend on them for the needs of our society. At the Institute of Mechanical Solutions, with the blessing of Her Majesty, we have developed something to aid in this situation."

He gestured with one hand to the machine, and everything clicked for Painter. Even before the assistant scholars poured rocks on the ground around it, he knew.

"What are they *talking* about?" Yumi asked.

She'd see soon enough. The tallest scholar held his pose for an uncomfortably long time as his assistants fiddled with the contraption. Finally he glanced toward the group, and one of them rushed up to speak in his ear.

Harsh whispers followed, along with animated gestures. Then the head scholar turned back to the crowd. "The demonstration," he said, "will naturally come after we've had proper time to set up and relax from our arduous journey."

"But demonstration of what, honored scholars?" the mayor said, bowing again.

The lead scholar smiled. "Our machine," he said, "for stacking stones."

Chapter 21

T'S AN abomination," Yumi said, pacing through Painter's room. "Worse, it's *blasphemy*! A dead thing can't summon the spirits. And if it did, it would be like lying. A deception. It . . . Why are you smiling?"

"Oh, no reason," Painter said, leaning back on his altar. "Please continue the rant."

"You disagree with me," she said, stalking up to him, her eyes narrowed. She was so angry she hadn't even changed out of the sleeping clothing, so they matched. "Out with it. Why do you disagree?"

"Well," he said, "I just find it poignant. The way you describe stacking—always focused on the idea of precision—is so mechanical. You complained every time I injected emotion into it, and once said you'd be better if you were a machine. Now . . . here we are."

She breathed out through her nose, then folded her arms. "I *forbid* you to find irony in this situation, Painter."

He raised his eyebrows.

"But only in my world," she added with a nod, "where my rules apply." She stalked in the other direction, trying to sort through the host of emotions arrayed to assault her.

A machine. To stack stones.

A machine to . . . replace her.

If it worked, would that mean no more yoki-hijo? No more girls spending their lives trapped by the invisible walls of expectation and responsibility?

But it was an *honor*.

Would it be so bad if no one had to bear that honor?

The spirits are in pain, she thought. *They want me to do something to save them.*

"I'll bet," she said, turning toward Painter, "*this* is why the spirits asked me for help. It's to stop that abomination." She gasped softly. "That's why they sent someone useless to hold my body . . . I needed to fail to stack . . . so these scholars would come and I could see their evil plan unfold!"

"I'll ignore the wisecrack about me being useless," Painter said. "I don't think those scholars are evil, Yumi."

"They are creating devices to replace the honest efforts of good people!" she said, spinning on him. "What if they made machines to harvest crops? To sew clothing? Soon *no one* would have anything useful to do with their lives! People would wither like fruit dropped to the ground."

"Uh, Yumi," he said, "where do you think those pajamas came from? The dresses you bought?"

She looked down at the clothing. She *had* noticed the incredibly precise stitches.

"We have the things you mention," he said. "Machines to help with planting and harvesting crops. Machines to make clothing. That shower you love so much? Another machine. Same with the viewer. And guess what? People in my world still have useful things to do. Machines require workers to build and maintain them, along with others to cultivate and position the hion lines. Your people will be fine."

"Your machines don't replace a holy purpose," she said. "The spirits will be offended."

"If they are, won't they just refuse to come to a machine's stacks?"

Well. Probably.

Unless something was deeply wrong. Something that prevented them from seeking help anywhere else.

Free us . . .

"Wonder how they're powering the thing," Painter said, standing up and glancing toward the room's light—which had a faint pair of twin colors leading to it, the ever-present hion. "Your people haven't discovered hion yet, have they?"

"I doubt it exists on my world," she said.

"Maybe they'll use something more ancient. Do your people have coal engines?"

She stared at him blankly. *Coal?*

"Guess not," he said.

"We're not primitive," she said, waving around the room, "merely because we can't make faces appear in boxes on the wall. *You* don't know how to make buildings float."

He didn't reply, so she moved a few stacks of painted bamboo and went about her morning routine. Once showered, combed, dressed, and the rest, she sat down with her ink and brush.

"I am ready for instruction, Master Teacher," she said, bowing deeply.

"Do you call me that," he asked, "because it annoys me?"

"Yes," she said, bowing again.

"You *admit* it?"

"Why *else* would I call you names you dislike?" she said. "I mean, I thought it was obvious."

He waved his hands and sat on his altar. "Isn't annoying people against the . . . spiritual girl code or something?"

"Your world," she said, raising her chin, "your rules. And from what I've seen, Painter, annoying people is basically a *religion* to you."

She *did* feel mischievous saying such things to him, and it would have been proper for her to stop. But . . . why was he so amusing to tease? If he'd bowed his head, she would likely have felt guilty. Instead he raised his hands toward the heavens and shook his head dramatically.

"I," he said, "don't understand you at *all.*"

"I am your humble student," she said, bowing once more, "in the fine art of painting."

"I suppose."

"And in the finer art of being aggravating."

This time he smiled. Which worried her. Despite her intentions, she was relaxing too much here, wasn't she? What else could she do? She needed to enjoy this less.

Focus on the work, she thought, picking up a brush. "What is my next lesson?"

"Bamboo," he said.

Yumi turned to look around the room, which was stacked with sheets of painted bamboo. They'd had to go to the supply store *three times* during the week. She felt she should clean the quarters, as she was severely adding to the clutter. Maybe she could have Painter ask Chaeyung and Hwanji for tips next time in her world. Cleaning up after herself was novel.

No. Don't enjoy it. And it's not right to talk to your attendants. You shouldn't even think of that.

"I have mastered bamboo," she said. "Yesterday I taught you something new. In return, you should also teach me an advanced technique."

"There's no reason for that," Painter said. "You just need the basics to defend yourself in case of a nightmare encounter."

"I can defeat this stable nightmare with . . . bamboo?"

"No," he said. "Once again, you're *not* going to face the stable nightmare. If we encounter it, we're going to *run*."

She sighed but bowed, this time sincere. She needed to listen to his wisdom—well, his experience—in this matter. So she launched into more painting. Until a knock at the door drew her away. A glance at the clock told her it was late in the day—at least as this society measured it. Although Yumi and he always rose at morning in her world, Painter kept a strange schedule in his world, working when many others slept.

It was dinnertime. Or breakfast, for the painters. The other painters generally met before or after shift to chat, and Yumi often had to turn down Akane's invitations to those gatherings.

She pulled open the door, prepared with another excuse for Akane. Instead the *entire* group was standing out there. Not only Akane—who was stylish even in the trousers and painting shirt she wore on duty. But also Tojin, with sleeves rolled up to show his muscles. Short Masaka, with a turtleneck, her glaring eyes shadowed and lined with excessive amounts of dark makeup. Finally Izzy, the long-limbed girl with the bleached yellow hair.

"This," Tojin said, "is an intervention!"

"We're here to rescue you from your books, Yumi," Izzy said, grabbing her by the hand.

"I don't need—" Yumi began.

"We've all been there," Akane said, "studying for the tests. Yumi, trust me. If you don't relax now and then, you're going to stress yourself to the point that your mind rots. You *need* a break."

"Gotta rest the muscles between reps," Tojin said.

"Oh, *great*," Painter said (lowly), stepping up behind her. "I'd almost managed to forget about the weightlifting metaphors."

"Just some food," Akane said. "It's Ashday. Even *we* get a half day off work, trading shifts with Department Three so they can take time off on another day."

"Get rid of them," Painter said, turning back toward the room with a yawn.

Yes. That was definitely what she should have done. But the thought of another day spent painting bamboo again and again and again . . .

She looked around by reflex to see if Liyun was there to disapprove.

"Very well," Yumi said in a soft voice.

"Really?" Izzy said, jumping up and down.

"Wait, what?" Painter said, spinning.

She told the others to wait, then closed the door and hurriedly threw on a dress instead of the oversized painting shirt and trousers she'd been wearing.

"Wait," Painter said. "I have to beg to get a *water break*, but you can go to a noodle party?"

"You told me I don't need advanced techniques," she said, pulling on her short jacket, then checking herself in the mirror and tucking a stray bra strap back in place. "I have bamboo down, right? So I don't *need* further training."

"I suppose . . ."

"Then," she said, her heart fluttering, "I'm going to eat with them." She paused and looked at him. "Can I? . . . Please?"

"It's up to you," he said. "Anytime you want to go, you may. I'm not your master, Yumi."

Her choice? She hesitated.

What was she doing? She reached to begin taking off her jacket.

"Go," he said. "Don't think about it, Yumi. Just *go*. It's all right. I want to see Design anyway."

And so she did. Nervous, elated, terrified. She joined the others as they led her to the noodle shop. They mentioned going to some other restaurant, but they noticed how she panicked at that idea and quickly decided against it. In minutes she was seated with them, her money out on the table—at Painter's suggestion, she'd offered to pay as a thank-you—a menu in her hands.

She ordered a flavor of broth she'd never had before. After all, if she was going to be terrified of the experience already, she might as well add more strangeness. A short time later, Design waved for Painter to go speak with her—leaving Yumi with four people who were practically strangers.

It was *thrilling*.

They chatted about their vacations, and their wages, and the foreman. A verbal thornbush of interlocking vines and spikes in which Yumi didn't *dare* interject. They seemed to understand that she was already daunted by going out, and they didn't push her into conversation. That let her watch. Up close. *People interacting.*

She'd never been allowed to do that. She was to remain distant. In the common way of things that are forbidden, that made them mysterious. She was fascinated by the ways that normal people conversed, and joked, and talked over each other, and laughed, and . . . and it was like a performance, each of them with memorized lines. How did they know when to speak or when to stop? When to tell a joke and when to share some fact?

To try to make sense of it all, she decided to focus on one companion. As she already felt she knew Akane a little, she turned her attention to Tojin. Painter had said the man was always showing off his muscles to women. Yumi assumed it was to entice them to mate.

Liyun said details of courtship would only distract her from her duty, so other than some little tidbits overheard when she was younger . . . she had no *idea* how people paired off. She'd had trouble picking a *dress.* How did you pick a *mate*? She hoped, from what Painter had said, that Tojin would illuminate her.

He certainly did like exposing his muscles. Except as the noodles arrived, Tojin leaped up from his seat and rushed over to some people who had started sitting down at another table. None of them women. One was as bulky as Tojin—she wondered what beasts they fought, that they needed such muscles.

"Gaino," Tojin said to the overly large man. "You were *right* about the lat press. Look." He proceeded to *take off his shirt* and flex.

Yumi watched with eyes wide. Yes, glimpses of Painter when bathing had been one thing, but this was . . . illustrative. She barely remembered to chew her noodles as several other very large men at the table clapped for Tojin.

"What were your reps?" Gaino asked.

"Four twenties," Tojin said. "But if you lean forward instead of back, you can really isolate."

"I'm plateauing," another guy said, then flexed one of his arms. "Need to lose at least another percent. See here, you can barely see my outline."

"You look great," Tojin said. Then he flexed *his* arm. "But maybe try some bench work with some reverse presses?"

Yumi couldn't tear her eyes away. It wasn't that this was *attractive*. It was more *enthralling*. She didn't even blush. Instead her jaw dropped. It was like something in her brain had gotten scrambled and her responses were mixed up.

"Tojin!" Izzy called. "You're breaking the new girl! Stop comparing sizes!"

He looked back at the table, then *he* blushed. He scrambled to pull on his shirt again. It *could* have all been a display for her and the other girls, like Painter had flippantly said. Yet that didn't feel right. He seemed more excited about talking technique with the other men. And when he sat back down, he apologized to her with what sounded like true sincerity.

"I didn't mean to make a spectacle of myself," he said, lowering his eyes.

"I . . ." Yumi stammered. "It . . . um . . . What kind of beasts do you fight?"

"Beasts?" he asked. "*Fight?*"

"Those muscles," she said. "You train for . . . war? Battle?"

Izzy laughed so much she was likely to shoot noodles from her nose. Tojin appeared embarrassed. He was . . . shy? Really? Why would a shy person make such a display of himself, if not for battle?

"It's not for anything like that," he said. "I just like to make the best of myself that I can. See how much I can do. Reach my limits, then *pass* them."

"To accomplish what?" Yumi asked.

"That *is* the accomplishment," he said, then flexed his arm in a very specific way that made his *veins* distinct. It was almost grotesque, yet somehow impressive all the same.

"Our bodies are the most incredible tools ever," Tojin said. "Isn't it odd that we'll fine-tune an engine until it purrs, but never do the same for our bodies?"

She barely knew what that meant. But she did notice Akane gazing at Tojin with fondness. And when the woman went to get some sauce for the noodles, she put a light hand on his arm and then let it trail away. Tojin gave her a goofy smile, then looked down, grinning.

He actually *was* shy about women. Either that or Yumi was completely misunderstanding—admittedly also very plausible. But now she felt she understood the way a woman might look at a man. Liyun might have tried to keep her away from people, but Yumi still had eyes. Akane's way of looking at Tojin wasn't the stare of a hungry woman wanting to feast. There had been more than a few of those around the room earlier.

Did he truly want muscles . . . just because? Was this what happened to a society that had hion lines to do all the hard work? Was that . . . a bad thing?

"It's so odd," Yumi said. "When my brother was talking about you, Tojin, he . . ." She paused, realizing that maybe she shouldn't say it. Indeed, all of them immediately looked straight at her, intensely curious.

Talking to people was hard.

". . . didn't explain that part," Yumi finished. "With the muscles. Why you're building them."

"I'm sure he didn't," Izzy said, with a smile.

"Where *is* he, Yumi?" Tojin asked. "If you don't mind me prying. I normally see your brother every night or two, patrolling near us. Foreman says he's on personal leave. But it feels like we should still see him now and then."

"He, um . . ." Yumi's heart started thumping. Could she go grab Painter and have him tell her an untruth? She decided on something that was close to what he'd said. "He has important work. Very important work."

"More important than his job?" Akane said, returning and handing the sauce to Tojin.

"No, no," Yumi said quickly. "It *is* his job." She leaned in. "He's hunting a *stable nightmare.*"

She expected shock.

Instead Akane rolled her eyes. Tojin paused, then shook his head, looking down. Izzy outright laughed.

"You don't believe . . ." Yumi said softly.

Why did everyone react that way to Painter? Was he really *so* useless? Strangely, the thought didn't make her angry as it had before. This time she felt sad for him. Along with . . . an odd sense of indignation?

Surely they're being unfair to him, she thought. *He might not be the best, but he's trying to learn stacking. And he picked it up quickly.*

Perhaps, though, she could see why he had some hard feelings for this group, if their first reaction to this news wasn't concern, but dismissiveness.

"Enough, enough," Izzy said, holding up some paper with words written all over it. Not a book. This was loose-leaf and made at an awkwardly large size. "Have you read this?"

"Please, no horoscopes," Tojin said, emptying what seemed to be half the bottle of hot sauce into his soup. They all appeared happy to move on, without looking back, from the topic of Painter and his ways.

"Horoscopes are *forbidden* at this table," Izzy said. "They're a competing product. But this isn't even a *drama*scope. They're launching the ship soon."

"They said that last week," Akane said.

"The shroud was too thick," Izzy said. "But it's happening for real this time."

"I bet," Masaka said softly, "they are *very. Very. Friendly.*"

"They?" Yumi asked, glancing around as she slurped up a noodle. "What are we talking about?"

"The aliens?" Akane said. "Who live on the star?"

Yumi immediately started coughing. She drank half a cup of barley tea out of embarrassment, then spoke. "The *what*?"

"Don't they have newspapers where you're from?" Izzy said. "We've been planning a launch! Of a ship that can travel the space between worlds. It's been building *forever*. But it's finally time for it to leave."

"*Friendly,*" Masaka hissed, leaning forward. "Aliens are *all friendly*."

"You really haven't heard, Yumi?" Izzy said. "That's wild. I need my notebook. This is good information for refining your dramascope . . ."

"Hush," Akane said. "Not everyone reads the paper obsessively, Izzy."

How did Akane remain so dainty when eating? Was Yumi supposed to be that way? It seemed hard to eat noodles without slurping. She'd never actually eaten in front of anyone but her attendants before.

"I'll bet," Izzy said, "the aliens are *hot*."

Yumi started choking again.

"Wildly hot," Izzy said, flopping back. "All the men dreamy. All the women sultry."

"How many dramas involve aliens these days?" Tojin said, with a smile.

"Like half," Izzy said. "And the aliens? Hot. All of them. Isn't it natural they would be though?"

"Um . . . why?" Tojin asked.

"I'm going to date an alien or two," Izzy said, lifting her chin. "It's in my dramascope. I'd never date one who isn't hot."

Yumi was glad for the others and their baffled expressions, so that she knew it wasn't only *her* thinking Izzy was strange. Even Masaka stared.

"Your logic, Izzy," Akane said, "is . . . um . . ."

"Terrible?" Tojin offered.

"I was looking for something more politic."

"*Allegedly* terrible?"

"You'll see," Izzy said. "When I have both a handsome alien hunk and a curvy alien knockout fighting over me."

"Excuse me," Yumi said. "I need to . . . um . . . go. For a little bit. For something."

She dashed off toward the bar, where Painter was chatting with De-sign. When she arrived, she found Design stretching something glowing between her fingers. Like a cord made of *light*. Yumi momentarily forgot what she'd been about, instead staring at that strange sight. A glowing rope, whose ends vanished into nothing.

"Your spiritweb," Design was saying, "knows what body is yours. It remains Connected to it, you see. You form Connections like that with everyone—and to a lesser extent every*thing*—you've known. Nifty, eh!"

"And that cord," Painter was saying, "is mine?"

"Yup!" Design said. "This won't cut it. Don't worry. I'm just lengthening it, and also checking it for problems. I couldn't think of much else to help—sorry, I'm incorrigibly useless at times. It's in my Pattern. But at least this will give you a longer leash, so to speak."

"What is she doing?" Yumi whispered to Painter.

"She's making it so that we don't yank each other around," he explained, "when we get too far apart."

"Technically you will still do that," Design said, "but the distance you can go before it happens will be much greater. I can probably get this to several blocks in length without risking any degradation to your Connection."

That sounded like a good thing, although something about it felt . . . regretful to Yumi. All these years, she'd been alone. Selfishly, a part of her had liked that there was someone who couldn't leave her by herself. She shoved aside such impious emotions.

"Painter," she whispered. "Do you know about this launch the others are discussing? A ship? Sailing the sky?"

"Oh, right," he said. "Yeah, it's more like a bus that rides hion into the sky. They've been discussing it for years. Off to . . ." He sat upright, then smacked his hand into his face. "I'm an idiot. It's going to your planet, Yumi."

"So?" Design asked. "Nikaro. You're not going to *sneak on board,* are you?"

"What? No!"

"Oh," Design said, sounding disappointed.

"It seems like a strange coincidence, doesn't it?" Yumi said. "That I should come here mere days before your people send explorers to my world. It could mean something."

"Wait," Design said. "Are you *sure* you're from that other world, Yumi?"

"No," she admitted. "It's Painter's theory."

"I kept noticing the star," he explained, "on the day when the swap happened. And, I mean, it makes sense. Her world, Design, has this enormous ball of fire in the sky!"

"Most do, Nikaro," Design said. "Like, practically every world but this one."

"They do?" he asked.

"Yup."

"Do they all have heat?" he asked. "From the ground?"

"Heat from the ground?" Design said, looking to Yumi, who nodded eagerly. "No, that's really strange."

"Could I be from some other place on *this* world?" Yumi asked.

"We surveyed the planet before coming here," Design said. "I didn't pay enough attention, so it's possible—but I think the entire thing is covered in the shroud." Design shrugged. "The theory that you're from that other world—the one that orbits with this one strangely nearby—is solid. You could be from somewhere farther out, I guess, but Connection on this level rarely spans that distance. It was, for example, super hard for me to leave my homeworld, given my Connection to it."

"Did you . . . see anything about that world in the sky?" Painter asked. "Before coming here?"

"Afraid we didn't stop there," she replied. "Heat from the ground, you say?"

"Yes, and plants that fly!" Painter added.

"Neat!" Design said. "Well, I might be able to confirm it to be sure. Your spiritweb's Connection to your world will be fainter than the one sticking you two together, so I can't see it without help. Hoid had some device somewhere in our luggage though . . ." She shrugged. "Give me some time. I'll try to dig it out."

"Regardless," Yumi said, "that group of people traveling from here to the other planet—probably *my* planet—might be involved in all of this. *That* might be why the spirits have done what they've done."

"I thought you were sure our swap had to do with that machine," Painter said.

"They could be related," she said.

Painter, remarkably, nodded slowly.

"You agree?" she asked. "We *agree* on something?"

"Not the first thing," he said.

"What do you mean?"

He smiled. "I'll show you. Tomorrow."

Chapter 22

THE NEXT morning, Painter awoke eagerly and stretched. The floor was faintly warm from the wagon having been lowered to the ground for the night. He could imagine how comfortable it must be on a cold night to settle down into that heat: blanket on top, radiance beneath. Like an ember crumbling into the bed of a fire. Though he wasn't ready to give up his soft futon yet, maybe there *was* something to Yumi's way of doing things.

Well, some of the things she did.

As she was drowsily sitting up and arranging her sleeping gown, Painter strode over to the door. It opened on its own, Chaeyung standing outside with a table and Hwanji beside her with a small tray of food. They arrived early and waited there, listening for noise so they would know when to enter.

Painter took the tray of food. "Thanks!" he said. "I'll eat alone today." He winked at them, then shut the door.

Behind him, Yumi gasped.

He walked back to his blankets and sat. Then he dug in, using the maipon sticks for the rice, though the attendants always used a spoon. Which was odd, but perhaps it was a ritual thing.

He looked up at Yumi's horrified stare.

"What?" he said, wiping his mouth. "Rice on my lips? Sorry. I was hungry." He dug back in, picking at all the little bowls of savory delights they always brought to augment the rice. That was a nice touch—made him feel like he was eating a huge feast, even though each side dish contained only a bite or two. Enormous variety, but in microcosm.

"Painter!" she said. "I . . . What . . ." Evidently she was having trouble speaking. Almost hyperventilating.

He paused. He'd expected her to be upset. He hadn't anticipated . . . well, this.

"Yumi," he said. "Breathe. It's all right. The world isn't going to end because I decide to feed myself."

She gasped more frantically. As if she thought, just maybe, the world *would* end.

He reached for her, but stopped shy of touching her. "Yumi," he said. "Look at what you've been doing in my world. Feeding yourself, moving around freely. The spirits *gave* that to you. They aren't going to care if I eat on my own."

She settled down nearby and held her head, not looking at him. That . . . really was a stronger reaction than he'd anticipated. Maybe . . . maybe he should call the attendants back. He turned to do so, but at that very moment the door swung open.

Liyun stood outside, immaculate as always, today in a bell-shaped maroon gown, her white bow tied tightly, not a hair on her head out of place. Though she appeared . . . more haggard than usual. Bags under her eyes. Had she not been sleeping well?

She stepped into the wagon, leaving her clogs outside, then knelt before Painter, studying him. "You look pale," she said. "It seems you have not fully recovered from your . . . malady last week. Perhaps you should lie down, then rise again, starting this day over. After you remember who you are."

"I remember," Painter said, then took another bite, out of spite. This woman . . . "Tell me, Liyun. As a yoki-hijo, is it my prerogative to choose to feed myself?"

"You are blessed by the spirits," Liyun said, enunciating each word precisely. "You are granted the *wisdom* to decide to *follow* their dictates."

"And if that wisdom leads me to eat on my own?" He took another bite. "I'm not on duty today; I'm just practicing. So if I feel that I should relax a little, what would you do?"

"I follow you," she said, "as is my responsibility. And *hope* that you are not becoming *unfit*."

Yumi's breathing became gasps again.

Painter didn't back down. Something about Liyun simply set him off. We've all had that experience with one human mosquito or another—if it's not the buzzing, then the leeching of our blood will do it. He hated how Liyun never said what she wanted, but instead left her intent to drip from cold words. Condensation of the pure essence of patronization.

"Do you think I'm unfit?" he asked.

"I do not decide fitness," Liyun said, bowing her head with what felt to him to be mock humility. "I only serve."

"Great," Painter said. "This is how you serve me today. Make sure I have peace and quiet as I eat. I want to consider the best way to recover."

"If that is what you wish," she said slowly, "and you are *certain* that you do not *instead* wish to follow *proper* protocol."

"Great, thanks," Painter said. "See you at the place of ritual. Appreciate your help."

She rose and lingered there, looming over him.

He took the hint. And tossed it back in her face. "Oh," he said, "would you get me a small paintbrush, some ink, and something to paint on? Leave it at the shrine. I feel like . . . painting today."

"Painting," Liyun said flatly.

"Painting. Yes. Thank you."

When he didn't respond to her looming, she—with obvious reluctance—withdrew. When the door shut, Painter left the food and crawled over to Yumi.

"Hey," he said. "Look, it's fine. She *has* to do what I say."

"I'm. Trying. *Not*. To scream. Right now," Yumi said between gasps. "Just. Leave. Me."

Well, all right. Her world. Her rules. Or something. He finished his meal, then threw open the door and nodded to the befuddled attendants standing outside. "Let's go."

They held up their fans and hurried along with him toward the cool spring. A moment later, Yumi was yanked out of the wagon after him. He paused. Hadn't Design lengthened that leash? They'd tested it, and it had worked . . .

She lengthened the leash between us on my world, he thought. *That must not apply here.*

Unfortunate, but Yumi *had* told him to leave her alone, so he said nothing. He continued on, all the way to the cold spring—Yumi trailing along behind. Once there, he stopped the attendants as they started to undress.

"I'll bathe myself as well," he said to them. "I'll take those soaps . . . Thank you. Oh, and you can put my clothing on that rock right there. Thanks. I'll call for you once I'm ready to proceed to the shrine."

They stood in place. He gave them a reassuring smile, then nodded toward the pathway out. Once they were gone, he began undressing. Yumi turned her back to him, like he did when she was changing—but with way more subtext. Hell, there was an entire encyclopedia down there.

He stepped into the cool spring with the plate of soaps, which was designed to float on its own. He knew the order of the soaps, and followed it correctly.

Yumi remained standing on the rim of the spring, not coming in. He was briefly tempted to yank her into the water, but resisted.

"I decided," he told her, lathering up, "that I'm going to do as you said. Embrace my place here."

She didn't reply.

"If I'm here," he said, "it's because your spirits decided to choose me. I've been thinking of myself as an imitation yoki-hijo, and that was wrong. I have been chosen just as you were. It merely happened to me a little later in life."

He went through the next soap, which was colored red and came as a powder. It scraped the skin, and he had to stand in a shallower part of the pool to reach his lower portions.

As he was stepping back into the water, Yumi sighed and turned around to face him, sitting on the edge of the pool. Painter hesitated because of his state of undress, but she was staring down at her feet trailing in the water, not at him. Besides, it was only Yumi. He continued on to the next soap.

"You claim," she said, "that you have started to *care* about all of this. You respond by breaking the protocol?"

"If I'm chosen by the spirits," he said, "can't I make decisions like this? Isn't that my right?"

"It is," she said, "but you *can't.*"

He shook his head. "That is (lowly) hypocritical, Yumi. If I can make the decisions—if I *legitimately* can—then you have to let me do so. Liyun has to let *us* do so, even when she disagrees. Otherwise they're not decisions. Otherwise, what she says about us being the ultimate decider? That is an untruth." He glanced at Yumi. "And I know how you feel about those."

Finally, she sighed and pulled off her bulky nightgown—he had no idea how they slept in something made of such thick cloth in this overly hot world—and undergarments, then slipped into the bath. He held the plate of soap out for her, so she could make spiritual versions. She liked that, for the familiarity of it, despite it vanishing from her fingers after a few minutes.

They turned to their standard ritual, bathing back-to-back in the ten-foot-wide pool, close enough for him to periodically float the soap plate her direction.

"I can't refute your words," she said. "Because the logic makes sense. Even though I know you're wrong."

"That's because you've lived this so long," he said. "It feels normal to you. It sometimes takes an outsider to point out how broken something is."

He heard her sink down to wash out her hair, then stand up again. He scooted her the soap as she glanced at him, then she wiped the water from her eyes and pulled her hair back. "So *this* is the mysterious thing you said we 'agree on'? You made me wait a day to find out that—for some bizarre reason—your 'revelation' is that you should ignore propriety and piety?"

"We agree," he said, washing his own hair, "that it's okay to relax a tad. You went to eat with the others. I decided to eat on my own."

"Opposite actions."

"Done for the same reason."

"I think it's a stretch that we *agree* on this."

"Well, it felt fun to say," he said.

"This much confusion is worth a chance for you to make a little quip?"

"Well, obviously." He smiled, glancing over his shoulder at her. "*I* thought it was funny, at least."

"Funny? How?"

He shrugged. "Just . . . funny?"

She shook her head. "That is not what humor is like, Painter."

(She was, of course, dead wrong. Remember what the poet said: "Never let something trivial, like a sense of humor, get in the way of a good joke."

The poet was me.

He said it right now.)

Afterward, they both rested on their backs and floated for a time to soak, and didn't say much. Eventually they climbed out of the bath. He held the clothing toward her so she could make a copy. This, fortunately, didn't vanish once donned. They didn't know why. (It has to do with them automatically incorporating the clothing into their vision of themselves at the time, but that's beside the point.)

The two turned back-to-back as a token nod toward modesty as they dressed. Which was amusing, since putting *on* clothing wasn't exactly the immodest part of the experience.

Painter found it aggravating how difficult it was to tie the bow on his outfit. He pulled it too tight, then tried it loose, and then looked flabbergasted at Yumi, who had tied hers into a basic knot like she often did. She shrugged.

"At least," she said to him, "I didn't dismiss the people who could have done this correctly for me."

A valid point.

A short time later, the attendants dropped them off at the orchard shrine, where trees drifted and bumped against one another like people in line for concert tickets. Painter felt bad every time they came here, as he knew for a fact they were interrupting the work of the orchard keepers. Then again, maybe the workers wanted an excuse to take a break.

Liyun was nowhere to be seen—the yoki-hijo was supposed to be alone during meditation—but she had done as Painter had requested, leaving a scroll, some painting ink, and a small brush for him. Judging by the symbol on the leather sheath for the brush, she'd commandeered them from the scholars. Well, they were probably too busy trying to make their machine work to bother with writing anyway.

"So why this?" Yumi asked, gesturing to it.

"Well," Painter said, "you keep telling me I need to clear my mind while meditating—"

"You do."

"—which is basically impossible—"

"It's absolutely not."

"—but I considered and realized there *is* a time when I mostly clear my mind." He held up his brush. "When I'm painting."

She cocked her head and watched as he rolled out the scroll, then knelt to begin painting. He started into it, expecting her to condemn him. If she'd hated it when he'd improvised earlier in the day, she would undoubtedly hate this doubly—as he was supposed to be worshipping the spirits at the moment. Or something. He still didn't quite get the point of this part.

"You're . . . actually trying," she said softly, surprising him. "You've given this some thought."

"A lot of it," he admitted, doing a quick painting. Just some flourishes of the brush to create curved lines.

She knelt beside him. "When I was painting those bamboo stalks, I . . . got into a rhythm. Time passed. Almost like I was meditating."

"So I'm right!"

"It's *wrong*," she said. "You're not supposed to *do* anything. But . . . it's right anyway, I think." She peered closer at what he'd done—a painting where he tried to capture a face in as few lines as possible.

"Is that Hwanji?" she asked, pointing.

"Yes," he said. "It's an artistic technique for practicing how to see shapes and lines in everything around you. You try to capture a person with only a few strokes."

"Looks easy," she said. "Like . . . you don't want to do all the work of a real painting."

"It's more difficult than it appears," he said. "It's like . . . like poetry written using the fewest syllables possible."

She appeared skeptical. "It's pretty, I suppose. But I do think it looks lazy. And it doesn't seem it would be of much use against the nightmares."

"It's not."

"Then why—"

"Hey," he said, "I'm trying to meditate here." He gave her a wink.

The stare she returned could have boiled water.

So of course he did a quick painting of that—her lips, eyes, the shape of her teardrop face. All done with quick flourishes of the brush to evoke the correct image. An artistic shorthand that had become a form unto itself.

She took this in stride. It was the kind of teasing he'd learned didn't bother her—or, well, it bothered her in the *right* way. If he wanted Yumi to play along, he had to tease *her*, not her station or the spirits.

He continued, and soon moved from faces—he preferred references for those—to his old standby. Bamboo. The more familiar the motions, the better he felt it would be for clearing his mind.

Somehow, an hour passed.

When Liyun arrived, he realized he'd filled the scroll with bamboo. A part of him was slightly disappointed—he'd hoped, contrary to what Yumi said, that painting would draw the attention of spirits. She said that although other arts could do it, painting wasn't one of them as far as she knew.

Yumi met his eyes, then glanced at the paintings. He could practically hear her thoughts—part of her had wondered as well. You didn't need to be in a place of ritual for the spirits to come; that was just where the rocks were stacked, where it was easiest. If skilled painting could accomplish the task, an hour spent here should have been enough.

Or perhaps his painting did not count as skilled.

Regardless, it had been relaxing. He smiled, tucked away his disappointment, and turned toward Liyun. "That was perfect," he said. "I'll want to paint like this every day, please."

"Why?" she asked.

"It is the will of the spirits," he said.

Though Yumi gave him a frown at that, he figured his words were true. The spirits wanted him here and meditating, so they would approve. Together he, Yumi, and Liyun left the shrine and crossed out of the orchard and through the town. At the edge, near the place of ritual, a large tent had been erected. He heard voices from inside—mostly sounding annoyed.

"Those scholars haven't gotten their machine working yet, I assume?" he said softly to Liyun.

"No," she said. "Their arrival was a surprise to me. It's an affront to us— bordering on blasphemy—for them to bring one of those here. I hate the things."

"Wait," Yumi said. "She *knows* about them?"

"You know about these?" Painter asked.

"It is nothing for you to worry about, Chosen," Liyun said with a wave of her fingers. "The efforts of the scholars are a novelty, nothing more." She hesitated. "Still, how *dare* they cart one of these to a village where we're on duty . . ."

She ushered Painter into the place of ritual, then roosted nearby, as if waiting for carrion. He settled down to practice, and was occasionally distracted by the arguments in the tent.

"That machine *is* why we're here," Yumi said softly. "I think we are to stop it, but we need confirmation from the spirits." She looked at him. "Well, keep practicing! No dallying. Just because you've decided to be insolent where protocol is concerned doesn't mean I'm going to let you slacken under my tutelage!"

He groaned, but went ahead and got to it, working hard on his stacks beneath the light of that strange sun. Why didn't it burn out? What *truly* kept feeding it?

After a solid few hours, the attendants brought him lunch. He again didn't let Chaeyung and Hwanji feed him directly, but—feeling magnanimous—he allowed them to sit and offer him utensils and napkins. Liyun's glare as she watched him could have boiled *stone*.

"I still worry she'll declare us unfit," Yumi whispered as the attendants left with their table. "She could send us to her superiors, for . . . special attention. It's what's done with yoki-hijo who grow too old, or otherwise infirm."

"What happens to her if she does that?" he asked.

"Well, she'll have to wait in line with the other unemployed wardens," Yumi said, "until she's given a turn with another yoki-hijo."

"Whom she'll have to train from childhood," he said. "Yeah, she's not going to take that step lightly, Yumi. I'd bet we could spend months, maybe *years*, practicing here before she gave up. She won't want to completely upend her life."

"She wouldn't want to," Yumi agreed, "but you need to understand: Liyun will do what needs to be done. She is strict with herself, not just me."

He wanted to dispute that, but . . . Yumi was probably right. Liyun seemed the type who drank her own poison. If only to build up her tolerance.

"I'm sorry today was hard for you," Painter said. "Maybe I should have talked to you about my plans. I figured you were fine shaking things up in *my* world, so I should have the same opportunity, shouldn't I?"

"Maybe," she said, rapping a stone to make him keep stacking. "But . . . it's different. You're wearing my body, Painter. What you do is seen as what *I* do. It's not the same way in your world."

He considered that, acknowledging that what he did affected her in unique ways. But he was increasingly certain he'd made the correct choice. If only for his own sanity.

He tried hard to do as she asked during training though, as a kind of . . . apology. He managed a stack of twelve that day—and not a strictly straight-up one either. It had quirks and some character. Still miles from Yumi's designs, but he felt proud nonetheless.

Liyun had left by that time to see to something, so the attendants walked him home. His body ached in that good way you feel after doing something difficult. Like walking a long distance. Or thinking of a really great pun.

Painter thought this ache might be what Tojin always talked about after lifting weights. Too bad Tojin wasn't here, actually. He'd have loved lifting these rocks; it didn't take long listening to him talk incessantly about reps and muscles to realize what an enormous nerd he was.

At his wagon, Painter nodded to his attendants. Chaeyung handed him his nightgown, laundered for the day. "You will . . . want to dress yourself, won't you?"

"Yes," he said.

"Leave your clothing outside, Chosen," she said, "so we can care for it." She bowed and walked off.

Hwanji, however, lingered. Painter hesitated in his doorway. He'd hardly spoken to the attendants, and to his embarrassment, he realized he barely knew them one from another—and any differentiation he *could* make was due to their looks. Hwanji was the shorter, more rounded of the two.

Yumi peeked around him, looking curious.

"Hwanji?" Painter asked. "Do you need something?"

To this, the young woman bowed herself formally to the ground—placing a small clog for her knee, using a cloth to rest her hand on the stone. The work these people had to do to not burn themselves was, as you might have noticed, legendary.

"Honored One," she said. "If Liyun asks, or . . . well, implies . . . will you make it clear that this new behavior of yours was not my fault?"

"Of course I will," Painter said. "But Hwanji, why would she even think that?"

"Oh!" Hwanji said. "Chosen, before entering your service, I was an attendant of the yoki-hijo Dwookim. She was . . . very vocal in the reform movement."

Painter glanced at Yumi, who shook her head and shrugged.

"The reform movement?" Painter asked.

Hwanji glanced up sharply. "I thought . . . you'd heard . . . The way you've been acting . . ." Her eyes went wide and she scrambled to her feet, turning as if to flee.

Painter seized her by the hand, stumbling and nearly falling onto the overly hot stones. "Hwanji," he said. "I've been so confused lately. *Please.* I won't tell Liyun, but I need to know."

The attendant looked back, reluctant. Painter dropped her hand, to let her go if she wanted. Instead she spoke in a small voice. "I thought you must have heard that . . . some of the other yoki-hijo . . ."

"Eat for themselves?" Painter guessed. "Dress themselves."

"Decide for themselves," Hwanji said, with a nod. "Live their lives, until they decide to retire? It is true."

"No," Yumi said, stepping down to the ground without clogs—but she didn't notice, so the heat didn't bother her. Being a spirit is like that. "No, she's . . . she's . . ."

"Lying?" Painter said.

"Honored One?" Hwanji said in a panic. "No, I would *never*. It's true. Everyone knows about the schism. Except . . . well, I guess, you . . ."

"Liyun trained me," Painter said, "and she never told me?"

"She and the orthodox wardens keep it from their Chosen," Hwanji explained. "It's vital to Liyun that she preserve tradition. Her kind try very hard. It is a good thing to remember the past."

"How many?" Yumi said, her voice hoarse. "How many of the other yoki-hijo are . . . in this reform movement?"

Painter asked.

"Oh," Hwanji said, looking away. "Most of them, Honored One. Of the fourteen current yoki-hijo, I think there is just one other orthodox. It . . . well, you wouldn't know this, but the reform movement isn't exactly *new*. It's a couple hundred years old now. Almost everyone else feels that there's no reason to be *quite* so strict with the yoki-hijo."

There were only fourteen current yoki-hijo? Painter found that tidbit interesting—Torio might be smaller than he'd imagined—but the other fact overshadowed it by far.

A schism in the religion.

A couple hundred years old.

Painter nearly laughed. He would have, if not for the horrified—betrayed—expression on Yumi's face. How could it be that nobody had ever *told* her?

She lives her life in ritual, he thought. *Who is there to tell her? Who is there to even (lowly) talk to her?*

His heart broke for her as she fell to her knees. "But . . ." she said. "But the spirits . . . They don't listen to these women, do they?"

As he repeated it, Hwanji spoke quickly. "No, no. Not like they listen to you. Don't worry, Honored One. You're the strongest yoki-hijo. Everyone knows it. Why, my old yoki-hijo, before she retired, she only averaged around ten spirits summoned per session."

Yumi wilted. "Ten. I . . . averaged around twelve . . . and most yoki-hijo draw no more than five or six, Liyun told me. So . . ."

So the spirits did not ignore a woman simply because she decided to eat on her own. Painter should have felt vindicated. Instead he felt miserable.

"The others . . . retire?" Yumi asked. "I was told . . . this wasn't possible. That they have to work even when infirm."

"They insist on being finished at age seventy," Hwanji said as Painter repeated Yumi's words. "And, well, I don't think the years until that retirement are quite as hard on them as they are for you. Since . . ." She winced. "They take days off. Whenever they feel they need them. Dwookim worked around half the days of the week during most of the time I served her."

"Days off," Yumi said, Painter repeating. "To do what?"

"Whatever they want," Hwanji said, with a shrug. "I'm sorry, Honored One."

"Thank her, please," Yumi said, bowing to Hwanji. "Thank her, Painter. For being the only person, apparently, to *care* if I knew the *truth*."

"Thank you," Painter whispered. "Deeply, Hwanji. I will pretend I didn't learn this from you."

She nodded and turned away, glancing all around her anxiously, as if frightened Liyun would pop out at any moment.

"It seems," Yumi whispered, looking up at him with tears in her eyes, "that you were right. Good job."

"Yumi . . ." he said, reaching toward her shoulder—then froze. He didn't want to inflict those feelings upon her. It felt like the wrong time.

"If you please," Yumi said to him, "would you go in and go to sleep? I have the *distinct* and *urgent* need to be someone else for a while."

Chapter 23

TWO DAYS later, when they awoke again in Yumi's world, she was feeling *somewhat* better. She'd spent her day in Painter's world meditating while he roamed the city, testing out the new freedom granted by Design's change to their bond.

How quickly and naturally he had returned to freedom. Did he feel constricted now that they were back in her world, where their tether was barely ten feet long? What did it say that she'd stayed in his room thinking the entire day?

She walked to the window, gazing outward while listening to Painter fetch his breakfast from the attendants. She watched the rising crops creeping ever higher in the sky as hotspots on the ground went from warm to scalding. The plants spun like children playing in a rare spring rainfall. She watched them soar, and she envied their liberty. Even cultivated crops were granted more independence than she.

As soon as she thought that, she quashed it. Crushing her longing, her wanderlust, her dreams until they were flat as paper, more easily filed away deep within her soul.

Despite it all, that's still my instinct, she thought, listening to Painter eat. *I know I've been lied to. Yet my training holds.* It's a depressing fact. Abuse is a more effective form of captivity than a cell will ever be.

A quiet banging came at the door, and Yumi turned, cocking her head.

Why was someone doing that? In all her life, when people wanted her, they simply entered.

Painter called for the person to enter. Liyun opened the door, dressed immaculately in white and dark blue, the long sleeves of her ceremonial tobok swallowing her hands.

She bowed. "Upon your pleasure, Chosen."

Painter waved with his maipon sticks for her to enter. She left her clogs behind and knelt before him in a posture that might have looked demure for someone else. Liyun, however, appeared unable to make herself fully bow her back, her elbows were too stiff on her knees, and she lowered her head barely a few degrees. A *technically* apologetic pose, by the strictest definition of the word.

She seemed sorry in the same way a tank commander might be apologetic after destroying your house. He might be in the wrong. But he *was* still in a tank.

"How," Liyun finally said to Painter, "did you find out?"

He continued eating, but glanced at Yumi, letting her take the lead. She nodded to him in thanks.

"Find out," Yumi said, "about what, Liyun?"

Painter repeated the words with an appropriate air of indifference. How did he manage that? She would have wilted beneath Liyun's glare.

"The reform movement," Liyun admitted at last.

Something had been straining inside of Yumi. It cracked fully when Liyun said the words. Until that moment, a part of Yumi had believed that Hwanji had been lying or confused.

"I . . ." Yumi said.

"Someone contacted me," Painter said, fabricating the lie with such ease it concerned her. "Someone who thought I was being treated unfairly. They left me a note a few weeks ago. There was no name. Just a random activist, I suppose."

Liyun swallowed this lie easily.

"You shouldn't have taught me to read," Yumi said, with him repeating the words. "I'd be a much better captive that way."

"You aren't a captive," Liyun said. "You are—"

"A servant, yes," Yumi said, with him repeating. "I know."

Liyun took a deep breath. "Is this the reason, then, for all the . . . strangeness these last weeks?"

Painter looked to Yumi.

"Yes," she said for him to repeat. "To an extent." The deception came easily to her as well. Frighteningly easy.

Liyun stood up and nodded. "Very well then." She turned to leave. "I shall meet you at the place of ritual, where I shall wait upon your needs for the day, Chosen."

"Wait," Yumi said through Painter. "That's it? That's the end? All you're going to say?"

"It is not uncommon," Liyun said as she slipped on her clogs, "for a younger person to seek to stride past their boundaries. I had hoped such a common attitude would not seize you, but we are all weak before the eyes of the spirits." She looked at Painter. "We are still the servants of the people. Even the most reformed yoki-hijo does her duty in that regard. So we continue. Besides, I know for a fact you were trained well. You will overcome this bout of petulance."

Yumi gasped softly. Liyun hadn't spoken to her in such a forward way since the first years of her training.

The woman turned to leave. Yumi found a word bubbling out, too hot to keep in. "Liyun!"

The woman glanced over her shoulder as Painter relayed the word.

"Do the others live with their families?" Yumi asked. "Do they go back to them? At least visit their homes?"

"It is not unheard of," Liyun said, "for a yoki-hijo among the more . . . liberal persuasions to spend a few weeks each year with her birth family." She paused briefly. "You'd hate it, Yumi. Nothing to do? Sitting each day with people you don't know? Strangers trying to pretend they're your parents? You would be miserable."

"Don't you think I would have wanted to have the *choice*?" Yumi asked through Painter.

"You have the choice," Liyun said. "You always have. Forgive me for not pointing you toward it, as it would have destroyed you."

She left then.

"I (lowly) *hate* that woman," Painter muttered.

"Please don't say that," Yumi whispered.

"You defend her?" Painter said, standing. "After what she did to you?"

"She's my . . ." She couldn't form the word. "She raised me. The best she knew how. And she is right; I'm still a servant of the people and the spirits. So nothing changes."

"Nothing?" he said.

"Very little of importance."

"Your happiness is nothing 'little,' Yumi."

"You think I'm happier?" she said. "Look at me and tell me I'm *happier* this way, Painter."

He met her eyes, then glanced away. "Well," he finally said, "I think you *will* be happier, once this difficult time passes. I think the spirits believe that too. Have you thought that maybe *this* is why they wrapped us up in this? So you could learn to be free?"

"Have *you* thought that maybe they approached me instead of any other yoki-hijo," she said, "because *I* was trained to be absolutely obedient to their will? Apparently that's rarer than I thought."

She stalked out the door that Liyun had left open. He followed behind, fortunately—because otherwise she'd have been yanked right back toward him.

At the cool spring, she tossed off her clothing and strode straight into the water, then dove underneath and let the soft coolness enwrap her. She turned over and floated to the surface, staring up into the sky filled with twirling plants, kept from drifting too far by the attentive crows and flyers. So far beyond reach that they might as well have been on another planet.

Painter stepped into the water himself, but didn't start washing. Instead he turned over and floated as well, quiet, drifting next to her.

Yumi squeezed her eyes shut and tried not to let him hear her sniffling. If he did hear, he didn't say anything.

"I'm glad," she whispered at last, "to know. Even if it hurts to realize how I've been lied to. Even if I'm not happier right *now*. I'm glad to know. So thank you. For pushing for the truth."

"I didn't do it to find the truth," he whispered back. "I was annoyed and reckless."

"That's what you needed to be," she said. "Maybe you're right. Maybe the spirits wanted this for me."

She had trouble imagining that to be true. Likely thousands of yoki-hijo had lived following the traditions she had. If the spirits had disliked this style of treating their servants, then surely they'd have done something about it long ago. The shifts in how her kind were treated seemed more cultural than doctrinal.

Though that raised an ugly question: Did the spirits care at all? She'd talked to them, interacted with them, petitioned them. They didn't think like people did. Didn't understand as people did. So why would they care whether she ate her own food or was served by someone else?

Before, her trust in the system had prevented these kinds of questions. Now no such barrier remained. Could she visit Torio City? Could she know her family? Have friends? Could she have something that resembled a normal life?

What even *was* a normal life?

"What is it like?" she asked softly. "Being able to decide for yourself what to do each day?"

"You've tasted it a little in my world. It's like that."

"It must be overwhelming," she whispered, "to simply . . . be able to do anything. To be able to make friends with whoever you want. Pick your profession. I can barely select a broth for noodles. You're so good at all of that, Painter. How?"

"It's . . . not as easy for me as you think, Yumi."

She turned her head in the water and looked toward him floating there, staring at the sky. What did he think when he saw the plants up there, so high? When he watched the flocks of butterflies scatter as crows soared past, sending individual plants spinning? Did he see freedom, or something else?

"Just because you *can* talk to anyone," Painter said, "doesn't mean you will know what to say."

"Is that why things are so strange between you and the other painters? You all have so many things you *could* say, that you don't know *what* to say?"

"Something like that."

"You could make other friends," she said.

"I've never really known how," he said, his voice low as he drifted. "It *should* be easy. Everyone else makes it seem that way. But . . . if that's the case . . . why didn't it work for me?"

"You didn't try hard enough, maybe?" she said.

"That's what my parents say," he said. "That I should just go . . . try. 'Just go talk to someone!' they'd say. So I would. I'd gather my courage, stumble over, and say the wrong things. I'd feel like an awkward fool, and people would laugh at me. After that my parents would say, 'Well, you shouldn't have done it *that* way, son.' But what *is* the way?"

He turned his head to look toward her. "I know it sounds ridiculous to you. I had all the opportunities. My life was easy, liberated. But . . . I always felt like I was standing on the other side of a large glass window. I could see the world passing beyond it, could even pretend I was part of it. But that barrier was still there. Separating me from everyone else." He looked away. "That sounds stupid, doesn't it?"

"No . . ." She closed her eyes. "I understand invisible walls, Painter."

She let her hand float outward, near his. She could feel him doing the same, reaching toward her, then stopping. And she wondered. She could touch the water, float in it, because she felt she *should*. She could pick up clothing for a similar reason.

Was there a version of this, a way of thinking, where she could touch him? She let her fingers brush his.

It didn't work—instead of feeling his fingers, she felt that shiver, that burst of warmth travel up through her arm and strike her to the core. She gasped, splashing upright at the shock of it. Then she sank down so only her head showed. He sputtered and turned toward her, water streaming across his face.

"Painter," she said, eager. "Let's break the rules. Even Liyun agrees . . . I can do that! Let's *try* it."

"Isn't that what I've been doing?" he said, wiping his face.

"Let's do something *more*," she said, her eyes wide. "Let's do something crazy. Something unexpected."

"Like what?"

"I don't know! You choose. You're the one with free will."

He raised an eyebrow at her.

"I might have it too," she admitted, "but mine is provisional. Come on. What are we going to do?"

He studied her for a moment, then blushed deeply. What was that about?

Oh.

"Seriously?" she said, splashing him. "*That's* where your mind went?"

"You're surprised?" he said, gesturing. "Really?" He shook his head, then began soaping up to start the actual bathing part of, well, bathing.

She considered, and soon felt foolish for her sudden impulse to violate rules. What would she have done if she'd been alone? Run through the town insulting people? Stare at each and every person instead of lowering her eyes? A part of her was tickled at the thought.

"What if," Painter said, "we figured out what those scholars are doing in that tent of theirs?"

"What?" Yumi rose and took some soap. "By asking them?"

"Um, no, Yumi." He smiled. "We would not ask."

"What would we do, then?"

"Sneak into their tent," he said, making sneaking motions with his fingers. "See what we can learn about their equipment. Maybe sabotage it."

She felt her jaw drop, gritty soap powder trickling through her fingers.

He noticed, pausing, and looked toward her. "What?"

"*Painter*," she said. "That would be *illegal!*"

"You wanted to do something transgressive!"

"Like getting dressed, then running out and hopping up and down in full sight of people in the town!" She wilted, thinking about how embarrassing that would be. "Maybe behind a fan or two."

"The spirits want us to accomplish something," he said. "And you're right—it's probably not you learning how to eat by yourself. You still think our task has to do with that machine?"

She nodded, dunked to rinse off soap, then rose. "I do."

"Then we need information," he said. "So . . ."

She stepped closer to him in the water, then found herself grinning, hands held close to her chin, elbows tight against her sides. "Let's do it."

After all, it was *probably* the will of the spirits. "But how? We'll be spotted for certain."

This would be a test. Surely if actively breaking the law didn't anger the spirits, then . . . well, nothing short of outright insulting them would do so.

"It's a good thing everyone leaves us alone for several hours a day, isn't it?" Painter glanced at her and smiled. "In a place nobody can approach, and where they've even helpfully cleared away the casual workers who might catch us sneaking out. Convenient, eh?"

She nodded, conflicted by how eager she felt. She could barely wait the time it took to wash off—going through the ritual soaps at blinding speed—and get dressed. Painter didn't seem nervous at all as Chaeyung and Hwanji led them down the path into the orchard, among the drifting trees, to the elevated shrine. But he ignored the painting supplies today, kneeling until Chaeyung and Hwanji were out of sight.

Then he looked to Yumi, who nodded eagerly, her heart—well, she didn't have one in this form, but she felt like she did—racing and her hands trembling. This was going to be so *wrong*!

The first thing Painter did was pick up his clogs, take off his stockings, then wrap the cloth around the wood. "Can't do much sneaking if I make a clop each time I step."

"Wow," Yumi said. "You know a lot about this."

He blushed. "It happens a lot in the dramas. There, people generally remove their shoes entirely. I thought maybe I should do this instead, to avoid screaming from pain at every step."

He tried on the clogs and found them significantly muffled with the cloth around them. (If you're trying to judge the heat of the ground in Torio, the stone in their settlements wasn't nearly hot enough to set cloth aflame. It could burn you if you left your skin touching it for an extended period, but except at hotspots a casual brush wouldn't do damage.)

He nodded to her, then hopped down off the shrine. She hesitated. This was the moment. Was she *really* going to do this? After a lifetime of training in proper behavior?

She squeezed her eyes closed and followed him, cracking one eye, then the other. Painter hadn't noticed her worry—he'd moved over to one of the larger trees and was pushing it with his finger, making it drift around on its chain.

"How do these trees float again?" he said.

"On thermals."

He nudged another tree with his finger. "They're so *light*. Even if they're floating, I shouldn't be able to move them around this easily." He touched one, then hopped back, looking at his hand.

"What?" she asked.

"I felt lighter when I touched it," he said, trying once more. Then he wrapped both arms around a trunk. "That's so *surreal*. I feel like a balloon."

"A what?"

"I'll show you sometime," he said, stepping back away from the tree. "The trees might float on thermals, Yumi, but they somehow make themselves lighter first."

(He was right. If you've been wondering how they work, this is a big clue. Plants on Yumi's world don't really defy physics so much as they sneak past while physics is distracted by a nice drama on the viewer. Probably something involving pendulums. Physics loves those things.)

Feeling an increasing sense of transgressive elation, Yumi followed Painter among the lazy trees, which opened and closed pathways as they drifted on their chains. She quickly realized that she had no sense of how the village was laid out, aside from the steamwell at the center, the hills with the cold spring off to the west, and the orchard to the south. Painter, however, seemed to have a better feel for it. Perhaps that was the sort of skill you picked up when you didn't always have someone to lead you everywhere you needed to be.

He managed to avoid sections where workers were harvesting nuts from the trees. Then he led Yumi to the edge of the orchard, near the eastern side of the town—close to the place of ritual. Here he crouched beside a tree.

Though he'd gotten them close, the tent the scholars had set up was still a good fifty yards away. Over hot stone, past the fence around the place of ritual. A set of three large trees had been chained to the ground near the rear of the scholars' tent to provide shade. That would give cover once they approached—but first they had to cross fifty yards of open ground.

Painter gazed down at the day's ritual tobok. The dress was bright yellow and red. "These stand out rather a lot, don't they?" he asked.

"That's deliberately the point," Yumi said.

He nodded. Then pulled his dress off.

Yumi gasped. Not for the common reason—they did bathe together every day. In addition, there were three more layers underneath. But those were *undergarments*.

"What are you doing?" she demanded as he shucked the *second* layer of skirt too. "Stop!"

He grinned and gestured to the final layer of clothing: thin silken trousers you might find reminiscent of pantaloons, dyed light brown, and a loose green overshirt. Also silken, shimmering, and way too revealing of his figure. Underneath that was the wrap around his chest, and that was it.

She silently prayed he wouldn't go any further.

"This," he said, "is remarkably similar to what men wear around here."

"Except not," she said. "Their outfits are completely different."

"Close enough. I think that from a distance I'll just appear like a worker leaving the orchard."

"If someone looks closely, they'll see *me*, practically naked and absolutely deranged! It's not going to work."

He gazed out at the tent, as if he was going to go striding out anyway, but didn't move. He glanced at her.

"I'll pull out now if you want," he said. "This *is* your life I'm playing with, Yumi. If I get caught, you'll have to live with it—assuming we swap back eventually. So . . . do you want me to stop? It's your choice."

Her choice? What a terrible idea.

But she felt reckless. And determined. Somehow at once. So before she could think about what she was doing, she threw off her overdress and second layer too, standing in her silks. "Go!" she said.

"Why . . . did *you* strip?" he asked. "You're invisible."

"Solidarity!" she shouted, then—taking a deep breath—started out across the stone.

Once, she would have assumed that she couldn't hide, no matter how good the disguise. She would have assumed that people would instantly know a yoki-hijo.

But she had lived in Painter's world. She'd been *normal* for a week and a half at this point. Well, at least during the half of each day she spent in his world. Perhaps . . . perhaps he was right and no one would notice.

She still felt like a field mouse. Yes, a little mouse that had dropped from its nest in the rice plant and fallen to the hot stones during the day, having to scurry for high ground in full sight of all the giant hawks and crows above. Burning up with each step.

She mistook every sound in the distance for a cry of alarm. She was certain every figure moving through the town was dashing to get Li-yun. Everyone would soon hear that the yoki-hijo was crazy and running around in her underwear.

Painter just plodded along.

"Hurry!" she hissed at him.

"Hurrying ruins the illusion," he said. "Trust me. I've seen this at least three times in the dramas."

"Three times? That's the extent of your experience?" She jumped, looking toward a shadow cast by several rice plants moving overhead.

This was misery. Intoxicating misery. And despite his apparent calm, Painter seemed unable to stop himself from speeding up as they neared the hiding place. He practically ran the last few yards and pulled up against the trunk of one of the shade trees.

The little stand of trees, as she'd hoped, provided some cover. They kept snapping their chains taut in the thermals—since this was near the place of ritual, the stones were extra hot. Painter wiped his brow, then shook his hand, the beads of sweat evaporating quickly on the ground.

"How you people survive in this place," he whispered, "I'll never know. But we . . ."

He trailed off as he saw Yumi, her heart thundering like the ritual drum, her nerves dancers contorting before the spirits, her eyes the blazing bonfires of a night festival.

"You all right?" he asked her.

"That was the worst thing I've ever done!" she said, throwing her hands into the air. "It was wonderful!"

"Girl," he said, "you *really* need to get out more."

"I'm trying!" she said, with an uncontrolled grin. Then she pulled her arms tight up beneath her chin, her eyes going even wider. "We could run away. Escape together. Off into the wide world, like in the stories Samjae used to tell me . . ."

"Usually," he said, with a dry smile, "I prefer to go on at least one date with a girl before I elope with her. Call me traditional."

"I didn't mean it like that," she snapped (lowly). "It's just . . . this feels so liberating. And terrifying. They don't care. The spirits don't *actually* care."

"I don't know about that," he said. He pointed around the trunk toward the tent, hovering a few feet above the ground on its platform. "The spirits give you things like that platform, right? No cost? No price?"

"No price," she said. "They want to help, once we summon them. I think they find us intriguing and enjoy watching us."

"Sounds like they do care," he said. "About you. If not about a lot of the things you all have made up about them."

She smiled. "Right, then. What next? How do we get into that tent without being seen?"

"I figure you'll simply walk over to it," Painter said.

"Me? Why me?"

"Yumi. You are *literally* a ghost at the moment."

"Oh!" She looked down at herself. And despite wearing roughly the same amount of cloth she did when in Painter's world, she blushed at her state of near undress. "I guess . . . that's useful, isn't it?"

"For spying? It seems like it might be an advantage, yes." He peeked at the tent. It was large, almost more a pavilion, and made of thick canvas. It had been set up on a wooden platform some twenty or more feet across that had floating devices underneath to keep it off the stones.

"I wonder . . ." Painter said.

"What?"

"It's just . . . this is what the nightmares do at home. Sneaking around, hiding, peeking in to watch people." His frown deepened. "They can go right through walls. I don't suppose . . ." He glanced at her.

Yumi nodded at Painter in understanding. Then, reminding herself that no one could see her, she slipped out from behind the tree and crossed the last bit of ground to the tent. She hadn't wrapped her clogs, so they continued to clop, wood on stone.

That sound wasn't real. She wasn't real, not completely. When she tried to grab things, her hands passed through them unless she concentrated.

So . . . upon reaching the tent, she bowed to the spirits underneath, then stepped up onto the edge of the hovering wooden platform. There, she determinedly stepped into the cloth wall.

It, with equal determination, pushed right back.

Yumi glared at the cloth, rubbing her nose. Maybe she wasn't showing it enough respect. She bowed to the wall as best she could from her narrow perch.

"O wall of cloth," she said, "grant me the honor of—"

"What are you doing?" Painter hissed at her from behind.

"Petitioning the wall."

"What?"

She spun toward him and gestured to the tent. "All things have souls, and the soul of the wall is akin to the spirits. All nonliving things are of them! That's—"

"Yumi!" he hissed.

"—why they become statues when we make requests of them! And why rocks draw their attention. It's—"

"Look at your hand!"

She hesitated, then glanced at her hand—which in her gesticulating she'd thrust straight through the cloth. Huh. Had her petition worked? Or . . .

Or had she just not been paying attention? Design said they touched things they wanted to—expected to. So perhaps . . .

She closed her eyes and stepped forward, not thinking about the cloth. Doing that, she walked straight through. When she opened her eyes, she found herself inside the tent. And wow, the scholars traveled in *style*. Thick rugs on the floor. Fine pillows and cushions for sitting on. A counter with various liquors, and those serving boys—likely scholars in training—to wait upon their needs.

The lavish display was interrupted by the enormous metal machine at the center, its valves and bars open and gaping, like a heart cut from a beast with the arteries severed.

The lead scholar had a pinched face and almost pointed head—like a blunt pencil. He paced back and forth, looking less intimidating without his hat. The bowl cut of hair didn't help. It was the sort of style you ended up with when you assumed that because you'd studied literature and engineering, you knew your hairdresser's job better than they did.

"We should try the vacuum pumps again," the scholar was saying as he paced.

"It's not the vacuum pumps," said a scholar who sat on the floor beside the machine, tinkering with it. "It's the power source, Gyundok-nimi."

"We never had a problem with the power source for the father machine," the lead scholar snapped.

"Pardon, Gyundok-nimi," another scholar said, lounging in pillows with a half-eaten fruit, "but we *absolutely* have had problems with the father machine's power."

"The Incident?" Gyundok said—and Yumi could sense the capital letter there. "Hasn't been an issue for years."

The three other scholars shared a glance.

"Fine," Gyundok said, his hands going to his hips. "If it's the power source, you prime it, Sunjun. This machine is small. It will be safe."

Sunjun—the scholar working on the machine—raised his hands and backed away from it. "Not a chance."

"We need a spirit," said the man lounging in the pillows.

"Is that all, Honam?" the leader said, spinning toward him. "Our machine that draws spirits needs a spirit to start, you say. What a *useful* observation."

"Maybe that yoki-hijo will call one," Honam said, taking a bite of his fruit. "We could grab it."

"Have you *seen* her stacks?" said Sunjun. "The only thing she'll be summoning in this town is an apology."

"You try starting it, Honam," the leader said. "Once it's primed, it will keep itself going. Should be enough energy in this town for that. As long as we don't turn it off, we'll be good."

"We don't even know that it will work for the severing," Sunjun said. "Maybe we should rethink this entire fiasco."

"If it doesn't work," the lead scholar said, "then we'll try something else. But *first* we follow my plan." He peeked out the parted front of the tent, toward the town. "This is dangerous, what's happening here. Honam, prime the machine."

"No," Honam said. "Not a chance."

"I order you—"

"I'll do it." The fourth scholar spoke from near the wall, where he stood partially in shadows. Yumi squinted at him, making out a man with a full beard on his chin but a mustache that was failing to keep its end of the bargain. He stepped forward, causing Sunjun to scramble farther back from the machine.

"It's a small machine," the fourth scholar said. "It will be fine. Just needs a little priming."

Yumi stepped forward, trying to get into a better position to watch as this last unnamed scholar knelt down in front of the machine and opened a panel. She had to pick her way between the others and lean in close—getting right to the edge of her tether to Painter—so she could observe as the scholar hesitated, then pressed his hand to a plate at the heart of the machine.

There, she was absolutely certain, two lines of light sprang into existence. One was a vibrant magenta. The other a liquid azure.

Hion lines.

She gasped, then clamped her mouth shut. *Then* felt immediately foolish. They couldn't hear her. So she leaned forward farther, inches from the man, to make certain she was seeing what she thought she was. Yes, those *were* hion lines. She couldn't mistake the distinctive colors. They connected the scholar's hand to the—

Another pair formed from her face, leading to the plate.

She yelped, jerking back. Lights went up along the machine's sides, and the scholar who had been kneeling relaxed visibly, pulling his hand away and wiping it on his trousers. The lead scholar and the lounging one cheered in excitement.

The one who had been sitting nearby though—Sunjun, the one with grease on his hands from working on the thing—ignored the achievement. He wasn't looking at the lights or his companions. No, Sunjun was looking right at Yumi.

She felt a sudden panic and scrambled away, grabbing the spirit of a blanket and holding it up in front of her. If they saw—

He continued staring at where she'd been. Not at her. She was still invisible.

"There's a spirit in here," Sunjun said, scrambling to his feet.

"What?" the lead scholar said.

"I saw a second set of lines," Sunjun said, pointing to where Yumi had been standing. "A spirit." He turned to fumble with some equipment, then pulled out a box with a trailing wire that he plugged into the larger machine. Yumi felt a coldness come over her. An actual *physical* coldness, not just a fear. The machine had stolen warmth from her.

Sunjun turned the box, and the needle on a dial atop it swung toward Yumi. She scuttled away, dodging around the scholars and running for the wall of the tent.

The needle followed her.

"There!" Sunjun said, pointing. "It's moving. Quick! Dig out the capture device!"

Terrified of whatever *that* was, Yumi closed her eyes and jumped through the wall.

Chapter 24

A S H E waited for Yumi to finish in the tent, Painter spent his time testing his theory about the trees. Though these shade trees were modestly large, most of their bulk was in their foliage, not their height. Minimal effort got him up into the branches and among the leaves, where he felt more hidden.

The chain tethering the tree was looped here around the upper trunk, fastened with a sturdy clipping mechanism. That chain was heavy, but it didn't weigh the tree down—it just held it in place. Something was making the metal lighter, he figured, like it made his body lighter. As before, the closer he stayed to the trunk, the stronger this effect was.

When he'd first climbed into the tree, his weight had caused it to sag and thump against the ground. But if he hugged it tight, his cheek to the bark—the tree was wide enough that his hands barely touched on the other side—it lifted once more. When doing this, it was as if he became part of its essence and added negligible weight to its bulk. If he moved farther out onto one of the branches, his weight returned, his own flesh noticeable on his bones, his clothing settling back onto his body.

The tree, in turn, slumped downward and hit the ground again. Remarkably, these plants had *adapted* to this place where the ground was so hot. They had barely any roots, merely some curled vestigial ones at the bottom, like gnarled fingers. How did they manage to—

Yumi burst through the wall of the tent. Running.

Painter dropped to a lower branch to look down at her.

"Scholars saw me somehow!" she shouted, frantic. "They're coming after me! They mustn't find me! Or find you! Everyone will see me like this and know that we spied on the scholars and that I've given up all semblance of sanity in favor of categoric hooliganism and malfeasance!"

Painter wasn't sure what shocked him more. The fact that she'd been spotted, or the fact that she'd actually used the word "hooliganism" in practical discourse.

Unfortunately, her alarm wasn't exaggerated. Shouts sounded from the tent, and one scholar popped out around it holding some kind of device—which he pointed toward the trees where Yumi was standing.

"They're going to find you up there!" she said, then began hyperventilating again. "You can't hide. I'm dead. I'm over. It's over. I-I-I—"

"Yumi!" he hissed, a desperate plan forming. The obvious one really, considering the circumstances. He held out his hand to her. With his other hand he grabbed the chain holding the tree in place, then he mouthed one sentence.

We go up.

"Painter, that's a very *bad* idea!"

But the scholars were flooding out of the tent, and she didn't have time to come up with something better. He gestured more urgently, and after the briefest moment she leaped up and grabbed the first branch.

He unhooked the chain, then climbed higher—where he was better obscured by the prodigious canopy—and wrapped his arms around the trunk, his heart pounding as he imagined their dramatic escape.

The tree began to drift sluggishly upward. Less dramatic. More torpid. But the scholars noticed too slowly, and by the time they started pointing toward it, the roots were barely out of reach. Painter buried his head among some branches so the scholars couldn't make out who he was.

In minutes the tree had gained forty or fifty feet, and the soft wind nudged them vaguely to the south—and the orchard—as Painter had hoped. Landing in there would make it difficult for any pursuers to gauge where to find them.

Yumi hauled herself up, gasping for breath. He looked toward her, worried, but couldn't move without jeopardizing their buoyancy. Thankfully, the tree didn't seem to notice the weight of a ghost.

"Yumi?" he whispered.

She twisted around, holding tightly to her branch, and he saw she was crying, gulping in breaths.

And laughing.

He relaxed.

"That is," she said, "the single most delinquent thing I've ever done. I don't know how to react! I'm shaking like a steamwell the moment before it erupts. Yet for some reason I feel *good*. Like I want to do it *again*. I'm broken!"

"No." He grinned. "You're human."

"We're still going to get caught," she said. "They'll watch where we land."

"Maybe." He twisted against the trunk, stretching out to add some weight. That made their ascent slow as they continued to drift toward the orchard.

They'd risen just high enough to reach the bottom layer of the sky's plants—mostly weeds and wildflowers here. The tree peeked up through the layer of foliage like it was breaking the surface of a lake. Flowers sprouting from the center of lily pads danced with bushes that spread limbs wide to catch the thermals. Leaves and florets—similar to the white sprigs that dandelions release on Scadrial, or duluko plants release here—swirled in the air. Butterflies exploded from a bush, fluttering to surround the tree.

The tree's motion caused eddies in the air around them, carrying the various fecund flotsam in swirls and patterns. Painter breathed out, momentarily forgetting everything else. The flowers, the petals, the butterflies, the sparkling light—it was like paint thrown on a palette by a master of some incomprehensible art form. A sudden improvisational beauty against the brilliant canvas of the deep blue sky.

Up here in the sky, beads of moisture condensed on fat, lush leaves. A certain wet decadence misted on his skin—like sweat but pure, tasting of something bright and clean.

That's why they rise, he thought. *The air is humid up this high, evaporated by the hot stone below. So the plants rise to reach it . . .*

In that moment he envied this world that had light in the sky, as fragmented sunlight caught the dew and made each and every plant seem like it was wearing its wedding jewelry. The scene changed and shifted, colors mixing and parting, all afire with sunlight, resplendent.

Yumi—farther out on her branch, almost joining the sights—seemed entranced. Her hair rippled around her, caught in the wind. She reached out as a butterfly landed nearby. It didn't see her, so she could lean in close to inspect its shivering wings.

She glanced toward Painter, backlit by wonder, and grinned. A plane of greenery bursting with colors expanded behind her like an infinite inviting highway. *Travel with us,* it said. Yet there was nowhere Painter wanted to go. Not when he had what he wanted with him right here.

"You're staring," she said.

He was a painter. Not a poet. But somehow he found the right words.

"I only stare," he said, "when I see something too beautiful for my eyes to take in at once."

She turned back out toward the landscape, apparently assuming that was what he referred to. "It's like another world," she whispered. "Always up here, every day. So close." Then she leaned out and looked upward toward the daystar. Painter's world. It caught sunlight. Shouldn't all of that darkness have made it black?

"If I'm to lose everything," she whispered, "I'm glad I saw this first."

"You're not going to lose anything," he said, recovering enough of his senses to lean out farther from the trunk and send the tree wafting down toward the orchard below.

"They'll find us," she said, turning toward him again. "They'll see where it lands."

He shook his head. "We'll be fine."

"How do you know?" she asked.

"Because this day is too perfect to be ruined now."

TWENTY minutes later, Liyun found him kneeling in the shrine, the very picture of innocence. If his tobok was askew, well, he'd only just started dressing himself—so it made sense he'd get it wrong. If he was breathing a little heavily, sweaty as if from an extended run, then he'd ob-viously been praying with vigor; communing with the spirits could be strenuous for the devoted. Finally, if there were twigs in his hair, well, the shrine was in an orchard. Those sorts of things fall from trees, I'm told.

Liyun folded her arms, inspecting him.

"Oh?" Painter said, turning. "Is it time already?"

"Did you see someone suspicious skulking through here?" she said. "There has been . . . hooliganism afoot in the city."

Ah, he thought. *That's where she got it. Makes sense.*

"I have been too busy with my meditations to notice," he said. "I'm sorry."

"It is . . . not your fault, Chosen. It is well that you are trying extra hard to petition the spirits, considering your failings lately." She gestured. "Shall we go? The scholars have gotten their machine working at last."

"Have they?" he said. "How unfortunate."

He rose and followed Liyun, Yumi trailing along behind him as if trying to hide in his shadow. Her expression kept alternating between ashamed and elated—the result of some strange emotional short circuit where both of her blinkers turned on at once and utterly confused every-one following behind.

"You're sure," he whispered to her, letting Liyun get ahead so the woman wouldn't hear, "you saw hion lines?"

"Absolutely," Yumi whispered back. "What does it mean?"

"Your people must be close to discovering how to harness hion," he said. "You're on the cusp of the industrial revolution. Things are about to change in your world, Yumi."

"Will it get dark," she whispered, "like on your world?"

"You mean the shroud? No, that existed before we discovered hion. Rather, before we learned how to harness it. Those were . . . difficult days. People wandering through the smoke, living only near bursts of light rising from the ground where plants could grow . . ."

He shivered, thinking about how it must have been. Traveling through the shroud via train was bad enough. Walking through it? Living in it? True, nightmares hadn't been as common back then, but still.

"I have a history book in my school things somewhere," he said to

Yumi. "You can read it when you're in my body. It will explain what might be coming for your people."

"What was that, Chosen One?" Liyun said.

"Just a prayer," Painter said, realizing he'd let his voice stray from a whisper.

Outside the orchard, they picked up Chaeyung and Hwanji—and for once Painter crossed the town without being gawked at. Everyone was gathered at the place of ritual. As he approached, they made way for him, letting him step up near the tent. Here, the scholars had deposited their four-foot-wide machine amid a large number of stones. These were generally smaller than the ones in the place of ritual, but the mechanical thing was moving with eerily smooth motions, making four separate stacks of rocks at once.

"We can beat that," Yumi said. "Look at how *pedestrian* those stacks are! Straight up and down."

Painter was intimidated anyway—even as the machine accidentally knocked over one stack and had to clear it away with three arms before starting again. Yumi might have been able to beat it, but his stacks were nowhere near as good as these.

Still, bolstered by her determination, he stepped into the place of ritual and set to work. He was surprised to find he welcomed the activity of stacking. A lot had happened in the last day, and this return to something normal comforted him. Which says a lot about the human ability to redefine what the word "normal" means.

He soon worked up a sweat—but his stack fell at the seventh stone. The next one only made it to six. He growled and slammed his fist into the ground, barely noticing its heat.

"Relax," Yumi said. "Meditate a moment. You can't stack if your hands are shaking."

He fought down his annoyance. She was right. He took a few deep breaths, then started over.

Hours passed, but most of the townspeople didn't leave. They seemed to sense something was happening here as Painter managed a stack of ten, then a stack of nine, then a stack of *twelve* all in a row. Leaving those three in a line, he started into a fourth one, wiping his hands on his skirt to dry them before placing rocks one after another—more bold this time.

And he *felt* something. Didn't he? A Connection to the land itself? It felt silly to try to express it, but something pulled on him. Tugging directly on his emotions; as he worked, he tugged back.

Something peeked out of the ground nearby. It vanished as he glanced toward it, but Yumi gasped, then clasped her hands before her, grinning like a maniac. She waved for him to continue, then apparently remembered her duty as a coach and encouraged him to breathe. To be calm.

That wasn't so easy, as the crowd was beginning to get louder, people murmuring and chattering. Painter launched into his eighth stack—remarkably without any of the others having fallen. He could *almost* visualize this one before he placed the stones. He'd make it the tallest of them all. He had the rocks, and knew how they'd fit together. He could make his tower appear to lean, but really be sturdy because of the weight of this rock here . . .

He felt that tugging again.

It was actually working.

It was all *real*.

An ethereal ball of light seeped up from the ground near the fence, roughly halfway between him and the machine. It glowed like a large glob of liquid metal, softly shimmering with the colors of hion.

Painter placed another rock, struggling to remain calm. The spirit lingered, then turned as if looking toward the clanking machine—though the spirit had no eyes. Part of it stretched in that direction, then the rest followed, like elastic snapping together. As the parts melded, it soared along the stone ground like it was swimming. It passed among the startled people who, their attention on the machine, hadn't noticed it first appearing.

It swam right up to the scholars.

"No!" Yumi cried, standing. "No, they *stole* it from us!"

Painter turned, letting his current rock slip. The tower toppled, destabilizing one of the others, which collapsed as well. Outside the fence, the townspeople cheered as one of the scholars picked up the glowing spirit, then raised it in his hands. People crowded around, cutting off Painter's view of what happened next.

"And now!" The man's voice drifted to where Painter slouched on the ground, barely noticing the heat from below. "See how we can make this spirit transform into a useful object via the pictures we present as simple inputs. Behold! It is done!"

"That took all day!" a voice shouted. Liyun? "Your machine will never replace the yoki-hijo. A competent girl can draw a half dozen spirits in a day! A master can sometimes get *dozens*!"

"And how many yoki-hijo are there?" the scholar shouted back. "Sixteen at most! We currently have only fourteen. How long did the people of this town wait between visits of the yoki-hijo? Months? Years? *These* machines can be placed in every town and village, working all day."

Liyun didn't reply.

"You will see!" the scholar said. "We'll remain here calling spirits until every need of every resident is filled."

Painter—exhausted, his fingers raw even inside his gloves—turned to Yumi.

"You did well," she told him.

"Not well enough. Yumi, I don't think I drew that spirit. I think the machine did."

"No," she said, firm. Then she hesitated and spoke a little less certainly. "It was maybe both of you. Spirits always come up right next to me when I'm performing, while that one was between you and the scholars."

"So the machine works," Painter said. "It drew the spirit."

"What you did worked as well, Painter," she said, kneeling beside him. "It was already obvious the machine works. They wouldn't have brought it here if it weren't capable of attracting a spirit. But its stacks are mediocre, barely viable. You can beat it, Painter, do better than it can. Get a spirit for us to talk to, to question."

He looked around at the many rocks. "More practice?" he said with a sigh.

She nodded.

In response, he took a drink from the canteen Hwanji brought him, shook the stiffness out of his hands, then got back to it. Though he didn't draw another spirit that day—and he knew it had been months between the first time Yumi had done it and her second—at least it was a nibble at success.

He hoped that would sustain him for however long it took to find his next taste.

A WEEK LATER, Yumi watched the most shocking thing she'd ever seen. Two people kissing. In *front* of her. In front of everyone, on the *viewer*. A man made from the blue hion lines, and a woman from the magenta.

Locking lips, intimate. Right *there*.

She gasped and pulled her blankets closer, up to her chin. "Can they *show* that?" she asked.

Painter just chuckled.

She threw a pillow at him in response—it didn't even disrupt his spirit, but it made her feel better. Then she leaned forward, eyes wide.

It had become her habit, after practicing her painting for several hours, to stop and watch a drama. It felt like a frivolous waste of time, but Painter said that it was important to relax now and then—and it *was* his world. His rules. She was basically *forced* to do this.

Besides, the story continued each night—and she *needed* to see what happened. She followed three separate dramas, but *Seasons of Regret* was the best. And the most scandalous. She cocked her head as the kiss continued. And continued. And . . .

"How do they breathe?" she asked.

"In a kiss like that," he said, "you share breath. You send the air back and forth, exhaling into each other's lungs. It can keep you going for a good fifteen minutes."

She believed it for the briefest moment, then saw his smirk. That earned him another pillow, this one straight through the head.

On the viewer, Sir Ashinata and Lady Hinobi broke apart. This was a "historical" drama, according to Painter. Which meant they were pretending to be from another time, before things like showers. Yumi sighed at how the two stared at each other, with the viewer showing their faces up close, tiny hion lines reproducing even their eyelashes.

That look. Could they really be faking? Painter must be wrong—these two actors must actually be in love. Because of that look. She had been *waiting* to see them look at each other like that for a week now.

Sir Ashinata was some kind of wandering warrior, and their pairing was forbidden. But they had finally admitted their love. It was *wonderful*.

"Now," Sir Ashinata said, "I must go away. Forever."

"What?" Yumi cried. "*What?*"

He spun and walked off, one hand on his hion blade. Lady Hinobi turned from him to hide the tears in her eyes.

"No," Yumi said, leaping to her feet. "*No!*"

But the ending music started playing. The hour was over. He was *leaving*?

"That's terrible!" she said, pointing. "We waited all this time, and now he's just *going away*?"

"He's ronin," Painter said. "That is the way of his kind."

Yumi glared at him, but . . . well, he turned away, wiping a tear from his eye. He didn't like it any more than she did. And Painter wasn't to blame for what the people who made the drama had done.

She collapsed into a heap of blankets and pillows on the futon. She'd discovered at last that it wasn't an altar. Painter had chuckled for a day after she'd finally thought to ask.

"But . . ." she said. "But why?"

"Some stories end this way." Painter stood up and stretched. "Depends on what the writer wants. It's good that they're all a little different. You don't want them all to be happy."

"Yes. I. *Do*." Her voice grew softer. "They could create anything. Make anything. Why would they make something *sad*?"

"I've heard people find it more realistic."

"Is it?" Yumi asked, pulling her blankets tighter. "Is sadness realistic?" That felt more depressing than the ending itself.

"I used to think so," Painter said. "And Yumi, many things in life are sad. So it's realistic at least to some experiences. It's good that some stories are happy, some are sad. That part *is* realistic."

She shook her head and dried her tears in the blanket.

"Sometimes," Painter said, "the more you think about it, the better an ending like this seems. It can be right, even if it's painful."

"There's still hope," Yumi said, fierce. "The program isn't finished. Something might happen tomorrow."

"I don't know," Painter said. "That was the end of the arc—you can see it in the extra-long credits. Tomorrow they'll switch to a different set of characters."

"No," she said. "It's not over. You'll see . . ."

She said it with more confidence than she felt. Ten hours awake in each body made for an odd schedule in some ways, but at least she could catch a drama each day. This one could turn out to be happy.

Couldn't it?

Painter walked to the viewer to turn it off—he liked experimenting with what he could accomplish while a spirit. Yumi trailed over to the window to look out at the pure black sky. With its single point of light, distant as last night's dreams.

(Unfortunately, you're not going to get an answer for why "the star" could pierce the shroud when the sun and stars could not. I don't yet know. I have some answers about the shroud itself, and the nature of what was happening to Yumi's and Painter's lands. I'll give you those when it's appropriate.

But the way that one planet could filter through the darkness and reach longing eyes in Kilahito? No idea what was going on. I'm sorry to leave you with this mystery, but think of it as—instead of a hole—a promise for future stories yet undiscovered.)

"Want to get back to training?" Painter said, gesturing to the stacks of paper.

"No," she said, turning away from the window and putting aside silly thoughts about a silly drama, even if her eyes were still wet. "I think it's time for me to go out. Hunting nightmares."

"You're not ready."

"You've said this is all I need to learn," she said, waving to the stacks of painted bamboo. "You said I mastered it a *week* ago, Painter. You've been having me do nothing more than bamboo for days and days and days now!"

"Knowing how to paint," he said, "is different from being able to do it in a stressful situation. That requires reflex and instinct. Like hitting a ball."

"A ball?" she asked, picking up the small bowl of soup she'd forgotten as the ending of the drama arrived. She frowned as she sat down on the futon. "What ball?"

"You know," he said, making a motion with his hand—as if that explained it. "Hitting a ball? With a snap-racket? You . . . don't have that on your world."

"Obviously," she said, tasting her noodles.

Hey! They *almost* weren't terrible.

"Try this," she said, eager, holding the bowl toward him, pinching the spoon between two fingers and proffering it. He plucked the spirit of the spoon and was able to get a taste of the soul of the soup.

He looked up at her.

"It's only my second week cooking," she said.

"There is more salt in this soup than there is soup, Yumi," he said.

"It said to salt liberally," she said. "I didn't know what that meant."

"You could ask."

It was . . . difficult to remember she could ask for things. Beyond that, cooking for herself was a strange experience.

"Well," she said, holding up the bowl, "I consider this a success. It's quite nearly edible." She went to the sink and ceremoniously dumped it out. "But for all my weakness at cooking, Painter, I'm *certainly* better at painting. It's time. We should go out tonight and look for that nightmare."

He walked over. "You don't even believe this is the reason we're linked. You think it's that machine and the scholars."

"Yes," she admitted. By now they'd seen that it could legitimately draw its own spirits, without help from a yoki-hijo. It merely did so very slowly, at a rate of one or so a day. "But what if I'm wrong?"

He met her eyes.

"I don't understand any of this," she said. "Painter, *you* said you thought that stable nightmare was the reason. So we need to pursue it. We need to try to find it."

He shoved his hands in his pockets to think, his brow creasing. Unfortunately they'd nearly run through his meager savings—and his suspension would soon be over. He'd need to immediately go back to work and prove himself to his superiors so that he didn't get into further trouble.

Therefore, either she needed to start doing his job, or they needed to solve this issue, ending their bond.

Did she want that?

Well, of course she did. She had duties—and more importantly, the spirits had called her to a special task. She needed to see that through to help them. Then she had to return to her life. Improved, yes.

But still irrevocably alone.

She didn't want to confront that. At least . . . at least there was that flying ship from his planet, traveling between their worlds. That meant something. For the future.

"All right," he said, standing up. "Let's pack the painting supplies."

She nodded firmly. Today she'd dressed in sturdy work clothing. For *working*. Something she'd never truly done, but it felt right. Leggings under her dress, a thicker jacket than her lightweight one—short, not even down to her waist, but solid, with numerous metal clasps and buttons on it. Almost like armor.

"Something's off about this," Painter said, strolling over as she packed the painter's bag. "Yumi, that stable nightmare should have been spotted by now. It's been weeks. The Dreamwatch should've been sent for, should be working in the city. But if they were, it would be on the news. The Dreamwatch arriving is such a big deal . . ."

"Wait," Yumi said, pointing at him. "Have you been *stalling*? Is *that* why you made me practice again all this week? You thought maybe someone else would catch the thing?"

He shrugged. She didn't want to think of him as cowardly, but there *were* moments like this when he seemed perfectly willing to let someone else do the difficult jobs. Admittedly, she'd spent her entire life doing very little for herself. To an uncomfortable extreme. So she figured maybe she shouldn't point fingers.

She shoved the last of the large canvases into the bag, then nodded. It was time, at long last, for her to try being a nightmare painter.

PAINTER made them wait past the time when shift started, just in case. He said he wanted to minimize the chances of her being spotted by the other painters—although eventually that would very much be part of their plan. That said, it would probably be okay if she happened to be seen. Someone else would be patrolling his beat until his suspension was up. However, he said that the area was wide, and painters often moved between sections as they patrolled, chasing leads. As long as she didn't encounter any painters up close who could identify her as Nikaro's sister, they should be fine.

The plan was simple. They needed to hunt for signs of the stable nightmare, see if it was still prowling these streets. If it was, they'd draw the attention of one of the groups of painters patrolling nearby. Once they'd seen it, everyone could go to the foreman and corroborate what Yumi had told him. The Dreamwatch would be sent for.

It was a straightforward plan in concept, but each of the individual pieces daunted Yumi. She'd brought a device Painter said would make an emergency noise—it was a metal contraption with two round things on the sides that he said were bells. She'd seen bells though, and these weren't those. How was something shaped like a large biscuit a bell?

But she trusted it would work. Newer painters carried these to call for help. So she'd turn it on if they saw the stable nightmare. But what if no other painters were nearby? How would they get close enough to a nightmare to determine it was the right one, yet stay far enough away that it wouldn't attack her?

She voiced none of this to Painter. He was too nervous himself, evidenced by how he suggested—no fewer than three times—that she return to the apartment. She resisted, though she'd never seen the streets so empty as she did tonight. Soon she crept out past the last line of buildings—built almost like a fortification, with windowless walls in a ring.

Here she *finally* got her first up-close look at the shroud: a shifting, seething wall of darkness. It was blacker than common night; night didn't swallow light. And night didn't feel like it was looking *back*. Her nerves failed her, and she didn't dare walk all the way up to the shroud. Instead she hovered near the last line of buildings, staring at it.

She hadn't expected it to *shift* like that. Turbulent. Undulating. Yet because of the lack of color, it was impossible to distinguish details. That gave it the appearance of something much farther away. An impossible visual.

"Do you ever get used to it?" she asked softly.

"You grow accustomed to it," he said. "Like a persistent noise. In the same way, you occasionally notice it anew—and suddenly it's alien again. Terrifying again. You have to get used to it all over. It's almost like making friends with someone who keeps changing personalities. One who stares at you in a way that makes you think they're eventually going to try to kill you . . ."

She ripped her gaze away from the shroud, instead looking along the buildings here. Whitewash covered the bricks of many portions—a plainly deliberate design choice, a wall of white to ward off the wall of darkness. And on many of those whitewashed portions were paintings. Large murals painted with the ink of a nightmare painter—monochromatic, but incredibly detailed in contrast and subtlety of shade.

"What are those?" she asked.

"Painters put them up when they feel like it," he said. "One section per painter."

"Where's yours?"

He shook his head. He didn't have one then? Perhaps no one would be impressed by another painting of bamboo.

They started their patrol, walking back from the shroud through the nearer rings of the city streets. Despite what she'd said earlier, he hadn't made her spend the last week *only* on bamboo. They'd talked about patrolling and about protocol for painters. So she understood what it was he did at night—how he watched for nightmare signs.

He still spotted the first sign before she did. "There," he said, pointing ahead. To the corner of a wall by the street, about five feet up in the air. A smoking black spot marked the bricks there.

That high? She'd been watching the ground. They approached to find black smoke steaming off what appeared to be black tar—a piece of the shroud—covering a hand-size section of the corner. A sign that a nightmare had passed this way recently, brushing the building and leaving a trail.

"How did you spot that?" she hissed.

"Practice," he said, "and luck."

The less you have of the first, the more you need the second.

Though he'd taught her that the next step was to follow the trail, looking for other marks, he continued studying this one. Then he peered down the nearby alleyway.

"What?" she asked.

"This is a blatant mark," he said. "Right on the street, obvious and bigger than most. Feels like another painter should have spotted this. Yet I can see the next mark on that fire escape right inside the alley. No painter."

"So no one's noticed this yet," she said. "We're first. What's the problem?"

"No real problem," he said. "It's just that I had a horrifying thought. The foreman thinks I'm a slacker."

"A what?"

"He thinks I haven't been doing my job for months now, starting long before you arrived. That's why he put me on suspension; me claiming I saw a stable nightmare was the final stroke in the painting he'd made of me in his head. Point is, he believes I've been slacking off, yet no one else ever reported any problems with this region . . ." He looked to Yumi, perhaps seeing her confusion.

"I'm worried," Painter explained, "that the foreman *didn't* replace me on this beat after suspending me. We've been short-staffed, and from his perspective, this beat is a quiet one. I'm worried he assumed other painters were covering the region, or that it's a section nightmares don't often visit, which allowed me to supposedly goof off instead of doing my job."

"And if he *didn't* assign a replacement . . ."

"That would explain why the stable nightmare was never spotted," Painter said. "Why it could spend weeks prowling the city and never be caught. Most nightmare painters patrol and watch for signs only near the rim of the city, because nightmares have to pass through there to get farther inward. If this nightmare always entered through my section of the perimeter, it could move through the entire city unchallenged."

A disturbing thought indeed. He waved her along with him into the alley, though she couldn't see the second sign he'd spotted. As they walked, she whispered to him carefully, "Painter? Why is it that the foreman assumed you haven't been doing your job? Why is everyone so ready to assume you were lying?"

Painter glanced down. And her instinct was to reprimand him, to *insist* that he explain himself *immediately*. His reaction was an obvious sign of guilt.

Yet had that ever worked on him as well as it had on her, when Liyun had treated her that way?

Had it ever *truly* worked on her? Demands, guilt, verbal punishment? She remembered days of exhaustion when all she'd wanted was a kind word, a teardrop's worth of empathy.

Choice. She had a *choice*.

You don't have to be like her, Yumi thought. *You really don't.*

Such a novel idea, and so much harder to do than she would ever have assumed. Still, Yumi forced out the words. The ones akin to those she always wished she could have heard.

"It's all right," she whispered. "I know you're trying. That's what matters."

Pay attention. At times, *this* is what heroism looks like.

Painter glanced at her, then let out a long breath. "Thanks," he whispered. "But you're right about me. It's hard sometimes, you know? Keeping on doing the same thing every day, feeling like you're getting nowhere?"

He pointed at a fire escape—a metal lattice that ran up alongside a building. She squinted, and barely made out a trail of smoke coming off one of the metal corners on the second story. They started upward.

"In school," he whispered to her, "the teachers always talked about the *importance* of our job. They'd preach about the meaning of art, about theory. They said painting was about passion and the whims of creativity. They teach us we're supposed to see the *shape* of the nightmare, and paint that.

"Then you get into the real world, and find that it's hard to be creative like that every moment. You realize they didn't teach you important things, like how to work when you *don't* feel passion, or when the whims of creativity aren't striking you. What then? What good is theory when you need to feed yourself?

"In the real world, you realize you can do your job by making the same thing again and again. Bamboo captures nightmares just fine. Whatever they say. All of those high-minded aspirations from school fade before the truth, Yumi, that sometimes . . . it's just a job."

They stopped on the landing. She said nothing, though it was hard for her. Merely nodded for him to continue.

"So I got into a bit of a rut," he said. "Yeah, guess I can say it. I only did bamboo, day in and day out. Foreman Sukishi didn't like that. He never liked me. I wasn't . . . well regarded in school, as I told you. So he's thought the worst of me. And he always assumed I was doing bamboo because I wasn't actually finding nightmares."

They reached the second story of the fire escape, near the sign of the nightmare. And as he looked toward her again, Yumi realized that she understood. She'd made different choices, putting perhaps *too much* of herself into her work instead of backing off like he had. Still, she could legitimately see how doing as he had wasn't laziness; it was something more personal, and far more relatable.

"It's really hard to be a great painter," he whispered as they knelt beside the nightmare sign. "But it's (lowly) easy to be a fine one. Regardless of what the foreman thinks though, I did my job—and I didn't let anyone get hurt. I would never allow that. I . . . I might not be some warrior, like you wanted. I'm not the person *anyone* wanted. But I'm trying."

She nodded to him and put her hand toward his shoulder for comfort, though she didn't dare touch him.

"Get a good look," Painter said, pointing to the smoke wafting from the corner where two small metal beams met. "The more of these you see, the easier it will be for you to pick out others when you're patrolling."

She leaned in close to inspect the metal—and the black coating. It looked like blood, in a way. Blood that evaporated.

"Why don't they leave trails on the ground?" she said. "Like footprints?"

"Once in a while you'll see a footprint," he said. "But not very often. We've never been able to figure it out."

Curious. It seemed likely the nightmare had left this sign when it had brushed the corner while walking up the steps. "Maybe it has to happen accidentally," she whispered. "Like when I went through that wall . . ."

Painter nodded, thoughtful. Then he pointed toward the top of the lattice, where another wisp of smoke was clinging to a bar near a window, all of it highlighted by the reflections of hion lines close above.

"Painter," she whispered, "are they actually dangerous?"

"Of course they are."

"But if the stable one has been free for weeks . . . why hasn't it killed anyone?"

He didn't answer, just stared upward at that window.

"Maybe what you know is wrong," she said. "I thought I understood my life, but it turns out I've been profoundly lied to. Is it possible the same is true for you?"

"No. I've seen pictures of cities destroyed by these things."

"How could one creature, even a nightmare, destroy a city?"

"They're hard to stop when stable," he said. "And they call to others. One reaches stability, and then others follow." He paused. "We think."

"You think?"

"The most recent city this happened to was decades ago, and the few survivors couldn't explain much. Dozens of nightmares rampaging." He looked at her. "But I promise they're dangerous. I've personally seen a child bleed after being attacked by one of these things. Maybe I don't have all the answers, maybe there are holes in our understanding, but I know they're a threat."

She nodded to him, took a deep breath, and started to climb up to see what was in that window.

Painter, however, waved for her to halt. "My turn to be the ghost," he said. "Have the bell ready in case. It's wound—all you need to do is flip the switch, and the ringing should carry far enough to reach the nearby sections."

She wanted to argue, but his point was valid. She shouldn't risk herself if he could potentially sneak up on the nightmare unseen. He'd let her know if they'd found the stable one, or if they needed to keep searching.

Painter moved silently up the last two stories, then peered in through a window at the top. Yumi waited, anxious, clutching the bell in one hand and the strap of her large canvas bag in the other—barely conscious that by pulling it tight like that, it was cutting into her shoulder. She didn't dare think, and instead focused on her breathing, in and out.

In and out. In and out.

Painter returned, shaking his head. "There's a nightmare in there, but it's not ours. We can move on."

He started down the steps, but Yumi remained in place, looking up. "What happens," she whispered, "if we don't stop it?"

"It could become stable," Painter admitted, halfway to the next level. "It takes many visits."

"You've been off your patrol," Yumi said, "for over two weeks now." Twenty-seven days. "And there might not be a replacement doing your job. What good does it do for us to hunt this stable nightmare if we just allow a host of others to feed and become real, step by step, while we do nothing?"

"This nightmare might stray into other regions on future nights. It will eventually get caught."

"And if it doesn't? I could stop it now."

"Too dangerous," he said.

"How? If it's not stable, it can't hurt me. Right?"

He stopped next to her. "They feed on people, Yumi. Our dreams, yes. Also on our thoughts, our minds. Besides, it's possible it has some stability. You can't always tell by its appearance."

She met his eyes, then started climbing the steps. She had trained for weeks. If not for this, then why?

Painter groaned behind her, then followed her up. She crept to the window, steeled herself, then looked in. An elderly woman lay on a bed there, frail. The light shining in through the window formed a square that framed her body, the shadow at its edge falling across her face. The voluminous bed seemed to have swallowed her.

The nightmare perched on the headboard. Yumi's breath caught. She'd imagined something humanlike. A shadow of a person. This was more arachnoid, with legs made of twisting smoke that clawed down around the old woman like a cage. It was (lowly) big. Large as the largest of the great hawks that hunted the skies. With those leglike tendrils stretched out fully, it would easily be fifteen feet across.

Yumi froze, a powerful anxiety seizing her in its grip. She wanted to bolt, to scramble down the steps, to run until her strength gave out. But she couldn't move.

Something buried deep inside her recognized that monstrous figure. And that piece of her was *terrified*. A primal instinct told her that you *did not mess* with a creature that saw humans as prey.

"Right," Painter whispered. "Carefully remove your supplies and think calm thoughts, like I told you. It will focus on its victim, assuming you don't get too afraid."

"How do I—"

"Meditate, Yumi. And get your supplies out."

You couldn't meditate *and* pull out supplies. That wasn't the way it worked, at least not for her.

She remained still and tried breathing exercises. That seemed to help.

"As long as you don't make sudden motions or speak too loudly," Painter said, "it won't be drawn to you. With luck, you can get the painting going without it ever disengaging its victim. You can banish it quietly, and that poor woman doesn't even need to know what happened."

Yumi didn't move.

"Yumi?" Painter said. Then a little louder, "*Yumi.*"

The nightmare shifted, then turned what *might* have been a head in their direction, with a face that dripped liquid darkness toward the ground. There were no eyes . . .

Or were those tiny white spots eyes? Like pinpricks swirling scratchily into infinity. The thing quested out with four of its many legs, stretching them across the room toward the window.

It had *seen* them.

No . . . it had *heard* Painter.

"Wait," Painter said, backing up. "Wait, it's pointing toward *me*. Did it (lowly) see me?"

Yumi finally found her strength. She looked down, frantic, and dug into her bag for the jar of ink. With trembling fingers, she tried to unscrew the lid—but found it fastened tight, as if bolted in place.

"You can *hear* me?" Painter said louder, stepping forward.

The nightmare paused and withdrew its legs. Then it balanced its bulky body in an impossible posture on only two of them as all the rest stretched again toward the window—slowly, carefully elongating—as if the night itself were reaching to swallow Painter.

"You do see me," Painter said. "I guess if Design can do it, it's not so surprising that . . ." His voice drifted off, then he made a strained sound, prompting Yumi to look.

To find him beginning to disintegrate.

Painter had gone rigid, his eyes wide, as parts of him became smoky and indistinct—his form *fuzzing* toward the nightmare. His essence twisted, coalescing into twin vortices of smoke like miniature tornadoes. One blue. One magenta.

Hion. His *soul* was becoming hion. And the nightmare—spreading its many legs around the window and drawing its center bulk toward Painter, pinprick white eyes facing his direction—was *feeding* on that energy.

Yumi screamed.

He'd told her not to do that. Some weaker nightmares did react to sudden sounds, but a painter's job wasn't merely to frighten them away—it was to deal with them so they didn't assault someone else. Still, a loud noise could disorient and frighten off a nightmare, and was a last resort for a painter who was out of supplies or otherwise indisposed. Not that this was her line of thinking.

Her line of thinking amounted to: "*AAAAAAAAAAAAAAHHHH!*"

There are things a classroom can't teach. For those, you need a good scoop of field experience plopped right on your plate, glistening like grease. Everyone at least *feels* like screaming their first time.

In this case, the nightmare drew back, its legs curling in. Then it darted away, fleeing through the opposite wall—leaving Painter to shake himself, his form snapping into place.

"That," he said (lowly), "was unexpected. It could feed on me like it does a sleeping person."

"How can you be so calm!" Yumi said, frantic.

"I'm probably just numb," he said. "Thank you for frightening it off."

"P-painter?" a voice said from within the room. The elderly woman had sat up and seemed disoriented.

"Tell her you're simply checking on her," Painter advised. "And you got startled by something. Nobody wants to *know* they've been fed on. It . . . is better this way."

Feeling overwhelmed, Yumi did as he suggested. Then, blushing deeply, she grabbed at her bag. Her body was still electric, pumped full of every frenzied cocktail it could make. She felt like she should be doing something, even if it was more screaming.

Fortunately, Painter was calm, as if the incident was over. He wasn't looking in the room. What if the thing returned?

Yumi's shameful failure made her want to scrunch up and vanish. Had she really been thinking of *him* as a coward earlier?

"That could have gone worse," he said.

"What?" she said, shocked.

"Everyone has trouble their first few times," he said, turning to her and smiling. "Don't fret. I couldn't sleep for days after my first field encounter—and I was shadowing two experienced painters. I think you did fine."

"I did *nothing*."

"Which is better than running," he said, then frowned. "Though I suppose *that* is going to be a problem . . ."

It took her a moment to realize what he was indicating. He'd moved to the railing and was pointing below. Two figures had entered the alleyway, worried, to check on the scream they'd heard.

Akane and Tojin.

Chapter 26

PAINTER TRIED to calculate whether there was a way to escape without Yumi being seen—but it was too late. Tojin was already pointing, and Akane called up. Yumi, looking sheepish, stepped to the railing of the fire escape landing.

Yeah, he'd worried about being seen by the wrong painters. He'd hoped that Tojin and Akane would find Yumi only *after* she had accomplished their goal and proven the existence of the stable nightmare. How would he explain any of this?

Akane came scrambling up the steps, Tojin in tow. "Yumi?" she demanded, taking in the painter's bag Yumi was holding. "What are you . . ." Akane trailed off as she saw the old woman through the window. "Sorry!" she said. "Um, merely some routine training of a new recruit! Please pay us no mind." Akane seized Yumi by the arm and towed her down the steps, past a befuddled Tojin.

Seriously, where did they find clothes that fit him? Did they just stitch two regular shirts together? Painter sighed, following the group. Yumi looked back at him, her eyes wide, panicked. He shrugged, as he had no idea what to say. Worse, his head was starting to pound from that encounter. Who knew that a ghost could get a headache?

"What (lowly) are you *doing*?" Akane repeated at Yumi as they reached the street. "You haven't been to training! You aren't authorized to be out here!"

Yumi looked at the ground.

"She's trying to cover for him," Tojin said. "Nikaro is on 'personal leave.' I'll bet he's been goofing off, not doing his rounds. It's like . . . before, Akane." He walked over and met Yumi's eyes, giving her an encouraging smile. "You're trying to help out. Do your brother's job, eh? Because you know it needs to be done, even if he's too much a coward to do it himself?"

"Oh, *Yumi*," Akane said, one hand to her forehead. "That's sweet of you to try, but girl, you *can't* just go out and cover a painter's shift. It's not like Nikaro works at an assembly line."

"Painter's not a coward," Yumi said softly. She looked up. "And I'm not completely without training. He showed me a few things."

Painter stifled a groan. She probably thought that would help, but it wouldn't. They'd think him reckless for teaching her anything. And maybe he was.

Akane locked arms with Yumi and towed her away, more by force of personality than force of arm. "Tojin," she said, "see if Ito and his team can cover for us tonight. I think we need to stage an intervention."

"Sure thing," Tojin said, jogging off.

Painter trailed behind the two of them as Akane steered Yumi—who was visibly shaken—toward the old familiar noodle house. And . . . Painter was surprised by how much at peace he felt with what was coming. He'd been dreading it, deep down. The truth had been burning at him like a fire that refused to go out no matter how much water he dumped on it.

Yumi was going to find out what happened to him in school. And . . . well, the fact that it was coming was actually a *relief*.

As they walked, Yumi choked out the story of what she'd seen. Which was good. It meant that Akane would double-check on that elderly woman—probably post a watcher from among the swing-shift painters— to make sure that when the thing inevitably returned, it would get painted out of existence.

The sole loser tonight was Painter. And . . . well, he'd really lost months ago, if not years ago. As they reached the noodle house, he realized that any hope he'd had of impressing Akane or reconciling with the others was long dead and gone. They thought that in his laziness, he'd sent his little sister to go out untrained and potentially get herself hurt.

It was over. He didn't have to worry about his former friends anymore. There was a freedom in watching that door shut, entirely, forever.

Sure, it *hurt*. Like acupuncture gone wrong, all over his body, spiking him through the nerves and into his heart.

At least it was over. At least he knew.

Akane got Yumi seated and ordered her some warm broth to sip. The others arrived soon after. Tojin with arms exposed. Izzy in white and Masaka in black. They settled around Yumi in their usual places, and Painter took a seat at a nearby unoccupied table, gazing at Yumi as she came out of her shell. Food, warmth, and friendship soon soothed away the nerves of her first nightmare encounter. The others knew what that felt like. It was why they'd been willing to trade shifts to come talk to her.

He glanced at Design as she emerged from the kitchen, then returned to watching Yumi. She had such a reserved smile. Sure, there was something to be said for a smile that was given away freely—but he preferred Yumi's. Revealed only when truly earned, her smile had a unique value. A currency backed by the irresistible power of her soul.

Design sauntered up to him, then huffed. "I'm supposed to act jealous," she said, "that you barely look at me anymore. Maybe these curves are faulty. The math could be off. Is that a thing that happens with mortals?"

"You're as perfect as ever, Design," he said. "I'm just having an . . . unusual few weeks."

She settled in a chair beside his. "I'm not truly jealous," she noted. "I'm kind of a god, to some people at least. Envy would be unbefitting of me. But when he gave me this form, Hoid said I was supposed to watch how humans interacted. How they paired off."

"Why give you *that* instruction?" Painter asked.

"I have some wildly inaccurate ideas about the ways humans form bonds," she said. "It's endearing and amusing."

He looked at her; she grinned back. And he wondered: was she actually some bizarre inhuman thing like she claimed? He would have scoffed at the idea, except for . . . well, everything lately.

Design nodded toward Yumi. "Why do you like her?"

"I don't. We're forced to work together."

"Nikaro. Do you want to try that again, and make it sound persuasive or something? Because I've only had eyes for a few years, and even *I* can see straight through you."

He leaned down, crossing his arms on the table and resting his head on them. He didn't argue. What was the point?

"Can't you feel it?" he whispered.

"What?"

"The *heat*," he said. "It radiates from Yumi, like from the sun on her world."

Design looked closely at him, narrowing her eyes. "Are you all right? She's not on fire. You might be hallucinating."

"It's a metaphor, Design," he said. "Yumi's *warm* because she's *intense*. She has given everything she has to become the best at what she does. Stacking rocks, an activity so bizarre it makes her *more* fascinating. Because there's nobody else like her."

"Wait," Design said. "Weren't you complaining the other day, down here, about how intense she is?"

"Yeah." He smiled.

"You can't like it and hate it all at once."

"Your friend is right," he said. "You do have some inaccurate ideas about mortals."

"It's endearing and amusing."

He basked in that heat one last time. "I love that Yumi understands. She's been there. She's one of the only people I've met who knows how it feels to give yourself to art . . ."

"That sounds like a terrible reason for liking someone," Design said.

"It's the way we humans do things."

"A stupid way," Design said.

"How would you do it?"

"With a formula," she said. "Find complementary sets of attributes that fit into a proper matrix."

He shook his head, smiling. "I wish there were a formula, Design. If there were, I could fix this."

She cocked her head. ". . . This?"

He nodded toward the table, to where Akane had put her arm around

Yumi's shoulders. "Yumi, dear," Akane said, "we need to have a talk about your brother. And the things he's done."

"We know you look up to him," Tojin said. "We don't want to interfere . . ."

"I do," Izzy said. "I *absolutely* want to interfere. You have to know. Your brother is a liar."

Painter stood up, feeling strange that the motion didn't push back the chair—he instead simply passed through it. He gave Design a smile.

It had been nice, these last few days. But he would find it liberating to be done. To know the door was closed. Not only with his old friends. But with Yumi.

That's a lie, the honest part of him thought. *This is ripping you apart.*

No more than he deserved though. He trailed off, enjoying the extended leash Design had given him, and went wandering through the night.

. . . know he sometimes tells untruths," Yumi said to the group. "I've heard him speak them. I think they're mostly just to avoid hurting people's feelings. He's more reliable than he seems."

The others shared glances. Yumi didn't know what to make of their behavior. Tojin wouldn't meet her eyes, looking like he wanted to be anywhere but here. Akane kept her arm on Yumi's shoulders, as if to give her support.

It was Izzy who started explaining first. Yumi had mostly taken the yellow-haired woman for frivolous, but now her voice was dead serious.

"Yumi," she said, "do you know what the Dreamwatch are?"

"Sure," Yumi replied. "They deal with stable nightmares."

"They're the elite painters," Tojin said, hands clasped tightly before him, as if he were trying to squeeze juice from the air. "The best of the best. The finest artists; the most respected of our kind. Every painter dreams of joining them."

"They're the actual warriors," Akane said. "The rest of us, we're like . . . the house dress you wear at home, while they're the ball gown. Understand?"

"That makes no sense," Masaka said.

"I understand," Yumi said. "But why does this matter?"

"Your brother," Izzy said. "He wanted to be in the Dreamwatch. Badly. Too badly."

Yumi cocked her head.

"He lied," Izzy said. "Back in school, he told us he'd gotten in. Tryouts were a year into our two years of training. He told us he'd been selected—and he managed to convince our professors somehow, although they should have known who got in and who didn't. Nikaro left class half the day to 'train' with the Dreamwatch."

"We were going to be his crew," Tojin said softly. "Each member of the Dreamwatch gets a team, called companions. Nikaro promised us that we'd be his. It . . . would have changed a lot. Not just money. But . . . I mean, I told my family."

"We all did," Akane said, squeezing Yumi's shoulder.

"I'm extremely confused," Yumi confessed.

"One year into our training," Izzy said, "Painter tried out for the Dreamwatch and told us he'd been accepted. He spent the entire next year *pretending* to go train with them, giving us promises, making us hope. Then . . . at the end of the year . . ."

"We found out," Masaka whispered, "that he'd been lying the entire time. He *hadn't* been going to special classes. He'd been going to the library and just . . . sitting there. Not even reading or studying. Just sitting. Staring at the wall."

"A whole *year*," Tojin said, wringing his hands.

"That (lowly) man," Izzy said, punching the chair with a clenched fist. "Sitting in the *library*. He shouldn't have graduated at all. Unfortunately, they needed painters, and he was capable."

"A capable *liar* at least," Tojin said. "Should have sent him to the law school after an extended con like that."

Yumi felt her stomach wrench. She . . . thought she was following this. But it didn't make sense. "Why would he just sit there? Maybe he made it into the Dreamwatch, but then washed out at the end?"

"Nope!" Izzy said. "He didn't get accepted at all. He lied to us for an entire year."

"Broke our hearts," Tojin said softly. "We found him there in the library, after finally getting smart and realizing he'd never introduced us to any of the other Dreamwatch recruits. We confirmed it with the administration. He never. Got. *In*."

Yumi looked up and met each of their eyes in turn, except Tojin's—he was staring at the table, seeming concurrently angry and embarrassed.

"I was going to be famous," Izzy said.

"It's not even that," Akane said. "It's that . . . Yumi, it's hard to explain how it felt. After all that time. To find out . . ."

"I can understand what it's like," Yumi said, "to uncover profound, extended deception by someone you love. I'm so sorry he caused you that agony."

"Nikaro is unreliable, Yumi," Akane said softly. "He's done his job this last year since graduation, but . . . well, you need to know. This story he tells about the stable nightmare? It's just a way to make himself look important."

"What if it's not, though?" Yumi asked.

What if it was?

She . . . had no proof he'd ever seen such a thing.

"It's *absolutely* a lie," Izzy said. At her side, Masaka nodded firmly. "If he'd really seen a stable nightmare, it would have attacked by now. They don't skulk and hide once they've formed. They start murdering."

"It's proof," Tojin said. "He said he saw one . . . what? Two weeks ago?"

"Twenty-seven days," Yumi whispered.

"Right," Tojin said, with a nod. "Over two weeks. It would have attacked by now."

"He goes out at night, doesn't he?" Izzy said. "He tells you that he's hunting it, right? He encouraged you to take his patrol because he was *so busy* tracking a super dangerous nightmare? Well, I promise you. He's going to some café somewhere. Staring at the wall. Letting you *dream* while he just *sits there*."

The table fell silent. Yumi could practically *feel* their sense of betrayal. Their frustration, anger. Even hatred? And who could blame them?

She wanted to defend him. She couldn't find the words. They were ephemeral, like a prayer she had heard only once.

"What I don't get," she eventually said, "is why you thought he would even make it into this Dreamwatch. You said they only take the best artists, right?"

"The best of the best," Masaka whispered.

"So why would you think they'd take Nikaro?" Yumi said. "I mean, he's capable, but . . . surely the Dreamwatch wants someone who can do something more than paint bamboo or the occasional face from a few quick lines."

The others frowned, and Akane pulled back, looking at Yumi with a frown.

"Huh," Izzy said. "I assumed his family would know. Something else he lied about, I guess."

"What?" Yumi said.

"Yumi," Akane replied, "Nikaro is the single *most talented* artist I've ever met. He's amazing."

"The rest of us," Tojin said, "we came to painter school on a whim. We showed some aptitude, took a class or two, and got selected. Nikaro? He'd dedicated his *life* to getting into that school—to doing this job. He showed us things he'd done as a child. He'd been painting from the day he could hold a brush."

"I believed him," Akane said. "After seeing what he could do . . . I absolutely believed, and still do. He said he'd given everything, every day of his life, to learning how to paint so he could join the Dreamwatch. That's why we believed him. When we met him, it seemed inevitable he'd get in."

"The Dreamwatch must have seen something we didn't," Tojin said. "Still seems strange they rejected him. But who knows. Maybe he didn't even go to the audition? Wouldn't be the biggest lie he's told."

"Yeah," Izzy said, "or maybe they can just smell a liar. The Dreamwatch are about protecting people's dreams—not crushing them. Nikaro would eventually have wandered off and let someone get eaten by a nightmare because he found a neat wall to stare at."

Yumi took it all in, feeling overwhelmed. A stack of stones gone way too high, and teetering with every shift in the breeze. "Excuse me," she said. "I . . . need some time."

She fled, and they let her. Minutes later, she tore into Painter's apartment and rushed to the trunk at the foot of his futon. She tossed aside the supplies and pulled out the portfolio at the bottom. She'd promised not to open it. But what was a promise made to someone like him?

She ripped it open.

And found wonder inside.

Gorgeous paintings of startling skill. She gasped, putting a hand to her lips. Dozens and dozens of amazing pieces, incredible in their variety. Streets that seemed to come alive. People with glittering eyes, smiling from the page. Architecture that made her feel small. Then intricately detailed pictures of flowers that made her feel she was a giant.

He could somehow make the ink flow through a thousand different shades to give a *feeling* of color. An *impression* of liveliness. A *semblance* of motion. Frozen pieces of time, committed to the page, with even the distant people in the background conveying emotion with the slope of their posture and the shades of the light around them.

Here, buried at the bottom of a trunk, were *masterpieces*.

"I knew it would go poorly," Painter's voice said from behind.

Yumi jumped, spinning to find him standing in the doorway. She blushed, caught right in the act, but he didn't say anything about her violation of his privacy. He merely leaned against the frame of the open door, his eyes distant.

"I was going to go walk the city tonight," he said, "but then I realized where you'd come. So I thought it best to just get it over with, you know?"

"I . . ." What did she say? She didn't know how to ask someone to pass the salt. She couldn't handle *this*.

"I knew it would go poorly with the others," he repeated. "That it would blow up on me, back in school? I knew. I recognized the anger they'd feel when they found out. How my lies would ruin and break everything. I knew. Over the months, I've wondered: Is it better? Better that I *understood* what I was doing? Or would it have been better if I'd somehow done it by accident?"

"Why?" Yumi finally whispered. "Why didn't you just *tell* them that you didn't get accepted to the Dreamwatch?"

"Why, why, why . . ." He slumped against the doorframe. "I've asked that *every day*. Why didn't I just *say* something?" He looked away, out the window, his gaze vacant. "When we first met and they saw my art, it was the first time anyone had ever been *excited* by what I could do. My parents didn't want a painter. It's a low-class job. They hated that all I wanted was ink and a page . . ."

He shrugged. "I met Akane first; you know how she is. I soon had a whole group of friends, adopted right in. And they gushed over what I could do. They *cared* about it. We spent that entire first year planning. Talking about what we'd do in the Dreamwatch—me as the central soldier, them as my companions. Everything was pinned on me getting in."

He looked at her, his eyes glistening. "Then . . . I didn't make it. Not good enough. Poor style. Bad grasp of perspective. Even still, I can't see my flaws. I can't understand why. I'm so bad at art that I can't even *see* why I got rejected. It crushed me, Yumi. It *destroyed* me.

"I went to the others. I knew I needed to tell them. I *knew* it. Stupid, stupid, *stupid*! Everything would have been different if I'd simply *said it.* But I had just been ripped apart, and I saw the hope in their eyes, and I couldn't crush it. I couldn't do to them what had just been done to me. I . . . I *couldn't.*"

"So you *lied* to them? Making it worse?"

"I know!" he said, throwing his hands into the air, standing up and stalking into the room. "I thought that I'd tell them the next day. The test happened to be on Akane's birthday. Why ruin the party with bad news, I thought. So I let them *assume* I'd passed. Didn't say it, but didn't really say anything.

"After that though, there were end-of-year tests, and I didn't want to distract everyone. Then . . . it just kind of continued. I believe . . . something was truly wrong with me back then. I moved through a haze those first few weeks, my hopes lying around me with slit throats, my emotions a cloud as dark as the shroud.

"I remember genuinely thinking that maybe I could simply keep it *going.* There was a desperate edge to those thoughts, a terror that I didn't want to confront. Couldn't confront? I wasn't thinking straight, Yumi. It wasn't normal, what I did. But I just *had* to keep it going. Watching it grow. A tumor. Not on my lungs or my throat. But on my soul."

He stepped over to her and knelt beside the portfolio. He methodically, gingerly, began taking the souls of the various pictures and packing them back in.

"What about these?" she said. "You don't paint like this anymore? Why not? You don't need to be in the Dreamwatch to do art."

"You know," he said softly, "they say true artists create, even if nobody is watching? They're *truly* driven. I thought that was me. For years. Funny, eh? Me. I got to school and found an audience, then realized that it's so, *so* much more satisfying to create *for* someone.

"Shows how much of an artist I actually am. Akane and the others were my audience. I loved showing them the new pieces I made. I loved the joy, the delight, the . . . the praise too, I guess. But then I just . . . lost it all." He bowed his head, pausing as one of the souls of the pictures evaporated in his fingers. "I had friends for the first time. For a little while."

He gestured at the pictures then, pleading. So, reluctantly, she put them away.

"There's no point anymore," he said. "No point to *any* of it. No matter how much I pretend and tell myself I'm something important." He smiled at her. "I was willing to do it again to you. I jumped right into the lie. Willing to let you believe I was some hero, even though you'd inevitably find out. At least it only took you a couple weeks!"

She looked up to him, and her heart broke to see the tears on his cheeks. Phantom, ghostly tears. She reached up and hesitated right before touching him, then put a finger to the tear—wetting her finger.

He glanced away. "Well," he said, wiping his eyes, "this is who those spirits stuck you with. I wonder what got into them. Shall we . . . I don't know." He sighed, then walked toward the door. "I'll leave you alone. I can do *that* right, at least."

"Painter," she said. "*Nikaro.*"

He stopped near the door, shoulders slumping. He . . . expected a rebuke, she realized. The kind that would set even the stones ablaze. He deserved one, didn't he? She'd been warned against lies, and this was a monumental one. The biggest she'd heard of—except the one told her by the very person who had taught her to never lie.

What a mess it all was. Emotions swirled in her, like quartz in a stone cut in half. Frustration at him on one side. Agony for him on the other.

She'd tasted friendship in the others. And she realized in that moment that she would lose them too. When this was all over. She'd never see Akane or Tojin again.

"Nikaro, look at me," she said, standing up.

He turned around, and she stepped up to him, close. Dangerously close.

"Let's go out," she said softly.

". . . Out?"

"Go out." She waved her hand toward the window. "Let's *do* something. Just us. Something that doesn't involve nightmares, or spirits, or machines, or betrayals. Let's just . . . just go. For one night."

"You know what I am, Yumi," he said. "What I've done. We have to confront that. Deal with it."

"Do we?" she asked, her voice growing small. "Do we really *have to*?"

"Ignoring my problems is what got me into this situation."

"What are we ignoring?" she said. "I heard what you said. I heard what they said. I know." She met his eyes. "I *know*. We've confronted it. There. Done. Let's go out."

"But—"

"Maybe I don't want to be responsible tonight! Maybe I don't want to *have* to be the one who solves problems. Please?"

He held her eyes. Then he turned away, ashamed.

"We're going," she said anyway. She walked around him to the hallway, then held out her hand. "Come on. Tonight we're not a painter or a yoki-hijo. Tonight we're just people. I've wanted for *years* to visit the big city back home, and I was always denied. Will you deny me too, Nikaro? Would you break my heart like that?"

Finally, wonderfully, he stepped forward. "I could never," he said softly. "I guess . . . there is that carnival running to celebrate the trip to the star."

"Great. We'll go there."

"You don't know what a carnival is."

"Are you coming with me?"

He hesitated, then nodded.

"Then," she said, "I don't particularly care what it is."

Chapter 28

THERE IS something universal about a carnival. You'll find them almost everywhere. On planets where the most advanced form of power is a hitch that can hold six horses. And on planets that are literally illuminated by free-flowing lines of light in the sky. Because carnivals don't need electricity, Investiture, or other forms of power. The *people* are the energy of a carnival.

Excitement bleeds. It flows like rivers. Ask any carnie, and they'll agree that there is a frantic *current* to a carnival. Yes, it's completely fabricated. So is the electricity that powers a light bulb. Being artificial doesn't mean it isn't real—it only means it has a purpose.

It's this power of excitement that carnivals tap, feed upon, exploit. And for all that people call carnivals a scam or a con, they're nothing of the sort. We go to them to *be* exploited. That's part of the charm. While you're there—among the dizzying overload of lights, chatter, excitement, sticky ground, and thronging people—you feel that there *must* be more than enough energy to go around.

Human exhilaration is a renewable resource. And you can generate it with cheap stuffed animals and fried foods.

Painter was surprised at how busy the place was. But they'd left patrol early, and the night was young yet. People packed the carnival, heady with the knowledge that within a short time, news would come back with finality. They were not alone in the cosmere. It's an important revelation for a society, second only to realizing that the rest of us have been visiting for quite some time now but never got around to explaining. That sort of thing tends to cause a lot of unfortunate paperwork. Sometimes also panic.

It's true that Painter's planet isn't among the most cosmopolitan or relevant to the cosmere's political or economic landscape. I still recommend you visit. Trust a guy who spent a couple years there as a statue. Few can throw a party like a planet confined to an eternal night.

(In his language, by the way, they obviously didn't use the actual word "carnival." Like with everything else, these are my words to describe their world. You might be interested to know that the word they *do* use roughly translates, in your language, to "place of a million lights." Their term for the workers there? "Light keepers.")

Painter strolled alongside Yumi, trying to keep from being walked through by members of the crowd, since he found that unnerving. Yumi took in the sights, her eyes reflecting the spinning hion of rides and the twinkling rhythms of the large bulbs on the fronts of stalls—like on a runway, trying to guide a person in to land in their particular trap. Was the gaudy mess nauseating to her?

"It's wonderful," she whispered. "It's like someone broke the sun itself into a million pieces and threw it in the air like confetti. This has been here all along?"

"Well, it usually only runs on festival and rest days," he said.

"We could have come and seen it? Why don't you come *every time* it's open?"

He shrugged, enjoying her wonder.

"What are all of these?" she asked, pointing to the stalls.

"Games."

She cocked her head.

"Games?" he said. "You play them?"

"Like an instrument?"

He stopped in place, staring at her. "Your (lowly) life was so ridiculous, Yumi. You've never played a *game* before?"

She shook her head, so he waved for her to walk up to one of the stalls with a line. That way the carnie would be focused on the customers, not a random gawker. Yumi watched with fascination as people tried to knock down boxes by throwing a large ball.

"So . . ." she said at his explanation, "it's . . . a challenge? Like trying to stack a pile higher than you've ever done?"

"Yes!" he said, pointing. "Yes, that's it. Games are fun challenges."

"These people are having fun?" she asked, as a man at the front of the line cried out after getting all the boxes down but one.

"Well . . . it's fun when you win . . ." Painter said.

Someone in the next stall walked away with a large stuffed creature. Yumi watched that with even more consternation.

"So . . ." she said, "you knock the boxes down, and you get one of those beasts."

"Yes."

"And they're extremely valuable?"

"Um . . . well, no. They're pretty cheap, actually. We could go to a store and buy a dozen of them for the price of a nice pair of shoes."

"I am *so* confused."

"It's not about the prize," he said, gesturing for her to follow him as the carnies started eyeing her. "It's about *winning*. The prize is proof. A memento? To remember the day? It becomes more valuable because of the good feelings it evokes. Beyond that, people just like to have things sometimes."

"I think . . . that might make sense," she said, strolling alongside him, holding to the strap of his painter's bag over her shoulder. He'd told her to bring it because sometimes if people knew you were a painter, they treated you with deference. Might convince some carnies to look elsewhere for easy prey.

"I like my clothing," she said. "The first thing I've ever owned. I like *having* it. The dress reminds me of Akane and that day shopping."

"See?" he said.

For some reason though, she was growing morose. Was she remembering the things Akane had said about him? With a sudden desperation, he wanted her thinking about *anything* else. But before he could speak up, she smiled, then spun around, arms extended.

"Your job, Nikaro," she declared, "is to escort the yoki-hijo on her first—and likely only—trip to a carnival! You must make it an *experience!*"

"I thought you said," he told her, ducking around a couple sharing fluff candy, "we weren't painter or yoki-hijo tonight."

"Then you escort just the yoki part! The girl at a carnival for her first time! Present it to me, man from another world. Wow my primitive mind with your advanced alien technology and lights!"

"Well, fortunately," he said, stepping in front of her and gesturing to himself, "you've come to the right person. I've been visiting carnivals since I was a child, and I can eagerly introduce you to every *unique* aspect of the phenomenon."

"Excellent," she said, strolling forward, Painter walking backward directly in front of her—occasionally passing right through people. If they thought a lone painter talking to herself was odd . . . well, they thought painters were odd anyway. So who cared?

"Where do we start?" she asked.

"With the food," he said, dancing to her right and pointing to a stall with fried pop'ems. "It is the most incredible, delectable, *amazing* food you will ever eat—"

"Wow!"

"—for the first bite."

She looked at him, frowning.

"Carnival food," he said, "has this strange property. Each bite you take tastes increasingly artificial, oily, and overly sweet. Until you get done, and (lowly) wonder why you *ate* all of that. It's truly magnificent."

"You're exaggerating."

"Am I?"

Five minutes later—her fingers sticky with the remnants of powdered sugar, an empty bag of pop'ems in her hand—she looked toward him with a nauseated expression. "That was *awful*," she said.

"Isn't it?" He grinned.

"I need another."

He directed her to get some cheese powder rice puffs, as they tended to last a little longer before the gross part reared its head. Once she was happily chewing on them, he led her toward the center of the festivities.

"I'm *modestly* impressed," she said. "But you're going to have to do better than strange foods, Painter."

"Well, we also have rides."

She looked at him, then blushed. "I don't know what those are either. I'm sorry."

"They're . . ." Huh. How to explain. "Have you ever been in a bus—or a wagon I guess—that was out of control?"

"Once. It was terrifying."

"It's like that, but *fun*."

"I'm not convinced you have any idea what that word means."

He grinned. "Remember the flight on the tree?"

Her eyes went wide. "You have flying trees here?"

"Not exactly," he said. "But things sort of like that. Less magical, maybe, but also safe—so you get the exciting part without the dangerous part. But you get to *pretend* they're still dangerous, so you can be afraid. In a fun way!"

"Wonderful food that is also gross," she said. "Experiences that are at once terrifying and not. Are all of your modern wonders self-contradictory?"

"Contradiction," he said, "is the *core* of modern life." He smiled at her. And he loved the way she smiled back.

He gestured, and led her past several of the performers—a strong man lifting impossible weights. A "living statue." (Bad imitation in my estimation.) A fire-breather. Yumi appeared to legitimately love each of these.

"You have experts," she whispered while watching a performer swallow a cane four feet long, "in the *strangest* things." She tossed far too large of a tip to the man and bowed formally to him.

From there, the games. She was terrible at them. But he found it fascinating how she tried each one in the row, then settled on one—the game where you knock down the boxes—and paid the carnie for *ten* tries.

"We're going to run out of money quickly at this rate," he said, leaning against the counter as she concentrated and threw the ball, missing. "You should have picked the balloon popping game."

"That one is random," she said. "You can't win it except by accident." She narrowed her eyes, throwing another ball. It bounced off the boxes.

"And that is bad?" he asked.

"I must be presented with a challenge of skill and not fortune, Painter."

"Well then, try the coin toss," he said, as she threw again and the ball bounced free. "This one takes strength like Tojin has to win."

"No it doesn't," she said, then threw the ball and got a lucky hit, toppling all of the boxes.

"Ha!" the carnie said, leaning down. "You can take the small prize . . . but do *that* four more times, and you get the largest prize!"

"Yes," Yumi said. "I read the rules."

Then she proceeded to knock over four more stacks of boxes in a row. The carnie's jaw dropped.

"Oh, (lowly) incredible," Painter said, smacking his forehead. "It's a balancing trick, isn't it?"

"Yes," she said. "One of the boxes is weighted on the bottom in such a way as to make the entire thing seem less stable than it is. Getting that one is key." She pointed at the largest of the stuffed animals—a dragon eating a bowl of noodles. (Quite fanciful. The dragons I know prefer steak.)

"Advice," Yumi said as the carnie handed her the dragon—which was nearly taller than she was. "Don't put the weighted box in the same corner each time. It makes the pattern easy to exploit."

The carnie scratched his head, then grinned at her. "You've still got two throws left."

"Give them to the next child who visits," she said, then walked off, head held high, Painter trailing. "You're right," she said to him. "This trophy feels . . . satisfying. And soft. How do they make it so *soft*?"

"By tradition," he said, leading her to a less populated section, "you now must give it a name."

"Hm . . ."

"A *silly* name," he added.

"Why silly?"

He gestured at the giant pink dragon.

"Right," she said. Then she blushed. "I . . . don't do silliness very well, Painter."

"No problem. It's one of my more impressive features. Let's see . . . silliest name . . ." He grinned. "She shall be known as the fearsome Liyun Noodleface."

Yumi gasped. "Painter! That's irreverent."

"Perfect," he said. "Job done." Then he turned, picking out one ride in particular. The highest in the carnival—the massive Jotun Line. You don't have anything quite like it here, though on some worlds they build rides like these as wheels that slowly carry people in a lofty circle above the carnival.

In Kilahito, they'd ended up designing something that was similar, but not circular. Instead the seats went straight up along a tall steel post, then paused at the top for the best view before turning and coming down the other side. It moved slowly, with a near-constant rotation of two-person pods.

Painter gestured to it. "I might have located the best local equivalent of a flying tree."

She tipped the dragon to the side, having trouble seeing while carrying it. Her eyes widened as she saw the ride. Then, remarkably, she gave the dragon to a little girl who had been standing nearby gaping at it.

"Farewell, Liyun Noodleface," Yumi said, waving as the little girl hopped off with the giant plush over her head. At Painter's curious look, Yumi shrugged. "I think I'm a little too new to owning things to have an enormous pink dragon."

He smiled, then led her to the ride. There was a long line, but as they approached, the ride conductor spotted her—or more specifically, her painter's bag.

"Painter," he said, waving her forward. "Thank you for your service."

Everyone in line politely clapped as he ushered her into the next cab, letting her have the two-person seat to herself—which was convenient, as it left room for Painter to slide in beside her. She put the bag by her feet as their cab swung into position and inched slowly upward along the post as other cabs were unloaded and filled.

"Is that common?" she asked him. "The way they treated me because they thought I was a painter?"

"It happens now and then."

"I thought you'd said that no one cared."

"They care about being safe," he said. "They care that someone is out there doing what I do. At the same time, we make them uncomfortable.

We're a reminder that things lurk at night, feeding on their nightmares." The cab inched up to the next stop. "We're not like yoki-hijo. There are only a handful of you, but it's easy to train a nightmare painter; basically anyone who goes through the schooling can do it. You don't have to be a master to make something that will trap a nightmare."

"But you are," she said softly. "A master."

"I thought I was." He paused, then looked at her. "Would it matter to you if I was?"

She gave it some thought. Someone else probably would have responded immediately with assurances he was good enough. He liked that she didn't do that, though he found himself waiting, breathless. And not just because he didn't breathe anymore.

"It matters," she said, "that you've stopped painting. It doesn't matter that you didn't get accepted by the Dreamwatch."

"But it does," he said. "If I'd gotten accepted, my whole life would be different."

"Would it have changed who you are?"

"I suppose not," he said. "Maybe my failure is what told me who I really am. The man who would lie to his friends. Maybe it's better I didn't have those when I was younger. Fewer people to betray."

He looked toward her and found her eyes glistening, teary. "I'm so bad at this," she whispered.

"What?"

"I was supposed to be distracting you. Yet here we are again, having the same conversation."

"No, Yumi," he said (highly). "It's fine."

"It isn't though. We did everything wrong, Painter. I wasn't supposed to fixate on winning that prize—I was just supposed to throw and enjoy the company. I see that in the way others are acting down below. I . . . I don't know how to be a person, Nikaro. You have to explain to me how to have *fun.*"

"I like explaining things," he said, causing her to look at him again. "Yumi, I'm a painter. Do you remember why I said I loved it?"

"To share it," she whispered. "To see the delight of your creations with your friends . . ."

Painter gestured as they continued upward, high enough that the chaos of the carnival instead became a *pattern*. Flowing pathways, spinning rides like fanciful geometries. Lights, once garish and overwhelming, became twinkling accents to a wonderful tapestry.

Her eyes widened.

"Not quite as breathtaking as flying," he said.

"No," she whispered, "but I love it. I love not feeling afraid. I love being able to linger." She stared for a time, but then saw one of the other couples in their cab pass, coming back down the other way. Those two cuddled up close with a jacket around them.

"We can't do this right, Painter," she said. "We—"

"Yumi," he interrupted, feeling an unfamiliar emotion.

Contentment. How long had it been? Years? Even with everything else, even in their strange situation . . . being in that cab that night, with light dancing beneath them . . . was perfect.

She looked at him, cocking her head.

"Are you happy?" he asked softly. "Right now. Worries ignored. Problems forgotten. Are you *happy*?"

"Yes," she whispered.

"How long has it been?"

"I don't think I can remember a time," she said. "There are . . . vague memories. Of laughter. A home. A place where the floor was never too hot, and where someone held me. I might have just imagined all of that . . . You?"

"My birthday," he said, "first year of upper school. About a month before the test to join the Dreamwatch. The following month was awful, stressful as I tried to prepare every last moment. That day of my party though—with friends and my paintings, a place I thought I belonged . . . Masaka made me a hat."

"Was it black?"

"More like a helmet," he said, smiling. "With spikes. She said it was a birthday hat."

They stopped in place as the ride paused for the couple at the top of the pinnacle to have a moment. Painter felt warm, even though it was colder up this high. He felt as if he were wrapped in a blanket. With the best view in town. And he wasn't looking at the city.

"Maybe," Yumi said, with a smile, "it's all right if we do things the wrong way. As long as it's the *same* wrong way."

She rested her hand on the bar in front of them—right near his—as the ride brought them up into the top position. He wanted so badly to be able to hold her, but had to content himself with moving his hand an inch closer to hers—until he felt the *barest* sense of electric warmth at their touch.

It thrummed through him, like magma injected into his veins. If he'd looked closely, he would have seen two little lines—like electric sparks—connecting his skin to hers. Magenta and azure.

Together they enjoyed the silent presence of one another, drinking in the moment. It's said that everything you eat, even the air you breathe, becomes part of you. The axi that make up the matter you take in come to make up *you* instead. I, however, find that the *moments* we take into our souls as memories are far more important than what we eat.

We need those moments as surely as the air, and they linger. Potent. Yes, a person is more than their experiences, stacked up like stones. But our best moments are the foundations we use to reach for the sky.

Eventually, after what felt like a lifetime that passed too quickly, their cab reached the bottom. Yumi slipped out, settling the oversized painter's bag against her back. Wordlessly, the two of them strolled away from the carnival. Now that they'd been to the sky, the chaos at ground level seemed distorted. Like a painting seen so close-up you could no longer make out the meaning.

They trailed vaguely in the direction of Painter's apartment. The streets grew quiet—the carnival receding into their past—as they entered sections of the city that acknowledged the late hour. Even the homes felt sleepy, the drawn drapes drooping eyelids. Only the ever-present hion lines floating above lit the way, painting cobbles and concrete.

Neither of them wanted to break the moment. Until finally Yumi stopped and dug into the painter's bag. She pulled out the smaller sketchpad and knelt, taking out a small paintbrush and a jar of ink.

"Yumi?" he asked, leaning down.

She held up a finger to still him, then unscrewed the ink jar—twisting it the correct way this time—and dipped her brush. Then she proceeded to paint a picture of what they'd just experienced. A view in the first person, looking out at the landscape below. In front of that, their hands on the bar of the ride's cab. Except in this, their hands overlapped.

It wasn't a very good painting.

Considering the experience of the one responsible, that won't surprise you. But for a person who'd first picked up a brush twenty-three days earlier, it was quite remarkable—in the same way that the drawing of one eight-year-old might be better than that of another.

Regardless, here's the thing: art doesn't need to be good to be valuable. I've heard it said that art is the one truly useless creation—intended for no mechanical purpose. Valued only because of the perception of the people who view it.

The thing is, *everything* is useless, intrinsically. Nothing has value unless we *grant* it that value. Any object can be worth whatever we decide it to be worth.

And to these two, Yumi's painting was *priceless*.

"I realized something earlier," she said. "When we were talking about owning things. I realized . . . I don't own anything. And never will . . ."

"The clothing—"

"Will stay behind, Nikaro," she said softly. "When this is all over."

Right. He hadn't considered that. Once . . . whatever had happened to them was through . . . once the spirits decided to end the Connection . . .

Well, Yumi would wake up one day in her body. And he in his. On separate planets.

She stood up holding the painting, letting it air-dry. Her eyes large, like pools of ink awaiting a brush. She smiled again, a different smile. Not joyful. Melancholic.

"This," she said to him, "is for you. To remember me when I am gone. What did you call it?"

"A memento," he whispered. "To remember the day."

"Valuable because of the good feelings it evokes," she whispered, then carefully folded the dried painting and tucked it into the inside pocket of her jacket. "If we wake up tomorrow and it's all over, you'll have this. So you don't forget me."

"I could *never*. Yumi, maybe we could . . ."

What? Travel the space between planets? Even if the government allowed a couple of youths to do something like that—which was highly unlikely—she was still a yoki-hijo. One of only fourteen on her whole world.

She couldn't have a life like he had briefly let himself dream she could.

"I want you to know," she told him, "that *I* don't think you're a liar."

"I literally did lie though," he said. "It's a fact."

"Why did you do it?"

"Because . . . I was too weak to tell the truth?"

"Because," she said pointedly, "you didn't want to hurt the people you loved."

"I lied to you."

"Again," she said, "because you wanted so *desperately* to be the thing I needed. You wanted to help me, Painter. And yes, maybe you wanted to pretend to be someone great. That's not the action of a liar, but a dreamer." She nodded sharply. "I was taught that a liar is someone who takes advantage of others to get gain. That's *not* you. It's never been you."

She leaned closer to him, as close as they could get without touching. "I don't blame you, Nikaro. Maybe stop blaming yourself. You see, I've learned one thing from your world, more than any other."

"Which . . . is?"

"Answers," she said, "are not simple. They never were."

He smiled back, then closed his eyes, taking a deep breath. It was strange how much of a difference those words meant. That someone didn't judge him. That she knew exactly what he'd done, in all its horrors, and . . . didn't care? Didn't blame?

Perhaps he should have been strong enough to come to a similar conclusion on his own. Perhaps he should have been a lot of things he wasn't. But in this case, having someone say it—someone who *mattered* . . .

It was like a painting he could share. He opened his eyes . . .

To find Yumi stumbling backward, eyes wide, lips frozen in a mask of terror. He spun to see something lurking from the alley behind them: a nightmare of jagged blackness, fully eleven feet tall, with claws that sliced the wall in large gouges. Eyes like pits of white, and a mouth with actual teeth.

The nightmare. It was fully stable now.

It had, inexplicably, come *looking* for them.

Chapter 29

T WAS Yumi's second time seeing a nightmare.

The other was to this one as a puppy was to a wolf. The stable nightmare reared on two lupine legs, powerful and somehow more *real* than the previous one she'd seen. Its darkness had coalesced, hardened, its skin spines, and those eyes—voids of anger. It towered over them, and when it stepped the nails on its feet tore gouges in the pavement.

"Run," Painter said. "Yumi, *RUN!*"

His voice sliced through her terror, and she recovered enough to turn and dash away, clinging to her painter's bag—not because it would be helpful, but because she needed *something* to hold on to.

The nightmare gave chase. Silent save for what sounded like metal on stone. Painter ran out in front of her, looking as frantic as she felt—she thought he was leaving her, but no. He was *leading* her. He waved as he dashed for an alley just ahead of her. She followed him in, nearly tripping at the hard left turn.

The nightmare beast, far more bulky, responded less quickly. It skidded past, then had to heave itself back after them. Yumi—against her better interests—glanced behind her as she ran, and saw it darkening the mouth of the alley. It reached in with two enormous hands, one against each wall, raking the stone and cracking a window. Then it fell to all fours and began charging again.

"The bell!" Painter shouted as they burst out the other end of the alley. "Ring the bell!"

They crossed a street, entering a wide open place with smooth stone ground that held sections full of wood chips and strange erections of metal and wood. The first time she'd seen one of these, she had thought it might be some kind of art installation—and had laughed when she was told it was a sports court and playground.

Painter led them past some of the playground equipment, perhaps thinking it would slow the beast—but the nightmare ripped through the metal, tossing a jungle gym. Hopefully the noise would attract someone. Yumi added a belated scream to the cacophony, and almost pulled the bell free—but a chunk of metal hurled by the monster clipped her, knocking her to the ground. Her bag skidded out of her hands.

A *crack* followed, then ink stained the bag, flowing from the opening.

The beast hesitated, seeing that.

"Come on," Painter said, hovering near Yumi, waving urgently.

She found her feet and turned toward the bag.

"No," he said. "Leave it."

Trusting his instincts, she ran with him across the playground.

"Head this way," he said, pointing down another alleyway. "The nightmare can see me. I'll lead it to the south. You curve around the block, then sneak up and grab the bell. Ring it. *Don't* try to confront the thing. Understand?"

She nodded, too terrified to trust her voice. If she opened her mouth, she'd scream.

Out in the playground, the thing had given the ink a wide berth, but now came for them again. Painter took a deep, wide-eyed breath—even though he was a ghost—then ran back out. He didn't wave at the thing to draw its attention; he just *ran*. The thing turned after him, and Yumi didn't wait to see the result of their chase. She did as Painter had said, running down her own alley and ducking around the rear of a building, breathing heavily.

There, she stood trembling, spine pressed to the bricks, sweating and taut—every muscle like a rope trying to haul a tree from the sky. She knew she needed to keep moving. She needed to sneak back and grab the bell.

She should move. Painter was running for his life. *Move!*

Her body refused.

It's difficult for one who hasn't experienced it to understand how powerfully the body can react to trauma like this. Seeing something so terrible come for you—*knowing* it intends to not merely harm you, but likely *feed* upon you—goes against all rational experience. You end up reaching someplace deeper than your thoughts can go, sinking to instincts hard-coded into your very essence.

Overriding those is not simply a matter of willpower. It requires training and experience. So Yumi trembled there, huffing, dazed—and had to *fight* to keep herself from running away as fast as she could. It is to her credit, not her condemnation, that she remained frozen. The only viable alternative her body would accept involved mad, uncontrollable flight.

A hand grabbed Yumi on the arm.

She bolted upright, finding a large figure standing beside her that had approached completely unseen—not because it had been particularly quiet, but because she hadn't been able to concentrate on anything other than her fear.

Hysterical, she swung her fist at it—and it grunted. Then . . . then said her name? Her eyes focused, and she saw for the first time that it was . . . Tojin?

Yes, the painter Tojin, sleeves rolled up, shaking her arm and saying her name. Again. Again. Finally she registered it, and emerged a tiny bit from her frenzy.

"I told you it sounded like her," Tojin said over his shoulder. Calm. Too calm. He *didn't know*.

Akane walked up, arms folded, painter's bag over her shoulder. "Yumi," she said. "You promised you wouldn't go out anymore. We *told* you how dangerous this was."

Technically, Yumi hadn't promised she wouldn't go back out. They'd just lectured her on it, and had assumed compliance from her contrite bows.

She wasn't in any state to argue that point. "How?" she said, her voice hoarse. "How did you find me?"

"We tailed you," Tojin said, "when you left the apartment earlier. We . . . well, *I* thought you'd go back to it."

"I trusted you had more sense than that," Akane added.

"We lost you for a while there," Tojin said. "Did you go to the carnival *specifically* to lose us?"

"Tojin . . ." Akane said, squinting in the dim light. "Tojin, look at her. She's *terrified*. Yumi, did you see another one?"

Yumi could only nod.

Tojin sighed. "This is *why* we said to not go out again. This is a duty for a painter."

Painter.

The bell.

Yumi knew, even after one experience with the nightmare, that Akane and Tojin alone wouldn't be enough to defeat it. They needed every painter in the region—hundreds, if she could find them.

And Painter, *her* Painter, was in danger.

"Bring your ink!" she said, then tore out of Tojin's grip and went scrambling back down the alleyway. She didn't see his bemused expression, nor the roll of Akane's eyes. Because of course they didn't recognize the danger. They'd done this hundreds of times. A nightmare, to them, was nothing terrifying.

Yumi reached the mouth of the alley and looked out at the torn-up playground—ghostly in the hion light. Still and empty. Several lights turned on around nearby buildings, then quickly shut off. This was painter business. Thank you for your service.

Suddenly apprehensive, Yumi crossed the playground onto the sports court, where her bag had fallen. She searched in it and found it sliced apart by claws, the bell broken and covered in ink. As she was struggling to comprehend this, something dark emerged from within a piece of fallen playground equipment. It grew to eleven feet tall, stalking up to her from behind.

Painter had eluded it. But this thing was *smart*. Dangerously crafty. Beyond that, there was a deeper problem. An issue Yumi and Painter couldn't have anticipated. This thing could *feel* Yumi's presence.

It knew where she was. Always.

This was why it hadn't rampaged. Yumi didn't know it yet, but this was what the creature had been doing all those weeks. It had been drawn to her. Had been watching her. Waiting for a chance to attack.

She felt it before she heard it. She spun and—too frightened even to scream—gasped as it rammed a clawed paw into her chest. The claws pierced her straight through, though they fuzzed right before they struck.

It would have killed almost any person, but Yumi had something this beast wanted. Power, Investiture, *soul*. Where it had needed to lap at others, here it could *guzzle*. Instead of spearing her physically, it let its blade-claws become incorporeal as they touched her—and this allowed it to draw out her essence.

Yumi felt an icy cold expanding from her core, as if her heart had been frozen—like the ice in drinks Design served—and was pumping frost through her body. Her gasp wilted, and she slumped to the ground, breathing out a cold mist.

She *felt* herself dying. Going to a place where there was no warmth, and could never *be* warmth. And . . .

And . . .

And she would *not* go without a fight.

Her emotions—the primal nerves that had been sending her into a panic all night—backed up against the wall of death. And from within her welled, like the fierce anger of a geyser, a *refusal* to be taken like this.

With a trembling hand—shaking like that of a woman a hundred years her senior—she reached to the side. She picked up a chunk of concrete torn up by the beast's passing.

Then she stacked it on top of the one beside it.

The beast hesitated. The flow of power out of her slowed.

Yumi somehow found another chunk, though she was fading now, her burst of strength giving out. It is not a light thing to have a piece of your soul forcibly consumed—trust me.

With numb fingers, she placed the stone.

The monster didn't appear frightened, but it leaned forward, no longer feeding. It stared at the stones with bone-white pits for eyes. Something in it seemed to . . . remember.

A second later a scream made it spin. Tojin had finally ambled out of the alleyway and—horrified by the sight of a fully stable nightmare—he fell backward to the ground. Akane screamed from behind him. Yes, they'd seen nightmares before, but never anything like *this*. It had an air about it, a debilitating sense of primeval danger.

The nightmare ripped away from Yumi, leaving her slumped against the ground, trembling. Her vision began to darken at the edges, her body going frigid as if she'd been left for a day in a blizzard.

She could only watch as the thing reached Tojin and Akane. These two it could kill. These two weren't even worth a *bite*. These it would rend, destroy. It raised a claw to strike Tojin, who lay terrified on the ground.

Then Painter arrived.

Her Painter. He stepped over Tojin's supine form, having rounded the street behind, looking for Yumi. He placed himself directly between the thing and Tojin and thrust his hand to the side, where a large paintbrush burst from his essence and formed as if out of silver light. He wouldn't remember creating it, and after the fact wouldn't have been able to tell you how he'd done it.

Akane had dropped her bag, breaking the ink jar, in her haste to get away. She'd tripped and fallen in the alley, and now—remembering Tojin—was trying to crawl to him in a panic. Neither of them could see Painter.

But Yumi could. Her angle was just right to look past the monster, looming on hind legs. To see the terrified Painter clutching his brush, confronting the thing. To see his shape itself begin to warp and fuzz, as it had before, crumbling like a statue whose outer layers were being scraped off by a terrible wind.

That Painter. Shaking. Breaking. Overwhelmed.

That Painter rammed his brush down into the ink spilled from Akane's bag and began to paint.

A long line on the concrete. Knob on both ends. A sprig of bamboo. The shape of the nightmare twisted for a second, then—eyes going wider, deeper, *whiter*—it surged forward at him, driving him to take a step backward.

Painter, now inches from the thing, went pale. His figure crumbling. Eyes wide. But then Tojin whimpered from below, and something steeled in Painter. He rammed his brush back down, and—with a look of consummate determination—swept it out in front of him at the monster's feet. And began to paint.

No, not just paint.

Create.

Sweeping arcs around him and Tojin, staining the ground with phantom ink. He met the monster's gaze, not even looking down as he drew with his brush.

The nightmare stepped back. And Painter *advanced*. One step after another, driving the thing back with each twist of his brush, creating an artistic masterpiece that burned away behind him as he walked. The ink wasn't real, Yumi thought. The brush should have vanished too, shouldn't it?

But no. At that moment, Yumi understood. The brush was an extension of Painter. It belonged to him. As natural as his own heart. Lying there—watching him drive the thing back by force of skill, art, and sheer *will*—Yumi realized something. She'd been right at the start of all this.

The spirits *had* sent her a hero.

The nightmare began to shrink, twisting in a horrific way, enormous claws shortening, skeleton seeming to *pop* as it constricted. Its face narrowed as it was forced to conform to Painter's vision of it, the one he painted on the concrete. Not a monster at all. Something friendly, with four paws and a wagging tail. The thing recognized this vision for it and let out a howl—fully stable enough to actually *speak*—then turned and loped away, its terrible form restoring as it broke from Painter's spell.

Defeated, embarrassed—but not destroyed—it vanished into the night.

Painter fell to his knees, overwhelmed, the paintbrush finally burning away in his fingers. Behind him, Akane reached Tojin, helping him sit up. The two of them stared out after the nightmare, baffled as to what had driven it off.

Painter looked with a wan smile toward Yumi. Then at last he seemed to notice that she wasn't moving.

"Yumi!" he said, but his voice sounded distant, like she was . . . was deep underwater . . .

She tried to reply, but her teeth only chattered together. Her body shivered and spasmed, and her vision was fading—darkness at the sides creeping in further.

"Yumi!" Painter's anxious face above her. "What's wrong?"

"So . . . cold . . ." she whispered, her breath puffing.

He knelt above her, panicked, holding up his hands.

The darkness closed in.

Painter *seized* her in an embrace.

His essence mingled with hers. His self and her self mashed into one. A shocking, intoxicating, sensual concoction.

Heat *detonated* within Yumi, a dying fire suddenly given air. It surged through her. His heat. *Their* heat. She gasped with the force of a drowning woman and went rigid.

Painter pulled back, his face streaked with sweat. She caught herself before falling to the ground again, then kept breathing in deep gasps, no longer frozen. Together they sat there, trembling, until Akane and Tojin arrived to help her stand.

Perhaps *now* they would believe.

Chapter 30

A N HOUR later they sat in the noodle shop again, Painter at his
own table nearby, watching the others in their nervous huddle. They
constantly asked Yumi if she was all right, as if the answer would change
moment to moment.

She did *seem* all right. At least she wasn't dying of the cold any longer.
The others had tried to take her to the hospital, but she'd insisted she
wanted something warm to eat. And a warm place to sit.

So they'd come here, and she was on her second bowl of broth for
the night—spiced and heated to boiling. How she could eat that without
burning herself baffled him, but then again, people from her planet had an
odd relationship with heat.

Painter felt tired. That thing had drawn something from him, and holding Yumi had done the same. Fortunately, it didn't feel like anything per-
manent. Hollow fatigue, like he hadn't gotten enough sleep. Never before
while in spirit form had he felt drowsy.

He was trying to figure out why the shop was so crowded at this hour,
beyond its usual complement of painters. But before he hit on the answer,
Tojin arrived and rushed over to the others. They were all there—Masaka
and Izzy having been called from their patrols.

"The foreman believed me," he told them. "Particularly after I showed
him what had happened to the playground. The Dreamwatch has been

summoned. There is a contingent of them in Jito; they'll be here within a few hours."

"That is wonderful," Akane said (highly). "They'll deal with it, Yumi. They'll find it."

"Sorry," Tojin said, settling in next to Akane, "for not believing you earlier."

Yumi met Painter's eyes. Mission accomplished. The stable nightmare would soon be dealt with. If that was why the spirits had paired them, then their job was done.

"We're to go three per patrol," Tojin continued, "until the thing is caught. We're also not to tell anyone."

"I hate that part," Masaka muttered. "The city's people deserve to know."

"You just relish the idea of telling them," Izzy said, poking her in the arm. "Because it's horrific."

"I *hate* horrific things," Masaka said.

"You think nightmares are cute."

"They *can* be," she said. "They can be anything."

Akane glanced at Yumi. "You all right, Yumi?"

"Yes," Yumi said softly. "Better, now that I have something warm in me."

"That was brave of you," Akane said, "to go out to try to prove that your brother wasn't a liar. But it was also *exceedingly* stupid. You realize that now, don't you?"

Yumi nodded.

"He ran, didn't he?" Izzy asked. "When he saw it weeks ago? He ran away to another city. That's why we haven't seen him lately; why he went 'on leave.'"

"No," Yumi said, fire in her eyes, her objection vigorous enough to make Painter smile through the fatigue. "I saw him earlier today. You're all wrong about him. So very wrong."

He blessed her for that, but also didn't miss how the others shared looks. She would never persuade them. That didn't hurt as much as it once had. After all, he still wasn't certain if she'd persuaded *him* or not.

These last few weeks spending time—invisibly, yes, but actual time—with his old friends had reminded him how much he'd enjoyed being with them. He acknowledged how his bitterness had poisoned his mind, like mold on a painting, ruining the true details. He'd been uncharitable in his descriptions to Yumi. Painfully so.

The truth was, these were wonderful people. He appreciated the way Akane kept them all together, like the glue of a collage. So careful never to let anyone feel left behind. He found it endearing, the way Tojin was so enthusiastic about his bodybuilding but also shy about it. Painter even liked how he could never figure out if Masaka was genuinely interested in the macabre, or somehow just oblivious.

He even appreciated Izzy and her . . . Izzy-ness. They might not be his friends anymore. But he could be *their* friend. In secret. If he let go of that awful bitterness.

Design came bustling over, hands on her hips. "I'm going to find out," she said to them, "what you're hiding from me."

"Sorry, Design," Akane said sweetly. "Painter business. It's the rules."

"Rules don't apply to me," Design said. "I'm not a person. Or truly alive." She shook her head. "Well, sorry about the crowd. Though it *is* to be expected."

"Expected?" Tojin asked.

"Because of the broadcast?" Design said, cocking her head. "The landing? The spaceship? Have you forgotten that your people are about to make *first contact*? Officially at least. Noodle shop owners with nice butts don't count, apparently."

The landing.

That was *tonight*?

Painter turned, seeing the crowd with new eyes. People chattered with an air of excitement, waiting for Design to turn on the restaurant's hion viewer—which she did shortly after leaving their table. Painter rose and stared at the lines of light behind the glass—hung high on the wall so everyone could see. The hion began to shake, then formed into the shape of the lead explorer in his command chair—broadcast all the way from the space bus near the star.

"We've completed our orbit of the planet," the lead explorer said. "It matches the visual inspections via telescope. We get no radio signals, even this close, but our surveys indicate settlements. There are very few land masses though. It seems like these people might spend most of their lives sailing the oceans, for we see many boats."

Boats?

Yumi stepped up to Painter, her eyes wide as they watched.

"Extending our hion lines now toward the surface," the explorer said. That was what had carried them all this way—a pair of mobile hion lines connected back to their planet, capable of letting a space vessel travel like a train, constantly powered, pushed by the lines. How they strengthened the lines enough to stretch all that way was beyond Painter.

"Have you," he whispered to Yumi, "ever visited the oceans on your planet?"

"The what?" she said. "I don't know that word."

"Water," he said. "Enormous bodies of water, like the cold spring, but huge. We have a few of them here—our cities run to the edges of them." One of those oceans could take an entire *day* to cross, he'd heard, using a hion-line boat.

"Water like that would boil away," she said. "There aren't enough high grounds for more than the occasional cool spring. Unless . . . maybe it's out beyond the searing stones? In the cold wastes, up high?"

He felt a mounting worry as they watched the explorers in the cockpit guide their vessel. He listened to their observations, heard the rattling of the ship as it rode the hion lines all the way to the ground and finally touched down.

The door opened. And the camera turned, in the hands of an explorer, to show the view outside. There, curious beings were coming up to inspect the vessel. Limber, tall, with four arms, the explorers described them as having chalk-white skin. They most certainly *weren't* human.

Though you might have guessed this, Painter was stunned. Yumi wasn't from the star.

She never had been.

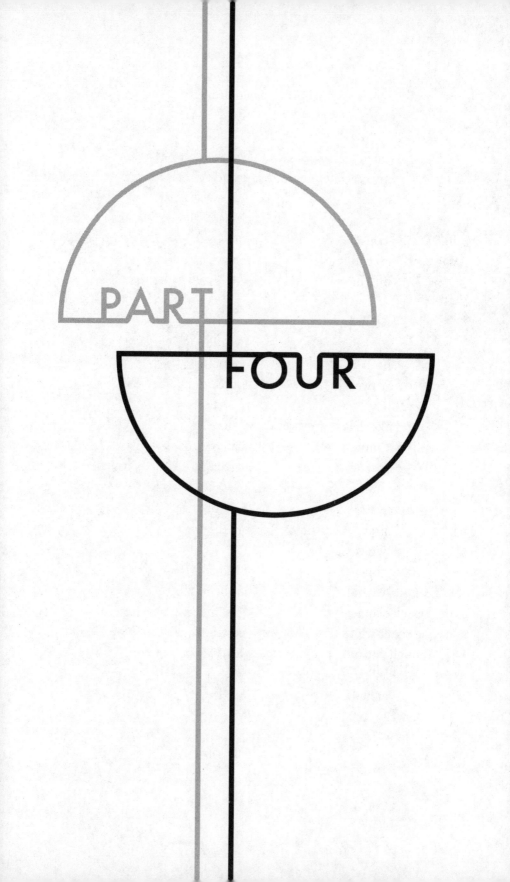

PART FOUR

Chapter 31

MAYBE IT'S time travel," Yumi said, half walking, half floating as she paced in the cold spring. Strange how she'd begun finding the cool water refreshing instead of shocking.

"Time travel?" Painter said, skeptical where he sat in the cold spring with arms out along the stones, resting back, toes peeking from the water.

"You have an advanced level of technology," she said, ticking things off on her fingers. "While we are just beginning to build machines, you have ones that can travel to the *stars*. Our languages are close. Even without the strange gift of the spirits that lets us understand one another, I can see it in the familiar way your writing looks. We are both human. Maybe we're from the *same* planet during different *times*."

"Yumi," he said, beads of water glistening on his bare chest, "this is *not* my planet. The ground is scalding, the sky is too high, and there's no shroud. Your plants *float*. I think I'd know if plants floated on my world."

"It could be the *distant* past," she said. "A lot can change over time, Painter. We should at least consider the possibility."

He frowned, but nodded. She paced back the other direction, water chill as it washed across her thighs and waist with each too-light step. Her theory frightened her. If she was right, the distance between her and Painter would change from incredible to *impossible*. Another world was daunting. Another time . . .

He met her eyes, and seemed to be thinking the same thing. Perhaps there was another possibility, and she tried to send her mind that way instead. How bizarre that she'd come to relish this time in the cold spring—the renewing water, mixed with the familiar sun and its comfortable warmth. The quiet time alone with Painter. That should have been unremarkable, with how Connected they were, but it felt like every other moment was filled with things they should be doing.

Or . . . she admitted to herself . . . maybe that sense of anxiety at other times was just her. Feeling guilty for not being of use when Painter would have preferred to simply relax.

Either way, the bath was a peaceful time for her. Hair wet against her back, the tips trailing in the water behind her, skin prickling as the top half of her dried while her legs remained in the water—which somehow felt warm by contrast. The most surreal part—the part that only struck her when she stopped to think about it—was how natural it felt.

The last few days, she'd hardly considered the fact that she was bare. Painter seemed to react the same way, no longer staring, no longer embarrassed. He merely floated comfortably, thoughtful as he gazed at the sky and the spinning flowers high above. What had once been the single most stressful moment of her entire life was now just . . . normal.

"Maybe we're still from different planets," Painter said, "but they're farther apart. Design is from somewhere else. You could be too."

"Maybe," she said, trailing her fingers in the water as she walked. "But Design said she thought that was unlikely. If you think about it, we decided on a whim that we were from two different planets."

"I was looking at the star when the strange event happened."

"Which was completely coincidental. If you'd been looking at a bowl of noodles, would that imply that I came from the land of the noodle people?"

"That's a *perfect* explanation for you." He raised a finger. "Stiff and rigid until you soak her in water."

She gave him a flat stare.

"Come on, Yumi," he said. "*How* long did you spend in the shower yesterday?"

She clasped her hands behind her back and turned away, strolling lightly on her tiptoes, buoyant in the water. "You're right about Mrs.

Shinja," she said. "She *really* gets mad about running out of hot water. Why do you suppose I like cold springs in my world and near-scalding warmth on yours?"

"Variety, I guess," Painter said. Then in a lower yet dramatic voice: "Cold noodles with ice for hot days, warm noodles with broth on cool ones. The noodle princess must be master of both realms."

She splashed a huge wave of water at him, and it was satisfying how he cringed—even though it was spirit water and flew straight through him. She smiled, then continued her strolling.

"I'm *trying*," she said, "to solve our problem. Please make an effort to pay attention."

"But we've solved it. Nightmare is dealt with."

"And if the nightmare isn't what caused the spirits to reach out to me? It could still be the machine."

Those scholars *were* suspicious. She wanted to be wrong—she wanted it all to be over now, finished as soon as the Dreamwatch did their jobs—but she was *afraid* she was right. She couldn't let go, not until she knew.

"I suppose," he said, resting back, the tips of his feet popping up out of the water again. "I guess we can solve the problem no matter if we're from different times or different planets. Nothing changes except . . ."

She slowed, then met his eyes and again saw the unspoken tragedy he acknowledged in them. Neither of them dared say the words. That they didn't *want* this to end. How crazy was it that they would rather live in limbo like this, disorienting though it was, so long as it meant they could be together?

Why couldn't she form the words? Why didn't she dare speak them? Was it because she was afraid if she acknowledged what she felt, she would somehow ruin it? Send whatever it was that was growing between them flying off, like flower petals in a thermal?

Or was it something worse? Something that terrified her more than a nightmare? The worry that maybe he didn't feel the same way. What if her assumptions when looking in his eyes were untrue? What if he *wanted* this to be finished so that he could have his life back, no longer forced to deal with the imperious demands of a yoki-hijo who didn't know how to person correctly?

She struggled to say something. But all she could think of was waking up one day alone, not knowing where he was.

It's going to end poorly, isn't it? she thought with mounting dread. *There's no way for it to work out. It can't work out, not for the yoki-hijo.*

Her life, as Liyun had always promised, was not one of joy. Her life was not her own.

Her life was service.

The two eventually climbed out of the spring to begin dressing. "How long do you think it will take," she asked him, "before my people invent bras? It's difficult to return to this time, wrap a band underneath my chest, and pretend that's good enough."

"I don't know," he said. "You'll need elastic for bras first, right?"

"How should I know?" Maybe *she* could invent them. Sketch it out, tell everyone that the spirits had shown the garment to her in a vision—which, in comparison to some of the ways she'd been forced to distort the facts recently, would be remarkably close to the truth.

They finished and then followed the attendants out to the shrine. There they found a small line of people—as per Painter's morning request. By this point, Liyun had given up on trying to bully him into doing things the proper way.

The townspeople shuffled, confused, as Painter called the first of them forward. Then, looking to Yumi for support and getting a nod in return, he started painting. He kept the art simple, like he'd done other days in the shrine, but he now had models to use—and so even these simple paintings were more skillful, more realistic. More a test of his talents, even if these weren't the powerful, dynamic paintings she hoped he'd someday return to.

She was satisfied as he became absorbed by the work. This *was* a form of meditation for him. She could say the prayers for both of them, and she did so, kneeling and whispering quietly. Like a chorus to accompany the soft sounds of brush on canvas. Music of the most personal variety.

Whatever else happened, this was an accomplishment. A brush in his hand, creating something other than bamboo.

She finished her basic prayers and moved on to meditation. Clearing her mind. Yet when she soothed away everything else, she was left with a sense of dread. None of her usual tricks—counting her breaths, repeating a phrase over and over, humming to herself—banished it. Each time she sank toward the deep waters of nothingness, she found that same sensation of doom. Impenetrable. As if it were the natural state. The color and texture of the canvas, once the paint had been washed away.

Something was still profoundly wrong. Solving the trouble with the nightmare was not nearly enough. And their time was running out. She wasn't certain how, but as she beat her mind against the dread, she knew it to be the case.

"Painter," she said, opening her eyes.

"Hmm?" he asked as a townswoman bowed to him and moved on, carrying a bemused expression and his painting of her.

"What's beyond the shroud?" Yumi asked.

"I don't think anything's beyond it," he said as the next townsperson stepped up. "It covers everything."

"Are you sure?"

"I . . . I guess I'm not. And Design wasn't *that* certain either. We learned geography in school, but it talked only about Nagadan. There are some other nations out beyond ours, smaller. Around a dozen of them, and they're always squabbling. I didn't learn much about them. Beyond those . . . well, we never actually covered that in classes."

"What if there's an *end* to the shroud?" she said, scooting closer to him, excited. "What if Design is wrong and *this* is what's beyond? You have bamboo in your land, Painter. And rice. Where does rice come from?"

"Plants with four leaves," he said. "I've seen them in fields."

"Same as ours."

"But not flying."

"So the vegetation of our lands is similar," she said. "You could merely have a . . . a strain of it that was made by the spirits to live without the heat of the ground."

"It's possible, I suppose," he said. "Maybe we could get some maps in my world? See if maybe those have holes or blank spaces that could hold your land? How big *is* Torio?"

She didn't know, although the fact that she traveled it in a loop—visiting villages all along the way—made him think it was smaller than his nation.

However, it all seemed farfetched. Two societies like theirs living side by side for centuries, never discovering one another? But . . . maybe there was one of those oceans he mentioned in the way? Or some other natural feature?

The possibility comforted her. She closed her eyes and focused on the sound of brush on paper, the occasional tapping as he dipped in the ink jar . . . She sank down and pushed through the sense of dread at last, entering a state of utter stillness. A nothingness where all time, self, and nature were one.

Then, as if placed there *deliberately* from outside, an idea struck her.

She cracked her eyes, hurled out of her meditative state to find the line of townspeople gone and Painter cleaning up his tools. The entire hour had passed just like that, which wasn't uncommon when she meditated.

That thought, that *idea*, was remarkable.

"I know what to do," she whispered, then looked at Painter. "I know something we can try!"

"Okay . . ." he said, frowning.

"We can't wait for you to get good enough at stacking. I'm sorry, Painter, but it's true. Your progress is remarkable, but we have to move faster."

"I don't understand."

"I'll show you." She reached her hand toward his—then, remembering she couldn't touch him, simply waved instead. She hopped down off the altar onto the spirit of her clogs, then waited impatiently as he tied his on. They soon emerged from the orchard, passing Chaeyung and Hwanji, who jumped to follow. Yumi felt only the smallest stab of guilt at not remaining in the shrine until she was fetched, as was proper.

They passed through the now-familiar town. It was the first time since her childhood training that she'd stayed in one place long enough to learn where everything was. One might have assumed this would make the place feel kind of like home. Yet as Yumi thought about it, the word "home" conjured images of a cluttered little room with a futon, lit by the hion lights outside. It was alien, and yet it was the place where she'd learned what she actually liked. Dramas on the viewer. Clothing that was her own. Noodle soup, light on the salt, chicken broth with a single egg and a pinch of pepper.

Here she was the yoki-hijo. There she was *Yumi*.

And because of who she was, she felt guilty at that realization. It was *exactly* what she'd feared would happen. She had grown accustomed to the delights of his world. She did not regret—could not regret—letting herself indulge. But she *would* pay for that indulgence once this was all done and she lost not only Painter, but her home, her friends, and even her newly discovered sense of self.

You cannot let yourself be happy, a part of her warned. *Because happiness is far, far too dangerous.*

Perhaps that was why she felt such an urgency to finish this before the break became too painful to endure.

As they rounded the steamwell, the air wet and misty from a recent eruption, Yumi was distracted by a farmer fiddling with his flyer—which, like a giant insect with wings outstretched to the sides, buzzed and hovered in front of him, then dropped. The farmer grabbed it before it hit the ground. Then he finally got it moving, soaring up toward the crops above.

Painter walked on past, but she hesitated, bothered. "Painter," she said, "would you ask Hwanji and Chaeyung if something is wrong with that man's flyer?"

The two women appeared embarrassed at the question. "It's nothing, Chosen," Chaeyung said.

"Chaeyung," Yumi said through Painter, "you've known me for years. You can talk to me. It's all right."

They shared a look, then Chaeyung leaned in and spoke softly. "It's the creations of those scholars," she hissed. "They don't work as well, Chosen One."

Hwanji nodded. "Far be it from us to speak poorly of such honored guests of the town. But something's wrong with their creations. That's *fact*, Chosen."

The way they talked—there was an eagerness. Not only because of the topic. They seemed excited by the idea of talking to her, now that she'd given them leave. And . . . why not? They'd been companions for years, yet they didn't chat. She'd never considered whether that would be painful for them, serving a woman they never truly got to know.

They continued on to the place of ritual, where—right outside—the machine was set up, chugging away and stacking its stones. It worked all day to draw one single spirit; but as the scholars promised, it could work all the time. It might not beat a yoki-hijo, but a hundred of them would far, *far* surpass what the women could create.

Still, Yumi folded her arms—rumpling her tobok—and glared at the machine. Painter stopped beside her and said softly, "It's not bad *just* because it's technology, Yumi."

"Conversely," she said, her eyes narrowed, "it's not *good* just because it's technology. Disliking this machine doesn't have to mean I'm against progress or the wonderful things of your world. I simply think that *this* machine in *this* situation is wrong."

He rested on the fence that encircled the place of ritual. "You're right," he said. "I'm sorry I generalized." He stepped into the place of ritual, Yumi trailing behind. "So, do I get to hear this grand idea now?"

"Pick a rock to begin a stack," she said, pointing.

He shrugged and put on the kneepads and gloves, then settled down near a pile of stones of a variety of sizes. He did a good job picking his foundational stone, then set it on the ground in a shallow nook—one that was practically invisible, but able to add stability.

He *had* learned. In fact, in the last thirty days he'd managed to learn a good portion of what it took to be a yoki-hijo. Unfortunately, perfecting that took *years*. Like the stone, all he had for now was a solid foundation.

He picked up a second rock at Yumi's urging, but before he could place it she stopped him. Then she took the soul of the rock from his hands and weighed it, tested it, *knew* it. She set it down in place, then looked at him, smiling.

"Match that," she said.

He paused, then smiled as well and set his real rock over the spirit one—moving it, twisting it—until they aligned perfectly. Again his training was invaluable. He didn't know enough to be a master, but he now had the basic training necessary to *imitate* one.

Excited, Yumi placed a third stone, then a fourth—with him matching her exactly. Together they built high. Up. Out. Into a sculpture of stone, carefully balanced, beyond anything Painter had managed on his own. At thirty stones, he looked to her with a grin on his face.

"You're not ashamed," she said, "to need help?"

"One of the first things you learn in art school," he said, "is how to imitate the styles of the great masters. It's only once you can keep up with them that you develop your own. I'm just glad I can keep up here." He met her eyes. "This is going to work, Yumi. Let's do it."

They dove into the task, and sculptures grew around them—guided by Yumi, but she let him choose the stones. Let him place the first of each stack. He started placing stones on his own, then looking to her as she adjusted her version in roughly the same position—except better.

If only I could have been trained this way, she thought, feeling as if she could see his skill increasing moment to moment. Working together, their fingers occasionally brushing.

This was *her* meditation. This was something *she* had missed. She realized that over the weeks, she'd lost this—this connection to the stones, the spirits, and even her own heart. She might have been *made* a yoki-hijo, but the art was *hers.* Or together, *theirs.*

The scholars noticed, as did the townspeople. At one point she heard a gasp, and glanced to see Liyun outside the fence, hand to her lips and *tears* in her eyes. Liyun had been looking more haggard lately, worn down, exhausted. It was encouraging to see her so happy today. It probably seemed like a miracle from the spirits to suddenly have her yoki-hijo back. Perhaps it was.

The scholars started arguing. Their machine then started stacking more quickly. They moved frantically, except for the lead one—who was holding the boxy device Yumi had seen last time. The one that let him detect a spirit.

He was staring directly at her.

He knows, she thought. *Somehow. He knows.*

Beside her, Painter had gone stiff. She first thought maybe one of their stacks—they'd done a dozen already—was about to fall. But now his eyes were on the ground, where a glowing red-and-blue teardrop was rising.

Immediately the spirit began to distort. The scholars shouted, and their machine moved even faster. The colors swirling in the spirit agitated, and it began to be stretched and pulled toward the machine.

"No," Yumi said, bowing her head. "Please. *Please.* We have summoned you, spirit. I am your yoki-hijo. Tell me. What do you need? What must we do?"

It forcibly pulled back—like a glop of liquid metal, pooling the bulk of itself near her and Painter as one end was stretched out an impossible length toward the scholars.

"Please," it whispered, the word vibrating through her. Painter's eyes went wide. He could hear it too. "Please. Freedom. *Please*."

"How?" Yumi begged. "How."

"Stop," it whispered, "the *machine*."

Then it was pulled away, gathered in by the scholars' device. They called for a supplicant to receive the boon, though the lead scholar remained where he was, hands clutching his nefarious box. He didn't look pleased or self-satisfied for having stolen her spirit. Instead he looked concerned.

Behind him, the scholars made the spirit into a pair of repelling statues for lifting a home. They were smaller than the ones Yumi had made in the past.

The machine, she thought, *keeps a piece of the spirit's soul. That's why the gifts the scholars create don't work as well.* It was collecting strength. To maintain its power. Or . . . for some other purpose?

"Yumi!" Painter cried. "You were right!"

She shook herself and tore her eyes away from the lead scholar, focusing on Painter. Right?

She'd been *right*. About the machine. About the needs of the spirits. After all that doubting, after all that uncertainty, she'd . . . been right?

She'd been *right*.

This would all end when she and Painter destroyed that machine.

Chapter 32

I'S ABSOLUTELY, most definitely, assuredly *not* time travel," Design explained to the two of them, resting her elbows on the bar.

"How do you know?" Painter asked.

"Because time travel into the past is impossible," Design said. "I can show you the math."

"Wait," Yumi said. "Time travel into the future *is* possible?"

"Um, yes, dear," Design said. "You're doing it now."

"Oh. Right."

"We can slow or speed up time relative to other places or people," Design said. "That's easier in the Spiritual Realm, where time flows like water into whatever container you provide. But you can't go *back*. Nobody, not even a Shard, can do that."

"What's a Shard?" Painter asked.

"Yeah, we're not going to get into *that*," Design said.

"Very well," Yumi replied, "but many things I assumed impossible proved to be entirely *possible* recently. So perhaps something is happening that you don't know about, Design."

The buxom woman—well, entity—sighed. "You need proof, eh? All right, let's read your aura, little girl." She ducked down and began fiddling with things under the counter.

"Read my aura?" Yumi whispered, leaning over to Painter.

"It's a carnival thing," he explained. "Izzy loves readings. You know how she's always trying to use dramas to guess what people's futures are? It's like that. Old lady sits in a room and squints at you, then tells you what kind of job you'll like. It's . . . mostly nonsense."

Design popped back up and thumped a large piece of equipment onto the bar. A black box with some kind of . . . glass portion on top? Like a viewer?

"Is this normally part of it, Painter?" Yumi asked.

"I've . . . never seen it done like this before . . ." he said as Design took Yumi's hand and put it onto the glass plate.

A customer came up for food, and Design shooed him away. When he didn't leave, she stood up tall and snapped, "What? Can't you see that I'm talking to a ghost and reading his girlfriend's spiritweb? Go sit in the storming corner until I'm ready for you."

The man frowned and trailed away. Painter, however, was shocked. Girlfriend?

"Took me longer to find this thing than I wanted," Design said. "Hidden among all his junk. Guy needs a sorting system."

(I have one. It's called my brain.)

Design moved some dials, then hooked the machine up to the bar's hion lines for power. While he waited, Painter reached over and took the spirit of Yumi's soup, pulling it in front of him. He got two bites before it evaporated. He didn't get hungry while a ghost, but he *did* miss Design's cooking.

"Okay," Design eventually said as something began to glow inside the box. "This fabrial will give a far more accurate reading of your spiritweb than I can on my own. Let's see . . ." She leaned back, frowning, then leaned forward again, studying some . . . were those words? The waving lines that appeared on a smaller plate at the side?

"Huh," Design said.

"What?" Yumi and Painter said in unison.

"The readings are going haywire," Design said, "because you're *highly* Invested. Like, *super* Invested."

Painter blinked. Then waited for more. Then looked to Yumi, who shrugged.

"Storms," Design said. "Yeah, this is like . . . Returned-level Investiture.

No, more. Elantrian-level. The device isn't built for that kind of reading—and you're screwing with the system something crazy. It's kind of fun. Oooh. I wonder if you'll explode when you die."

"What?" Yumi yelped.

"Highly unlikely," Design said. "But possible!" She grinned. "This is awesome."

"We have *no idea* what you're talking about," Painter said.

"Investiture is what souls are made out of," said Design. "Well, everything is Investiture—because matter, energy, and Investiture are the same. But souls, as you'd call them, are parts of our beings that are pure Investiture. Like . . . fire is energy. This table is matter. Souls? Investiture."

"And Yumi's spirits?"

"Likely Investiture too," Design said. "I haven't met them, so I can't say. But the nightmares are. Pure Investiture. They're probably *terrified* of you, Yumi."

"We've met several," Yumi said. "And they were very *not* afraid of me."

"Well, they should have been," Design said. "You could maybe consume them, at least screw with them in all kinds of fun ways. Investiture—raw Investiture in particular—is kinda wahoopli."

". . . Wahoopli?" Painter said.

"Word I just made up," Design said. "It means weird. Hoid says I should be more literary. He makes up words all the time. So I'm trying it out."

(I do *not* make up words. I have no idea where she was getting that part.)

"Anyway, raw Investiture," Design said, "responds to thoughts. Emotions. *Especially* the thoughts and emotions of heavily Invested beings. Painter, when you paint nightmares, it's your *thought*—your perception of them—that causes them to transform. It's not the actual painting. They can literally become anything, and because of that they have a weakness. Through concentration, you can force them to become what you envision."

"Huh," Painter said, shocked by how much sense that made to him. Considering how conversations with Design often went.

"Regardless, back to Yumi . . ." Design said, squinting—not because she needed to, but because she was picking up human mannerisms. (Which was, I can proudly say, part of the point of making her "human" in the first place.) "Yumi, have you experienced any memory loss lately?"

"I don't think so," she said. "Should I have?"

"It's difficult to read your spiritweb," Design said. "You glow like a bonfire, girl. Obscures a lot of things—but I *do* see an excision here. Some of your memories have been bled away."

Both of them again stared at her blankly.

"Everyone imprints memories in their Investiture," Design said. "It's why a Cognitive Shadow remembers everything the body did, if the body dies? Storms, you people don't know *anything*. Look, in highly Invested individuals in particular, memories get spread through your whole soul, okay? And you've lost some. They were cut out. Not many. Maybe a day's worth? Hard to see details, though the scar is right here."

"I . . . got touched by that stable nightmare," Yumi said. "It seemed to drain something from me. Maybe that was it?"

"That sounds reasonable," Design said, then clapped once, loudly. "All right, done. No more data here. I could stare all day and get nowhere. Like trying to understand one of Hoid's more obtuse jokes."

(Completely uncalled-for.)

"You," Design said, gesturing at Painter as she shoved Yumi's hand off the machine. "Your turn."

"Me?" Painter said, feeling threatened. "I'm not real! I mean, I don't have a body."

"This thing reads souls," she said, pointing.

Reluctantly—but unwilling to appear cowardly in front of Yumi—he put his hand on the machine. He wasn't sure if it was because he expected it or for some other reason, but he could touch the cool plate on the top of the device.

Design watched the vibrating lines on the side. "Ha!" she said, turning so he could see them better. "See?"

"I can't read that, Design," he said.

"You've got a normal soul's worth of Investiture," Design said. "Exactly the level we'd expect for this planet, which has no Shard in residence and where the people haven't been specifically granted extra. Shroud and Splinters of Virtuosity notwithstanding."

"Again," Painter said, keeping his hand on the device, "Shard? Splinter? Virtuosity?"

"Still not getting into it," Design said. "Regardless, I see no evidence of Connection to the past in your spiritweb. Nikaro, you—absolutely, assuredly, conclusively—have *not* been time traveling. This is definite."

"Do I have a Connection to another world?" Painter asked. "Can you read that?"

"Neither of you," she said, "have been traveling to other worlds. You're from this planet, both of you. I can see *that* easily. Though . . . Yumi has fewer Connections to other people than I'd expect. That's not related to her power; it feels more like . . ."

"Like I don't know anyone?" she whispered.

"Yeah, that!" Design said. "Never seen a person with so few Connections. You're a very private individual, I take it."

"Yes," she said, looking down.

"I wonder what that's like," Design said. "But I don't wonder it enough to try it."

"How did you see her Connections to others?" Painter said. "I thought you said you couldn't read her well."

"I could see *that*," Design said, rolling her eyes as if they were supposed to understand why. "She's Connected to *you*, obviously. I could see that without the device. And a few others. Then there are these thirteen odd lines . . ."

"*Thirteen?*" Yumi said, standing up from her stool.

"Yup!" Design said. "Connection lines are easy to see at times, but notoriously hard to read. I don't know what these are Connected to. Didn't look like family though. More a thematic Connection . . ."

"Yumi?" he asked.

"There are currently thirteen other yoki-hijo," Yumi said. "Where? Where are they?"

"I can't read that," Design said.

"Then what good is this?" Yumi said, gesturing to the device.

"What good is . . . Yumi, do you understand what a *miracle* this fabrial is? It's reading things that until very recently you'd need a highly specialized individual who could—"

"Are they here?" Yumi asked. "This world. Nearby?"

"Definitely this world," Design said. "That direction, somewhere." She waved vaguely to the west, toward the near portion of the shroud where Painter patrolled. "But . . ." She sighed as Yumi dashed from the building.

Painter scrambled to follow, caught off guard. "Yumi?" he shouted, stumbling out onto the street. "Yumi. You promised the others you'd stay away from . . ."

She was running down the street and seemed not to be listening. He took off after her, catching up, then joined her as she eventually emerged from the outer ring of warehouses onto the road that circled Kilahito. She slowed here, walking up to the shroud—dangerously close.

"Yumi?" Painter said, approaching from behind, and reached out—but stopped just short of touching her.

Finally she sank to her knees and bowed her head. He walked around to her side and crouched there, worried.

"I'm sorry," she whispered. "I thought . . . Actually, I wasn't thinking. I *felt*. That I wanted to see them. Be with them. It overcame me." She looked at him. "I knew one of them, when I was a child. We were trained together. Did you know that?"

He shook his head.

"Then they took her, separated us," Yumi whispered, "when we were growing to know each other too well. Wasn't good for me, Liyun said, to form an attachment. In the years since, I've never met another one of them."

"What, really?" he said. "Not even in passing?"

She shook her head.

"That feels tragic," he said, settling down beside her and staring at the shroud. Black on black. He knew it was shifting and moving, but he *felt* it more than he *saw* it.

"How did you deal with the loneliness?" she asked softly. "When you were younger?"

"By painting."

"When you make art," she whispered, "it's easy to forget."

"Until you don't have anyone to show it to."

"I never had that problem," she said. "But my audience was never human. I often wished that after it was all done for the day, someone would be there to tell me I'd done a good job."

"Hey," he said.

She glanced at him.

"Good job."

"I didn't mean right *now*," she said (lowly).

He grinned at her anyway. And eventually she grinned back. Then she idly picked up a few pebbles and broken cobbles from the ground. Unsurprisingly, she began stacking them.

"We're missing today's episode of *Seasons of Regret*," she said. "I didn't even remember. Considering all the . . ."

"Insanity?"

"Yeah," she said, balancing another pebble.

"Ask Izzy," he said. "She'll know what happened. And will explain. In detail."

"I almost . . ." she said, balancing a fourth pebble, "would rather not. I'd rather imagine it for myself. So I can pretend it turned out happy in the end."

Painter glanced to the side. This wasn't the best place for a conversation. At the very least, they risked running into Akane and Tojin, who would *never* let Yumi . . .

He frowned, then stood up.

The shroud was *changing*. Rippling. He almost shouted for Yumi to run, thinking a nightmare was coming out. But then the shroud drew *back*. *Away from them.*

Like darkness before light. Like water evaporating before a terrible heat. The shroud retreated in a kind of curve, bowing inward. He glanced at Yumi, who stacked another pebble.

The shroud pulled back farther.

"Yumi!" he hissed, then pointed.

She followed his gaze, then gasped softly. "What is happening?"

"The stacking," he said. "The shroud is responding to the stacking."

To test this, she placed another—and the shroud pulled back more. It was responding only in a small region, maybe ten feet across. But Painter found the behavior bizarre—until he realized there was an obvious correlation.

"That's how it responds to hion lines," he said, looking toward Yumi. "It's how we survive; hion pushes back the shroud. We build new settlements by extending the lines into the dark."

Yumi selected another handful of pebbles from around the area, then settled herself with a determined expression, stacking one after another, working faster than he'd have dared. Not a single one of her miniature towers toppled. Behind them, he noticed Design approaching, still wearing her apron. It was an odd sight, and he realized he had basically considered her to be a fixture of the restaurant—seeing her was like seeing the bar itself rip up and come sauntering out onto the street.

Design wordlessly joined them, watching the shroud. The darkness lurched with each pebble, but then started to churn and bubble, like water boiling.

"Yumi . . ." Painter said at this new behavior. "Maybe . . ."

She increased her speed, building with both hands, growing her towers higher, higher, making the shroud churn and froth and agitate and ripple, then *split*. Right down the center, revealing a human hand, then shoulders and a face—a woman, dressed in the bright tobok of a yoki-hijo—reaching out to them with a voiceless scream. The shroud surged forward again, swallowing her, then bulged out toward the three of them.

Painter yelled and leaped back. Yumi scattered rocks in her haste to get away. Even Design—who had long claimed to be some kind of immortal unaffected by common fears—scuttled away until all three of them pressed their backs to the nearest wall: Painter's whitewashed but unpainted one.

"What (lowly) was *that*?" Painter demanded.

"Your world is *really* weird," Design said. "I have a number to explain how weird. It's high. Super high."

"That was a yoki-hijo," Yumi whispered, looking at them both. "In the darkness. Why?"

Painter shook his head, baffled.

"Could be a nightmare," Design said. "Taking the *shape* of a person—because you were thinking about them. Don't trust anything you see made from that darkness, kids."

"Good point," Painter said. "This could be some kind of trap. Even if it's not, isn't this a distraction right now? The other yoki-hijo are on your mind, Yumi, but what would they want you to do?"

"To follow the will of the spirits," Yumi said. "The scholars' machine— we have to figure out how to destroy it."

"I suggest hitting it," Design said. "Very hard. Preferably with something that is *more* hard. I'd offer myself, as I make an encouragingly mediocre sword, but there are . . . complications."

"We could just use a rock," Painter said. "Stalk in there and hit the machine while the scholars are confused. What are they going to do? They're a bunch of spindly academics."

Yumi looked horrified. "I couldn't do that!"

"You wouldn't have to," Painter said, glancing back at the shroud— which was stilling. In mere seconds, it appeared identical to how it had before. "I can destroy the machine, Yumi. Maybe that's why the spirits sent for me. They need someone who doesn't care about your society's rules. Someone who can simply walk into that tent and do what has to be done."

"Maybe," Yumi admitted. "But we don't move in haste. We should plan first."

Of course she wanted to plan. "Yumi, you said this is getting worse. You said our time was running out. I don't think we're going to be able to come up with a better plan than just sneaking in and smashing the machine. We aren't soldiers; we have no resources."

"You could be right," she said. "But I can't help thinking we should go into this with more information. Design, you surveyed this world before you landed. How sure are you it was all covered in the shroud?"

"Not that sure," she replied.

"Do you have maps?" Yumi asked. "A way to tell what's out there in that darkness?"

"I don't," Design said. "But . . . I might know someone who can tell us. Someone who has traveled it extensively."

DESIGN LED them back to the noodle shop. They snuck in quickly, trying not to draw the attention of the many painters coming off shift and gathering at their usual tables. Namakudo, one of Design's assistant cooks, had been forced to come out of the kitchen to take orders.

Design led them through a kitchen full of boiling pots into a small room at the rear filled with . . . numbers? Yumi stood in the center and frowned, looking at the walls, which were ornamented with long stretches of numerical sequences that flowed and circled around; it was hard to tell where one ended and another began, or if they formed an infinite loop.

"Ah . . ." Design said. "It feels so good to come here and be near *real* art. Be back quicker than a chasmfiend gobbles a chull." She darted away, leaving Yumi and Painter.

"Do you think she's getting more eccentric?" Painter said, sitting on the floor. "Or is she just comfortable enough with us to let it show?"

"The latter," Yumi said, looking up and finding numbers written even on the *ceiling*. "Definitely the latter."

Design returned a few minutes later with Masaka in tow. Short, too much dark makeup, black skirt and her customary black sweater, collar all the way to her chin, hands lost in her sleeves.

"Ha!" Painter said, leaping to his feet. He pointed. "*Ha!* I knew it. I *knew* she wasn't human."

"Yumi," Design said, "meet Chinikdakordich, the sixtieth horde of the Natricatich strain."

Masaka pulled into her sweater a little farther, like a tortoise seeking the safety of its shell during the heat of the day. "We prefer the name Masaka," she said softly. "We're being human, Design. We're getting very good at it."

"I know you are," Design said, patting her.

"So it's true?" Yumi asked, feeling intimidated. "You're . . . a creature like Design?"

"Not entirely like her, but yes," Masaka said, looking down. "Is it . . . so obvious, Yumi? We're figuring out many things. Human girls like cute things. We like cute things." She looked up, and almost seemed ready to cry. "We made *such* a good human. You can't even see the seams in our skin, so long as we wear makeup, and clothing with long neck portions! The trick is to make the entire face one piece. Took years of breeding."

Breeding? One piece? *Seams?*

Uh . . . Yumi steeled herself.

Painter, laughing, sat back down. She shot him a glare, but he shrugged.

"Yumi," he said, "Masaka being an alien is *literally* the first thing about any of this that has made sense to me."

"I think," Yumi said to Masaka—who evidently couldn't see or hear Painter—"you are doing an excellent job. You're, um, a very cute young woman."

"We are?" Masaka said. She smiled, then stepped closer. Yumi forcibly prevented herself from backing up as the girl—thing—took her hand. "Thank you, Yumi. *Thank you.* Here, this is for you." She slipped something from her pocket and handed it to Yumi. A . . .

A knife.

"Very good at cracking shells," Masaka said, pointing at the hooked end. "And prying out the insides. Look, look." She pointed at the handle. "Flowers inscribed here. Very cute."

"Very cute," Yumi repeated.

"Don't tell anyone what we are, please," Masaka said. "We are tired of people being scared of us. We are tired of wars. We like painting. Please."

"I . . . won't tell anyone," Yumi said. "But please, we need help. You . . . know about what's out in the darkness?"

"No horde," Design said, holding up a finger, "settles on a planet without knowing *everything* about the terrain. I'll bet she's been sending out . . . um, scouts. Little scouts. To investigate the entire place."

Masaka looked out at the kitchens, then shut the door. "Is it important?" she asked Yumi. "As important as Design said?"

"Yes," Yumi said. "I think it really is."

Masaka took a deep breath. "We . . . I am not so paranoid as others, Design. I *am* trying to be human. To avoid the conflicts. But I have sent hordelings out. Most of the landscape beyond the cities is wasteland, enveloped in this strange Investiture. Like the slag castoffs of half-refined souls. But there are places we cannot go."

"Cannot go?" Yumi asked, looking at Painter. "What do you mean?"

"Hard places," Masaka explained. "Walls in the blackness, where the Investiture has become solid. Rising up high in the sky, into the atmosphere. Like columns. One vast one a few miles away. Other small ones, circles all of them, like . . . fortifications."

"Around towns?" Painter asked, standing up, then waving for Yumi to say it—which she did.

"No way to tell," Masaka said. "I can't get through." She wilted. "I am young. I am not so . . . eager as some of my kind. I don't have the knowledge, have not gathered the power, to deal with things like this. I came here to hide."

"It might be enough," Yumi said, "if you draw out a little map of it, maybe? Where these places are?"

Masaka nodded, and Design went to fetch some paper.

"Towns," Painter repeated, stepping up beside Yumi. "Those circles she found. They're your towns!"

"It's impossible," Yumi said. "I'd *know* if I'd been living in little enclaves inside a vast darkness. We can see all the way to the horizon!"

"The shroud can look like anything," he said. "Design said it could fool us. And you yourself said that people from your lands rarely travel between villages because of the heat of the stone in between. So it could all be some kind of strange cover-up."

"And you really think," she replied, "that of the thousands upon thousands of people who live in my kingdom, none would stroll out and find one of these barriers? That a flyer would never smack into an invisible wall in the sky? You think this could have been hidden from all of us for such a long time?"

"I . . ." He winced at the implausibility of it all. "Yeah, all right. But I would bet you the biggest bowl of noodles you can eat that if we overlap Masaka's map with a map of your lands, we're going to find a correlation."

Masaka had watched all of this with interest, but didn't seem to find a woman talking to herself to be all that odd. When Design returned with a paper, Masaka knelt down with a fine brush and sketched out a large circle near one edge of it.

"Kilahito," she said, pointing to the circle. "Where we are now." She drew another circle of similar size across the page. "The largest of the impassable zones." Then she drew out several other smaller circles, about a dozen. Yes . . . those *could* be the size of towns. "The other ones."

"How accurate," Yumi said, "are these distances you've drawn?"

"Hordes have incredible spatial awareness," Design said. "Comes from having bodies that can spread out to the size of a nation. Her guess will be more accurate than most people's instrument-measured surveys."

"Here is a scale," Masaka said, drawing a line at the bottom with some numbers on it. "It is exact."

Painter knelt and studied the painting in detail, then measured the distances using his palm and fingers, something he'd taught Yumi to do for measuring parts of a painting.

"You ready to sleep?" he asked her.

"I'd prefer to eat first," she said. "I never did get dinner."

He nodded. "I'm going to memorize this drawing. See if I can reproduce it exactly. Shouldn't take me too long. After that we can get back to your land and fix this once and for all."

Yumi nodded in return and wandered out to the main room, taking advantage of the longer leash. Design, having put off her customers too long, came out and took charge of the restaurant. So Yumi sat at the counter, watching Masaka join the rest of the painters. They noticed Yumi and waved.

Fix this once and for all.

It might be . . . the last time she saw these people. Her last chance to be a normal person rather than the collected hopes and needs of an entire people. And so she let herself leave the bar, then trail across the room to the others.

"Yumi, Yumi," Tojin said. "Look at this." He flexed, stretching his . . . neck muscles? She hadn't ever even thought about the fact that people had muscles in their necks. "What do you think?"

"Your head," she said, "looks small by comparison." She blushed immediately, as that felt rude.

Tojin, however, grinned widely. "Thanks!"

Akane sat nearby, gazing at the ceiling as Izzy kept talking. About dramas, of course. "So it turns out," she was saying, "he *didn't* leave. He thought he had to because he was being *threatened* by his *evil brother.*"

Yumi's breath caught.

"His brother," Akane said, "that you *just* told me was dead."

"He *is* dead!" Izzy said. "He set it all up *before* he died! Using people who hate the honor of ronin."

"So . . ." Yumi whispered, "Sir Ashinata came back?"

"There was an extra episode," Izzy said, "that they didn't tell us about." She raised a finger. "This proves my theory of the importance of dramas. I'm writing a book on their relevance for improving mental health."

Tojin frowned. "What about . . . drama-horoscope-figgldygrak—whatsit?"

"Old news," Izzy said. "I'm going to be a viewer critic instead. It's going to make me *famous.*"

Nearby, Masaka had settled into her seat. And though she didn't say much, Yumi could see her contentment. She understood that. Being an outsider, then finding a place. Being alone, then finding friends.

"I wish," Yumi said, trying to hold back the tears, "that I'd been able to meet you all sooner."

"It's your brother's fault," Tojin said. "He could have invited you at any point. Only did it when he wanted someone to try doing his work for him."

Yumi felt a sudden, *burning* anger.

"I'm surprised," Akane said, "that he didn't try to recruit her to go to his classes for him in school. Considering that all he wanted to do was take time off. He—"

Yumi leaped to her feet, cutting her off. "You," she said (lowly), "do *not* know Nikaro!"

"We . . . know what he did to us," Izzy said.

Tojin nodded.

"I know he hurt you," Yumi said. "I know it was hard. But did you think about how hard it was for him?"

"Hard for *him*?" Akane asked. "He was quite literally sitting around doing *nothing*."

"Wanting to fix things," Yumi said, "and not knowing how to do so is the most *excruciating* experience *I've* ever had. You don't know him, Akane. You really *don't*. Do you know what it's like to feel the pressure of needing to succeed, not for yourself but because everyone else depends on you? Do you know what it does to someone to realize that your value is wrapped up—almost exclusively—in what you can do for people? To know that if you fail, you become *nothing* to the ones you most love?"

They shied away from her. All but Akane, who leaned forward. "We never thought he was nothing, Yumi," she said softly. "He wasn't our friend *just* because of what we thought he could do for us."

"Did you ever tell him that?" Yumi asked. "Did you ever wonder how he felt? Can you tell me, honestly, that you think he lied because he *wanted* to hurt you? Do you *actually* think he was *enjoying* himself? Sitting alone? Staring at the wall? Trying desperately to think of a way to not let you down? To not fail you?"

"He should have told us," Akane said.

"He should have," Yumi agreed. "He agrees. I agree. You agree. We all (lowly) *agree*! But he *didn't* tell you. It happened. It's over. I'm sorry." She sighed, her rage waning like the last jets of a drowsy steamwell. "You were his friends. He failed you. He ruined your lives. But did you ever think how unfair it was that *he* was *responsible* for *your* lives?"

"I can't pretend," Tojin said softly, "that he didn't hurt me."

"I know, Tojin," Yumi said. "But he loves you all still; I can see it in him. He cannot change what he did, but he is a good person, trying very hard. You don't have to forget what he did. But did you ever think that maybe instead of constant wisecracks and snark you could simply . . . try to understand? On that day, when he was rejected from the Dreamwatch, Painter lost everything. Every hope, every dream. He lost his love of what he did. But I think losing you as his friends was the worst of all."

She met each of their eyes in turn, and they glanced away, not contradicting her. Akane, last of all, looked down.

"Thank you," Yumi said, "for the kindness you've shown me these past weeks. I truly appreciate it. But I'm going to be leaving now. So maybe spare some of that kindness for someone who needs it even more."

She bowed to them, the most formal bow she knew, as if to the spirits themselves. Then she turned away, joining Painter, who had just come out of the kitchen.

"Come on," she said, walking toward the door.

"But dinner—"

"I've lost my appetite," she said. "You're right. It's time to end this."

Chapter 34

I DON'T KNOW why you require this, Chosen," Liyun said, kneeling bleary-eyed before Painter in the shrine. "I have fetched it, but . . . it is one of several *very unusual* actions you've been taking lately."

Painter settled down, listening to the shivering and shaking of the trees, bumping into one another in the wind like a crowd at the carnival. He'd been harsh toward this woman in the past, but . . . well, he thought he was coming to understand her.

"It's a hard duty, Liyun," he said, "being the warden of a yoki-hijo. If something goes wrong, nobody can impugn the girl chosen by the spirits; she is beyond recrimination. But someone must pay. Perhaps the one who guided her poorly."

Liyun looked up, shocked. Then nodded. "You've grown . . . wise, over the years, Chosen."

"I appreciate your service," Painter said, reaching to take the rolled-up piece of paper she'd brought. "If you're worried about my unusual actions, you can be content that they've helped more than you can know. After all, my work yesterday proves that I'm returning to myself."

"You . . . still sleep over twelve hours a day, Chosen."

"What's better?" he asked. "A yoki-hijo who cannot work at all, or one who is slowly returning to herself?"

Liyun nodded again, her head bowed.

"Know that if your Yumi returns," he said, "it's because of what you have done. Your faith in her. Thank you."

Liyun stood, and he was surprised to see tears in her eyes. He'd thought her as likely to cry as a rock was. She bowed to him again, then withdrew, her clogs sounding on the stone until she vanished down the path between the trees.

"That was sweet of you," Yumi said, kneeling next to him. "I know how she riles you."

"I'm thinking that maybe I understand the pressure she's under," he said. "She could be less a personification of a crusted-over paintbrush, mind you. But . . . I can empathize."

He held up the scroll that Liyun had delivered, then looked to Yumi and took a deep breath. They'd waited to do this until after bathing and their meditations. They'd needed his paints, after all, at the shrine.

With a firm hand he unrolled the scroll, revealing a map of Torio, Yumi's kingdom. This was the map used by the driver of Yumi's wagon to get from town to town. He studied its scale and nodded. Then, from memory, he painted a copy of Masaka's drawing at the same size as the map, using some grid lines as guides.

He laid his copy atop Liyun's map to find that they overlapped perfectly. The circles Masaka had drawn—each of which represented an impenetrable wall inside the shroud—were *directly* around some of the larger towns on Liyun's map. Kilahito wasn't represented in the map of Yumi's lands, naturally, but the circle that Masaka had drawn indicating the biggest of the walled-off regions was listed on Liyun's map as Torio City. The capital, seat of the queen, home to the university.

(If you're curious about the scale, both nations were relatively small by modern reckoning—less than fifty miles across. There wasn't a lot of life on the planet. Painter's people were quietly content with a small and intimate collection of cities. While Yumi's nation could grow no larger than the steamwells allowed. On these maps, then, Kilahito and the town they were currently in were less than five miles apart.)

Yumi leaned forward as she studied the two maps—his done on thinner paper, so the lines beneath showed through. "Painter," she said, her wonderful eyes so wide they could have been canvases, "you were right. This time *you* were *right*!"

Right. He was right.

Their lands were somehow the same. Cities in Torio existed in the dark space *between* the cities of his nation. No overlap of actual living spaces, but many of them were shockingly close.

"It seems impossible," Yumi whispered. "We're both in the same place. Existing right *next* to one another."

"Like we're overlapping," he said. "Two peoples. One land . . ." He sat back, proud of having been able to see this. At the same time . . . what did it change? There was only one way forward. "I need to destroy that machine."

"We need a plan," Yumi said. "One that isn't you simply walking up and trying to beat the machine to pieces with a rock. They'll think we've gone insane—and no matter how spindly those scholars are, you won't get far with all four of them piling on top of you."

"What else do we do?" he said. "Like I said before—we don't have any resources."

"No," Yumi said. "There is *one* resource we have that we haven't tried using in a while. The truth."

He frowned at her. "What are you saying?"

"You've shown me," she said, "that I have more power than I ever dared to wield. The spirits brought you here so that I could realize it. *We* are the ultimate authority in this town. Not those scholars, not Liyun, not even the local officials. The yoki-hijo can ask for anything. Demand anything."

"So we just walk up and insist that the scholars let us break their machine?" he said. "I think they'll ignore us, yoki-hijo or not."

"Then we don't give them any other option."

They locked eyes. The truth. The (lowly) truth. He wished he'd been brave enough to use it more in his own life. He nodded. "Your world, Yumi," he said. "Your rules. Tell me what you want me to do."

"Thank you," she said, moving her hand next to his, almost touching. "*Thank you*, Painter."

She had him quickly step down from the shrine and slip on his clogs. He left behind his paints, including the sketches of townspeople he'd done while waiting for the map. This wasn't a task for a painter, but for a girl of commanding primal spirits.

He found Liyun outside, chatting softly with Hwanji and Chaeyung. Together they bowed as he approached, by now accustomed to the way he decided when his meditations were done.

He stepped up to them, braced himself, then spoke the words Yumi had prepared. "The spirits came to me," he said, "and asked me to destroy the machine that the scholars brought. I do not entirely know the reason, but I believe it is hurting them.

"This knowledge is partially to blame for my erratic behavior lately. I've been trying to figure out how to navigate my duties, the social norms I've been taught, and this strange demand of the spirits. Today, it is coming to a head. I want you to support me in gathering the people of the town. Then, together, we're going to go to the scholars and demand that the machine be destroyed."

All three stared at him. He tried not to wince. And yet, saying it like that . . . felt good. Actually, it had been easier than he'd imagined.

It was a test with dangerous stakes. How far did Yumi's authority go? How far could he push these people?

"Are you *certain* about this, Chosen?" Liyun finally asked.

Yumi stepped up beside him and spoke, with him repeating the words. "I have never been so sure about something in my life, Liyun. This is what the spirits wish of me. You *will* help me. Either that or you will remove me from my position—but you would have to physically restrain me. Because I am going to deal with that machine right now."

Painter blinked at the force in her words. He'd thought *that* kind of sternness was reserved solely for wayward stone-stacking trainees.

Chaeyung and Hwanji looked to Liyun. Who, at last, bowed.

"You are the yoki-hijo," Liyun said. "If you have *carefully* considered the ramifications to both yourself and to our order . . ."

"Even if I'm right," Yumi said through Painter, "then others will undoubtedly see it as jealousy. They will paint me as erratic, someone who has lost control of her emotions and her mind after seeing the machine replace her. I will likely be removed from my position. I know, Liyun.

Nevertheless, this *is* what the spirits have demanded. So I serve—as you taught me so well."

"You might," Liyun whispered, "spend the rest of your life in . . . captivity. Serving only under lock and key, stacking with strict oversight."

"And you will be disgraced," Yumi said through Painter. "I know, Liyun. I *know*."

Liyun hesitated, then bowed, a deep and flowery bow. "Chosen," she said (highly). "We are your servants."

"Ha!" Hwanji said, grabbing Painter by the arm. "I *knew* something was wrong with those scholars, Chosen. We had other scholars from the university come to my home village, and they were kind and quiet men who helped us with the disease upon our crops. These men though, they spend all day sneaking around. Shooting everyone dark glances."

"Quickly, woman," Liyun said. "Go and fetch the town officials. We will need their bailiff to execute this command. Assuming it pleases you, Chosen?"

"It does please me," Painter said. "Thank you."

Within half an hour, they marched through town with not just the town's bailiff, but twelve of its strongest men, who carried hammers for breaking stones. Painter walked at their head, Yumi at his side, seeming nervous but relieved.

"It *is* a better plan, isn't it?" she whispered.

He nodded. "You're wrong about one thing though," he said back softly. "You said the machine would replace you. It can't."

"But—"

"It can summon spirits," he said. "But it can't create art. Art is about intent, Yumi. A rainbow isn't art, beautiful though it might be. Art is about *creation*. Human creation. A machine can lift way more than Tojin can—doesn't make it less impressive when he lifts more than almost any human being."

He smiled at her. "I don't care how well a machine piles rocks. The fact that *you* do it is what matters to me."

She smiled back, brushing her hand against his, causing their arms to radiate warmth. But then they reached the scholars' tent. It was time. The machine wasn't in its place out front, but they often rolled it into the tent for brief maintenance. As the group arrived, the lead scholar—Painter couldn't remember his name—was stepping out, wearing his tall hat. He froze when he noticed them all.

"Scholars," Painter said. "By the authority of the spirits themselves, we have come to destroy your machine. Step aside."

The scholar cocked his head, then called into the tent.

"Sunjun! They're here!"

Sunjun, the most engineering-minded of the scholars, popped out of the tent. "Already?"

"Indeed," the lead scholar said. "Looks like it's time for a confrontation."

Sunjun sighed, then took out some device and activated it. Painter couldn't see what it did, but this wasn't the reaction he'd been hoping for. They didn't seem frightened, or even surprised. More . . . regretful. Perhaps they were stalling. Honam poked his head out of the tent, then handed the lead scholar something. A pair of goggles. He affixed them to his face, then looked at Painter.

"Stand aside," Painter said. "And relinquish the machine."

The lead scholar instead studied him. "So," the man said. "This is the descendant of the nomads. You've done quite well for yourselves, as a people. Tell me. What is it you think is happening here, boy? The division between our nations? The fact that you have entire cities nearby that can't visit ours?"

Painter froze.

They knew?

He felt cold. Yumi pulled closer to him, and the scholar looked at her, *seeing* her. It was the goggles maybe?

Painter swallowed. The bailiff and the others had frozen. Even Liyun just stood there. Completely motionless. Were they waiting for something from him? Their orders were to go in and destroy the machine if the scholars refused to surrender it. Yet nobody moved.

"Different dimensions," Painter finally said to the scholars. "That overlap somehow. That's what's going on. We exist in the same space, but can't see each other or interact, except in specific ways."

"Oh, that's an *excellent* theory," the lead scholar said. "You hear that, Sunjun?"

"Sure did," Sunjun said as the two other scholars rolled their machine out of the tent, onto a large plank that sloped to the stone ground. "The theory has problems, but it's pretty good for a kid without any real context. He'd have made a good scholar."

"Indeed," the lead scholar said.

"Doesn't matter," Painter said, pointing. "Bailiff, take that machine."

"Painter," Yumi said, "maybe we should get more information first."

"First," he said, "we at least . . ." He trailed off, noticing that the bailiff, the city officials . . . Liyun, Hwanji, and Chaeyung were all just standing there. He noticed for the first time that their immobility seemed unnatural. They weren't even blinking.

"Liyun?" Painter asked. "Chaeyung?"

"I regret to be the one to reveal it," the lead scholar said, "but you have *no idea* what is happening here, child."

Painter seized Liyun by the arm, shaking it. And her very shape—clothing included—began to *shift*. Darkening. Giving off wisps of blackness. She looked at him, and her eyes had gone white. Like . . . like holes drilled in her head.

Painter screamed, his voice joining Yumi's own cry. He jumped away, wiping his hand on his tobok.

"What did you *think* they were?" the lead scholar asked as the machine started up.

Painter, desperate, grabbed a rock. He rushed the machine, but the scholar grabbed his arm. Contrary to what Painter had assumed before, this man was *strong*. In desperation, Painter slammed his rock against the man's head.

The scholar's head shifted, its color bleeding away before darkness, his eyes becoming ivory bores into eternity.

"No," Painter said, pulling out of the thing's grip. "You too?"

"I'm afraid so," the lead scholar—nightmare—said.

"Painter!" Yumi cried, backing up toward him, cowering as the entire *landscape* began to change. Buildings turning black, giving off wisps of smoke. The ground. Even the light in the sky darkened.

"All along?" Painter asked, pained. "Were they just . . . puppets? Nightmares, with no thoughts?"

"No, the machine let them be themselves," the lead scholar said, his face distorted, made of shifting wisps of smoke—still wearing goggles, oddly. "It's what happens when it needs us. It's hard though. To walk the line between the memory of what we were and the reality of what we have become. They have to be kept from understanding their natures. Otherwise there are . . . complications."

The thing that had been Liyun turned toward them, and her form took on a lupine cast. With spiked sides, inky darkness. Painter recognized this thing; it was the stable nightmare he'd been hunting.

Liyun was the *stable nightmare*.

Unlike the scholar, she suddenly appeared to have no memory of who she'd been—or who Painter was. She prowled toward him, going down on all fours, growing to enormous size.

Painter tried to stand between it and Yumi. "You won't take her."

The thing stopped, and for the briefest moment seemed to recognize him.

"Child," the lead scholar-nightmare said. "What is it you think you're protecting?"

He froze, and his heart became ice. He turned to find Yumi had fallen to her knees. She was distorting—far less than the others, but still twisting, her skin turning to smoke. She looked at him, horror warping her features in an unnatural way.

"No . . ." he whispered. *No.*

He . . . he couldn't think.

Yumi. Yumi . . .

"Nikaro," she said, her voice hoarse. "I . . . What is happening . . . to me . . ."

"Tragic," the lead scholar said, stepping forward and seizing Painter by the arm. "I admit, this was an excellent ploy by the spirits. Connect one of the girls to an outsider to anchor her soul? Prevent us from altering her memories? It might have worked."

He heaved Painter back, slamming him against the machine, where the other scholars—also having become nightmares—were tweaking it.

"I'm sorry this took us so long to do," the creature in front of Painter said. "The delay makes it more cruel, I understand. Regrettably, this machine needed to charge up—our power source didn't work. And beyond that, some rogue spirits had to be captured. How they escaped is . . . distressing. Thank you for helping us return them to their prison."

"Please," Painter said, then reached toward Yumi, his heart wrenching at the sight of her huddled on the ground in a fetal position of pure terror. Darkness streamed off her as she clawed at her arms, as if to tear her own skin off. "*Please.* Let me help her."

"The machine is lord now," he whispered. "I'm sorry."

The scholar nodded to the others, his hollow eyes expanding. They turned some switch on their machine, and Painter felt a surge of *coldness* wash through him. Followed by a distinct, terrible *snap.*

Whatever it was that had linked him to Yumi broke. Painter felt himself hurled away from the scene. They shrank, and he smashed into a blackness—like he'd plunged into the ocean. Only he was still moving, an arrow in flight.

Darkness.

Hion lines like a flash.

A blur of buildings.

Then *slam.* He hit something.

Incredible pain followed, coursing through him, accompanied by sickening pops and a sound like leather being stretched. When it finally subsided he found himself lying in his apartment, covered in sweat.

Once again occupying his own body.

With Yumi nowhere in sight.

Chapter 35

YUMI HAD always considered the appearance of the daystar to be a good sign. An omen that the primal hijo would be open and welcoming this day. In fact, the star seemed extra bright today—glowing with a soft blue light on the western horizon as the sun rose in the east.

A powerful sign, if you believed in such things. There's an old joke that mentions that lost items tend to always be in the last place you look for them. Strangely, by converse, omens tend to appear in the first place people look for them. (Even if you're doing so for the second time.)

Yumi did believe in omens. She had to, as an omen had been the single most important event in her life. One that had appeared right after her birth, marking her as chosen by the spirits. She settled herself on the warm ground as her attendants, Hwanji and Chaeyung, entered. They bowed in ritual postures, then fed her with maipon sticks and spoons—a meal of rice and a stew that had been left on a hotspot outside to cook.

Yumi sat and ate, not being so crass as to try to feed herself. This was a ritual, and she was an expert in those. Though she couldn't help feeling distracted. Today marked one hundred days until the big festival in Torio City, the seat of the queen. And this was also nineteen days past her nineteenth birthday.

A day for decisions. A day for action.

A day to, maybe, ask for what she wanted?

First she had duties. Once her attendants had finished feeding her, she rose and went to the door of her private wagon. As they opened the door for her, she took a deep breath, then stepped down into her shoes.

Immediately her two attendants leaped to hold up enormous fans to obscure her from view. Naturally, people in the village had gathered to see her. The Chosen. The yoki-hijo. The girl of commanding primal spirits. (Yes, it still works better in their language.)

This land—Torio—had a dominant red-orange sun the color of baked clay. Bigger and closer than your sun, it had distinct spots of varied color on it—like a boiling stew, churning and undulating in the sky.

This bloody sun painted the landscape . . . well, just ordinary colors. The way the brain works, once you'd been there a few hours, you wouldn't have noticed that the light was redder than yours. But when you first arrived, it would look striking. Like clay fresh from a potter's kiln and bearing a distinct molten heat.

Hidden behind her fans, Yumi walked on clogged feet through the village to the local cold spring. Here she put her hands to the sides and let her attendants undress her for . . .

For . . .

She cocked her head. Something was . . . odd about this experience. Something was wrong. Wasn't it?

Something was *missing*.

She opened her mouth to ask, then bit her tongue. Speaking to Hwanji and Chaeyung now would shame them. Yet as the bathing progressed, she felt oddly out of sorts. She found herself glancing at the side of the cool spring, expecting . . .

Someone is supposed to be there, she thought, incongruously. That would be *terrible.* Shaming. Why would she want someone to watch her bathe?

Instead she closed her eyes and let her attendants continue their work.

PAINTER scattered his stack of rocks in frustration. As with his previous attempts, the shroud remained immobile. A wall of mottled black, indifferent to his inferior stacking.

Painter tried to meditate, as Yumi had always taught. He found any semblance of calm impossible, as closing his eyes only made him think of her huddling in terror, looking at him, pleading as the horror consumed her.

He still couldn't make sense of any of it. Was it some kind of trick played by the scholars? That couldn't have been Yumi . . . Yumi *couldn't* be a nightmare . . .

If she was, what did that mean? Had he fallen for someone created by his own . . . his own perceptions? Like a painter loving his own painting?

No. No, she'd been real. She *was* real.

And he was going to help her.

Somehow.

Painter forced his eyes open and grabbed his sack of rocks, collected in haste on his way to the shroud. He calmed his frantic breathing and started stacking, and each stone placed reminded him of her. Yumi would have been proud of the twelve-stone height he obtained, and the way he chose rocks of irregular size, looking to make not only a pile, but a tower.

The shroud didn't move. Though it had bowed for her, it didn't notice him. Painter was forced to admit the truth. Yumi had been special. Being yoki-hijo wasn't merely about stacking rocks, but about the power the spirits had given her. He could do nothing to disrupt the shroud without being Connected to her, just as he could never have attracted spirits without being Connected to her.

He sank back onto his heels, slumping his shoulders.

"Please," he whispered. "Just let me see her. Let me help her . . ."

"Nikaro?" a voice asked.

He turned with a start to see Akane walking past. She'd stopped, staring at him. "Nikaro," she said (lowly), striding toward him. "Where have you been? It feels like . . ." She frowned, seeing his face. "Have you been crying?"

He stumbled to his feet, knocking over the stack of rocks.

"Nikaro?" Akane demanded. "What have you *done*? Where is Yumi?"

Unable to face those condemnations, he grabbed his sack of rocks, then turned and fled, running through the night.

* * *

A short time later, Yumi's attendants led her to the shrine among some floating trees, knocking together. Here, once more, Yumi hesitated. This was . . . familiar. Why was it familiar? She'd never been to this town before. She moved to a new one each night.

Her attendants halted, looking worried but not speaking, lest they shame her. So she continued forward. But again she was shocked, to see someone standing at the shrine.

"Liyun?" Yumi asked, stopping. The woman didn't usually first approach until after Yumi had done her prayers and meditations. "Is something wrong?"

"I just wanted to let you know, Chosen," Liyun said, bowing, "that we passed Ihosen and came here instead."

"Ihosen?"

"The town we were going to visit? This is the next in line." Liyun put her hand to her head. "I . . . can't remember why we changed. I thought I should mention it."

"It is, of course, wisdom in you," Yumi said, bowing—though she mostly just felt confused. Why did Liyun think to inform her? The woman never mentioned other towns they visited.

"I wanted to tell you," Liyun said, "that I might not be here later tonight to guide you. Go, do your service, and then have the attendants escort you to the wagon."

"Liyun?" Yumi asked. "Protocol . . ."

"I know, Chosen," Liyun said, bowing reverently. "Unfortunately, I've been called to do something else. I don't fully remember what, but it is important. Someone must be . . . dealt with. So do your duty, and I will see you tomorrow."

Yumi bowed. Then she rose and watched Liyun hurry away. What an odd interaction. Why—

Liyun paused, then glanced back. She looked like she wanted to say something, then cocked her head as if she'd forgotten it.

She was gone moments later.

Yumi realized she hadn't been able to ask for the thing she wanted most. To visit Torio City for the festival. That would be . . .

Hollow? Why would she suddenly feel that to be hollow? She'd been planning to ask for that trip for weeks. Yet now she couldn't muster the effort to care.

She decided that perhaps she was abandoning her selfish streak. At long last, she might be becoming the yoki-hijo that Liyun had always wanted her to be.

She knelt to begin her prayers. Content that, with effort, she might finally be able to serve with her whole heart.

Chapter 36

PAINTER SAT on his floor, huddled in his blankets, staring at a stack of plates, cups, and utensils that Yumi had made a day before.

He pulled the blankets close because warmth felt right to him in a way it never had before. Because the last time someone had held these blankets, it had been her. Sitting with him. Watching the viewer and caring *way* too much about the lives of fictional people.

Maybe, he thought, *I can get a hion expander and go striking out in the shroud.* He could hunt for those walls that circled her towns. And . . . and do what? Be surrounded and killed by nightmares?

He didn't even know what her towns *were*. Masaka had said those walls were impenetrable, but Painter had apparently been living half his time inside one. He was so far beyond his depth that he couldn't see the surface.

The scholar had been right. Painter didn't have *any idea* what was going on anymore.

Except that he had lost Yumi.

No. I won't let it be forever. He stood up as an idea struck him. A very terrible idea. He followed it anyway and left the apartment, the sack of rocks over his shoulder and something special tucked into his pocket.

Nightmares often returned to the place where they'd last fed. Looking for another easy meal, perhaps. Or just working by instinct and following the same emotions that had led them to prey the time before. Painter gambled on this, and returned to the broken playground near the carnival.

Here he settled down to wait. Determined. And frightened, though more of what he might lose than of nightmares. So he was *relieved* when he saw something darkening the alley nearby.

He'd been right. He stood up, feeling exhausted as the nightmare flowed from the alley, slicing the ground with thick claws. It approached him, careful, perhaps remembering their last encounter.

"We first met before the swap happened," he said to the thing. "Was that a coincidence, or were you looking for me even then?"

It reared up, blackness so deep it could only be imagined. Eyes of scraped-out hollow white. It reached for him.

"Liyun," he whispered. Remembering the lupine form she'd taken during the confrontation with the scholars.

The thing froze, then crouched close to the ground.

"Have they taken your memory, Liyun?" he asked. "But why?"

The answer struck him immediately—remembered words of the scholars leading him to a single conclusion.

They were afraid of Yumi.

"Is that what is happening?" Painter said. "Are the towns some kind of . . . charade for *her* benefit? To keep her confused, or disoriented, or simply placid?"

The nightmare began to slink forward again. So Painter knelt and began to stack. As earlier, his stacks were impressive for him—though not nearly on Yumi's level. But he felt proud as he placed the stones. And as he'd hoped, the nightmare that was Liyun stopped once more. Drill-hole eyes fixated on the stacks.

"I know," he said, "I don't have whatever power or endowment was given to Yumi. Yet I saw you recognize me before—even after someone had robbed you of your shape and your mind. A piece of you is still Liyun. Perhaps the deepest, most important piece. That's what the scholar said. That you were allowed to be yourself again for a time. When with Yumi."

The thing stepped forward, its eyes fixed on the stack.

"Remember, Liyun," Painter whispered. "*Remember.*"

The beast—hulking, like a boulder of black smoke—reached out a claw toward the stack. But stopped before touching it.

"I remember," it whispered in Liyun's voice.

"Is she all right?" Painter asked, pained.

"She forgets," the thing said. "As we all forget . . ."

"That," Painter said, "is why I brought this."

He took something from his pocket. A piece of paper, painted with a beginner's skill. It depicted two hands, overlapping each other, above a sea of lights. Yumi's memory, for him, of her.

He bowed before the beast that was Liyun. "Can you give this to her?"

"I will forget. I . . ."

"Liyun," he said, intent. "Do you remember your duty?"

Those white holes fixated on him.

"Serve the yoki-hijo," Painter whispered. "Protect her. *Give her this.*"

"I want to be a person again," Liyun whispered. "So badly. It has been so long . . ."

"How . . . long?" Painter asked.

"Since before your people made cities," the thing whispered. "Since the days when this land had a sun. Centuries."

The weight of that hit Painter. Centuries.

Yes, it meant Yumi had been right. Kind of. They hadn't been time traveling. But these people had somehow been trapped, unchanging, for *seventeen hundred* years.

"Yumi . . ." he whispered. "She'd lost memories. But only one day."

"One day," the monster whispered. "Over, and over, and over, and over. That same day, erased each night, so she can live it again the next. For centuries. Millennia . . ."

It reached out, delicate, and pinched the sheet between two claws. "I have failed to kill you," it whispered. "But the machine will not make this mistake again. It will send one who does not know you, who cannot be influenced. With that one will come an army."

"What . . . kind of army?"

"There was a city once," Liyun whispered. "I remember wisps of it, as I travel here to feed, to try to remember. Whenever the machine lets go of us, we come to your land, to seek ourselves. Futinoro. You know that name?"

"A city," Painter whispered, "that was destroyed entirely by stable nightmares."

"It happened because the spirits managed to contact the people there," the monster said. "The machine ordered the city wiped out as a result, to prevent anyone from knowing the truth. It sent dozens of my kind to achieve it. I was there. In a dream, I was there."

Painter sat back and released a long breath, his eyes wide. They'd assumed that failure had come from the painters not doing their jobs. But if it instead had been a direct assault . . .

That changed everything. He snapped his attention back to the beast. "They're coming here?"

"From the west," Liyun said. "A hundred nightmares. Strong as I am. Fed by the machine to make them dangerous and stable. Flee. Flee and pray to the spirits."

Her eyes lingered again on the stack, and then she withdrew, taking his picture with her.

Chapter 37

YUMI DREAMED.

And had nightmares.

Yes. The irony is so thick, you could spread it on your toast. Don't focus on that. Focus on what she heard. Because unlike most nightmares, this one was only sounds.

Voice one: "She's breaking through the patch."

Voice two: "Strengthen it."

Voice three: "We should cut these memories out with the machine. All of them, stretching back the entire month."

Voice two: "We don't have the strength for that. And if we did, she'd notice. It would upset the balance."

Voice one: "And if she breaks through?"

Voice two: "We deal with her, then try again."

And . . . after that . . . nothing . . .

Yumi awoke feeling exhausted, which was not a good sign. But the daystar was out, bright in the sky. And she'd always considered its appearance to be a good sign. An omen that the primal hijo would be open and welcoming today.

There's an old joke that mentions lost items always being in the last place you look for them. It doesn't say anything about memories though. Those, once lost, are the sorts of things you don't even know to look for.

Yumi stretched, then settled herself on the warm floor to wait for her attendants.

Who never came.

Eventually Liyun opened the door, looking frazzled, her hair messy and her bow untied. Yumi was shocked. Liyun breaking protocol? They'd done the exact same thing for what seemed like forever. Now Liyun came to her door before Yumi even had breakfast?

"The town," Liyun said, "is sick."

"Sick," Yumi said. "The *entire town*?"

"Yes," Liyun said, then put her hand to her head. "I . . . don't remember how I discovered it. But something has happened, and . . . and you need to remain inside today. In prayer and meditation. Yes, that is what you need to do."

Yumi leaped to her feet. Was this her chance? Protocol broken. Could she ask? Strangely, she found her timidity completely absent. Though she'd worried for weeks about even asking, now it came out easily.

"I," she said, "would like to visit Torio City for the festival in a hundred days. You will see that it is arranged?"

What was (lowly) wrong with her? To say it that way? So forceful? To make *demands* of Liyun? Surely the spirits would strike her down this instant for such an act!

"Yes, all right," Liyun said absently. "As you wish, Chosen. Is that all?"

Yumi gaped. No lecture couched in questions? No glare of anger? Maybe everyone *was* sick in this town, and Liyun had caught it. She certainly appeared disoriented.

"I will . . ." Liyun said. "I will get you breakfast myself. Where did Hwanji and Chaeyung go? Yes, breakfast. I . . ."

She walked to the door, then stopped.

"Liyun?" Yumi asked.

"What is my duty?" the older woman asked.

"To guide the yoki-hijo."

"Yes, yes," Liyun said, then moved to step down into her clogs. Again she halted. "But that is not all, is it?" She moved her arm with a stiffness that made Yumi think it was pained. She reached into the pouch at her belt. And took out a folded piece of paper.

Liyun stared at it, then dropped it to the floor of the wagon and fled out the door in a rush.

What extraordinarily odd behavior. Yumi walked over to watch Liyun leave through a town that seemed completely empty. Not a soul to be seen. Even the crops were unattended.

Was the sickness *that bad*? No wonder Liyun was so worried. Yumi knelt to say a prayer to the spirits, then saw the piece of paper.

Painted paper.

She cocked her head, then spread it out.

Those two hands . . .

One was hers.

One was . . . *his.*

Memories assaulted her with the force of a collapsing tower of stones a hundred feet high.

PAINTER counted building numbers in a frenzy, hoping to the depth of his core that he remembered correctly. Hion lines behind him cast his shadow, doubled, against the door as he reached the appropriate house.

He pounded on the door. Then pounded again, after not waiting long enough. He'd raised his fist to pound a third time when the door opened. Judging by the formal painter's uniform—with a tighter coat than he wore, short in the front, and made of a vibrant blue—he'd come to the right place. Painter had made an educated guess as to where the Dreamwatch would be put up. They rated an entire house, and the Painter Department owned only a few of those.

"Stable nightmare," Painter said between breaths. "I . . . ran . . . all the way . . ."

"Oh, you saw it, did you?" the man at the door said. Tall, he had such an incredible beard that it made sense he was bald—the hair on the top had been intimidated into hiding. His coat indicated he was a companion—not a Dreamwatch member himself, but one of those chosen by a full member to be on the team. The role that Painter's friends had hoped to fill.

The companion opened the door with a yawn and waved Painter in. Painter had worried that the Dreamwatch would all be out scouring the city for the stable nightmare, but he appeared to be in luck. They were in, perhaps holding a strategy session or interviewing contacts.

Even with everything that was happening, Painter felt a thrill at being ushered into their headquarters. Even this little brush with their world was awe-inspiring—more so when he stepped into the main lounge of the building and saw not one, but *three* full Dreamwatch members. Dressed in black, marks of their stations sewn into their jackets. Painter couldn't help staring.

They were playing table tennis. Two of them at least, a man and a woman. The third one lounged in a seat near the viewer, watching *Seasons of Regret*. Various companions lounged around the room, doing what Painter imagined was official work. Reading. Keeping score for the ping-pong game. Um . . . taking naps . . .

Relaxing, Painter told himself, *between bouts of hard work.* He had explained to Yumi the value of that.

The woman at the game table glanced up as he entered. "Was that the food, Hikiri? I ordered the barbecued . . ." She frowned, noting Painter.

"He says he saw the stable nightmare," Painter's guide explained. "Ran all this way to tell us."

"Oh," she said, and seemed disappointed that he hadn't brought her food. "Well, that's good. Take his statement, Hikiri. Put a pin in the map. Do we have the map set up yet?"

"Getting to it," said the companion who was reading a novel at the side of the room. "I've got it in my pack somewhere."

"Well, write down the address where he saw it," the Dreamwatch member said, then turned back to her game.

Painter took a deep breath, then stepped forward. "There's a hundred of them coming, sir," he said. "The nightmare told me. An invasion of night-mares. Like what happened in Futinoro. From the west. Please, you *must* defend the city!"

The woman glanced at her two colleagues. The one playing table tennis with her rolled his eyes. The other kept staring at the viewer.

"An army of nightmares," ping-pong woman said, strolling over to him.

"Please believe me," he said. "*Please.*"

She nodded to his jacket. "You're a painter?"

"Yes. I was the one who found the stable nightmare in the first place."

"You look like a real go-getter," she said. "Interested in the Dream-watch, eh?"

"All my life," he said. "I tried so hard to get in. I'm . . . not good enough. That's why we need you. To defend the city. They're coming—maybe soon!"

"We'll take care of it," she said (highly). "Nice work out there. Thank you for the warning. Keep this up, and you might turn into Dreamwatch material yourself." She gave him a firm pat on the shoulder, then nodded to her bearded companion, who took Painter by the arm and tried to guide him out the door.

Painter lingered though. The Dreamwatch member turned back to her ping-pong game. Maybe . . . maybe that was how she meditated.

Now, you've probably caught on more quickly than Painter did here. You might be thinking at this point of the old adage that says having heroes is not worth it. There are variations on it all around the cosmere. Cynical takes that encourage you never to look up to someone, lest by turning your eyes toward the sky you leave your gut open for a nice stabbing.

I disagree. Hope is a grand thing, and having heroes is essential to human aspiration. That is part of why I tell these stories. That said, you *do* need to learn to separate the story—and what it has done to you—from the individual who prompted it. Art—and all stories are art, even the ones about real people—is about what it *does to you.*

The true hero is the one in your mind, the representation of an ideal that makes you a better person. The individual who inspired it, well, they're like the book on the table or the art on the wall. A vessel. A syringe full of trans-formational aspiration.

Don't force people to live up to your dreams of who they might be. And if you're ever in the situation in which Painter found himself, where your ideals are crumbling, don't do what he did. Don't make it slow. Walk away and patch the wound instead of giving the knife time to twist inside.

"Come on," Hikiri the companion said, pulling him again by the arm. "Let me get your statement."

"Did she mean what she said?" Painter asked. "About me being Dream-watch material? Could I still join them?"

Hikiri rubbed his temples. (An action he did so often it's a wonder he didn't have calluses there. Such was the life dealing with the Dreamwatch.)

"Do you like being a painter?" Hikiri said softly.

"I guess," Painter said.

"It's a good job," Hikiri said. "Stable. Respected. Not too dangerous. You should enjoy it."

Painter could read the tone of the man's voice and understood. *You have no chance here, kid.* Of course he didn't; he'd known that. He took a deep breath to plead anyway, but something else came out.

"I have friends," he said. "Great painters, loyal. When I was in school, we all thought I'd get into the Dreamwatch. They were going to be my companions, but I let them down. I wasn't good enough. It's always felt unfair to me that they got punished because I couldn't paint well enough. Do you think . . . there is a way they could be companions still? Are your Dreamwatch soldiers here recruiting?"

Hikiri shook his head, seeming bemused. "You thought you'd get into the Dreamwatch, did you? Were a skilled painter, I assume? Best of your class?"

"So I thought," Painter said. "Why are you looking at me like that?"

Hikiri pointed at the woman at the game table. "Do you know who she is?"

Painter shook his head.

"Tesuaka Tatomi," he whispered. "Daughter of the senator?" He pointed at the next. "Son of the main investor of the new wing of the college." The third one, by the viewer. "Old money. He's fourth-generation Dreamwatch."

Fourth-generation? That must be a very skilled family. Or . . .

Yes, in this regard, Painter was nearly as permeable as a bank vault. But three key cards and one pressure lock later, his eyes widened.

"The Dreamwatch," he whispered, "is about *who you know*?"

"Of course it is," Hikiri said, finally steering Painter away. "It's the most prestigious position in the painters. It's more appointment than it is job." He looked regretful as he said it. Those were the eyes of a man who had seen more than one young person hurl themselves at a target that, unbeknownst to them, was behind bulletproof glass.

"Then who fights the stable nightmares?" Painter asked.

"They do," Hikiri said. "Just with plenty of help from companions who do a lot of training." He smiled comfortingly to Painter. "You and your friends have good jobs. Enjoy that. We'll get around to hunting your stable nightmare soon."

"But the army of nightmares," Painter said. "They *are* coming, Hikiri. I . . ."

Hikiri didn't believe him. Of course he didn't. Why would he believe something so outlandish? Painter tried to think of some proof, but they'd reached the doorway, and Hikiri firmly pushed him out of it. He nodded to Painter, then shut the door.

I never could have joined them, Painter thought, numb. *No matter how skilled my painting, no matter how hard I worked, I would never have been accepted. I'm a nobody from a small town.*

The others and I . . . we never even had a chance.

There was a point in Painter's life when this discovery would have been the biggest he'd ever made. But today, it was a pale second to the more daunting realization. That he was completely alone and would have to prevent the destruction of the city by himself.

Chapter 38

YUMI BURST from the wagon in her nightgown and clogs, her eyes wild. She remembered. All of it—from the moment she'd woken up with Painter in her body to the day they'd taken him away. The last thirty days were clear in her mind.

Ironically, that was the only part of her life that made any sense. What was she? Was any of it real? She could feel warm sunlight on her skin, see the twirling plants high in the sky. The air was wet from the steamwell, the smell of sulfur lingering. What, if any of this, could she trust?

She searched through the empty town. Where was everyone? Why did it feel like the empty set of a drama after the actors had gone home? Finally, she scooped up a rock and went stalking toward the place of ritual, clogs slapping stone.

It was time to try Painter's idea. Find the machine. Hit it hard. Hope something vital broke. But when she reached the place of ritual, there was no tent. No scholars. No machine. Had that part all been fake too?

No, she thought, turning about. *The machine actually did something to Painter. It was here.*

Perhaps they'd carted it away. Yet in her dreams she'd heard them talking—saying they might need to use the machine on her. They'd keep it close, wouldn't they?

She lowered her stone. Then started walking through the walls of buildings.

It worked. Those walls weren't actually real. *She* wasn't actually real. Both were made of . . . well, whatever nightmares were made of. The rock she carried, however, seemed to really be a rock—at least, it resisted the first time she walked through a wall. As she tugged harder and pulled it through, the wall briefly distorted into amorphous smoke, then returned to looking like cut stones mortared with geyser mud.

Her search didn't take long. There were only so many buildings in the town; she strode straight through them, one after another, until she found the machine hidden inside the bailiff's home. The terrible, many-armed device continued quietly doing its work—a mere two arms stacking rocks, but the entire thing vibrating with a soft energy.

The scholars were here. Four nightmares with only the vaguest human shapes. Like shadows on a very cloudy day, indistinct, melding with the darkness in corners and beneath furniture. As she entered, they turned toward her with shocked postures, which gave her a moment to act.

She dashed forward and swung her rock at the place on the machine where she'd seen them power it on before, that day that seemed so long ago, when she and Painter had flown on a tree to escape. She smashed her rock down over and over, using both hands, breaking the latch on the front, exposing the internal mechanism. She crushed this, screaming, sweating, venting a lifetime's worth of stress. Like steam suddenly released after nineteen years of building beneath the ground.

The machine let out a whine, almost like it was in pain. Glowing white smoke erupted from the front where she'd pounded it. Then the legs locked up, the vibrations ceased, and the lights glowing from within it extinguished.

Yumi dropped the stone and fell to her knees. It was done.

"What," the lead scholar asked, "do you think you are doing, child?"

"Fulfilling the wishes of the spirits," she said. "Ending this machine. Saving us."

"You think . . . *that* is the machine?" the scholar asked. Though he had no mouth, the shadow of his head moved and distorted as he spoke. "Child. That little thing is not what rules us. It is but a bud compared to the tree."

Yumi slumped down. A part of her had known, after all. She'd heard them talking before, and could piece it together. There was another machine. The father machine.

"Where?" she asked.

The lead scholar didn't reply. He stalked forward, joined by the others. Yet she realized she knew.

"It's in Torio City, isn't it?" Yumi asked. "The festival. Did you turn it on during the festival?"

Another of the scholars spoke up, tentatively. "One thousand seven hundred and sixty-three years. Yes . . . festival day. The day we would create power for our people from the spirits themselves."

"And yet," another said, "it instead drew power from us. From our souls. From the lives of our people."

"And thus," another said, holding up a smoky hand, "we became these."

Seventeen hundred years? Yumi reeled, trying to comprehend that. "But . . . where did hion come from?" she whispered. "So much of this is confusing. How much of my world was real, and how much fake? What even *are* we?"

All four turned to her, as if seeing her anew. Their darkness lengthened, their white eyes glowing. They went from willowy shadows to full nightmares in a smooth transition.

"No!" Yumi said. "Don't let the machine control you! We can stop it."

"Why?" the lead scholar asked.

"We created it," another said.

"It is our purpose."

"Our energy."

"Our *art*."

As they spoke, their figures blended together, their voices losing individuality. Though she'd been able to tell them apart at first—hearing in their voices the men she'd spied on in the tent—now they just became nightmares.

"It is life."

"All obey. All souls."

"All of us."

"Except . . ." one said, hesitating.

Again all of them fixated on her.

"Except for the yoki-hijo," one whispered. "All obey the machine. Except . . . those who are too powerful. Except those who have been blessed by the spirits. You it cannot control. You, it must keep captive instead."

Emotion welled up inside Yumi. It meant . . . it meant she was real. Or had been real, until that day centuries ago when they'd activated the machine. When they'd brought the shroud and hion alike. It meant that she was herself, but somehow centuries old? Still, that daunted her.

"My memories . . ." she whispered.

"Scrubbed each day," the nightmares hissed in unison. "You've lived nearly two thousand years in the same town, Yumi. Doing the same things. Thinking the same thoughts. You are both incredibly old and eternally naive."

"And now that you do not accept our treatment—"

"—more extreme measures must be taken."

Their eyes widened, white bores directly through them. Their forms darkened further. As they rose and began to move toward her purposefully.

Yumi ran.

Chapter 39

ALL RIGHT. At this point, some of you might be confused.

If so, you're in good company. Because all of this confused the hell out of me when it began. Let me go over it again, laying out the threads as I've been able to gather them. Together they might present for you a tapestry of understanding.

Seventeen hundred years before our story started, a machine was activated at the great Torish festival of the spirits. Not the tiny machine you've seen; that was a prototype. The real machine was something far greater. Scholars had crafted it to stack stones, attract spirits, and then use them as a power source.

They'd miscalculated, however, because the machine saw *all* souls— not just the spirits that lived beneath the ground—as a viable power source. When first turned on, it was *hungry*. It needed strength to follow its instructions to stack stones, and it wanted an overwhelming amount of power to jump-start its work. No spirits were available. So it instead reached out and seized the nearest sources it could find: the souls of the people of Torio.

Let this be a lesson. When you Awaken a device like this, be very, *very* careful what Commands you give it to follow.

This machine immediately began feeding on them, destroying their bodies and harvesting their Investiture. The result was the shroud, sprayed into the air, left to rain down and blanket the land. A dark miasma literally crafted from the dead, everyone's Identities evaporated and transformed into this dark force. Imagine it like . . . the tar that decomposed bodies sometimes turn into over many years of incredible pressure. The shroud is that, except souls, left as refuse from the machine's initial activation.

A soul cannot be destroyed; it can only change forms. The machine, then, didn't use people up so much as transform them. They lingered as this blackness, a churning soup made of tens of thousands of souls subject to the machine's domineering will, held in eternal bondage to something they'd created.

Delightful, eh? Progress, it is said, always disrupts one industry or another. Well, in Torio, progress took a running leap—and instead of just disrupting industry, decided to disrupt the entire planet. Permanently.

Before long, the machine burned through the relatively weak souls of humans and moved on to the spirits themselves. Drawn by the machine's incredible stacking abilities, the spirits were handily trapped by its power. It eventually gathered each and every remaining free spirit in the land. They finally satiated it, providing a more . . . vigorous power source. That was its purpose, and the thing fulfilled it with excellence.

Unfortunately, there was almost no one left to appreciate it.

Only wandering refugees who survived the machine's initial activation— nomads from the edge of civilization. Lucky survivors who eventually came across the results of the machine's efforts: hion stubs provided in some of the former locations of Torish towns. The blood of enslaved spirits, hidden away, the source of this power never understood.

PAINTER stepped alone up to the shroud, holding his painter's bag with sweaty fingers, watching the shifting darkness. This was the west side of town—where the nightmares would come. It was near his patrol route— the place where Yumi had once pushed back the darkness ever so briefly.

When the nightmares arrived, they would find only him. A single painter.

He trembled, knowing how it would play out. A rush of dark things surrounding him. If he worked frantically, perhaps he could lock down one of them before he was killed. Perhaps even two or three. Then they would rip him apart. Leave him in pieces, like in the stories of what had happened to the painters of Futinoro.

After he was dead, the nightmares would descend upon the unsuspecting city. Rampaging. Maybe . . . maybe the Dreamwatch would recognize what was happening. Maybe they'd resist. But . . . but after meeting them, he had to acknowledge how frail a hope that was. How many people would die tonight because he hadn't been able to persuade the Dreamwatch?

He bowed his head.

Then thought, *What am I (lowly) doing?*

This was stupid. There was another way.

Yumi's way.

YOU still have questions, don't you?

All right, let's delve a little deeper. Let me show you a few events again—but this time through the eyes of someone *other* than Yumi or Painter. Someone who had been involved in both stories from the beginning.

Here I must admit to you that I've lied about one crucial item. Remember how I told you I'd been hearing voices, seeing flashes of images—sometimes as full pictures, sometimes just as lines that quivered in my vision? Glimpses of events as they unfolded through Painter's or Yumi's eyes? Well, that part is true, but it wasn't the whole truth.

There's a *third* person whose eyes I'd been seeing through.

Liyun.

In fact, for me, this story began with her. Baffling flashes of her life. (I think that the spirits were watching Liyun in particular. Then some irregularities about my . . . specific nature tapped into the Spiritual communication, letting me see what was happening.)

The machine evaporated the population of Torio, feeding upon their power and spitting out the shroud as a byproduct. Well, as Yumi and Painter had both guessed (despite lacking all the information), there were some people the machine couldn't harvest or control: the yoki-hijo.

They were superficially killed during the machine's initial activation like everyone else. However, after a short time these fourteen souls pulled themselves free of the shroud and *re-formed*. They came back from the dead, refusing to be controlled.

All fourteen women were beings of incredible willpower. Highly Invested at birth by the spirits, they presented a legitimate threat to the machine. It could not harvest their energy and could not keep them contained in the shroud. The most the machine could do to them was siphon off a tiny bit of their memories.

So, to control them, it created prisons in the form of fake towns. Servants, compelled by the machine, emerged from the shroud. Buildings, plants, and vehicles were recreated from the substance of souls, and a careful perimeter was erected. The walls Masaka found? Those projected (by making images out of the shroud) a perfectly realistic, yet fake landscape.

These places were fourteen nature preserves, you might say, each designed for a single occupant. The yoki-hijo were placed into these prisons, with their memories erased each night. Then they were given a single day to live over and over, calling fake spirits formed from the shroud.

A clunky system, yes, but it worked. For centuries it kept these extremely dangerous souls captive not by force of arm, but by pure force of *mundanity*.

Their keepers were the souls of those they had once known. Best I can tell, Liyun spent the last seventeen centuries or so living the same day over and over. She was exactly as presented. That was her, the actual person, the exact soul that raised Yumi. Released from the shroud, partially controlled by the machine, partially given self-governance.

Liyun was one of hundreds of souls forced into this strange half life. Their memories were, of course, erased each day—but I think part of them understood that something was wrong. Because each night, while the yoki-hijo slept, the machine would let its will slacken. Its attention no longer on these servants, they would lose their shape and sense of self, becoming vague blobs of blackness.

Each night, during this time of slumber, some of these servants would break free. They'd stalk the land, ghosts without memories, on a prowling search for meaning. For understanding. For *life*. And like most unbound Investiture—like the spirits themselves—the souls of the dead were drawn to the imaginations of the living.

These nightmares forgot how to be people when not compelled directly by the machine. But they longed, *lusted*, for the lives they'd lost. Maddened by their state of half-existence, they'd sneak into cities, hunting dreaming minds with powerful imaginations. There, Painter and his kind would trap them into some semblance of physicality and banish them back to the shroud—where the machine, each day, would recycle them again and set them to work in its prisons.

This was Liyun's life. The machine didn't mind that she prowled at night as a nightmare; why would it? The job was done, the yoki-hijo contained. Theoretically. A curious aspect of machines, even ones partially Awakened like this one: They don't *plan*. They don't think about the future. Most machines can only react to the state of things in the now.

Therefore it didn't, couldn't, account for Yumi spending *centuries* perfecting her art. Yes, her memories were wiped each day, but something remained. Muscle memory. Skills that sank in deep, infusing her soul, like rum in a cake. Her skill couldn't be separated from her; she had earned it.

So it was that on the day our story began, something remarkable occurred. Seventeen hundred years of repeating the same day, and something finally snapped. Because Yumi, her skill reaching a crescendo, stacked so well that she pulled a single spirit *away* from the machine.

This changed everything.

That spirit, grateful for a moment of freedom, yet knowing it would soon be captured again, contacted her. Looking for a way out. At the same time, Liyun—unnerved—*knew* something strange had happened with Yumi. She went hunting that night as a nightmare, stronger than she'd ever been before. And the briefly freed spirit watched her, followed her, until she encountered Painter.

He wasn't anyone special, at least on paper. Yes, he was of above-average painting skill, but that wasn't what drew the attention of the spirit. Instead it was the fact that he saved the life of a young boy.

Turns out that was enough; the spirit found in him the soul of a hero. It wasn't the boasts, the pretending, the superficial actions. It was the fact that when he could have just headed home to relax, he'd instead turned back. To protect the people of Kilahito, even when he didn't feel like it.

You know the rest. Painter and Yumi linked. And Liyun? Her disquiet grew. She escaped each night, prowling Kilahito, searching for her yoki-hijo. She didn't know who she was during these times—only that there was a Connection driving her to search for this young woman. She absolutely had tried to kill Yumi when she had found her after the carnival, and she might actually have managed it. This wouldn't have solved the machine's problems, as then Liyun would have absorbed all that power and become a danger. But it would have ended Yumi's problems, technically—by leaving her dead.

You'll have to forgive Liyun for the near-murder of someone she loved and was sworn to protect. She wasn't feeling like herself at the time—in fact, she hadn't felt like herself for seventeen hundred years.

YUMI scrambled through the town, frenzied, hunted. Remembering that unyielding coldness from the night when the monster—Liyun—had nearly absorbed her. Yumi felt echoes of that icy death. Like she'd been submerged, sinking far, far, far from the heat and light.

The four scholars, no longer the least bit recognizable, followed her. Nightmares on the prowl, hideous creations from the dreams of people's deepest torments. Shaped by fears, given substance by the terrible machine. She couldn't outrun them. She couldn't paint them, not without tools. Would they respond to stacking? Would she even get a chance to put two stones upon one another before they reached her?

She almost tried. But then she thought of a better way.

Painter's way.

She ran for the place of ritual, passing right through the fence. The sound of claws on stone chased her farther, to where the scholars had once kept their tent. Chained behind that spot, to give the tent shade, were several trees.

Yumi leaped for the first of them and pulled out the pin holding its chain to the ground. With a cry, she held on tightly to the tree, her eyes squeezed closed. Anticipating the arrival of the nightmares and the feeling of their claws on her skin.

When it didn't happen, she cracked her eyes and saw four dark shapes on the ground below. Looking up. Having arrived just a fraction too late for the second time in their lives.

PAINTER found his friends in their usual place at Design's restaurant. He blessed his luck. This would have been a terrible night for them to go out for dumplings instead. He stumbled up to their table, then threw himself to his knees and bowed, his head touching the ground.

"I'm sorry," he whispered.

Stunned silence.

"I know it's late for apologies," he continued. "I realize I hurt you deeply. I . . . didn't want to do that. Hurting all of you was the *last* thing I wanted. I just couldn't think, couldn't process what had happened until it was too late. And I foolishly kept thinking if I could put it off, I would be able to find some way to prevent you from suffering the terrible loss that I felt."

He continued kneeling, listening to them shuffle, a pair of maipon sticks clinking together as a bowl on the table shifted.

"I know you have no reason to believe me ever again," he said. "You're fully justified in ignoring me. But I'm *trying* to do better, and so I'm going to tell you the absolute truth. These last weeks, I've been interacting with nightmares. They have souls. They're people somehow, from long ago.

"I thought things were going well, but now . . . Now we're in danger. One of them told me, just a few minutes ago, that a *hundred* of its fellows are coming to Kilahito. To destroy it, like they did to Futinoro. Because of me, and what I know, an army of stable nightmares is on its way to the city right now, and the Dreamwatch won't listen to me.

"I've lied to you in the past. I've hurt you. But this is *not a lie*. Nightmares will destroy everyone in this city unless we stop them. I'm begging for your help. So I don't have to face them alone."

He squeezed his eyes shut, head to the floor, tears dripping to stain the wood.

"You *talked* to a nightmare," Akane said.

"Yes," he whispered.

"And it said an army of other nightmares was coming to destroy Kilahito."

"From the west," Painter said. "It sounds ridiculous. But it's true."

Tense silence. Though other patrons continued to eat, it was like this one section of the room had been muffled. As if nothing there lived. As if he were still alone.

"Suppose we'd better go with you then," Tojin said, and stood.

Painter looked up, his heart leaping.

"You *believe* him?" Izzy said, gesturing to Painter. "Really?"

Tojin shrugged. "What's the worst that could happen, Izzy? If he's wrong, we get a little embarrassed and have to come back and eat our noodles cold." He looked at Painter. "If he's right, and we don't go, then what?" He took a deep breath, then offered a beefy hand to Painter.

Painter took it and was hauled to his feet.

"I agree," Masaka said softly, from within her thick sweater-and-scarf shroud. "I think we should go. Just in case."

"If there are a hundred nightmares," Akane said, "then we won't do much to stop them."

"Takanda owes me a favor," Tojin said. "We'll bring him and his painters out to help. And Yuinshi always likes a good laugh—he'll want to watch this. He can bring some more."

"I suppose," Akane said, "I could ask Ikonora to come as well. And she could probably gather a few . . . We won't have a hundred painters. But maybe twenty or thirty."

"Yes, *please*," Painter said. He clutched Tojin's hand. "Thank you."

"The other night," he said, "when the stable nightmare attacked . . . it turned away, for no reason, and fled. When it did, I thought for the briefest moment I saw you there." Tojin smiled. "I realized my mind was playing tricks on me. Been thinking about it anyway, and it occurred to me that you're the only one who ever took this life seriously.

"Maybe if I'd been a little more like you, I wouldn't have fallen down and nearly been taken by that thing. I thought, maybe it's all right to pretend you're in the Dreamwatch, you know?" He shrugged. "There are worse lies to tell. Anyway, come on. Let's see how many companions we can gather for you."

ONE FINAL bit of explanation. You might be wondering what the spirit did to Yumi and Painter.

Well, by building that Connection between them, it protected Yumi. For when she was in spiritual form, she was immune to the machine's touch. (Much like the hion lines.) The spirit who Connected them hadn't had a plan beyond this: the hope that Yumi, once protected, would be able to help. The spirit hadn't actually expected Yumi and Painter to begin swapping—but when you play with things like Spiritual Connection, irregularities pop up.

This meddling by the spirit placed the machine in a predicament. Suddenly one of the yoki-hijo couldn't have her mind erased. While machines can't generally plan, they *can* assess a situation in all of its complexities and quickly devise a solution. The solution in this case? To keep the narrative going. To let Yumi "travel" to a new town each day and simply continue her life.

Thus, as she slept, it evaporated the previous town and created a new one using imprints left long ago on the shroud. At first, it thought creating a new town for her each day would be enough.

However, she refused to move on. She stayed in that second town for weeks, acting irregularly. The wrongness compounded, and the machine reassessed. Yumi was dangerous, and there was something distinctly odd about her behavior. So the machine called upon its most dedicated servants, the scholars: its creators. They had been kept apart from the soup of the shroud and held in reserve, their wills dominated but their minds left partially free, for just such a situation.

The scholars had been sent, therefore, as agents. They'd played a role like everyone else, reenacting things they'd done seventeen hundred years before. Showing off their machine prototype to the small towns. However, they'd come with a secondary mandate: to discover what was wrong in the town and to fix the problem, no matter what that required.

That brings us, finally, to the present. Where Yumi had a different problem. The tree she was flying on was made from the shroud.

That made sense to her. The buildings hadn't been real, nor had the people. Why would the plants be real? It had all been a charade orchestrated to control her. Better if every element, then, could be controlled exactly.

As she rose higher in the air, the tree started to warp beneath her fingers. Wisps of smoke began to trail from it. Being created from the shroud, the tree was subject to her enemy's control—which meant the machine could make its form vanish back into the shroud. Something it was starting to do, if more slowly than the machine would have liked.

She soon hit the invisible wall around her little town. Here the shroud had been painted to give the illusion of a landscape extending forever. Once she touched it, that wall warped and bent—letting her pass through. For the first time in almost two thousand years, she physically left that pocket of land and entered the shroud proper.

The darkness was strangely transparent to her. (And she didn't even have to burn tin.) Perhaps this was because she was made of its same substance. Once she was within it—hovering on a tree that was shrinking by the minute—she saw a dark and ruined landscape below. Nothing growing—just dark stone that had been hidden from the sun for millennia. Behind her, the town faded. She could see it retreating, a column with a dome on top. A piece of her broke when she realized even the sunlight she'd basked in and loved—even the sight of the daystar itself—had somehow been fake.

(She was wrong, by the way. The sunlight, actually, was real—the domes over the cities let sunlight through in one direction without allowing light back out the other way. So while what she felt was authentic, those of us surveying the world from above didn't spot these prisons. In addition, the heat from the ground was real, created by the machine using a concentration of Invested essence.)

From this height, Yumi could make out other dome-topped columns in the distance. These too were transparent to her eyes, lights standing out like candles on a dark night. The prisons of the thirteen other yoki-hijo. And in the middle of it all, a brilliant larger light that she figured must be Torio City, the capital. Home of the festival. Seat of the queen.

Yumi was drifting away from it.

That was a much smaller problem than the fact that her tree was unraveling faster now—joining with the smoky blackness. Beneath her, dark shapes gathered. The scholars had not given up. Indeed, she flew like a banner out here, hard to miss. She started to drift downward as her tree continued to cease being a tree. She clung to it, eyes closed, resting her forehead against the wood.

Please. Please, spirits. Let it continue.

The bark beneath her forehead hardened. The tree stabilized in the air. Yumi opened her eyes, surprised—and embarrassed by that surprise. She'd prayed. The spirits had answered. It was just . . . she didn't usually see them answer so quickly . . .

She started to fall again, the tree unraveling.

No! she thought. And again it recovered. Because . . . *Because what I believe to be true is true,* Yumi realized. *This tree is created from the shroud. And by thinking of it as something else, I can force that to be the reality.*

As she thought this way, the tree indeed became even more solid.

And the wind, Yumi thought forcefully. *I am lucky. Because it blows the right direction.*

The tree shifted in the wind, turning the way she needed it to go, toward Torio City. Toward the machine.

AN hour later, painters gathered at the western edge of the city, laying down stacks of canvases and large jars of ink. Favors had been cashed in. Promises given. Debts incurred. In total, thirty-seven had come.

Painter watched it all with excruciating anxiety, worried that the assault would come while they were still preparing. But now that he had them all organized—a good ten to fifteen percent of the city's total painters—he found himself overwhelmed with gratitude. His friends had not gone halfway in their efforts. It was still a small force, considering what was coming. And not one of them save him had any experience painting stable nightmares.

But it was a far, far cry from where he'd been before, standing here alone.

"All right, Akane," a lanky painter called. "What are we doing here again?"

"Waiting," she said. "Something might be coming. Something dangerous. Have your paints ready."

The others settled in, chatting in groups, some sitting with their backs to the wall of warehouse buildings around the city. Painter turned his eyes to the shroud and waited.

And waited.

And waited.

A full hour with all of them gathered there, grumbles increasing. His anxiety rising. What if he'd picked the wrong location? What if the others got bored and left right before the attack happened?

What if . . .

While Tojin placated one of the leaders among the other groups, Akane walked up, hands clasped behind her back. She looked tired.

"Nikaro," she said, "is your sister safe? Please tell me she's staying, for once, in your room."

"She's . . . not going to be painting. I will explain eventually, but you don't need to worry about her." *I'll do enough of that for all of us.*

Telling the truth was one thing. Explaining what had been happening with him and Yumi . . . well, that would have to wait. Akane glanced out at the shroud, concern written across her face. Then she looked back at him. "Tell me again what we're waiting for?"

"They'll come," Painter promised her before she could continue. "A hundred nightmares. It's going to happen."

"It's all right if it doesn't, you know."

"You all put your reputations on the line for this," Painter said. He'd noticed the glares from some painters as they realized he was involved. The others had left his name out of the recruitment efforts. Wisely.

She shrugged. "Like Tojin said. We might get embarrassed for a little while. Nothing we can't live down."

"Akane," he said, "I know it sounds strange, but I *did* speak to a nightmare. I . . . I can't explain it all. I promise though, this is really going to happen."

"And . . . if it doesn't, Nikaro?"

"I wouldn't lie to you," he said, his voice strained. "Not again."

"I'm not saying you would," she whispered. "But Nikaro, what if . . . maybe you imagined it. What if you . . . need help? Because sometimes, things you want to be real *feel* real?"

"I—"

"Please," Akane said. "Consider it."

He forced himself to. For her; for the effort they'd given him. He closed his eyes, and actually wondered. The things he'd experienced seemed so incredible, even outlandish. There *was* an easy explanation.

He'd wanted so badly to be someone special. He'd viewed himself, all these months, as a lone warrior wandering the night, looking for people to save. Could he have just . . . made it all up? Formed everything out of the shroud? Or even worse, simply imagined it?

He rebelled against the thought, but a calmer part of him—the part that had survived the shame of his previous lies—stood fast. Willing to examine this. If it was true, if he'd devised all of this, then Akane was right. He needed help. It wasn't a lie, or even a moral failing, to admit that.

"If it turns out," he said, opening his eyes, "that nothing comes of this . . . then yes, Akane. I'll get help."

She nodded toward the others. "Why don't I tell them this was a drill of sorts? Us trying to figure out how quickly we could gather a force to protect the city in an emergency."

"No," Painter said, taking her arm. "Don't lie to them. If you decide you need to dismiss them . . . tell them the truth. That you were humoring me. In remembrance of our former friendship."

She hugged him then.

"I'm truly sorry," he whispered, holding to her. "About everything I've done. Said. And the things I haven't said most of all."

"We know," she said, pulling back. "I can't speak for the others, but I forgive you, Nikaro. I know you didn't want to hurt us."

He smiled.

"Uh, *guys*?" Masaka said, hurrying over. "Have you ever seen it do *that* before?"

Painter turned.

The shroud was undulating. Agitating, *frothing*.

"Grab your things!" Painter shouted. "They're coming!"

People scrambled to their feet, gaping. Stunned.

As the nightmares began to emerge.

YUMI knew, as she approached Torio City, that she needed to let the tree land.

She couldn't defeat the machine while dealing with the nightmares who were still down there hunting her. She needed to confront them first. Instinct propelled her, but also good logic. Because she remembered something Design had told her.

Her tree floated down, unraveling as it lowered. As she landed, she stepped free, allowing it to vanish fully. Four ghastly figures stood before her, blocking the way into Torio City. All around was eternal night, barren stone veiled by a pervasive black smoke.

The four nightmares came for her and slammed their claws into her. Seeking to draw out her strength, to sap it, to freeze her.

But she was stronger than they were.

You could consume them.

As they tried to pull her strength away, she simply . . . refused.

"I am the one who the spirits chose," she said, feeling their claws pass through her harmlessly. "I am the thing you had to lock up."

They stumbled back from her, shrinking. As nightmares sometimes do when no longer feared.

"I am the one that nightmares fear," she said, imagining them. Knowing them for what they were. Forcing the figures to coalesce into four spindly scholars. "And *you* shall bow to *me*."

Color flooded them and they gasped, falling to the ground.

Yumi walked to the lead scholar, who sat up first, looking at her with frightened eyes. She didn't attack him though. She sat before him in a pose of meditation.

"Tell me," she said softly, "how to destroy the machine."

"You . . ." He glanced toward his colleagues, who lay in a lump. "You can't. I'm sorry." He bowed his head and began to shake. "I'm sorry . . . Oh, what have we done? What have we done . . ."

"It's all right," Yumi said. "What has happened is in the past. I am the yoki-hijo. My word is law. You may rest, once this is through."

"Thank you," he said, taking her by the hand. "But you can't stop it."

"There is no need to protect the machine. You are free from its control. It cannot hurt you, no matter how much it wants to."

"You don't understand," the scholar said. "It doesn't *want* anything. It's not alive."

"But the way everyone has acted," she said. "Something *is* controlling them."

"That is because of the instructions *we* gave the machine," he explained. "We built it to protect itself and to harvest energy from the spirits. These are not the machine's wishes, any more than a tree *wants* to grow. But once it started drawing on us, on all of us . . . we defended it because . . . because we were then part of it somehow."

She frowned, looking beyond him into the city. A shining, beautiful city full of buildings like towers, with fountains, trees, red roofs, and sculptures of dragons. Empty of people.

"It uses our souls as energy," she said.

"Originally it did," the scholar said. "Now it uses the spirits, which are trapped eternally to fuel the machine. Oh . . . what have we *done*?"

"Our people became but memories," another of the scholars whispered, eyes down. "Their souls as smoke."

"Our shame," another said. "Our sorrow. Powered perpetually by the spirits now, the machine will never run out, never shut down on its own."

"We *must* turn it off," Yumi said.

The lead scholar shook his head. "It is shielded. Protected as per its core instructions. There is no plug or hion line to remove. It self-perpetuates, fed by thousands of eternal spirits. I'm sorry. I wish . . . wish we could have left you alone. It's incredible that you made it this far."

"But worthless in the end," another scholar said. "It will wipe out the city of Kilahito now. Any trace of what happened with you and that boy will be annihilated."

"No," Yumi whispered, standing. "My world. My rules."

She stepped forward and commanded her nightgown to change. Black smoke swirled and she emerged from it wearing the dress that Akane had bought her.

She strode past the scholars, and at long last—seventeen hundred years after the first time she asked Liyun for the privilege—entered Torio City.

And found rubble.

"NIKARO!" a shrill voice shouted.

He tore away from his current painting, leaving a nightmare on the ground, curled up in the shape of a sleeping cat. The painters had formed an irregular circle, shoulder to shoulder—but some faltered. Painter rushed across the center of the circle, to the side of a painter he barely recognized. She was breaking, trembling, turning away from the nightmares in a panic.

Painter stepped in and slammed the tip of his brush down, ignoring her canvas. With a powerful swirl, he created a flower on the ground itself—a lotus, floating, opening its many petals to the air like a fist unclenching.

The nightmare shrank into the shape, forced to conform to his will. But like every other nightmare they'd faced tonight, it didn't evaporate away as usual.

In all honesty, the painters probably should have been slaughtered. But the machine was distracted by Yumi, and the nightmares were momentarily confused, surprised at the unexpected resistance. They prowled around the ring, looking to feed on the painters, but not rushing in a throng to attack. That didn't make it *easy* on Painter and his team, as the nightmares were terrifying and mostly stable. But these minutes of confusion made resisting them *possible*.

Still, the humans were *not* prepared for such a fight as this. They had to ward away each nightmare that came close—had to face down stable monsters and not break. They painted with trembling hands, and kept stopping and staring, panicking. Painter had to watch for this, because he had a sense the sole thing keeping them alive was this unified front. This collective force of painting, not allowing any one nightmare to attack the circle and break it completely. Even as he finished his lotus, he noticed Izzy freezing in terror.

Painter shoved her aside and attacked her nightmare with a painting. "Hold the circle!" he shouted as he crafted a bird, seeing that in the shape of the nightmare. It looked a little like the great ravens he'd seen in Yumi's world. "Keep painting! See how most of them mill around, distracted by our work. They cannot take us so long as we are painting! You've fought nightmares before. These are the same!"

But they weren't. These were bigger, their forms more terrible. Those eyes like the hollow insides of bones. The scraping of claws on the ground. Worst of all, none of them vanished when painted. They shrank down, but smoldered there like embers—then started growing again once attention was no longer on them.

Paintings alone weren't enough to hold these. His one consolation was that instead of continuing in through the city, the monsters had surrounded the circle. For now, Kilahito was safe. But as Painter finished helping Izzy, a scream rose from across the circle. He spun to find Nanakai—a painter in her forties—falling in a flash of blood as a nightmare seized upon her nervousness and pushed forward, attacking.

Two others grabbed her as she stammered on the ground, staring with horror at the gouges across her side and arm. Painter had to leap over her and hold the line, but he needed to capture three nightmares at once. And so, without thinking, he defaulted to bamboo. Simple bamboo.

In that moment, it was actually what he needed. It froze all three nightmares briefly, long enough for someone else to step in and help.

He couldn't stop the entire army himself. He couldn't stop them at *all*, not permanently. It was only a matter of time.

*   *   *

RUBBLE. The beautiful city she'd seen outside was an illusion, a veneer painted on the surface of the wall protecting the place. Perhaps that was how it had once looked, hundreds of years ago.

Now Yumi walked amid fallen stones and crumbling walls. Roofs had long since decayed away. Turned out she couldn't visit Torio City itself. Only its grave.

One structure remained at the very center of the city. Yumi imagined it as a grand exhibit hall, with banners out front for the festival of the spirits. Where the scholars had unveiled their amazing new project: a machine that could summon spirits and provide a new form of energy. Hion.

It would change the world.

From the top of the steps, Yumi turned to gaze out through the shroud. In the distance glowed the points of light spaced around Torio City.

"It cannot defeat us like the others," she whispered to herself. "Remember that." She stepped inside the building.

The machine was there, dominating the interior like a fat mushroom overgrowing all its siblings. Fully thirty feet tall, with hundreds of legs, it piled stones on all sides in an eternal process—other legs knocking them over as it went. It would have long since broken down, but Investiture— the smoke—repaired each worn joint, replaced each cracked limb. It was, you might say, an undead machine.

Thousands of spirits surrounded it, just beyond the ring of stones. Shimmering entities of liquid light, blue and red in swirls. Imagine them like frozen orbs of water, yet undulating, moving in a rhythm. Like an audience at a concert. Or a sermon.

Yumi steeled herself and stepped forward . . . before planting face-first into an invisible barrier right inside the doorway.

She pressed her hands against it, then looked through, trapped outside. This place was shielded, as the scholars had said.

"WE can't hold these!" Tojin shouted, pulling Painter by the arm. "It's not working! They recover after we paint them!"

Painter glanced toward the center of the circle, to where six of their colleagues now huddled with various dire wounds, bleeding out blood like ink on the ground. One woman wasn't moving at all. Others groaned in pain.

Nightmares had flooded the street around them—a churning, seemingly endless mass of black punctuated by those sickly white eyes. Pressing in, shrinking the circle. Growing increasingly bold as they recovered from their momentary confusion.

The painters were running out of canvases. The ground was covered in ink, such that stepping was slick.

"What do we do?" Tojin asked, panicked. "Nikaro, what do we *do*?"

"We paint."

"But—"

"We paint!" Painter shouted. "Because if we do not, they get into the city. Without us, the people die."

"The people ignore us!" another cried. "They turn off their lights. They sleep."

"Because they can't do anything else," Painter shouted, starting his next painting. "We are the line between their fears and their flesh. *We are the Dreamwatch now.*"

"We are the Dreamwatch now," Tojin said, raising his brush. "We are the Dreamwatch now!"

Others took up the cry as a particularly large nightmare loomed over the group. At least fifteen feet high, but familiar.

Yes. *Familiar.*

Lupine. Smoky shape like jagged edges of glass. Liyun was here . . .

Liyun. Painter's eyes widened.

That was the answer.

YUMI knelt, defeated, at the invisible barrier surrounding the machine's hall.

Rocks bounced off the shield when she tried to break it down. Her shouts did nothing.

All this way. For nothing.

Pain stabbed at her. But not her own. She frowned and stepped back outside to look . . . toward something?

Painter, she thought. She could feel him, faintly. The Connection had not been entirely severed.

He was frantic, fighting.

Nightmares will come. Endless nightmares. To destroy him, and all he knows. All that he might have told.

It was not a thought but an impression. Knowledge of what the machine would do to protect itself. The scholars weren't *completely* right about it having no will. Any object as Invested as it was would take on at least some trappings of self-awareness.

Painter would die. If he survived this first wave of nightmares, others would come. Thousands upon thousands, until Kilahito was rubble.

Yumi turned back to the awful machine, tears in her eyes. It, in turn, continued its eternal stacking. To it, one pile was the same as another. Things to build, knock over, then build again. The walls inside, the floor, much of the stone beneath had been chopped up to continue feeding its efforts. Beneath lay the sand its earlier stones had become over the centuries.

It didn't care what it made. All it did was keep going, maintaining its hold on the spirits for power.

It *didn't care.*

Yumi stalked away from the hall of the machine and down the steps, dress flowing and rippling in the wind. At the grand courtyard in front— once magnificent, now rubble—she knelt.

And started stacking.

PAINTER didn't try to force Liyun's nightmare into the shape of a bird, or cat, or even bamboo. He didn't look at the shifting darkness to find some vague impression. He didn't need that crutch. He knew what she was.

He *knew* her. Stern and unyielding, yet deep down just wanting to help. Those frown lines, those twin blades of hair, that bell-shaped dress . . .

He didn't look at her as he painted, but he felt the effects of what he was doing as the others nearby muttered. You weren't supposed to paint nightmares as people. A person could still kill you. The goal was to pick something innocent, harmless.

Liyun was anything but harmless. Yet he *knew* this nightmare at its core. That changed everything. As he finished his canvas with a flourish, he looked up to find her kneeling outside the ring of painters. Hands stained by the ink on the ground, gasping for breath.

And as Painter grabbed another canvas from their dwindling stack, Liyun did *not* revert back to a terrible monster like the others had. The nightmares were *people.*

He needed to treat them as such.

STACKING.

You might not call it an art.

You might find it the strangest idea. This is what Yumi's people revere? This is what they consider the highest aesthetic achievement of their culture? *This?*

Yet all art is meaningless without those to admire it. *You* don't get to decide what constitutes art. But *we* together *do.*

They'd taken Yumi's memories from her. Fortunately, as I've said, some things run deeper than memory. In many ways, despite the centuries, she was still a girl of nineteen. Her lived experience and her maturity aligned on that count.

But her skill . . . well, that had been growing. Day after day. Year after year. Ability distilled, like water drops forming stalactites through the course of primordial eons, she'd built something inside herself.

She wasn't just good at stacking.

She wasn't merely a master.

Yumi was literally the best who had ever lived. With twenty or more lifetimes' worth of practice.

When she let loose, everything changed. For in her was a power far beyond that of hion.

PAINTER didn't know the other Torish people as well as he did Liyun, but he had painted some of them recently, during meditations. He started there, with broad sweeping lines, crafting the shape of the town mayor.

Out among the sea of nightmares, one changed. Transforming, becoming *himself* again. With a shout, Painter got several others to paint the nightmares between him and that one, shrinking them so he could see it better. As the details manifested, he was able to get more accurate.

The nightmare wanted to be a person again. Painter could *feel* it, and as he outlined the general shape, the mayor fed him other details. Until Painter left the balding man huddling on the ground, terrified and cold, but also harmless.

It was a slow process. But the others took heart as they saw what was happening—that somehow Painter had found a way to make progress, instead of just treading water. They surged with strength, Tojin and Akane calling encouragement, holding back the tide—freezing each nightmare in turn as it tried to break through. Giving Painter room.

One at a time. Person after person. He shrank them down to themselves. Until, exhausted—his fingers cramped, his arms aching—he gave a final flourish to finish Hwanji's hair, and dropped her to the ground. He blinked to realize that the street outside the city had fallen still, save for the moans of the wounded painters and the exhausted sighs of the others.

It was over. Somehow, they'd done it. They'd finished their painting—and in so doing were left with a hundred very confused, very cold Torish townspeople.

Painter let his brush tumble from his fingers and clatter to the stone. He looked west, toward the shroud. Through it. Toward someone he felt beyond.

Someone who was concentrating with incredible focus.

Chapter 41

Y UMI STACKED.

Dozens of stones. Hundreds of them. She moved without thought, yet with *Intent*, building towering formations around herself from the bones of a broken city.

Sculptures of fifty or more stones. Sixty. Heights so incredible she had to climb up on top of nearby chunks of rubble to finish. She created a spiraling design from the towers, stacks of stones like seeds blown from a spinning flower, flowing from the center of the fallen courtyard.

Each piece fit with the others, and each stack built upon the others. Stone flowed as if it were water. Piles of seemingly impossible balances. Shapes to intrigue the mind. To make you gasp.

Time lost meaning to her. This was her meditation. This was her purpose. This was *creation*. Hundreds of stacks, born from a sublime flow. Sculptures working together on the grandest scale, yet still fascinating in the smallest detail.

This was art. Something the machine, however capable in the technical details, could never understand. Because art is, and always has been, about what it does to us. To the one shaping it and the one experiencing it.

For Yumi, on that transcendent day, she was both. Artist and audience. Alone.

Until the spirits joined her.

Ripped from the technical marvel that was the machine, they flowed out through the stones and emerged. One at a time, surrounding Yumi's creation. Eventually she felt a trembling as the machine panicked and picked up speed. A stack toppled, and she used its stones to create something even better.

A dozen spirits joined her. Two dozen. A hundred. Then hundreds. Each stolen from an increasingly reckless machine. One by one, those that had been transfixed by its precise motions instead turned toward her with awe, rejoicing in her organic creativity. Each was freed from their subjugation by something more beautiful. More meaningful.

At some point, picking up momentum, Yumi realized what she was doing. What this would mean. The machine had created the shroud, and was keeping it in place. Maintaining it, and hoarding all those souls in its clutches, ready to be deployed if needed.

No machine meant no more shroud.

No more souls held captive.

No more . . . Yumi.

This was true, unfortunately. Though the yoki-hijo had forcibly returned to life from the shroud, they'd only been able to do so because the shroud itself was being maintained by the machine.

Regardless, she did not stop. This time it wasn't about omens, or what she'd been "born" to do. This time, *she* decided: Service to her people. Service to the spirits. And last of all, service to someone she loved. No nightmares meant that Kilahito—and all it contained—would be safe.

So as she placed the final stone and the last spirit was pried from the grip of the dying machine, she looked up. Eastward. Toward someone she could feel out there.

Someone frightened. For her.

Behind Yumi, the machine at last fell still. Slumping, disintegrating as the pieces of it that hadn't been real—most of them, by now—evaporated away. Self-perpetuating, it had needed fuel to keep going. Fuel she had stolen away.

Thank you! the spirits said. *Thank you!*

Yumi sat back on her heels, closed her eyes.

It was finished.

* * *

THE Torish people started to evaporate.

By now, others had come to investigate the strange disturbance. Police, EMTs, even reporters. They'd given medical attention to the wounded painters. They'd listened, incredulous, to the accounts of those who had fought in the battle. Nurses had given blankets to the strange people who spoke a language that—without the bond that Yumi and Painter shared—was unintelligible to modern ears.

But then those former nightmares began to fade away, disintegrating into smoke. At first, Painter worried that they were becoming monsters again. He leaped to his feet, casting off his blanket and dropping his tea. But the people just continued to fade.

Each one smiled as it happened. He met Liyun's eyes and she grinned, then turned her eyes upward.

The shroud was undulating again. Different this time. Hissing . . .

Unraveling.

Yumi? he thought. *Yumi! What is going on?*

I've done it . . . she thought back.

How? he thought, amazed. *You broke the machine?*

Yes, she replied.

I'm coming to you, he thought, running up to the shroud as it— amazingly—began to crumble away. *Where are you?*

In return, he sensed only regret.

Nikaro, she said. *Do you remember . . . what you said about sad stories . . .*

"No," he whispered, falling to his knees. "No . . ."

YUMI felt herself going as it all unraveled.

I'm sorry, she thought to him. *But sometimes . . . sometimes it has to be sad.*

Her arms became smoke, her beautiful dress melding with the pieces of her as they streamed off. For a brief moment, she felt the thanks of the other yoki-hijo, finally relieved from their service, allowed to vanish. And the others beyond them, the thousands upon thousands of people who had made up the shroud. Their souls were now free.

Why? Painter asked, so pained it made her shudder. *Why must it be sad?*

Because this is what I have to do, she whispered back, feeling her entire essence unravel. Memories vanishing. Experiences vaporizing. She couldn't remember her own face any longer. She was . . . just smoke. From that smoke came old thoughts, echoes. Lies drilled into her from long ago.

I was created to serve, she said. *My life is not my own.*

It doesn't have to be that way, Painter sent to her. *Your life* can *belong to you. It should.*

Around her, the spirits continued to exult, their emotions so strange to her in contrast to her own pain.

I'm losing myself, Nikaro, she thought. *No one knows me anymore. I don't even know myself. I'm sorry. It was always a dream. Such a wonderful dream. Perhaps the first such ever given by a nightmare . . .*

Yumi, he sent. *I love you.*

Finally a good emotion.

I love you, Painter, she thought back. *Please. Remember me.*

And at last, the sole remaining yoki-hijo—chosen as a baby, designated to give her life—did exactly that. Evaporating away into nothing.

Epilogue

W HY DO we tell stories?

They are a universal human experience. Every culture I've ever visited, every people I've met, every human on every planet in every situation I've seen . . . they all tell stories. Men trapped alone for years tell them to themselves. Ancients leave them painted on the walls. Women whisper them to their babies.

Stories explain us. You want to define what makes a human different from an animal? I can do it in one word or a hundred thousand. Sad stories. Exultant stories. Didactic morality tales. Frivolous yarns that, paradoxically, carry too much meaning.

We *need* stories.

I'm sorry I had to bring this ending to you. But the more you think about it, the more you'll realize that our tale today had to end in such a way. Stories demand certain endings. It's part of their nature.

I wish I could have explained this to Painter, kneeling as he did on the cobbles, staring out as his world turned upside down. Because he didn't understand.

He thought the story wasn't finished.

Painter stood up, then seized his brush in fingers that ached from his extended battle. He took Akane's ink as she cowered down, looking up as the sky opened and the darkness vanished. He strode past terrified police, among wounded painters, past people who cried out at the strange light. He reached a blank wall. The one that had been left for him. The masterpiece he had never finished.

There, as a city panicked—full of people seeing the sun for the first time—he started painting.

Horribly inconsiderate of him. We were all ready to go home. The story should have been done.

He just kept on painting anyway.

A painting is, of course, a story too. Not a still fragment of one as you might think, but an *entire* story. Every painting moves, full of life, if you know how to look at it.

Here he painted a picture of a beautiful woman sitting on the branch of a tree. Soaring high in the sky, flowers bursting behind her like fireworks.

"I know you," he whispered.

The curve of her hair as it curled around the sides of her head to spill down her back. The line of her chin, the defiant confidence in her eyes. The smile. *That* smile.

"I *know* you."

Painter didn't have two thousand years of experience. But in some ways, what he did have was better. Because art requires intent. Art requires passion. And among all the painters in the city, you would never find a person with more of either.

As the city trembled and people panicked all around him, Painter worked calmly. The shroud vanished in large chunks, leaving behind wisps of darkness. He seemed to paint from this smoke itself, using the ink of the soul.

Her dress, the shade of the sky that day, captured in inkwash greyscale. The blazing sun, a section with no paint at all, contrasted by the streaks around it.

Painter finally had a reason for his masterwork.

For him, audience had always been so very important—and today he had a singular audience. One person. The most important one.

Something touched him on the arm. Unseen, yet warm, sending a thrill of heat through him as he painted the flowers. Smoke from the dying shroud clung to him, one of the few patches remaining. No one noticed it. They were too busy dealing with what they assumed was the end of the world.

Another touch. On the other shoulder.

A final flourish, the dots that were her pupils. Then he turned to find smoke behind him, spinning like a vortex. White on the inside, an infinite hole, the eye of a nightmare. Within it a dark shape reaching toward him.

Painter dropped his brush and reached in.

And took her hand.

I . . . Her voice. *It's not right . . .*

"Yumi," he said, tears in his eyes, holding on tight. "We decide what is right. Nightmares can be real. Why not dreams? You have power granted by the spirits. Your whole life—your *dozens* of lives—you've used it to serve. Use it for yourself this once."

But . . .

"Our world, Yumi. Our rules."

I don't . . .

"Our *world*. Our *rules*."

Our . . . world.

"You deserve to live."

Our rules.

"You deserve to be happy."

I . . . deserve to choose. I deserve love.

Her other hand emerged from the smoke and seized his. They held to each other as the city trembled, the smoke died, and the world changed. They clung to one another as light from above rained down and shone on her face.

The last wisps of darkness vanished.

And at the end of it all, when someone finally thought to check on him, they found Painter huddled against the wall beneath a masterpiece of incredible caliber, holding a young woman tight in his arms.

As real as anyone else. Because she wanted to be.

Another
Epilogue

RIGHT ABOUT then, I woke up.

Design was waiting for me, lounging behind the bar, smirking at me in the most unbearable way. Why I ever gave her a face, I'll never know.

"About time you loosened up a little," she said.

"Shut up." I shook off the dozen or so coats that had been hung all over me, then pulled off the hooks and other things she'd attached for the purpose.

I had to blink *paint* out of my *eyes*. Storming Cryptic.

I kept the crown though. It was a special kind of awful.

"What happened?" she asked.

"Remember that time I got my memories stolen?"

"Yes. It was hilarious."

"It was humiliating," I said. "I instituted protection protocols to defend me if something tried to play games with my soul. When we landed here, that machine tried to draw my Investiture. My protocols activated."

"And turned you into a statue?"

"It . . . wasn't *exactly* what I'd hoped would happen."

She smirked at me. *Insufferable* creature. Then she waved around with two eager hands. "I started a restaurant!"

"Yes, I was aware for much of it," I said.

"Sounds awful!"

"You have no idea."

"Nope! Any desire to stick around until the next pickup in three years?"

"None whatsoever."

Outside the front window of the shop, Painter and Yumi passed, supporting one another. They looked like the way it felt to spend three years being a coatrack. In other words, *terrible*. They paused just outside and kissed, but we'll get to that.

"How are we getting away?" I asked Design.

She disappeared behind the counter, then emerged with a large stack of papers. "I have a *plan*."

"Delightful," I said, finding a handful of individually packaged condiments in my pocket. Who had put *those* in there?

"Yup. You imitate one of their astronauts. We steal their ship. It should be able to get us to Iron Seven Waystation."

"You need all of that?" I asked, pointing at her huge stack of papers. "To explain such a simple plan?"

"What? This isn't my plan. These are my *recipes*."

"Wonderful."

"They mostly aren't. You have no idea how many different combinations of edible ingredients produce something completely *in*edible! It's fun."

"No it's not."

"It's fun," she said, "if someone else is tasting them."

I smiled. "Let's go steal a spaceship."

"Finally!" she said, grabbing her recipes. "I'm ready."

"No worries about abandoning your restaurant?"

"Nope! I willed it to someone. Well, two someones."

"Can they cook?"

"Who cares? Let's go!"

And so, I escaped that dreadful planet. Such was the *actual* point of this story, if you hadn't noticed. Pay attention. And stop encouraging rogue participants to go off script.

I suppose, though, you want some loose ends tied up. Design gets letters from Masaka once in a while with updates, and I was able to send some inquiries to get more details. You should be thankful to her and the others, as this is the type of story I'm only able to tell you because I have the permission of those involved.

You'll be happy to know the planet, Komashi, survived. (Find it in the UTol system, in dual orbit with the planet UTol—which you might have heard about for other reasons.) The emergence of the sun didn't cause an utter catastrophe on Komashi, though they did learn the hard way about sunburns.

Turns out, a number of the spirits liked being hion lines, and were persuaded to continue in that service—with proper payment. That kept the heat of the ground down to something manageable. There were plants in the ruins of Torio City they could use to start new strains of crops, and the old ones would still grow by hion, if kept in the shade.

It was difficult for a while, but society didn't collapse. Evidently the sky can fall and most people will still get up the next day and go to work. I hear the planet is delightful to visit these days. Warm floors. Flying plants. Neon nights. I wouldn't know, as *I'm* never going to go back.

If you do go, though, stop by the Noodle Princess. I hear it has some of the best food around. And of course there's the attached art gallery. Full of paintings and stacked-up stones. Just don't sneeze.

Painter and Yumi, well, they never told anyone about what had happened to them—though they did eventually manage to convince their friends that she was his secret girlfriend from another city, not his sister. A fact confirmed by his parents when they arrived in a tizzy, worried about what had become of their son during the upheavals.

Nightmares went away forever, at least the living kind. Which meant no more need for painters. Those poor Dreamwatch members had to get jobs at their mommies' and daddies' corporations instead. At Painter's insistence, his friends told everyone that Usasha—the only painter to die in the attack—had been the one to mobilize everyone. She was given the honors.

At the end of it all, Painter and Yumi just wanted a quiet life with each other. Who would have guessed? If you visit, tell them I sent you, as Yumi and Painter do like offworld visitors. Just don't overstay your welcome, try not to out their story to the locals, and be sure to tip your server well. And if you think of it, point out how humanlike she's acting. Masaka is increasingly comfortable with others knowing what she is, but she—like all people—still appreciates a compliment now and then.

Oh, and if you're worried, the planet didn't end up needing yoki-hijo to appease the spirits anymore. Turns out the things really, *really* like historical dramas.

To this day, no one on the planet knows what Yumi actually is. They think of her as the eccentric cook of the best noodle place in town—the woman with the odd accent who can stack a hundred bowls on top of one another, with silverware balanced on each tier.

That should cover it.

Oh. Except the kiss.

That first kiss, outside the noodle shop, bathed in sunlight. Lips together, sharing a deeper warmth, her hands to his face, his arms pulling her tight—as if to never let go. Pressed so close their very souls seemed to mix. And in the case of these two, those souls did at least mash together with a blast of abiding warmth.

That said, it wasn't a very good kiss.

Considering the limited experience of the ones responsible, that won't surprise you. Yet for two people whose only previous brushes with romance involved some particularly aspirational daydreams, it worked well enough.

Plus, here's the thing. A kiss doesn't need to be good to be valuable. It doesn't serve any real purpose. It's valued solely because of the person you share it with.

Things only have the value we give to them. And likewise, actions can be worth whatever we decide them to be worth.

And so, to these two, that kiss was *priceless*.

The End

Postscript

THIS IS my personal favorite of the Secret Projects. I don't normally pick favorites among my books, so that's an unusual statement for me to make. However, this book in particular felt like a special gift to my wife, who is often encouraging me to feature more romance in my novels.

This one also has some fairly personal inspirations to me as well—indeed, ones you might not expect. For example, the biggest inspiration is a video game.

One of my favorite video games of all time is *Final Fantasy X*, directed by Yoshinori Kitase, which hit me just at the very right time in my life—I love the story of that game. One of the things that has stuck with me all these years since playing it is how the two main characters in it have fantastical jobs. (One plays a cool fantasy sport, while the other's job is to lay spirits of the dead to rest.) It's not something we see enough in fantasy—people with jobs that are suited to the specific style of worldbuilding done in the story.

For years, I've wanted to write a book focusing on the everyday duties of people who had a job in a fantasy world. A job that—to them—was normal, but which would seem strange to us as readers. This idea stewed in the back of my mind for years, as I looked for the right place to explore it.

The second inspiration actually came from my friend, and editorial VP, Peter Ahlstrom. I don't read a lot of manga, but he loves it. For years before I hired him, he was involved in the fan translation (then eventually, the professional translation) community for manga. During our time just after college, he was involved in a fan community working on a manga called *Hikaru no Go*, by Yumi Hotta, with art by Takeshi Obata.

I read that out of solidarity for Peter—and found that I really liked it. That manga focuses on a ghostly master who teaches a young new player to play the game Go. The dynamic is fun because the master, who is haunting the young man, can't play the game—because he has no physical body. But he loves it. The young man doesn't really care for Go at first, but through the coaching of the master, comes to love it too.

From this I took the idea of two people from different walks of life who had to teach each other to do their fantastical jobs. I loved this dynamic—I imagined their frustration at not being able to do the job right, and instead needing to teach someone else to do it well. Two people who need to trade places and learn from one another, not just when it comes to their jobs, but in their lives as well.

This relationship really kicked the story off for me, and I spent a great deal of time planning their romance. I also have a vague memory of a story I read in college about two people who share a bunk on a space station— where room is tight, so people can't have their own sleeping space. But they never see each other, because they work opposite shifts by design, each leaving notes for the other. They fall in love just through the notes they leave. This idea of people who develop a romance unconventionally was extremely appealing to me.

Because two of my influences were Japanese in origin, I decided to lean into this, basing Yumi's culture on historial Korea and Painter's on a more modern Japan. I leaned into some tropes (like the hot spring) from manga and anime—and this also dovetailed nicely into the "trade places" concept I'd been considering. Some excellent anime (*Your Name* by Makoto Shinkai being the standout in my opinion) uses this idea—that of two people needing to live one another's lives.

That said, one thing that was important to me in this story was interaction. *Your Name*, and that story I can't remember, both depend on people growing fond of one another in absence—and while that's a neat dynamic, I wanted something different. I wanted plenty of interaction. Indeed, I wanted to isolate them from other people, and focus the two inwardly, as they grew together. This romantic goal, again inspired by things my wife has said about stories she loves, is what drove me to write this story in my free time, as a gift for her.

One we're both pleased that you now get to share.

Brandon Sanderson